CORNERED

BY
HELENKAY DIMON

© HelenKay Dimon

Printed and bound in Spain
by CPI, Barcelona

MILLS & BOON

® and ™ are trademarks owned and used by the trademark owner and/or its licensee. Trademarks marked with ® are registered with the United Kingdom Patent Office and/or the Office for Harmonisation in the Internal Market and in other countries.

Published in Great Britain 2015
by Mills & Boon, an imprint of Harlequin (UK) Limited,
Eton House, 18-24 Paradise Road, Richmond, Surrey, TW9 1SR

© 2015 HelenKay Dimon

ISBN: 978-0-263-25309-2

46-0615

Harlequin (UK) Limited's policy is to use papers that are natural, renewable and recyclable products and made from wood grown in sustainable forests. The logging and manufacturing processes conform to the legal environmental regulations of the country of origin.

"I don't want you to go."

The pleas tugged at him, made him think about doing stupid things that didn't fit with his life or the need to keep her protected. "You'll be safe with him."

Her other hand went to his lap. Smoothed up and down his thigh. "You make me feel safe."

The touching, the sound of her voice, the pleading in those big eyes. He was ten seconds from breaking. "Don't do this."

She nuzzled her mouth against his neck. Blew a warm breath over his skin. He fought it until he couldn't, then he turned his head and kissed her. Right there in another man's house, in a place with security but no connection to Cam.

It took every ounce of his strength and self-control to pull back. When that didn't give him enough space, he stood up. Paced around and thought about airplanes. Anything to take his mind off her face and the touch of those lips.

"Then I'm going with you."

"I don't know, Anne."

The cigar tipped a little, made him think about doing found thing, angry ... lit with on his ... He tried to keep his composure. "I'll be alright."

Her other hand went to his lip, and other ... and doing a slight ...

The ... him, the shape of her ... the pleading in those ... eyes. He was ... seconds from ...

He ... her mouth against his neck, blew ... warm breath over his skin. He thought it ... then he ... his head and ... Right there in another ... place with ...

He ... every ounce of his strength and will ... to pull back. When that didn't give what enough ... he stood up. He ... around both ... held on tight, ... his hands ... her and the rough ...

"I'll ... come with you ..."

He ...

HelenKay Dimon, an award-winning author, spent twelve years in the most unromantic career ever—divorce lawyer. After dedicating all that effort to helping people terminate relationships, she is thrilled to deal in happy endings and write romance novels for a living. Now her days are filled with gardening, writing, reading and spending time with her family in and around San Diego. Stop by her website, www.helenkaydimon.com, and say hello.

For all the readers who asked for more Corcoran Team
books—thank you! I love these guys, too.

Chapter One

A crack of gunfire echoed through the towering trees. That sort of thing would have sent Julia White scrambling for her cell phone and dialing for the police back in her normal life. But not on Calapan Island, the tiny strip of land miles from Seattle and accessible only by ferry. Here people fired weapons for sport, as a warning or just because it was Tuesday.

She didn't know the reason this time and didn't much care. Rather than flinch or worry, she stayed kneeling in the dirt, weeding the overgrown rectangle of roots and vines that had once been a garden alive with color.

The summer sun warmed her bare arms as the breeze lifted her hair off her shoulders and kept it dancing in front of her eyes. Needing a drink of water and a barrette, she stabbed the end of the sharp shovel into the ground and stood. A break sounded good after an hour of getting nowhere on the massive yard-work project.

She made it two steps before shots rang out again, this time multiple and in bursts. At the sound of the rapid rat-a-tat-tat, she spun around, trying to judge the distance between her and the bullets. Her gaze zipped from one end of the open yard to the other. A thunder of noise she couldn't identify filled her ears and grew closer as she scanned the part of the two acres she could see without moving away from the protective shield of the house.

A tangle of trees blocked her view to what lay beyond her father's falling-down property, but she didn't hesitate. Living in Seattle for the past two years had taught her one thing: don't invite danger. That meant moving. Smart women knew when to run.

She took off for the back porch as she tapped the pockets of her cargo shorts in search of her phone. Empty. Maybe that was for the best, since what passed for police on the island didn't exactly fill her with a sense of security. More like dread.

Her foot hit the bottom step right as the hair on the back of her neck stirred. That only made her jog faster. Anxiety rocketed through her as she reached for the door. Just as she tugged she heard it—heavy breathing, and not hers. She whipped her head around in time to see someone barreling toward her. Broad shoulders and big. Male and fast.

Her hand slipped on the knob, but she turned it. She managed to open the door an inch before a man's hand slammed against the frame by her head. The heat from his body radiated against her back as panic swamped her. She opened her mouth to scream, but a hand clamped over her face, blocking the sound.

"I'm not going to hurt you." The harsh whisper brushed across her ear.

Yeah, no way was she believing that.

She kicked out and shoved. Flailed and tried to run again, this time for the tree line. She would not go out like this. She'd always joked that if she stayed on Calapan she'd die. She refused to let that prediction come true.

She elbowed him in the stomach and heard him swear in response. Another shot or two like that and she might be able to put some distance between them and get inside. Gathering all her strength, she drew her arm forward again and pushed back. She hit nothing but air.

One minute she stood locked in an epic battle on the porch. The next, her attacker reached around her and got the door open. He propelled her forward, slamming the door behind them and locking them both inside.

He held up his hands as he stared at her with big blue eyes. "Please listen to me."

He could beg all he wanted. The dimple, those shoulders, the objective cuteness…she wasn't buying any of it. She'd never been charmed by a handsome face before and wasn't starting now.

If he wanted a fight, fine. She'd give him one. Without thinking or analyzing, almost on autopilot, she ran for the small family room on the far side of the kitchen. Guns didn't scare her, because they were a way of life on Calapan. Growing up here, she'd learned how to shoot. Cans, mostly, but she didn't plan on telling her attacker about that limitation.

Footsteps beat in time with hers. She ran. He stalked. He kept talking—something about needing her help— but she blocked it all out, her only thought being to find that rifle. There was a Glock around here, too.

"Ma'am, slow down for a second."

Not likely. She put a couch between them as she tried to remember where she had left the guns after she moved them around this morning. Her mind flipped to the fireplace, and a quick glance revealed one leaning against the mantel. The same fireplace mantel next to the attacker and not her.

Her mind raced with directions. *Draw him out. Let him talk.* She skipped all of it. "Get out."

"I will not hurt you." He hadn't lowered his hands.

That didn't mean he couldn't. Her gaze dipped to the gun strapped to his hip and the trickle of blood running down from the edge of the sleeve of his navy T-shirt. "Then leave."

"My name is Cameron Roth."

As if she cared. "Fine. Leave, Cameron."

"I work for a group called the Corcoran Team."

She didn't even know what he was talking about. Her mind stayed focused on the gun, the blood, the shots and the fact that a stranger stood in front of her. The combination was all her brain could process at the moment.

"I don't know who this team is, but you can go find them." She bit back the tremble in her voice and tried to get the words out as quickly and clearly as possible. "I'll pretend this never happened, but you need to leave now."

"I can't."

Looked as though logic wouldn't work on this guy. She mentally measured the distance from her to the gun and wondered if she could get there before he put his hands down. "You mean won't."

"I need you to stop worrying."

That voice, all soothing and calm. It called to her, but she refused to trust it. Not when it promised a one-way ticket to getting injured…or worse. "That's not going to happen with you standing in the middle of my house."

"I'm one of the good guys."

"Says the man who grabbed me and dragged me inside." Her gaze traveled over him and she thought she made out another weapon tucked into his jeans and outlined by his slim tee. "Were you the one out there shooting?"

All emotion left his face. His blank expression didn't give anything away. "There was a problem."

Forget the weapon—with that nonanswer the guy should be a lawyer. "I'll give you the keys to the car. You can take it and—"

"No." At his bark, she took a step back and he moved in, closing the gap again. "I'm here on assignment."

"What are you talking about?" She had no clue.

This was the nightmare that wouldn't end. She should have stayed in Seattle and let the house stand abandoned. Her father was gone and she didn't owe anyone on Calapan anything.

"I rendezvous with my team in fifteen minutes."

Again with the team thing. "Be extra punctual and go now."

The corner of his mouth twitched. "I would, but I don't want to be shot."

She wasn't sure if he was laughing at her or with her but didn't like either option. "That makes two of us, Cameron."

Some of the tension left his shoulders as he nodded toward the couch. "Sit."

He had to be kidding. "No."

"I'm at a disadvantage here. What's your name?"

This guy just kept talking when she needed him gone. "You aren't going to be here long enough for that to matter."

"There are some nasty people after me." He lowered his arms, but his hand didn't venture near the gun. "I'm just hiding out here for a few minutes."

"Who?" If there were more people out there with weapons, she wanted to be ready.

His eyes narrowed. "What?"

"Who is after you?"

His gaze went to the rifle and lingered for a second before returning to her face. "Let's just say some of the people on this island can't be trusted."

Yeah, that was a lesson she knew all too well. "Understatement."

"What?"

She ignored the question because she had bigger problems. Now he knew where all the weapons were. That left knives, and grabbing for those gave her the shivers. "Just so we're clear, you're running around the island shooting and being tracked by someone and have no trouble manhandling me—"

"That didn't actually happen."

"—yet I'm supposed to trust you." Her voice got louder as she went on.

He had the nerve to smile at her. "Yes."

"I'm not an idiot." Sure, her brain kept malfunctioning and waves of fear crashed over her every two seconds, but she was not letting her world end like this.

"I never said you were."

"And I have a phone." She lunged for the landline. It had been disconnected months before, after her father died. But this Cameron guy didn't know that...at least, she hoped he didn't. "The police can come and you can explain your problem."

"That's not going to work."

She'd read somewhere that trying to form a bond with an attacker sometimes helped humanize the victim. Since she was the victim, she was willing to try anything. "Tell me why, Cameron."

"You can call me Cam."

Apparently the bond thing worked. She shook the phone. "Talk or I'm dialing 9-1-1."

"That would be a mistake."

There was something about the way he said it. "Why?"

"The police are the problem."

A crack shattered the glass behind her, spraying it over the room. She ducked. Probably screamed. Just as she crossed her arm over her head, a heavy weight crashed into her. She hit the floor and skidded across it with Cameron on top of her.

When they stopped, he pinned her down. The second their bodies touched she started moving. She shifted her legs and tried to knee him anywhere it would hurt. He caught her leg and held a hand up as if to tell her to be quiet. The whole time his gaze scanned the room and his gun dug into her stomach.

Through all the kicking and squirming, the silence finally registered in her brain. She picked up his breathing and heard her own hammering in her ears. Other than that, nothing. No more shooting. No yelling.

He leaned up on his elbow and glanced down with their faces only inches apart. "Are you okay?"

"No."

He lifted his body off her and looked down the slim space between them. "You're hit?"

"I mean mentally." When she realized Cam's body shielded hers, that he was protecting, not attacking, she let the backs of her hands fall against the dusty floor. "I don't understand what's happening."

"That makes two of us." He shifted his body to the side as he slipped the gun out of its holster.

"Who is shooting at you now?" And why had Cam brought the person to her doorstep?

He crawled over to the one remaining intact family room window, ignoring the broken glass from the previous chaos and the crunching under his knees. "Your police chief."

Chief Kreider wasn't her anything. The guy had the whole old-boy thing down, all entitled and drunk on power...except for those times he was actually drunk. She was not a fan.

Following Cam, because he seemed like a good guy to hide behind, she sat on the other side of the window and peeked out. Three random men stood out there, armed and dressed in some sort of law-enforcement uniforms. None of them looked familiar and they all wore lethal shoot-first expressions.

That fast, she lost her ability to breathe.

Cam pulled her back down. "Be careful."

She only caught a glimpse, but... "You said you were fighting the police chief, right?"

"The guy standing in the middle of your yard."

"None of them is the police chief."

Cam's mouth dropped open. "What?"

"I think your problem just got bigger."

"And I think, since you're trapped in here with me, I'm not the only one with a problem." He reached behind his back and took out a second gun. Before she could scream or bolt, he handed it to her. "Do you know how to use this?"

"Yes." She took it but wished she didn't have to.

"Good."

"Not really." Something collapsed inside her. "I hate this island."

This time he did smile at her, full and sexy and the exact opposite of threatening. He opened her hand and put the gun in it. "Looks as if we finally agree on something."

For some reason she didn't find the look or his cuteness comforting. "Julia White."

"What?"

"I figure if we're going to die together you should know my name." It actually hurt to say those words.

Not that they affected him. No, he winked at her. "You're not dying on my watch, Julia."

"You sound confident."

"You can consider it a guarantee."

Chapter Two

Cam slid his body up along the wall and stood up. With his back covered, he peeked outside again. The men outside hadn't moved, which struck him as pretty bad planning. If he were in charge of the attack party, they'd be surrounding the house and moving in by now.

Thank goodness for amateurs.

His gaze bounced back to Julia. He couldn't help being impressed with the way she held it together. He'd rushed her, touched her and forced his way inside her house. Acted in a way that he begged to be punched. He'd watched the fear come over her, and before he could calm her, she'd controlled it. Taken the energy pinging around inside her and focused.

It was sexy as hell. So was the long wavy brown hair and then there were those big chocolate-brown eyes. Not that he had the time to notice...but he did.

He reeled those thoughts in because he had no plans to die today. He'd just made a vow to Julia, so now he had to figure out a way out of this mess without too much bloodshed. He'd brought the firefight to her door by accident. Even if it meant taking a bullet, he'd get her out.

She peeked around the windowsill, then ducked her head again. "Why are they just standing out there?"

"Good question." Cam kept his focus on the men. If he flinched they could move out of his sight, and he could not let that happen. Three of them, one dressed as the police chief and two in flannel shirts, which made them stand out in summer.

"I have another question," she said.

This time he glanced over at her. Seeing the pale face and the way her hand shook as she brushed the hair out of her eyes sent a shot of guilt through him. Still, he wasn't used to a lot of conversation in the middle of a shoot-out. "Now might not be the best time."

She checked the weapon before looking up again. "Why did you think they were police?"

Looked as though she talked when she got nervous. He tried to contain the adrenaline coursing through him enough to keep up the harsh whispering. "The uniform, plus the other two were at the police station. The chief knew I was coming. The usual."

She frowned. "That's the usual for you?"

"Uh, yeah." It all made sense to him, but in hindsight he'd played it too safe in the minutes leading up to his meeting. He could have checked identities through facial recognition, but that wasn't standard operating procedure for a job like this. It was supposed to be an easy witness pickup, not a death match.

Her attention did not waver. It stayed locked on him. "Who are you and what do you do?"

They absolutely didn't have time for that discussion. "Later."

And really, there was no easy way to tell her he worked for an undercover operation hired out to corporations and governments to handle kidnapping and threat situations. It was the kind of line that sounded like nonsense during a pickup in a bar. In real life it meant he lived in a web of secrets, lies and death. Not exactly the kind of information that was going to put her at ease right now.

"I don't think so." Her tone suggested she might turn that gun on him at any moment. "How about now or I'll go out there with them?"

"You think you'll be safe with a guy pretending to be police?" She'd already proven she was smart and quick on her feet. He didn't doubt she'd reason this through and agree...at least, he hoped so.

"Probably not," she mumbled.

"Then maybe we can take care of the attackers before exchanging personal info?" Seemed logical to him. He was about to point that out when the banging started again.

His hand went to her head. He pushed her toward the floor with his body covering hers. Glass shattered and rained over them. Edges clipped the back of his hands, but his long-sleeved shirt protected the rest. Drywall kicked up and a lamp exploded to his left.

The rapid volley gave way to another sharp silence. His head shot up and he took another look. The men outside still hadn't moved. Other than holding weapons at the ready and the glass shower, nothing had changed. When he looked down, Julia was already moving.

She visibly swallowed as she sat up. "Okay, we'll talk later."

He liked her style. "Exactly."

"Now what?"

"That was a warning shot." If they wanted to do real damage, to shoot their way inside, they would have. For some reason they stalled out there, and Cam couldn't figure out why.

He'd deal with that later. Now he needed an exit strategy, and the options appeared pretty limited. Running out the back door might work if she hadn't been wearing a bright red shirt. That would stick out with her streaking through the woods. Which led to the other issue—she lived in the middle of nowhere.

This part of Calapan consisted of lush greenery, dirt roads and little else. Her cabin sat with the water on one side and towering trees on the other three. That made running for help problematic. So shooting their way out won as the best scenario. And that was not good news.

"What exactly did you do to them?" The hand with the gun fell on her lap as some of the color seeped back into her cheeks.

Anger and blame—good. He could handle those. "My job."

"Could you be more specific?" The demand for information was right there in her tone and the flat line of her mouth.

He ignored both. "No." When she started to talk again he put a finger to his mouth. "Do not move."

"Where would I go?"

He decided to wait until later to explain hand gestures and go over the definition of the word *quiet*. Making sure he was dealing with three men and not more trumped everything. He could take them down one by one, but only if another line didn't loom behind this one.

Crouched and keeping out of sight, he shifted with quick movements around the cottage. Checked the side yards and the one in back where he'd found her a few minutes ago. It took about a minute thanks to the size of her place.

By the time he made it back to the window with Julia, he knew they were in serious trouble. "They're getting smarter."

She shifted her weight and sat up with her knees tucked under her. "Meaning?"

"They're spreading out." They'd finally mobilized. There was no reason to do that unless an attack came next. Cam still didn't know what was happening on this island, but it wasn't good. "They'll likely come in firing."

With her palms on the hardwood floor, she leaned forward. "You brought these guys to my door. Take them away."

If only it were that simple. But he did have a plan, and it involved taking her out of the cross fire. "Is there an attic?"

She made a face. "What?"

"Julia, I need you to focus." She could be angry and frustrated later. Now he needed her with him, because when the quiet broke this time he sensed it wouldn't stop until bodies littered the floor. "An attic?"

She shook her head. "There's only a crawl space."

He'd make that work. "We need to get you in it."

"Where will you be?"

He liked that she didn't balk or question what he wanted her to do. "You go up and I'll cover the downstairs."

"One against three?" She sounded appalled at the idea.

"I've beaten worse odds."

"Cal—"

"Cam." His temper flared unexpectedly. For some reason her not remembering his name dug at him, but he pushed the feelings aside. "Do you really know how to shoot?"

He'd handed her a gun, which was a risk. Now he needed to make sure she wouldn't shoot him in the head by accident.

"Of course," she said.

"Anyone but me comes near you, you shoot." He heard a noise. Faint but there. The attackers were closing in. No question about it. "That attic space?"

"Right." She crawled on her hands and knees until she cleared the sight line from the window, and he followed.

Smart woman with skills. She became more intriguing by the second.

They got to the short hall leading to the bedroom and bathroom and she pointed up. No string, but there was a small handle. He rose to his feet, nice and slow, while waiting for a new round of shooting to start. When that didn't happen, he went the rest of the way. He lifted his hand and felt nothing but air. On the second try, he jumped and his fingers brushed the handle. Grabbing it, he brought the door down.

Before she could argue, he took her by the waist and lifted. Her feet left the floor and she let out a half yelp before clamping her mouth shut again.

With only the rustling of clothing as noise, her body and then her legs disappeared into the dark hole above. A second later her face popped into the space. "Be careful."

He shut the door before she could say anything else. Now to bury the obvious entry. After a short mental countdown, he jumped, using the wall as leverage, and grabbed the handle. The yank pressed the hard metal into his palm but didn't come off. He only managed to knock the handle loose.

The second lunge cut his palm but did the trick. With a crack the handle fell off. He stuffed it into his pocket and hoped the shadowed hallway would do the rest to provide cover.

Then he moved. The corner at the end of the hall qualified as the perfect place. He could squat down and wait for the inevitable. Problem was, Julia sat right above. A stray bullet could ricochet and hit her, and he couldn't let that happen. That meant moving into the open, being more vulnerable, but he'd take the chance.

The kitchen worked as an alternative. He pivoted around the edge of the small island and hunkered down by the stove. Now began the game to see who would flinch first.

These guys didn't disappoint. One kicked in the front door and another stormed in the back. With the size of the house, they could have run right into each other if they hadn't stopped their momentum. They whispered and traded theories on his location. Cam heard it all.

Not seeing them, he had to concentrate on the voices and the footsteps to plot their positions. He had two in the small family room and one unaccounted for. Close enough.

When one came within range of the kitchen, Cam still held his position. Not moving. The preference was to take them alive. Much easier to question a breathing man than a dead one. Then the one who acted like the sidekick almost stepped on Cam's hand.

He sprang to his feet with an arm wrapped around the guy's throat as he faced down the one dressed as the police chief. The one who had all the facts and who'd sat in the office, pretending to be the police chief, which raised a lot of questions.

"Put the gun down." Cam issued the order as he backed his hostage into the family room and away from the hallway where Julia hid above.

The fake chief wore a smile that could only be described as feral. "You have been a problem."

No kidding. That was exactly what Cam got paid to handle. "Not the first time I've heard that."

"Lower the weapon and we'll let the woman live." One gave the orders while the other tightened his hold on Cam's arm to keep from being choked.

They'd seen her or guessed. Either way, them knowing limited Cam's options even further. Pretty soon he'd be down to about one.

Still, there was no reason to make it easy for them. "What woman?"

"Don't play dumb, Mr. Roth." That sick smile widened. "Yes, I know your real name."

That wasn't good at all. That wasn't the name he'd given as cover for the witness pickup. If the guy knew who he really was, he likely knew that the Corcoran Team was on the island. The mission could be blown. The same mission that was supposed to be exploratory only and not combat.

Just what they needed—more danger.

Cam's heel hit the back of the sofa and he stopped. "Where's the real police chief?"

"You need to stop asking questions and listen." The guy used a man-to-man tone, as if they were having a chat about everyday things. "You have five seconds before me and my men tear this place apart and grab the woman. Then we'll see how fast you talk."

"I'm looking forward to seeing that." The third man stepped in from a room in the back.

Cam guessed he had found a window. Didn't really matter how he got there. Problem was, the odds had just switched to three against one. Not impossible but not his favorite. It meant he'd have to kill two and take his chances with the third.

He had to stop the chief first. "One more step and I snap your man's neck."

"You think I care?" He brought up his gun and fired.

The shot exploded in front of Cam. He felt a jerk and then the man he was holding fell at full weight against Cam's chest. He dropped him with a thud to the floor and came up firing. He nailed the one in the hallway in the shoulder and knocked him back. The chief dived to the side and Cam dropped down as he scrambled around the couch.

The scene moved in slow motion, but Cam knew it took only a few deafening seconds. As shots continued to ring out, he blocked the hammering of adrenaline through his body and the grunts and heavy breathing filling the room.

He turned to get off a covering shot and took a quick inventory: one dead guy on the floor and the chief missing. The wounded shooter stood in that back room and fired random shots into the family room that kept Cam ducking. He was about to take a diving shot when he saw the crawl-space door drop. Not the whole way but enough to be noticed if anyone was looking.

The creak of the hinges had the shooter looking up. It was the distraction Cam needed. The guy shifted just enough to aim his gun into the dark hole, and Cam fired. Nailed him in the head this time and sent him crashing into the wall and then sprawling to the floor.

Cam jumped to his feet and searched the family room

and kitchen. The place looked like a war zone. Shot-up walls and broken glass. A shredded curtain and papers scattered everywhere. He didn't even know where half the stuff came from.

But a clear inside didn't mean they were safe. He checked the porch and scanned the front of the property for any signs of the fake chief fleeing into the woods but didn't see anything, including the truck that had been out there a few minutes ago.

"Julia?" He didn't bother whispering or covering. The men knew she was there and now all but the fake chief lay dead on her floor. "Talk to me."

When she didn't say anything he stalked to the end of the hall and looked up. The gun appeared first, then her face. "That was pretty awful."

Her voice shook, but she wasn't throwing up, so he took that as a good sign. "Are you hurt?"

"I don't think so."

The shaking grew stronger and he worried about shock. "Any chance you could be more definitive?"

"My legs are never going to hold me to come down again. Maybe I'll just live up here." She glanced down at the guy lying below her, and her eyes widened. "Did you... Is he dead?"

"Very." And Cam didn't want her staring at the guy. Nothing good could come out of that. He tucked his gun into his waistband and picked a position that had her looking at him and away from the still body.

But she was already glancing over his head. "You killed two?"

"One. The guy in uniform took out his own guy and got away. So much for loyalty." Cam lifted his hands and caught her, easing her to the floor and not letting go until she found her equilibrium. "You need to grab a bag and change your clothes, or at least your shirt."

"Why?"

"You can't stay here." He pointed around the room. "This is a mess and I don't know why the guy was shooting, so I need you off Calapan."

"Normally I'd get indignant and tell you not to order me around, but I'm okay with it this time." She handed his gun back to him.

He slipped it into the back waistband of his pants. "I knew you were smart."

"We need to get to the ferry." She wiped her hands on her thighs and blew out a long breath. "We can take my truck."

Looked as though she had more bad news in front of her. He winced. "Was it blue?"

"Was?"

Cam didn't see a vehicle outside. Unless she had a secret hiding place, they could add another criminal charge to the fake chief's list. "The one who got away took it."

Her mouth dropped open. "Are you kidding?"

In light of the past few minutes, the response struck him as overblown. Probably had something to do with the reaction to violence. She didn't double over or hide in a corner, but she did latch on to odd things. He could handle that. "I'm thinking a stolen car is not the worst thing to happen to you today."

"It's a two-mile walk to the ferry and we only have four a day. We miss it and we're trapped here. On this island."

The bad news just kept coming. He pushed aside his plans to hunt the shooter down and focused on this problem. There was only one solution—call in the cavalry.

He glanced at his watch and pushed the button. The one that sent an emergency signal out to the rest of the men. "We'll rendezvous with my team and get you to safety."

"Alive?" She managed to load that one word with a heap of sarcasm.

He didn't let her tone derail him. "My promise to do everything to keep you safe still stands."

"I'm holding you to it." She stared at him as if needing further reassurance.

He didn't have anything other than his word, which was pretty damn solid, so he nodded. "Good."

Chapter Three

Julia led him through the woods. The trees soared above their heads, blocking the late-afternoon sun and casting a chill over her. Light filtered through the branches and spots of sunshine highlighted parts of the rough terrain, but for the most part they had to rely on her sense of direction as a guide.

As a kid she'd used the forest area as a playground. There she could hide from her father's alcohol-fueled rages and all the yelling. She'd breathe in the scent of the wet ground mixed with pine and be surrounded by calm, if only for a short time.

Being there now qualified as the exact opposite of calm. Her stomach tumbled and her nerves jingled, making her jump at every little sound. The chirping birds and the swishing as the wind blew the leaves around, usually soothing, just had her twitching.

Cam walked next to her, keeping their pace brisk. Every time she stumbled over roots or overturned rocks, his arm shot out and he steadied her. She appreciated the assist but really just wanted to get on a ferry and head for Seattle. Her father's estate and the selling of the house could wait. She'd figure out the truck and how to remove dead bodies later.

She shivered at the thought. When her brain hiccuped over the destruction and seeing all that blood, she turned to the very real issue that she had to let someone in authority know. That would lead to questions she couldn't answer and the possibility of getting in trouble.

But the police could question her in her small apartment back in her Belltown neighborhood, because she was officially done with Calapan Island. This time forever, because nothing and no one bound her there now.

The place was gorgeous but had never been anything more than a scary death trap for her. That used to be metaphorical in many ways; now it was literal. She'd had to walk over dead bodies with her backpack on her shoulders to get out of her father's old house.

But really, right now she needed something to take her mind off all the terror and violence. Mr. Tall, Dark and Oh-So-Good-Looking beside her needed to step up and help on that score.

"Say something." She issued the order and then went back to stepping over mounds of this and that on the ground.

He shot her a side glance before returning to his neverending scan of the area around them. "Your shirt is bright purple."

Not exactly what she'd had in mind, but the comment was potentially annoying and right now she'd take that over noticing his firm jaw and general hotness. "You're critiquing my wardrobe?"

"I was hoping you'd pick something that blended in."

A solid response, but not a request she could make happen. "Every shirt I own is a bright color."

He looked at her again, but this time his gaze lingered. "Why?"

"Because I'm tired of blending in." She'd spent her entire youth trying not to draw her father's attention at the wrong time. Since he drank almost nonstop, that had turned out to be always.

But she was an adult now and refused to be defined by her father's issues. She just wished she'd been stronger on that point and had confronted him before he fell out of his boat, hit his head and died. His death left her with a mix of guilt and regret and more than a little bit of anger over all she had lived through and the baggage she still carried around.

Cam shrugged. "I thought you picked it because you looked so good in bold colors. They suit you."

Her sneaker slipped and she lost her footing. One wrong step and she turned her ankle as she bit back a string of profanity.

"You okay?" He faced her with both hands on her forearms.

She bit her lip. It was either that or grimace. "Yeah."

"Julia, I need to know the truth here." His expression went blank and his voice grew serious. "I can always carry you, if needed."

"That is not going to happen." She balanced her body against his, digging her fingernails into his arms as she shook out the sore ankle.

"You sure?"

"It's just a twinge." One that made her vision blink out for a second and her head spin.

When she moved her foot to the right, pain screamed through her. She'd done this a million times. Years ago she'd stopped running because of weak ankles. Well, that and because of her absolute hatred of running. But she knew the pain would ease if she stayed off it for a few hours and iced it down. She sensed neither was an option.

"By your own calculations we have about a mile and a half left to go." He looked up. "Daylight will fade and the ferry schedule will get in our way."

"Can we flag down a car?" A risky thought with gunmen racing around, she knew, but it was an option. Cam with all his superhero skills might be able to tell a legitimate driver from an undercover gunman. At least she hoped so.

He stared at her in that way a man did when he thought a woman had lost her mind. "In a tree?"

For a second she forgot he didn't know the area. Despite the could-charm-any-woman dimple and cute face, he fit in here. Had an outdoorsy look to him, and his clothes blended in. Certainly better than she did.

"There's a dirt road for emergency vehicle use only. The wildlife enforcement guys and police travel it." As soon as she said that last part, an alarm bell rang in her head.

"I'm not exactly looking for a run-in with more police or people pretending to be police." His fingers squeezed around her arms, then eased again. "But if the path is clearer you'll have an easier time, so we can try it."

Last thing she wanted to do was drag the danger out. Sooner or later the ankle had to go numb anyway. "I can keep going."

One of his eyebrows lifted. "Your choice is the emergency road or I throw you over my shoulder."

The shoulders, the face, the general hotness—she liked it all. The bossiness? Not so much. "You need to work on your negotiation skills."

"Why? I just won, didn't I?" He guided her to an over-turned log and helped her sit down.

Before she could say anything or think of a comeback, he dropped to one knee with his hands up her pants leg. Warm hands slid along her calf, then down to the top of her short socks. With a gentle touch he rotated her ankle one way, then the other.

The whole thing left her breathless. She didn't even scream when the sharp shock of pain radiated up her leg. For a guy who could turn and shoot without blinking, he could soothe by the simple touch of skin to skin.

She swore her vision blurred a little as she watched him, but somehow she found her voice again. "You could leave me here and go get the FBI."

"Tempting." He shot her a smile that could melt butter.

"We can't take the shoe off or it will swell." She was just babbling now.

"I know." He stood up and held out a hand toward her. "Come on."

She struggled to stand and almost called a halt to the whole project until he put her arm around his neck. The move let her fall into his side with him shouldering most of her weight and not putting any but the barest bit on the toes of her hurt foot.

"Better?" he asked.

This close she could smell him. A mix of wind and woods. Very compelling and weird, since smelling guys was not really her thing. She worked in an office and an-swered phones. She dated, but not much since breaking up with the accountant who had waffled between bor-ing her and scaring her as he drank scotch after scotch after dinner each night.

She managed to nod. Not that Cam waited for her to

be healed or even ready. He had them moving again, this time at a slower pace, but not by much. They wound around piles of rock and across fallen branches.

With each step, the end of his gun dug deeper into her side. She didn't complain, because he was almost carrying her, all while watching the area and stopping every few minutes to check for something only he could hear.

When they reached the dirt road about ten minutes later, she slumped even harder against him in relief. "Here it is."

"This?"

She couldn't really fault the disbelief in his voice. She looked first down one side, then the other. The path was overgrown in parts. In others she could see the faint outline of tire tracks. But mostly they looked at mud and stones. Pretty big stones.

But she couldn't come up with another option. All the roads, some better than others, required a hike. Some of them serious hikes, complete with rappelling. She could barely walk. Jumping up and down mountains was out.

"It's the best I could do on short notice," she joked even though there was nothing amusing about their current situation.

He stared at her for a second as if trying to figure out her mood, then nodded. "This should be a bit more stable for you."

She didn't see how, but now wasn't really the time to argue. "Sure."

She moved away from him and put some weight on the sore ankle. It felt all twingey and only a few steps from shattering, but she tried to trick her mind into thinking it was no big deal. "I'm fine."

"That's convincing." He reached out and this time it looked as if he planned to carry her. "Come on."

The rumbling broke her concentration. The grinding of an engine and thumping and thudding as the wheels covered the trail. She'd never been so grateful to hear a vehicle. "A car is coming."

He stood stock-still. "No."

"What?"

"Truck." He wrapped his fingers around her elbow and pulled, half dragging her back into the cover of the overgrown trees.

Her feet slipped and the aching turned to a harsh pounding in her foot. But that was nothing compared to the knocking in her chest. Her lungs seemed to want outside her chest.

Pebbles skidded under her sneakers as she tried to gain traction. "How can you tell?"

"Different sound." He slipped an arm around her waist and lifted. "Come on."

Her body took flight and she wrapped her arms around his shoulders to keep from falling. She wanted to scream and argue, but that engine noise and the ambling of the truck drew closer.

They'd gone about ten feet in when Cam turned and dropped. His knees buckled and they went down. She landed on top of him in a bone-crushing thud. His landing had to be harder against the rough ground, but she didn't have time to think about it because the world started spinning.

He flipped her until she lay underneath him, covered head to toe by firm, muscular male. She looked up and followed his gaze. They lay sprawled behind two stacked logs. Peeking through the sliver of space between them, she could see the tires and a flash of blue.

It was her truck or one that looked very similar. Her fury at being robbed mixed with the very real horror of being found out here. She'd heard the threats the men made about her to Cam. They didn't need to use the exact words for her to know being caught by those guys was not an option. She'd go out shooting instead.

The truck door opened and black shoes came into view. The leg bottoms of the police uniform. Footsteps echoed on the dirt path as the guy walked from one side of the car to the other. When he bent down to touch something on the ground, her breath caught in her throat. Not a single cell moved within her body.

Cam also froze. His eyes darted as he watched the movements, but even his hands stayed still. He had a gun in one and she had no idea when he had brought that back out again after checking her ankle.

What felt like hours passed. Finally, the guy stood up again. She still refused to breathe. Her fingers tightened on Cam's shirt, balling wads of material within her tight fists.

She heard keys jingle. Probably *her* keys. And whistling.

The jerk.

When the guy got back into the truck and the engine revved, she finally let the air rush out of her lungs. Her head fell back against the cool ground and she inhaled the scent of peat moss. Getting her heart to stop racing seemed impossible.

It took another few seconds for the tension across Cam's shoulders to ease. Still, he didn't move. His head lowered and he looked down at her with his mouth hovering over hers. "You okay?"

She shook her head because that was all she could get out.

Chalk it up to the adrenaline or the moment or that face, but she gave in and did something totally unlike her. Her hands smoothed up his chest to his cheeks, and then she brought his mouth even closer. When he didn't bridge the gap between them, she did.

Her lips touched his and at first he didn't react. Didn't make a sound or do anything. Then his fingers slipped into her hair and held her still as he deepened the kiss. The touch hit her with a jolt of mind-blowing fever. He kissed her long and hard until that dizziness came roaring back.

When he lifted his head again, she could barely hold her neck up. Her hands dropped to the ground beside her head. "Wow."

He nodded. "Yeah."

But she had to be smart. "The kiss was a onetime thing."

"That's a shame." The corner of his mouth kicked up in a smile. "What was it for?"

"Not letting me die." Seemed simple enough to her.

Some man pretending to be a police officer was looking for them, and Cam hadn't hesitated. He'd tucked her body under his and kept her safe. He'd already killed a man rather than let him touch her. She didn't know how to thank him for those things or how to deal with the confusion rattling her, since he was the one who'd brought the danger to her doorstep in the first place.

"Now what?" She felt as if she kept asking that, but it still seemed relevant.

He brushed her hair away from her face. "We find my team."

"Are they like you?" She tried to imagine a whole group of hot undercover guys with guns, and her mind couldn't process it.

He frowned at her. "You don't get to pick another team member to stay with you."

"I didn't say—"

"You're stuck with me."

"You don't want to pass me off?" She really hoped he'd say no.

"You do talk a lot." His thumb rubbed over her temple. Much more touching and she'd forget they were outside and in danger and return to the kissing that felt so good. "You don't like talking?"

"Strangely enough, I'm starting to."

Chapter Four

She looked like death by the time they got within a quarter mile of the ferry landing. Cam called in the team to have them rendezvous at a new position because he doubted Julia could make it much farther.

Not that she complained. No, she never made a sound except for a grunt here and there. But when they started down the grassy hill behind them, he heard her sharp intake of breath and called a halt. No way could she take the slope from here to the water, and she all but punched him when he mentioned again the idea of carrying her.

He liked her spunk and the well of energy she kept finding. Most men he knew would have dropped at the sight of two dead guys on their family room floor. She'd hung in there.

But she needed rest, which was why they sat at a picnic table behind a grocery market with her sore ankle resting on the bench next to him. The employees likely used the space for breaks, but right now he claimed it.

From this position he could use his binoculars to scan the marina. Sailboat masts bobbled and a cool wind blew off the water. People lined up on the dock. A group of men talked with each person as he or she stepped into line for the ferry.

Cam didn't know what that was about, but the lack of uniforms and the fact that no one had performed those checks when he landed a few hours ago suggested it wasn't legitimate. More likely this group was part of the one that had shot up Julia's house.

He scanned the faces he could make out and body types for anyone who looked like the fake police chief. That guy struck Cam as the leader. If they cut the group off at the top, the rest should wither or at least be confused enough that wiping them out would be easier.

He glanced at his watch. Before he could read the dial, she piped up. "The ferry will be leaving soon."

"You'll be on it." For some reason that promise sliced through him. He felt the cut through his midsection.

Which meant he needed to get her on that boat now. She was a distraction. A long-legged, sweet-faced distraction with a butt that held him captive and a drive that enthralled him.

He'd watched as other members of the Corcoran Team paired off. Marriage, engagements, living together, serious dating. Strong men who vowed to put work first bowled over by compelling women they could not resist.

The Corcoran traveling team had made a vow, too— keep moving and stay bachelors. He had no idea how the promises broke down with the other members, but looking at Julia, watching her trace a fingertip over a crack in the tabletop as her long hair fell over her shoulder, he felt an odd tug. One he planned to ignore, and that started with a no-more-kissing rule.

"Do you plan to roll me down the hill?" she asked as the finger tracing morphed into drumming.

He almost laughed at that. "Might be faster than carrying you."

She looked up long enough to glare at him. "No to both."

"You need to get away from the island." Cam was starting to think everyone should leave, because no one would be safe until his team figured out the random pieces of what was going on and put them together in a way that made sense.

"Will that matter?" Her shoulders fell. "If these men know who I am, they can track me down."

He hated that truth but liked that she kept thinking it through, thinking about the angles. That caution would keep her safe. "You'll stay in a hotel and use cash."

"For how long?"

He wanted to tell her a day or two, but that could be a lie, and he refused to get her hopes up. "However long it takes to make sure you're okay."

She glanced off to the side. Stared at the trash cans without talking for almost a minute. "It's not my house."

Whatever he'd expected her to say, that wasn't it. "What?"

"The house was my father's." She drummed those fingers against the table again.

The steady rhythm started a ticking in the nerve in the back of his neck. He reached over and put a hand over hers. "Okay, back up. Where is your dad?"

"Dead." She delivered the information in a flat voice.

He wasn't sure what to say or how to read her mood, so he went with the obvious response. "I'm sorry."

This was not his area of expertise. His birth mother had lost custody before he hit kindergarten. She'd held on just long enough to make him too old and unadoptable, according to state officials. He'd spent the rest of his youth passed around from one foster home to another until he aged out of the system and turned to the military for a more permanent home.

"I was cleaning the house out for sale, though I'm thinking that might not be happening now." She sighed as she opened her hand and let his fingers fall between hers. "My point is, anyone who looks up the deed will trace my father to me, and me to Seattle."

He was still trying to process the news and what it meant in terms of keeping her safe. "You don't live on Calapan."

"Not since I was smart enough to run away at eighteen and not look back."

"Very smart," a familiar male voice called out from around the corner of the market just before he came into view. "I hate this place."

Shane Baker. The Corcoran traveling team member who was the most likely to make a joke to get through a tough situation.

Julia snatched back her hand and spun around. Looked ready to jump to her feet, which was the last thing Cam wanted her to do with that ankle.

Shane and Holt Kingston, the head of the traveling team, stepped into view. Cam hated to admit they'd gotten the jump on him. Hated more the idea they might have seen the whole hand-holding thing.

"Whoa there." Cam put a reassuring hand on her arm. "They're with me."

She sat down hard on the bench again and glanced at him. "Huh, you really all do look like that."

He had no idea what she was talking about. "What?"

"Nothing."

Cam decided to keep the focus on the problem instead of whatever might be running through her head, though he did wonder. "Holt Kingston and Shane Baker, this is Julia White."

Holt shook her hand, then moved in beside her on the bench. "Your hostage."

That was the last thing Cam needed to hear. If they thought he'd messed up, they'd never let him forget it. "It wasn't like that."

She looked at Holt. "It sort of was."

Shane joined the group at the table. He sat across from Julia and looked her over with a frown on his face. "You okay?"

"She sprained her ankle." He'd also scared the crap out of her and killed a man in front of her, which had to have her mind blinking, but the team knew that from his check-in, so Cam didn't repeat it now.

This time she aimed her sigh at Cam. "*She* twisted her ankle and *she* can speak."

Shane barked out a laugh. "I like her."

"She's a talker." Cam figured they might as well get that out of the way because Holt operated on the say-as-few-words-as-possible theory.

Shane's smile faded. "Oh."

With that done, Cam turned back to the case. "What do we have?"

"No identification on the deceased. Connor and Joel are working on it from the photos and fingerprints we sent."

She put a palm on the table. "Who are they?"

Something about the way she held her hand out had them all quieting down. Cam had never seen anything like it. The team members tended to talk over each other when it came to handling assignments. Connor and to a lesser extent Holt and Davis, the leader of the Annapolis home team, could demand the floor with absolute certainty.

Before Cam could give a personnel rundown, Holt jumped in. "Connor runs the Corcoran Team. It's his baby. Joel is our tech guy. Both are back in the Annapolis main office."

She held up one finger. "Okay, one more question—"

Shane whistled. "I see what you mean about the talking."

"—who or what is the Corcoran Team?" She ended the comment by glaring at Shane.

There was a long-winded answer about undercover, off-the-books work. Cam went with the easier response. "We are."

"That doesn't really clear anything up." Her last word cut off before she looked at Holt. "And did you say you checked the deceased? I'm guessing that means you went back to the house, though I have no idea why you'd want to see that scene."

Holt nodded. "Yes."

"Have we figured out why these guys tracked Cam and kept shooting at him?" she asked as she leaned in.

"Not yet."

Cam could have listened to her rapid-fire questions and Holt barely answering all day. It summed up their respective personalities. But he knew from experience Holt's patience would expire, and that was reason alone to end this.

"We came here to talk to a witness who reported some concerns. Raised some questions about illegal drug running on Calapan," Cam explained, trying to keep the intel as neutral as possible.

"Who?" she asked.

Shane shook his head. "I don't think—"

"Rudy Bleesher." Cam ignored the stunned stares from his teammates. He was surprised he'd shared that information, too, but nothing made sense on this job. They'd come here for an interview and ended up in a shoot-out. Not the usual assignment. "She's from here. We aren't."

She snorted. "If it's about drugs, Rudy will know."

Holt's eyebrows lifted. "Because?"

"We went to school together, and the guy knew all about drug dealing."

Finally a piece of the puzzle that fit for Cam. If Rudy had started out using and maybe dealing and now wanted to turn in evidence to cut a deal or get out of trouble or whatever, that made sense. And they were talking about drugs in serious amounts.

Cam had been with the team for three years and had never gone after a run-of-the-mill drug user. But word was the operation on Calapan was serious business and served as a source for moving drugs up and down the coast and into Canada, which made it Corcoran business.

"You're sure this is the same guy?" Shane asked.

She started drumming those fingers again. "The island is thirty square miles, and most of that is wooded and uninhabited. Yeah, I know Rudy."

"We need to talk with Rudy and get Julia off the island." Holt glanced down at her hand but kept talking. "The ferry isn't an option until we clear these guys out, which means we need to find the real police chief."

"You know about him?" she asked.

"They were there when I got shot at." Cam thought

that part had been obvious but he guessed not. "They were watching when everything fell apart."

Julia flattened her hand against the table. "Which time?"

"The first, the time that led me to you, but you make a good point." Back then Cam had called the scramble code and they'd scattered. At that point he'd still thought they could grab Rudy and be gone without trouble. Talk about a miscalculation.

Holt looked through the binoculars and Shane rechecked maps on his watch. Cam waited. He could tell something ran through her head. Maybe it was the way she gnawed on her bottom lip.

The quiet stretched on for a few more beats before she exhaled. "I can take you to Rudy's house."

"No way." Shane clicked on the GPS function on his watch. "Give us the address."

"You'll never find it," she said in almost an I-told-you-so offensive strike.

Cam sided with Shane on this one. "We're pretty good at this."

He wanted Julia long gone and far away when they tracked down Rudy. The man wasn't where he was supposed to be this morning, and all hell had broken loose because of that.

"Fine." She shrugged. "Go to the fourth turn past the group of willows by the water where all the kids went skinny-dipping in high school."

Shane stared at her. "Maybe a street name?"

"There isn't one, to my knowledge. Rudy lives in a shack." She sent Cam that I-told-you-so grin she'd all but promised. "Getting mail is the least of his concerns."

"You win." Holt slapped a hand against the table and got up. He pointed at Cam. "You take Julia and look for Rudy. Shane and I will find the chief or at least clear the ferry area of suspects."

She shifted to look up at Holt, who now towered over her. "How?"

He smiled for the first time since he had sat down. "We can be persuasive."

"But first." Cam eyed Holt.

"What?" She glanced around, looking more confused by the second.

"Right. Sorry." Holt bent over and picked up a bag. He took out a bandage, then an ice pack. "Cam is going to set your ankle."

Her gaze flipped to Cam. "You know how to do that, too?"

The woman needed to have some faith. "My skills are endless."

RAY MINER STOOD in the ferry's ticket-buying area, just inside the building, so he could get a good look at anyone approaching the marina. But he was looking for one person in particular—Cameron Roth. The guy was supposed to be some superstar pilot who was good with a gun.

Ray had some skills of his own and was pretty sure he'd impressed the guy by shooting the man he was holding from right under his arm. But now he was down two men and Ray didn't like that at all. Cameron would pay for that.

Two more of his men returned from their search of the ferry decks after the most recent unloading. "There's nothing and no one left on board, but the waiting passengers are getting antsy."

"Tell them there's a delay and to come back for the next one." When his men stared at each other but neither moved, Ray saw the positives in eliminating a few of his guys without Cameron's help.

Ned, the bigger of the two and the one who usually did the talking, cleared his throat. "They're starting to have questions."

As if Ray cared. "We have the captain tied up and the rest of the crew believing I had to come in from Seattle and commandeer the boat because of the transfer of illegal goods in one of the cars. Have the crew inform the passengers that there is a search ongoing at the moment."

"What if someone calls the real police chief?" Ned asked.

"He's busy running around the island right now, and we have control of the phones." Besides, Ray liked this cover. He could get used to wearing the uniform. It went with the gun. "My bigger concerns are Cameron Roth and Julia White, the woman with him."

Now Ray knew her name. Knew the boss wanted her tracked down and brought to him. Apparently Ms. White didn't live on the island and wasn't supposed to be there. She was the type who liked to stick her nose where it didn't belong. She'd learn the hard way what a bad idea that was.

"They can't get far. We have the marina in lockdown and they're about to run out of ferry service. There's only one more after this." The one who wasn't Ned delivered the information.

Ray didn't remember his man's name, because it didn't matter. The guy's job was to not mess up as he followed orders. "What about a boat on another part of the island?"

Ned pointed to the boats docked around them. "Possible, but they didn't come in with a boat, so that should lead them back here if they want to find one. We also have a few guys watching the water and checking private boats."

"Do we have the okay to shoot?" the other one asked.

The guy suddenly became more interesting. Ray liked where his head was in this. "Not the woman. The boss wants her brought in and this Corcoran Team guy taken out."

Ned's eyes narrowed. "Why?"

"Just do it."

Ned shrugged. "I'm just saying it would be easier to kill them both. Set up some sort of lovers' argument gone wrong."

Ray agreed, but he didn't have the final say. Not in this. He took care of logistics and security for the business. He was the reason they'd been tipped off about Roth showing up in the first place. A guy like that, with his reputation and background, made enemies, and when a DC business associate heard Roth was headed for Calapan, he'd passed the word on. Ray had taken it from there.

But whether he liked this Roth guy or not didn't matter. Ray knew the guy was dangerous.

"Don't underestimate them. This guy Cameron took down two of our men." Really only one but Ray guessed it would be bad for morale if he told them how expendable they were.

Ned stared at Ray. "Roth couldn't get to you."

Ray would not let that happen. He would win that battle every time. "Not me."

Chapter Five

The trek to Rudy's house went easier than Julia had expected. Probably had something to do with the fact that Cam hot-wired a car and drove them most of the way there. He insisted on using the word *borrowed*, but she preferred being factual.

The rocky drive ended a good five hundred feet from the shack. Not that she could see it. The place was so much worse than she remembered. Tall weeds and overgrown trees obscured the building where it sat in a small valley.

In her memory she saw a small one-story building with a front porch. Now that she was older and bigger, it looked like a shed someone might keep in their backyard to store lawn equipment.

Cam pushed away the tall grasses and forged a path ahead of her. The way he trampled down a strip in front of her made it easier to walk. So did the combination of the ice, wrap and painkillers.

Then there was the view. Cameron Roth was not hard on the eyes. Walking behind him, she could see the broad shoulders and how they fell in a V to a trim waist.

He picked that moment to glance back at her. "This is a house?"

She had the same reaction to the falling-down place, but something about his tone struck her the wrong way. "Not refined enough for you?"

He stopped and turned to face her. "I was in the navy."

Okay... She had no idea what he was trying to tell her. "Is that code for something?"

"I've been in the jungle, on a ship for months at a time, crawled through mud and sat point in a swamp for days." He hitched his thumb over his shoulder toward the house. "A falling-down house doesn't scare me."

Then he started walking again. Snapped right back into undercover-protector mode.

She'd caught a glimpse into the man behind the gun. The ship and navy part made sense. The rest sort of blurred as it sped by her. But that was the most he'd shared. The only personal thing he'd shared, actually. She wanted him to keep going. "What did you do in the navy?"

"Flew missions."

And like that the window slammed shut again. "That's specific."

"It's as specific as I can be." They reached the area where the tall grass gave way to a shorter unkempt stretch of lawn right in front of the house. "Anyone else live here?"

Cam had led them wandering off to the side. A group of trees blocked their direct view, but she guessed the real point was it shielded the view of them.

"I have no idea," she said as she looked for any movement around the place.

Cam backed her up into the trunk of the tree and shielded her body with his as he talked. "When is the last time you saw Rudy?"

"Graduation, so, like, eight years ago." The years had ticked by and she'd visited the island as little as possible, but some things never changed and Rudy was one of those.

Cam's eyes narrowed. "How do you know he still lives here?"

Spoken like a guy who didn't grow up in a very small town. "A guy like Rudy doesn't venture very far. He sticks close to home, never gets a real job and lives with his mom."

Cam pointed toward the ground. "Here?"

"She died a couple of years ago." Thanks to the internet, Julia had a direct line to gossip on Calapan…whether she wanted it or not.

"You're sure?"

Cam didn't stop leaning and Julia had to fight to keep from resting her palms against his chest. "She was the high school gym teacher and her car went off the road in an ice storm, so the news made the rounds."

With a nod Cam took out his gun and took a step toward the house. "Stay back."

She grabbed his shirt before he could get very far. "He'll recognize me."

"He could be dangerous."

"Only if you try to take his drugs." Truth was, the outside of this place made her more nervous than the inside. Who knew what lurked about out here? But the house couldn't consist of more than two rooms. Cam could cover that without trouble.

"Anyone ever tell you that you have an answer for everything?" He sounded more amused than angry.

"I'm the one who lives here and knows the people." And she still didn't want to sit out here by herself.

"Lived. Past tense."

She had to concede that one. "You got me there."

With a hand on her wrist, he moved her clinch from his shirt to his back belt loop. "Hang close to me but let me move."

They didn't head straight for the porch. Cam guided them out in a half circle and they came up the side of the porch and stopped next to the door frame. He never put them straight in front of a door or window.

She guessed that was a safety precaution thing. She supported him using any and all of his training to protect her.

"It's quiet," Cam said in a whisper.

She'd expected music. She remembered Rudy blaring music. "Maybe he's gone."

"Huh." Cam looked through the curtain-covered window at the top of the door. "Maybe."

He turned the knob and the front door opened with a creak. It sounded like a bad horror movie. Other than a strange humming sound, she didn't hear anything. Most of the house was cast in shadows, but a stream of sunshine sneaked in and dust danced wherever it shined.

But the smell hit her. Rotten meat.

"What is that?" She guessed Rudy had forgotten to pay the electric bills and ended up with a refrigerator full of ruined food.

The stench made her gag. She put a hand over her nose and tried not to breathe, but that didn't work. Then she buried her face in the back of Cam's shirt. Still, the smell got in her senses. It was like a living, breathing thing and it slowly choked the life out of her.

Cam started backing up. "Go stand outside."

"Why? I don't…" Her gaze landed on the shoe and traveled up the leg to a knee. "Is that a foot?"

With his hands on her shoulders, Cam pushed her against the wall and out of the direct viewing line of the body. Not roughly. More like to rest her back against something hard. She wasn't sure if it was for protection or out of a concern that she might fall down. Because that was her worry, as well.

She shifted until she stood by the front door. They'd closed it behind them and now she wanted to fling it open and run outside. She looked at Cam and had no idea how he stayed so calm. He loomed over the body without any reaction.

Then he bent down. His hands moved quickly, going into pockets and picking through the papers lying around the body by using the end of a pen.

When he stood up, he shook his head. "He's been out more than a day."

She wasn't sure what that meant for his assignment. Her main concern was for him to get whatever information he needed so they could leave. "What happened?"

"Looks like someone hit him in the head with something hard." Cam's footsteps tapped against the hard floor as he came toward her.

"It could have been an accident." She hoped. Part of her wanted this all to be one big misunderstanding. Better yet, one terrible nightmare, and as soon as she woke up the horrible pictures in her mind would blink out for good.

"I don't see blood anywhere but on him, and whatever hit him is gone."

He sounded so sure. So much in charge as he spouted off his expertise. Normally that would bring her comfort, but the more they talked about death and stood surrounded by it, the more her mind muddled.

She knew they should do something, but she couldn't kick-start her mind enough to figure out what. "So, we need—"

"We have to leave. Now." He caught her by the elbow as he made his way for the door.

She didn't slow him down. Last place she wanted to be was at this house with this awful discovery waiting inside. In two steps she was at the front door. She opened it, ushering in some needed fresh air.

Cam swore behind her. "I should go out there first just to check."

As far as she was concerned, he was lucky she didn't run out screaming. "Next time."

Her foot hit the front porch, and the lights registered, flashing red and out of the line of sight from the inside of the house. Chief Kreider stood there with a line of four officers, possibly every officer on the island. All had their guns up and ready to go.

She tried to make sense of what she was seeing and couldn't.

"Hands up!"

The order crashed through her. The words registered, as did all the weapons. The police were here, but instead of investigating what was happening with Rudy, they'd turned on her. Maybe on Cam. She couldn't really be sure.

Cam stumbled to the door behind her, and his eyes narrowed on their unwanted guests. "Wait. Who is that?"

She felt as confused as he sounded. The only thing that overwhelmed the confusion was the lump of fear clogging her throat. "That is the real police chief. Bud Kreider. Real name is Brian."

"Interesting choice to go with Bud." Cam stepped around her and out onto the porch. "We can explain."

If anything the wall of police officers closed in. Kreider moved to the front and his attention never left Cam. What had started out as an awful find morphed into something else. Julia's heart hammered hard enough to echo in her ears.

Kreider widened his stance as he took careful aim. "Put the gun down now."

"Damn." Cam made a face. Quickly, then it disappeared to be replaced with that blank, unreadable expression he seemed to have perfected.

Her gaze shot over to him. "What?"

"I have three more on me," he mumbled half under his breath.

She knew he'd come armed, but the answer seemed so odd. So unlike what normal people did and how they acted. "What?"

"Both of you, down on the ground now. I'm not asking again." Kreider and one of his men got closer. She and Cam had their hands in the air, but that didn't seem to matter to the police chief. He all but shook as he gave each order.

She rushed to explain, because between the anxiety welling inside her and the tension spinning around all of them, she sensed a rash action headed right for them. "We didn't do anything."

"Julia White?" Kreider lowered his gun as his eyes narrowed. "What are you doing here? You haven't been to Calapan in years."

Mundane chitchat. She could handle this. Maybe while

she did, some great plan would pop into Cam's head. "Cleaning up Dad's house."

"Out here?" Kreider shook his head. "You'll have to come up with a better excuse than that."

He might as well know. Refusing to look at Cam in case he disagreed with telling the truth, she answered, "We're looking for Rudy."

She held her breath and waited for the fallout.

"We? You know this man?" Kreider pointed toward Cam as he asked.

There was no good way to answer that question. She felt she did know him, sort of, despite only meeting hours ago. In the end she went with the answer that seemed closest to the truth. "Yes. We came to talk with Rudy, but when we got here and he was…"

"Julia," Cam said, his voice like a warning, and it was enough for her to stop talking.

Kreider was almost on top of her now. "What?"

He'd know in five seconds anyway. If he touched the door, the smell would hit him. Seeing the body, no matter how hardened he was from years on the job and all that drinking, should hit with a punch. She still wanted to retch.

"Rudy is dead." Saying the words didn't help. If anything they brought home the reality that he was gone.

Close or not, Rudy was a human being. Someone had decided to end his life. Julia was convinced of it.

Kreider snapped to attention. "On the ground." He motioned to his men with his head. "Check inside."

"Chief, this isn't what it looks like." It grated against her to show the guy any deference. He was younger than her dad, but she'd seen him in action. He liked to throw his weight around and threaten. Suggest he had more power than he did.

Cam took a step. The move didn't put him in front of her, but his body did shield hers. "You had a meeting with me earlier."

Kreider's eyes narrowed even further. "You're Gideon Rodgers?"

The name didn't make sense. How many did the guy have? "Cam?"

"You giving out aliases?" Kreider shook his head. "Julia, what would your daddy think?"

She had no idea. None of this made sense. She tried to replay every minute since she'd come inside after the attack. Cam had told her who he was. Cam had told her why he was on the island. Cam had brought a firefight to her door.

For a second she questioned him. Maybe Cam had set up this elaborate ruse all while protecting his drug operation on the island. She'd never demanded verification, which meant he could be anyone. And the extra name didn't help.

Footsteps sounded behind her and she glanced around to see a policeman on the porch. "Sir, we have a body."

Kreider took the gun out of Cam's hand and the other policeman started a pat down. "Is there anything you want to tell me, son?"

"I'm not Gideon Rodgers."

"Whatever your name is, you are under arrest for the murder of Rudy Bleesher."

She didn't understand Cam having multiple names and all the other pieces of his job, but she knew Cam had been with her all day and didn't have any idea how to get to Rudy's house without her help. The man she'd walked around with, the one who'd played rescuer every minute, could not also be a cold-blooded killer. She'd never believe that.

"He didn't do—"

Cam shook his head. "Julia, it's okay."

"That's not correct, but wait." Kreider pointed a finger in her direction. "You are one step away from being arrested."

Her breath caught in her throat. "I didn't do anything."

Alarms blew in the distance and a line of official-looking county vehicles headed toward the shack. She didn't understand how they got there so fast. Rudy's place sat away from the neighbors—who had called them? Unless things had radically changed, Rudy didn't have the type of friends who would check in on him.

"We'll go through everyone's statements down at the station." The officer cuffed Cam's hands behind his back and Kreider nodded his approval.

Cam shook his head. "I hate this island."

"That makes two of us." But hating Calapan wasn't new. Questioning her trust in Cam, even for a second, was, and she didn't like it.

Chapter Six

Cam knew he'd never hear the end of this. No way would Holt and Shane let getting arrested slide without giving him a load of crap. And he probably deserved it. He hadn't seen the setup coming.

That was what happened when a guy started thinking more about the woman by his side than the job in front of him. Lesson learned.

"You've been busy since you've been on the island." Chief Kreider flipped through the paperwork in the file in front of him. "You stole a car, we have all those weapons to deal with, and now we have three murders."

Julia's gaze switched from the chief to Cam and back again. "Three?"

She sat at the small desk outside of the cell. Cam watched her fidget in her chair. She'd crossed and uncrossed her legs ten times now and they'd only been in the satellite police office for about an hour. Long enough for Kreider to put together a file, apparently.

Good thing the Corcoran Team kept close tabs on that sort of thing. Anytime any name or alias got searched, it popped up on the screen back at the team's home office in Annapolis. That meant Connor and Joel and whoever else was there and not out on assignment were running checks and tracking his location.

Connor had put the elaborate system in place as a precaution. The work they did offered more danger than reward sometimes. Connor insisted they run drills, conduct fake searches to try to trip up the computer tracking system.

Basically, he wanted them ready at all times for anything. Cam appreciated his boss's paranoia now more than ever, because it meant Holt and Shane would have a position and some sense of what just went wrong.

"There are two bodies at your house, but I'm thinking you know that." Kreider spared her a frown before he went back to reading.

Not that Julia was content to be ignored. Her foot hit the floor and she turned in her seat, fully facing the chief now. "Those men attacked and Cam protected me."

"Cam as in Cameron Roth." Kreider nodded as he flipped another page. "Your friend here also has several names. Did he bother to mention that?"

Cam wrapped his fingers around the bars as he studied the small space. One cell and a place for a guard to sit, the place where Julia sat now. During the walk into this place, Cam had noticed an outer room and two doors leading to somewhere—he wasn't sure where—but this building on the outskirts of nowhere couldn't be a thousand square feet or house that many officers on a regular basis.

"I gave you the number to call," Cam said for the third time, suspecting Kreider would ignore him this time, too.

"Of your boss, who would explain. Yeah, I got it." Kreider shut the file. "I'd rather hear the story from you.

But first, you." He turned to Julia and didn't say another word.

She frowned. "Me?"

Cam's hands clenched tighter around the bars. "Leave her out of this."

"You're the one who dragged her into it." Kreider focused his attention on her. Didn't break eye contact. "Or do you and Cameron here have a relationship of some sorts that might keep you from being honest with me?"

Her eyes went dark. "What exactly are you asking?"

"I'm trying to figure out why Gideon...I mean, Cameron skipped our meeting and showed up at your house instead. Maybe this is a plan the two of you had." Kreider looked back and forth between them. "Though I can't figure out why you would want to hurt Rudy or what you two might be planning here on Calapan."

"You can't be this incompetent." Everything about this guy ticked Cam off. He had a look of practiced ignorance. From the oversize belly and stain on his shirt to the swagger in his walk. He looked like a man who had traded a favor for a comfy desk job long ago and hadn't worked in the field or on a real case since.

"I wouldn't call catching a multiple murderer incompetent." Kreider stood up. The look of satisfaction on his face mirrored the way he held his body, all confident and sure. "The Seattle police don't. There's a detective here to question you about some cases that look a lot like this one."

Julia stilled. Her feet stopped moving and her palms came to rest on the table in front of her. "What are you talking about?"

"He's making it up." But Cam knew he wasn't. At the mention of a detective, Cam's blood ran cold. He knew of one other man running around the island wearing a uniform and pretending to be in charge, and that guy was lethal enough, steady enough, to kill a man Cam was holding.

"You'll see when the detective gets here." Kreider did a little stretch, complete with a grunt. "He's been at the ferry waiting for you to get in. Apparently you slipped past him."

That clinched it. Detective, ferry…the guy who was after him was going to walk right into the station and grab him the easy way. Might just put a bullet through his head and end it. Cam feared what would happen to Julia then.

Now to convince Kreider. "You're being set up."

"Julia, now would be a good time for you to pick sides." Kreider nodded in Cam's direction. "Is this really the guy you want to tie your future to?"

"He saved me."

Kreider shook his head and shot her a look of pity. "Or did he make it look that way so he could really kill the two men with the Seattle detective? Maybe your so-called rescuer is really a man on the run and he's using you."

She slumped back in her chair. "You're saying the guy at my house really was police?"

Cam could not let her thinking wander in that direction. "He claimed to be you, Kreider."

"Did you hear him do that, Julia?" Kreider kept up that pitying stare. "You think about that and we'll talk more in a second."

Silence screamed through the room the minute Kreider stepped out. Cam had hated the guy before. He detested him now, but the reason had changed.

Looked as though he had underestimated the other

man, as well. A few well-placed words and doubt filled her eyes. Cam could see the change wash over her as she questioned every conversation. "Julia, you can't believe—"

The chair squeaked as she turned around to face him. "Who is Gideon…whatever the last name is?"

This part likely wouldn't make sense to anyone outside the business. Cam's brain scrambled as he tried to figure out a way to deliver the information without sounding like a bad television show. "Gideon Rodgers. My cover name."

"Why did you need cover if you were on Calapan on an official assignment?"

She asked the right questions and didn't just agree with whatever he said. The smarts were so hot, but right now they had the power to trip him up even though he was telling the truth. "We didn't know who was involved. Rudy's intel suggested powerful people on the island were in on the drug dealing. That meant assuming the police had been compromised."

She stood up and walked over to him. Stayed just out of touching range with her hands in her pockets. "You see how everything you've done and told me fits into Chief Kreider's scenario as easily as it does yours, right?"

"Yes." Cam leaned in, trying to get closer, to will her to believe in him. "But if I'm right, we're about to be in the middle of a bloodbath."

The wariness didn't leave her eyes. "What are you talking about?"

"If the guy who escaped at your house is who I say he is, then he is after us, or at least me, and I don't think he cares who he takes out in this station to get to me." That guy wisely saw Cam as a threat and wanted him out of the way.

The attacker had killed his own man to make a point. He'd go through Kreider and Julia and anyone else. Which was why Cam needed to get out, get away from her before she became collateral damage, and find his men. They had to piece together what they'd walked into the middle of, and fast, before it exploded on them.

Some of the tension left her face. "What do you want me to do?"

With that question, delivered in a soft tone, relief washed through him. He bent over slightly as he blew out a long breath. "Come close enough so I can grab you."

"What?"

"We'll make it look like I forced you to let me out. We'll play it for the cameras, but I won't actually hurt you." It was the only way to keep from dragging her deeper into this logistical and legal mess.

Right now she had deniability on the criminal charges. She could, and he would make sure she did, claim that he kidnapped her. Anything to take away the sting of her being an accomplice.

"You still have to get out of the building," she pointed out.

She wasn't wrong and he'd thought that through. Being on the run would stink, but it was better than going down in a hail of bullets in the corner of this cell. "This is a police outpost. There's barely anyone here. And this guy was dumb enough to leave us together even though he thinks he can turn you against me."

"Okay, but…" She rocked back on her heels as she chewed on her bottom lip. "Even if you make it to the outside, then what?"

"I'll figure it out." He could run fast and far and hide in the trees while he reconnected with Holt. "Julia, I know this looks bad and I'm asking for blind faith when you barely know me, but—"

"Be quiet." She put her head in her hands for a second. When she straightened up again, a new determination thrummed off her. She walked to the far side of the room and hit the button. The one that opened the cell.

He heard a click and the lock disengaged. The cell door moved under his hands.

But this was the wrong way to do this. "What are you doing?"

"Picking a side." She held out a hand to him. "Let's go."

He didn't argue. He should have, but it was too late. Anyone watching the security tape would see she'd staged the escape. That meant his sole task now was to protect her.

After a quick look out the door, they slipped out of the room. He wanted to go right and storm through the front door. He didn't really see another way.

She pulled him to the left. "There should be a door to the parking lot from here."

With quiet footsteps, they walked down the short hall and into what looked like a closet turned storage of sorts. One with three lockers and civilian clothes hanging on pegs on the wall.

They kept going until they hit the door at the far side. Cam disengaged the lock and waited for alarm bells to ring. Nothing happened.

With the door opened, they walked into the cool dark night. More time had passed than he thought, but he had a bigger question. "How do you know about that exit?"

They flattened against the outside wall. Cam stared

across the small parking lot. Only two cars and one official vehicle sat there.

"I grew up here. I've been in the police station before." Her voice stayed flat.

For some reason her comment made him smile. "Misspent youth?"

"More like picking my dad up after he got caught driving around drunk." She pointed toward the line of trees to their left. "This way."

"Hold up." He caught her just before she cleared the side of the building and walked into the open area. He peeked around the corner. "It's clear."

They ducked and ran. He didn't have a weapon to fire for cover and had no idea where the fake Seattle policeman was lingering about, so they took off. No talking. Just darted out.

They made it the whole way and dived into the trees on the side of the lot before he remembered her ankle. She paced around in a circle now with a slight limp, likely trying to walk off the ache.

Guilt smacked into him. "You okay?"

She nodded. "That wasn't too bad."

He had the exact opposite reaction. "Actually, it was too easy."

She froze. "Meaning?"

Incompetent police or not, there was no way they should have been able to escape custody that easily. An alarm hadn't even sounded yet. "We need to find a place to hide."

JULIA POUNDED HER fist on one of the towering double doors of the sprawling two-story log home with the A-frame front. She was tired and hungry and two seconds away from being full-on grumpy. Her ankle thumped and the realization that she'd broken Cam out of jail kept running through her head.

She'd likely have a criminal record now. She, the person who led her entire life by the rules and without fanfare. She looked over and glared at the guy who'd brought so much trouble into her life.

His eyes widened. "What?"

"As if you don't know."

She was about to say more, but the door opened. Sandy Bartlet stood there. Her father's friend and exact opposite. He had more gray around his temples and lines at the corners of his eyes, but he wore the same wide smile he always did as he ushered them inside and wrapped her in a giant bear hug.

He stepped back and looked her up and down. "You didn't tell me you were back in town."

"Only to clean up Dad's house for sale so I can settle the estate."

Sandy and her dad had grown up together, raised like brothers. She viewed him as the uncle she'd never had. The one stable force in her life when her mother left and her father's disposition turned more and more sour.

He was the one who had given her dad a job and cleaned him up when he fell down. He was everything her father wasn't—successful and dependable being the main two things. He'd owned the shipyard on the island and made a fortune when he sold it to the company that eventually ran it into the ground and put her father back on the unemployment line.

Sandy squeezed her one last time, then let his arms drop to the sides. "I would have helped you, but whatever you planned on doing with the house might be impossible now."

Something clunked inside her. She felt it around her stomach. "You heard."

"The news is all over the island." Sandy put his hands on his hips and switched his gaze back and forth between her and Cam. "What really happened?"

The move had her jumping to make an introduction. She was half-surprised Cam hadn't done it himself. "This is Cameron Roth."

The men shook hands as Sandy talked. "I assume you know something about the shooting."

The need to protect and explain rushed up on her. "I was there. Men came in, threatened me, and Cam protected me."

Still, Cam said nothing. He stood there, unmoving, with his hands linked behind his back. Maybe he thought Sandy would turn him in or was too stunned by the inside of the house. Sandy didn't exactly go for subtle. There were large-screen televisions everywhere and overstuffed sofas. The man lived in comfort.

"Well, then." Sandy clapped his hands together. "That's certainly a different story from the one Kreider is telling."

"You heard from him?" Cam asked, talking for the first time since they'd stepped inside.

"He called right before you came to the door. Told me this wild tale about a jailbreak." Sandy shot Cam one of those man-to-man looks. "But instead of hauling you in, it sounds as if I should be thanking you for keeping her safe."

Julia had no idea what was going through either man's head. Sandy looked impressed, though concerned. Cam's expression had gone blank, which was really not help-ful or new.

She zipped right to the basics. "We need somewhere to stay until Cam can figure this out."

"Maybe it's best if Cam explains to the police and you stay here."

Cam nodded. "Maybe."

"No." She was not going down this road again. He'd tried to lose her at the police station by making things look even worse for him. She couldn't let that happen. Not after the insane time they'd been through.

Truth was, she felt safe with him. And the tiny voice in her head kept repeating that she really didn't want him to lose her.

That part she couldn't deal with or understand. The guy thrived on danger. He was everything she wasn't. Still, the one place she wanted to be was by his side.

She pushed the topic. "Someone is framing Cam for Rudy Bleesher's murder."

"What?" Sandy's head snapped back. "Rudy is dead?"

"We found the body. That's where the police spotted us." It all made sense in her head, but as the words spilled out she could hear the oddness of it all. No wonder Krei-der had taken them both in. The only real question was why he hadn't thrown her in a cell, too.

Sandy looked over at Cam. "Seems death is follow-ing you."

Cam nodded for a second time. "It does appear that way."

The whole quiet act was working on her nerves. She needed Cam to stand up and defend himself. She planned to tell him that the second she got him alone.

First she had to make an ally out of Sandy, which

shouldn't be hard with their history. "Sandy, please help. We need a few hours without questions or being chased."

"I'm not sure what that last part means, but fine." He held up one finger. "For one night only, and then Cam and I are going to have a serious talk in the morning about how to fix this and keep your name out of it."

That was the last place her mind went at the moment. "I'm not worried about that."

Cam shot her an are-you-crazy look. "I am."

"And that answer just bought you twelve hours, even though I want to question you both right now." Sandy let out a long exhale. "Take the two rooms down here. You can go wash up and I'll make something to eat."

Relief swamped her, nearly knocking her down. "Thank you, and thanks for the reprieve."

She sensed it wouldn't last.

Chapter Seven

No way was he staying. Cam didn't like the look of the place. From the outside it looked spacious and homey, all lit up with security lights as the night fell. And with a very impressive security system. Cam recognized the name and wondered what exactly he was walking into and if he'd be able to get out again.

Now he stood in a bedroom and watched Julia slump down on the bed. The wise thing would be to wait for her to fall asleep and then sneak away. But after all they'd been through and the way she'd stuck up for him, that seemed like a pretty jerky way to handle the situation.

Then there was the timing problem. The ticking at the back of his neck said he needed to move. Sandy might claim to give them twelve hours, but his loyalty was with Julia, not him. In Sandy's place, Cam would get her to safety and turn someone like him—with the questionable story and police on his tail—in.

She smiled up at him. "I told you it would be okay."

Man, she actually believed it. That was why it was so hard to hit her with the truth. Well, part of the reason. The idea of leaving her made something inside him clench. He couldn't get wrapped up in her or her life. He should get her out of the trouble he'd created for her and move on…but the memory of that kiss kept smacking him.

He wanted her more with each passing second. The driving need threw him off. He didn't operate like this. He never got involved during a job. He met a woman, they went out, they had sex, it trickled to nothing and he moved on. Just the way he liked it.

But he knew forgetting her would not be that easy. Which was why he needed to get out now. Because of his attraction and the danger. Nothing pointed to a good reason for him to hang around.

He inhaled. "I'm not staying."

"Why?" She shot the word back at him before he even finished the sentence.

"He can keep you safe." Cam pointed out into the hall and the general direction of this Sandy guy's family room. "He'll turn me in."

"But he said he'd help."

Spoken like someone who never dealt in danger and lies. He liked that about her. The girl-next-door sensibility of living her life without fear. Family troubles or not, she was grounded and not looking for a fast fling. He got that.

"I don't trust easily, Julia. Don't ask me to trust this situation. Nothing feels right about any of this." He sat down on the bed next to her when he should have been walking out the door.

"He helped raise me."

Cam took her hand in his. Let his warmth seep into her cold fingers. "You, not me."

She twisted on the mattress to face him. "You have to trust someone."

"That's not an easy emotion for me." In his whole life that sentiment had never really worked for him.

The first time he'd found a home was with the Corcoran Team. Joel was his best friend. They saw each other less now that Joel was back together with the woman who made him happy, but Cam still tagged along. And he hung out with Shane and, to a lesser extent, Holt. They were a team and he entrusted his life and safety to them, but those connections did not extend to people outside Corcoran. Not for him.

"You think it is for me? I grew up with a rageful alcoholic. I didn't exactly have friends over for playdates." She shook her head as if trying to clear out all the old memories. "I don't want you to go."

The pleas tugged at him, made him think about doing stupid things that didn't fit with his life or the need to keep her protected. "You'll be safe with Sandy."

Her other hand went to his lap. Smoothed up and down his thigh. "You make me feel safe."

The touching, the sound of her voice, the pleading in those big eyes. Cam was ten seconds from breaking. "Don't do this."

She nuzzled her mouth against his neck. Blew warm breath over his skin. He fought it until he couldn't, and then he turned his head and kissed her. Right there in another man's house, in a place with security but no connection to Cam.

His mouth lingered over hers, caressing and coaxing, before he pressed deeper. The flash of heat hit him straight in the chest. The need churning inside him kicked up and his hands started to wander over her.

It took every ounce of his strength and self-control to pull back. When that didn't give him enough space, he stood up. Paced around and thought about airplanes. Anything to take his mind off her face and the touch of those lips.

"Then I'm going with you." Her voice sounded shaky.

He knew that wasn't from fear. He felt the trembling inside him and tried to tamp it down.

"Fine." But he didn't mean it.

He'd have to be that jerk. Walk away the second she wasn't looking. Leave her where it was safe and warm and hope that whatever connections Sandy had—and Cam assumed from the look of the place that he had some power—he'd use them to help her. If not, Cam would circle back and take responsibility so she could be free.

Her eyes narrowed as she stared at him. "Really?"

"Go wash up and then we'll find some food."

"Was that so hard?" She got up and kissed him on the cheek.

He tried to smile and make it look genuine. "Nope."

She went into the bathroom. He waited until he heard the water running, then constructed a floor plan of the house in his head. He tried to figure out the most logical ways in and out of the house by the layout of the rooms he'd seen and the look of the place from the outside.

The only question was the alarm system. Sandy hadn't reset it before he ushered them out of the foyer. Cam had to hope that was still the case.

Being careful as he placed his footsteps, Cam walked to the door and opened it. He could hear a television playing in another room and could smell food cooking in the kitchen. He ignored the growl of his stomach and slipped into the hall.

He stopped, trying to get his bearings. It was too risky to go out the front. And if the entry was that way, that meant a side or back door would be in another direction. He glanced to his right and saw what he suspected was a closet. A quick check confirmed the thought. His only solution then was a walk toward the noise.

Between the size of the house and the fact that it had sensor lights outside, this would not be an easy task. He tried to dream up an excuse in case he got caught. The need for fresh air. Probably as plausible as anything else.

The television grew louder as he reached the end of the hall. Sandy stood with his back to him as he used the remote to dial around the stations on the screen that seemed to take up a third of the wall in the massive family room.

At least that task had Sandy occupied. Cam didn't wait for another distraction. He slid along the counter and headed for the door on the side of the kitchen. The French doors by the dining room would take him too close to Sandy, but this one had possibilities. Cam just hoped it didn't lead to a pantry. Would be hard to explain why he was hanging out in there.

He waited to move until Sandy laughed at something on the screen. Cam placed each step carefully and didn't take his eyes off Sandy until he had the door open. Once inside, Cam smelled the faint scent of gasoline and spotted the two cars despite the dark. There was a wide-open bay and a door at the opposite side.

Getting over there took a few seconds. Checking for wires or any evidence of an alarm took another two. The alarm panel next to the door showed a green light. Cam hoped that meant go.

He turned the knob slowly at first, then yanked the door. Cold air and misty rain slapped his face. He glanced up and saw the searchlight aimed at the lawn beyond.

Now he had to play the game of beat the sensor lights. Dodge and weave, keep low and not make noise.

He'd just picked a path when a figure appeared in front of him. Round face, backpack and ponytail...and a glare that could melt steel.

"Forget something?" Julia asked through clenched teeth.

"No."

"If you had asked I would have told you there was a patio off the bathroom in my room." She exhaled and it sounded harsh and ragged. "The bathroom is the size of most people's family rooms."

That was a weird architectural choice and now he regretted not slipping in there to check it out. "Didn't expect that."

"Obviously." She tightened her hold on the strap of her pack. "This is where teamwork comes into play. We work together and you don't need to sneak around."

It sounded good. Too good. "You need to stay here."

"Not happening. See, I turned the alarm to pause. You have about five seconds to come with me before all these lights and bells come on again." She leaned in closer. "And this time Sandy will call the police on you."

Score one for Julia and her overwhelming hotness.

A smart man knew when he'd lost. "Let's go."

RAY SAT IN the front of the van with Ned. They parked a good distance away, on the other side of a small hill. They could move in without thinking, but they waited. Watched the woman and the man run into the woods as the rain started to fall around them.

He was getting tired of following these two. From the ferry. The police station. This house. It was getting old.

Ned wiped a hand against the fog on the inside of the window. "Why are we letting them go?"

This was not Ray's decision. If he had a say, these two would be splattered all over the street by now. Hell, he'd only pulled out of the woman's house that first time because the boss tracked his movements and sent a message saying to let the woman go unharmed. Up until then Ray had had it handled and could have taken Roth without any trouble.

But he wasn't in charge…yet. "The boss wants us to follow. Watch from a safe distance."

"Why?"

The questions skidded across Ray's nerves. It was bad enough he had to listen to directions from the boss. Hearing his inferior question every move just added to the frustration boiling in Ray's gut. "He thinks Roth is not alone."

"You mean the woman."

"He's convinced that kind of guy from that kind of team would come here with other men. If so, we need to find all of them. Round them all up." Made sense to Ray. There was no reason to clamp down on only one problem when more scurried about. "The boss wants them all off the island."

"Are we still supposed to save the woman?" Ned asked as he traced the rain down the window with his finger.

"If possible."

"So, we're letting them go on purpose."

Ray was not impressed with how long it took Ned to reason that out. Maybe he'd picked the wrong second in command. Problem was, his first choice was dead on the floor in the woman's house.

Not many people got the jump on Bob, but Roth had,

which even Ray had to admit made the guy appear more skilled than they'd all hoped when they found out he was coming to Calapan to talk with a witness. Roth had fired one shot, a kill shot. Around the corner and in the middle of darkened chaos.

That one shot was the only reason Ray had held off on putting a bullet in Roth now. Sure, he had the boss's orders, but he really wanted Roth to suffer. See the life run out of him.

Ned looked over his shoulder. "Ray?"

"The boss always has a plan." And so did Ray.

Chapter Eight

It must be nice to have close friends. They'd walked and then gotten in a car. It had just happened to be there with the keys under the mat. Julia figured Holt and Shane were behind this. She didn't complain or ask questions, because the thump in her ankle had kicked up again. Once they were settled—and she hoped that happened soon—she'd dig into her bag and find more of those meds Holt had given her.

Cam took one last turn, then drove the car into the bushes. Right in. He had the old sedan tucked in between rocks and trees and now surrounded by shrubs. It was an interesting hiding place. Effective except for the part where she had to get the door open…and she had no idea where he intended for them to hide.

She recognized this area even though it wasn't one where she spent a lot of time. They were a few miles from the old shipyard where her father used to work. She could smell fish and feel the pickup in moisture in the air as they got closer to the water.

The place, like everything on this part of the island, had fallen into disrepair. Sandy talked about buying the land back and revitalizing the area, but Calapan wasn't exactly open to a big tourist crowd, which made the task a pretty bad investment. From what she saw of Sandy's life, he didn't make a lot of bad investments.

Unless Cam planned for them to hide in a tree, she didn't understand why he'd brought her here. "You know it's going to rain again in, like, five minutes, right?"

"Welcome to the Pacific Northwest." He held out a hand to her. The other one carried a flashlight.

Even in the darkness, guided only by one beam of light, she could make out his strong fingers. She grabbed on and didn't let go. "Where are we going?"

"I thought you knew every inch of the island." He marched, forging a path for both of them.

"I never said that." Then there was the part where she'd specifically tried to stay away as much as possible over the years.

At first when she did come here, usually to visit her father in the clinic, she'd always expected to see new buildings and new restaurants. A turnover in stores and fresh faces. That rarely happened. People who grew up here tended to stay here, except for the few like her who escaped.

Not many people landed here without any ties to the place. Most of the land was owned by a few, and neighboring islands like Bainbridge offered more of a welcoming community feel than Calapan. Here, neighbors sat miles away from each other and didn't want to get involved. Poor Rudy had found that out the hard way.

She thought about him and her mind zipped back to all that had happened in such a short time. That took her gaze to their joined hands and then to the sturdy man beside her who cradled her hand in a gentle hold even as he marched them through the tall grass and overgrown branches.

They broke around a cluster of trees and she stopped. Stood frozen to the ground. In front of her sat something that looked like a construction trailer. Old, with a rusted roof and a broken front step. She had no memory of the building, but it could have come after her time, before the shipyard wheezed its final breath.

Cam glanced at her. "Impressed?"

Kind of stunned, actually. "For a guy who isn't familiar with the island, you sure knew how to find this place."

She waited for the doubts to hit her again. She'd been swamped by them at the police station and unable to wipe her expression clean before Cam saw it. The strange anxiety over trusting him hadn't lasted long or lingered. It was just that Kreider had talked and she had listened and the words had made sense.

Then she'd remembered she was dealing with Kreider, the same guy who'd brought her father in to dry out but never arrested him. Who sometimes even looked the other way while her father drove around the middle of town drunk. A good old boy who protected his favorites and hated outsiders. The guy who found reasons to lock up anyone who was even a little different.

The idea of Kreider being too incompetent or too full of hate to see Cam as a protector was not hard to imagine. Kreider and Cam were too different, and if it came time to choose between them or pick one to believe, well, there wasn't even a contest. She picked Cam.

He clicked a button on his watch, and the dial lit up. "I'd like to wow you with my brilliance, but the GPS did all the work."

A handy tool. She noted that for a future purchase even if it did seem a little anticlimactic for Cam. She half expected him to have an invisible plane. "Okay."

"Holt found the place abandoned and set it up as a safe house for us after he cleared the area."

She was starting to like Holt. "Does clearing the area involve shooting a gun?"

"More like checking for vagrants and animals." Cam squeezed her hand. "We have a no on both."

They'd been so busy dealing with the two-legged kind of trouble that she hadn't even spared a thought for critters. The size of the raccoons alone around here could scare a normal person to death.

"Holt also dropped off some supplies." They went to the door in single file as they walked on a board across what looked like a deep puddle of water.

"Maybe I should have stuck with Holt." The quiet hit her and she glanced up in time to see Cam's jaw tighten. "Kidding."

"Believe it or not, I don't find that funny." He dropped her hand as he reached for his gun but came up with air, since Kreider had stripped him of his weapons hours ago.

She tried not to take the loss of contact personally, but he sounded as though he was serious. His tone matched his frown and neither said happy or anything similar. The idea that a man like Cam, with his confidence and control, could need reassurance struck her as funny, but she didn't dare laugh.

She went for damage control instead. "I don't find him attractive. Just you."

"That's better." He winked at her. "Stay here."

"Yeah, I know the drill by now."

He stopped before taking the last step onto the broken staircase. "You know we've only been together one day."

"It feels like months." That wasn't an exaggeration. She felt as if she knew him. As if deep down they'd bonded on some level that allowed them to fast-forward through the getting-to-know-you stage. Maybe that was what happened when the initial meet consisted of a hostage and shooting situation.

"I'm going to hope that's a good thing." He moved, balancing for a second on the piece of a rotted stair before pulling his body up to the deck.

He took careful steps. With each move he'd put a portion of his weight down. Once he heard the crack or the creak, he'd go forward. Almost sprint across as if to barely touch the piece of wood.

It felt as if it took forever for him to get to the door, but the journey only lasted a few minutes. Without looking back he turned the knob, then slipped inside.

With him out of view, the sounds of the night amplified. Crickets chirped and the leaves and branches swished and swayed. She could hear something scurry nearby but decided not to think about that. She blocked the critter just as she blocked the terror racing through her at the idea of someone sneaking up behind her.

She thought about that possibility and whipped around to confront whatever might be out there. Only a breeze greeted her.

"Are you okay?"

Cam's voice cut through the night and the nerves jumping around inside her. She glanced up to see him standing there with his hands on his hips, looking every inch a man in charge.

"I'm good." That qualified as a lie, but if she told him about the shaking knees and chattering teeth, she might accidentally distract him.

He held a hand out to her. "Let's get you inside and off that ankle."

He remembered. Of course he did.

She lifted an arm just as he leaned down. He had his hands under her armpits and her feet off the ground in no time. She spun through the air with her body pressed next to his. When the world came back into focus, she balanced against his chest with her arms wrapped around his neck.

"You're carrying me." It seemed like an obvious comment, but she wanted to point it out just in case.

"Yeah." The breathiness in his voice mirrored hers.

Like everything else about him, that was way too sexy.

"I can stand." Not that she really wanted to at the moment. The feeling of his strong arms around her had that shaking inside her turning into something else.

"That's a shame." He pressed a light kiss on her mouth, then loosened his grip.

Her body slid down his. The friction had her breath hitching in her chest and her common sense in free fall.

Some of that shine of the moment dulled when they stepped inside. To think she'd made fun of him for demanding pristine accommodations. But this was not good. There was a cot with blankets folded and stacked on the end. She gave credit to Holt for that and the bag of food and duffel bag on the floor.

The rest of the place consisted of dust and cobwebs. Cleaning was not her thing, but neither were spiders. She shivered and not in a good way.

"It's set up to look abandoned," he said with more than a little amusement in his voice.

"Uh…" That sounded like crazy talk. A bit more in line with the scenarios she spun in her head about guys working undercover, but still a little weird. "What?"

"Holt cleaned it up, then added some charm. The idea

is that if someone comes looking tomorrow or any day soon, they'll see what they expect to see." Cam glanced around. "A stripped-down, no-one-lives-here building."

Now she was impressed. "You guys think of everything."

He shrugged as he stopped in the middle of the room. "Usually."

Something about that tone. She could pick up the nuance, which amazed her, since she missed all the subtleties of conversation at the office. "Meaning?"

He didn't say anything for long minutes. Just stood there staring down at the tip of his shoe. "Nothing prepared me for you."

Something spun around in her belly and she thought it might be fear mixed with a twinge of hope and a dose of excitement. "That sounds like a compliment."

He turned to face her. "Not that many things throw me off stride."

"Let me try now." Before he could say no or reason through the arguments, she had her arms around his neck and her lips on his.

The kiss dragged her under right from the start. She heard roaring in her ears, and excitement bubbled in her chest. Touching him, holding him, being this close filled her with a lightness she couldn't remember ever feeling before.

The throat clearing came a second before Holt's dry voice. "Am I interrupting?"

Cam jumped and put his body in front of hers. Actually held out his arms so no part of her peeked through except her head, which she kept moving to get a better view.

"Maybe I don't like Holt that much after all." She was only half kidding.

"That's what I was just thinking." Cam didn't sound amused at all.

HOLT COUGHED. IT was the worst fake cough Cam had ever heard. Didn't help that Holt laughed while doing it. Then he held up a hand. "Sorry."

Somehow Cam doubted that. "Are you?"

Holt walked into the building. His shoes tapped against the floor and Cam wondered where that sound was five minutes ago. No one got the jump on him. He'd been trained not to let people sneak up on him. He'd failed that test in the past few minutes.

Further proof that being near Julia put him in a tail-spin.

"Wanted to make sure you found the place and give you a status." Holt nodded to Julia as he talked.

"On what?" she asked.

Holt's mouth opened and closed again. Clearly the guy wasn't sure how to relay the information without debriefing Julia in the process.

Cam almost laughed at that, since this was the woman who had heard evidence against him and still sided with him. She didn't exactly cough up details in order to protect her own butt. She could be trusted, and he never thought that about anyone.

He could even admit it. "You can talk in front of her."

"Whoa." Holt made a face. "Really?"

Cam knew the reaction was about Cam's own issues, but Julia took exception. "Do you want a reference?"

"I wasn't... Never mind." Holt checked his watch. "The guy is following Shane."

"What are we talking about?" Julia sat down hard on the edge of the table. The confusion on her face came through in her voice.

"There's been a car shadowing you and Cam," Holt explained. "Shane managed a pretty stealthy switch and now the car is following him instead of you, but the driver doesn't know that."

An impressive maneuver and one Cam was grateful for. He'd picked up the tail early but didn't let his concern show. An emergency code to Holt took care of the problem, which explained why they worked in groups. Swinging some of these switches alone would be tough.

"Is it the police?" She did not seem even a little upset about the idea of tricking the police.

"Nah, it's a guy named Ray Miner." Holt slipped a piece of paper out of his back pants pocket. "Connor and Joel have been working on this."

Cam took the sheet and stared at the coded message. "Of course they are."

"This Ray is a mercenary type. Retired military who's had trouble in and out with drugs. He showed up on Calapan almost a year ago and now his bank accounts are flush."

"That's stupid." She looked back and forth between them. "Doesn't it make it easier to prove his guilt, if he is guilty of something?"

Holt shook his head. "They're hidden accounts. He's not an amateur and Joel had to dig to find them."

And that was the part that worried Cam. Kreider had ego issues. Cam didn't know what Ray had other than a uniform that didn't belong to him and some skills. "Ray is our fake police chief."

"Yeah, he clearly doesn't like you." Holt's voice grew

more serious as he talked. "He's been passing your photo around town, suggesting you're dangerous."

Julia linked her fingers together. Within a few seconds her knuckles turned white. "You think he killed Rudy?"

"Probably but he's not the leader type. Someone else is running this." Before Cam could ask, Holt filled in the rest of the details. "Kreider has gone missing. He was smart enough to remove the tracker I put on his car."

That did it.

"You're leaving in the morning." Cam stared at Julia but refused to debate this point. She'd stayed too long and he didn't trust Sandy. Cam wanted her back in Seattle in a hotel. The idea of her rolling around in crisp sheets did appeal to him. "First ferry. We get you to Seattle. If that's not safe enough, we put you on a plane to Maryland."

"Why?"

"The home office is there. The Annapolis group can watch over you. No one will think to look for you there." The more he thought about it, the more he liked the plan.

"One flaw." She held up a finger. "I've never been there and know no one there."

"That's what the team is for." Connor would watch over her. The women would take her in. Sure, he'd have to fight off all kinds of matchmaking attempts, but no one would be shooting at her, and that was worth it to Cam.

"You don't think that would be a little odd?" She looked as if she was fighting a laugh. "You dump me on these people and then stay here?"

"This is what we do." They rescued people and kept them safe. That was exactly what this would be.

"I wouldn't know what to do with myself."

She was missing the point, so Cam tried again. "This is not about comfort. It's about safety."

She rolled her eyes at him. "I knew you were going to say that."

This was not the time for this argument, but Cam was fine to have it. He took a step toward her, but Holt blocked his path. "Can I talk with you for a second?"

That sounded like a request, but it wasn't. Cam wanted to say no, but Holt would just threaten to kick his ass, and nothing good could come out of that situation to calm Julia's nerves.

Holt didn't even wait for an answer. He opened the door and stepped out on a solid plank on the deck. Cam closed the door behind him and joined his friend and team leader. And waited. A lecture would hit any second now. Cam could feel it.

"I like her," Holt said.

That was not where Cam had expected the conversation to go. But he was wary because Holt could easily be luring him in. "Okay."

Holt had both hands on his hips. "Anything you want to tell me?"

There it was. The circle around to the private stuff. Cam pretended he didn't get it and went right to the work angle. "We need to look into people in addition to Kreider. He has the connections, but I can't believe others would follow him. He's not the kind of guy who can command men for long." Cam wrote a list in his head. "There's this guy named Sandy—"

"No." Holt actually made a weird sound that came out kind of like a growl. "About Julia."

Yeah, this was The Talk. Cam braced for the rest of it. "She's pretty tough."

"Uh-huh."

"Bright, smart, confident. Doesn't scare easily." He

could go on but thought he'd said enough. Too much
and Holt would shift this conversation into a place Cam
didn't want it to go.

Holt's eyebrow lifted. "Pretty."

He said it, but Cam was not about to disagree. "True."

"Look, I've watched this whole scenario play out before. You're not the first Corcoran Team member to lose
his head over a woman."

Cam knew all about the Annapolis office and how
they got paired off one by one. Found amazing women
and surrendered their bachelorhoods. He and Shane and
Holt had joked about never drinking the water back at
the Annapolis office because there had to be something
in it that made reasonable men fall stupid in love. They'd
also promised they would not fall into the same trap.

The danger and the missions didn't really allow for
a home life. Cam wasn't quite sure why the Annapolis
office didn't see it. Not that the women weren't great.
They were. Every woman matched up well with one of
the members. But the point was anything could happen.
Cam didn't see a reason to take the risk when there were
plenty of women out there who were fine with a no-
strings relationship.

They were confirmed bachelors and Cam wasn't ready
to let that go. "That's not happening."

Holt smiled. "She's hot. Like, way hot."

That was the kind of smile, as if he was mentally con-
juring up Julia's face, that made Cam homicidal. "Holt,
get to the point. Now."

"You know what happens next, right? You fall, hard
and fast." Holt leaned in and his voice dropped lower.
"You get tied up and ripped apart."

Cam had watched Joel suffer and squirm. He'd loved

Hope and feared for her safety. The combination had him spinning in circles and miserable until he won her back.

Cam did not want a piece of that misery. "I'm not involved with Julia in that way."

"You looked pretty involved with your hand up her shirt."

Did that happen? Cam just remembered his palm hitting bare skin and his mind imploding. "You're spying on me now?"

"I was going to walk up to the place sooner, but you were in midkiss. And not to question your skills, but it's not as if you noticed me." Holt held up a hand. "Which brings me to my point."

Cam beat him to the punch because hearing the accusation just might lead to a punch being thrown. "I'm not going to blow the job. I have never messed up a mission or put anything before the team."

"When it comes down to a choice between her or the assignment, you need to think about what you're going to choose." Holt wasn't whispering now. His deep voice carried on the still night.

"She's the assignment." The words rang hollow in Cam's ears. He couldn't sell the argument, because not one part of him believed it.

"That's just it, Cam. She's not. You dragged her into this." Holt's shoulders fell as he blew out a breath. "You made her a target when you ran into her yard and brought her into this mess."

The anger simmering inside Cam spilled over. He knew he was responsible. Knew and hated it, and having it thrown in his face didn't make the situation better. "Don't you think I know that? If I could go back and replay that and keep her safe from the beginning, I would."

"I know."

"But being shot at messed up my thinking." And once he'd had her he couldn't bring himself to store her. He wanted her by his side. He said this was to watch over her, but there were moments when he knew that wasn't true.

"Then give some thought to how this is going to end."

Cam got lost in the vagueness of that one. "The job or with Julia?"

"See, the fact that you're asking that question proves my point." Holt took off down the stairs. If he was worried about his footing, he didn't show it. He stopped one step from the water. "And because I'm your friend and a good leader, I put a condom in the bag."

"What?"

Holt smiled. "You're welcome."

The idea of being free to touch Julia... Cam couldn't even let his mind go there. "You're sending mixed messages here."

"I know." Holt didn't bother turning around this time. He just waved a hand over his shoulder and kept walking. "I'm just waiting to see which one you're smart enough to follow."

The longer he stood there, the more Cam questioned the answer.

Chapter Nine

Julia opened the duffel bag hoping to find chips, maybe some candy. She shoved some T-shirts aside and something that looked like a bomb. She had no idea what that was about. Mixing food with ammunition should be illegal. With her luck she'd eat the wrong thing.

A bit more shifting and she hit more goodies. The packet on top of a new pair of sneakers was not food. Not even close.

She picked the condom up between two fingers and held it, not sure what to do next. Instead of being excited or even grateful, she felt anger filling her. But throwing a fit was not her style.

This was some sort of go-to bag Holt had delivered for an assignment, and it came with birth control. Shirts, bombs and condoms. It was like some bizarre college pack.

The choices made her wonder exactly how Cam operated on a job. A guy who kept his pants zipped and his mind on the operation wouldn't need condoms. Could be she'd fallen for a pretty face with a sexy line.

The door opened and Cam stepped back in with the push of cool wind behind him. He shook his head and drops of water fell from his hair. When he looked up at her, he froze.

She continued to hold the condom. "This is interesting."

With a small shake of his head, he unstuck himself from the floor and came over to her. Crouched down even with where she knelt. "That's Holt's idea of being helpful."

Cam made it sound so innocent. "He's your birth-control pusher?"

"He knows I'm attracted to you." Cam took the condom and slipped it into his front pants pocket. "He also gave me a lecture about keeping my mind on the job, so it's not clear what he wants me to do. Not that he gets a say."

Do... She'd been asking herself the same questions ever since that first kiss. Kept it private as she turned her options over in her mind. Knowing Holt and Cam were out there talking about her just felt wrong. "I'm trying to figure out if I should be embarrassed."

"No one was engaging in locker room talk or anything like that. Believe it or not, the condom is a new addition to the go bag. I'm trying to remember if Holt ever tried to help me out like that." He smiled. "I promise."

The twisting in her stomach started to loosen. Maybe she'd jumped to conclusions. Not trusting was a knee-jerk reaction for her. The doubting had become so ingrained it qualified as her go-to response. But, really, any person would wonder with those supplies.

Her father used to make a promise and then break it. She'd learned early on not to take anyone's word or operate on blind faith. Yet she'd done exactly that since meeting Cam. She didn't understand her reaction or how her attraction guided her when it came to him.

"I assumed that…" She flipped her hand around as she tried to find the right thing to say. It would be too easy to offend and she really didn't want to do that.

"Julia, it's okay." He reached over and slid his fingers through hers. "I get it."

"I guess it seemed like…" She groaned when the words refused to come. "Forget it."

"You have been hit with a lot of evidence that suggests I'm a liar and a jerk. Every time, you've assessed the facts with a cool head instead of jumping to conclusions." He caressed one of her fingers, then another. "You've listened even when it would have been easier for you to write me off."

The touch of his hand felt so good that she almost lost her train of thought. Almost. "And I've sided with you every time."

He shot her a smile. "I like that about you."

That sexy look had her insides melting. She didn't know how all the people he rescued withstood that. He turned on that grin, and the blood rushed from her brain. His effect on her senses had her breath coming out in pants.

"You don't seem so bad," she joked. And by that she meant he went to her head faster than any man she'd ever met.

"As for the condom, Holt's gestures, while well meaning, sometimes misfire." Cam sucked in air through his teeth, making a hissing sound. "He can be socially awkward."

Julia heard the respect and friendship behind the sound. "Does he know you say things like that about him?"

"I tell him almost daily."

The thought of the guys sitting around ribbing each other made her smile. "I thought maybe sex was part of the job."

Cam's eyes widened. "What?"

"You know, that you guys have a bet about who can score first. That you get together and plan strategy." She shrugged. "You hear about stuff like that. Usually when something goes very wrong or some poor woman finds out the hard way, but I see it here and there."

His frown didn't ease, but the touch of his hand against hers stayed gentle. "What kind of men do you know?"

She was starting to wonder that herself. "The usual twentysomethings. Guys I worked with. Went to school with. Friends of friends and setups. Randoms on the internet."

"That list makes me happy I'm thirty-three and not in the middle of the dating scene." He stood and drew her up beside him. "Come here."

She didn't say anything. She was too busy holding her breath when his hands landed on the small of her back and pulled her close.

"I am not married, engaged or involved," he said.

"That's probably a good thing in light of the things I've been thinking about you."

"I'm not— Wait, really?"

It was a nonstop action film in her head. She saw him and her, and there was nothing neutral about it. "Yeah."

He nodded. "Okay, well, you may as well listen to the entire list, then."

She took a big inhale and let it out slowly. "I'm ready."

"I have never, and I mean never, ever, had sex on an assignment. I do not go looking for bed partners from vulnerable people or people in danger." He shifted his legs until they straddled hers. "In fact, my attraction to you is a pretty big problem."

She tried to swallow but she forgot how. "Because?"

His fingers sneaked under the edge of her shirt, and his thumbs rubbed against her back. "I can't seem to control what I feel for you, and I keep trying. I'm thinking about you when I shouldn't be. What I see us doing together requires a bed and might result in traction. Possibly."

And just like that, any doubt still rumbling around her brain deflated and died. He wasn't a criminal or scamming her. He wasn't looking for a good time or boasting with his friends.

She could see the truth in his eyes and hear it in his voice. Under all that rescuing and protecting, past that dimple and that face that made her sigh, was a good guy. Decent and willing to do the right thing no matter what.

He cared about his team and would throw his body in front of hers without debate. She'd never known anyone like him. Growing up with her dad, she'd never understood that people like Cam existed. Not in her world.

But now she knew they did.

"I think we should break your rule." Her fingers went to the back of his neck and brought his head closer to hers.

"I don't understand." He whispered the words against her lips.

"That's because you have so many rules. Hard to keep track of them, I guess."

He smiled then. "Narrow it down for me."

"Maybe it's time you had sex on the job." Being bold

wasn't really her style, but with him she wanted to be honest and trust. To dive in.

He pulled back, but not far. "Julia, are you sure?"

"I'm attracted to you. You can tell that, right?" She brushed her lips over his chin and smiled at the way the scruff there tickled her lips. "It's wild and out of control and I can't think when I'm around you. That's a bad thing when guns are going off and I need to run."

One hand slipped up her back. "That sounds familiar."

"So, maybe if we just burn this off—do it and then it's over—that'll help." That was the least sexy thing she'd ever said, but she got the point across. Mutual attraction. Spontaneous and big.

His eyebrow lifted. "It's not going to burn off."

She had to agree with him there. She'd thrown in the phrase, thinking it would help make it make sense for both of them. She did not have a thing for sex and violence together and didn't want him to think that. "I don't think so, either, but we can try."

"I keep thinking about the word *burn*."

"Tomorrow something could happen and..." She nuzzled her cheek against his. "Well, I want a good memory."

Both of his hands found her shoulders, and his mouth went to her ear. "I'm not going to let anything happen to you."

His touch and scent, being this close and feeling so much a part of him, blocked everything else out. She forgot about the danger and men with guns. Ignored the horror she'd witnessed and the fear that still held her in its grasp.

She pushed all that aside and focused on him. "Right now I want something to happen to me."

"This is not smart." But his mouth traveled over her.

He kissed her in that space behind her ear that made her shiver. "Agreed."

"Anyone could walk by."

Her fingers tunneled up under his pullover jacket, skimming over his firm muscles. "Now you're reaching for excuses."

"You're right." Then his hands touched her cheeks and the rest of the world melted away.

She tried to hold on to the thoughts bombarding her brain but couldn't. Her body came alive with the sensations rocketing through her and around her. His kisses enticed her as his hands learned her curves. When he lifted her off her feet, she didn't hesitate. Her legs wrapped around his hips and she held on tight.

The room spun around her and a hit of warmth had her body tingling. He laid her down on the cot and climbed on top of her, balancing his weight on his elbows but never letting their mouths break contact.

The bed rocked and creaked. His head shot up. "Think this will hold us?"

"I don't care." She was too busy shoving his shirt and the one under that up his body and off.

The material fell to the floor, forgotten. She took a minute to skim her fingertips over his collarbone. He was firm and fit. Everywhere she touched, the heat of his skin burned through her. The kiss dragged on and his hands wandered. She felt the tug at her waist and heard the zipper of her pants screech.

She didn't care about any of it. She wanted her clothes off and her body rubbing against his. As if she said the wish out loud, he broke off the kiss and sat up. The cot wobbled, but he balanced his weight as he stripped her shirt off and unclasped her bra. He had his hands on her breasts and his mouth traveling down her neck before she could find her breath.

Then they went wild. Hands toured and legs shifted. She felt him kick off his shoes, and her hands went to his belt. The buckle clanked as she opened the buttons and slipped her hand inside. She held him, moving her hand over him.

"Julia, yes." He held her head as his mouth took hers.

The kiss blinded her. Waves of heat crashed over her as the air rushed out of her lungs. Every nerve ending popped to life as she tried to remember every touch. But his expert hands and those long fingers took over. He caressed her. Slid her pants down and off, then covered her body with his again.

She felt his erection press against her. The energy in the room had her buzzing as her heart hammered a frantic beat in her chest. She heard a rip and he pushed his body off her by an inch or two to reach down between them.

Wanting the moment to last, she debated helping him roll the condom on. Thought about prolonging the intensity and need swirling around them. But she wanted this. Wanted him.

She helped him shove down his pants and welcomed his hips as they fell between her thighs. Sensations bombarded her as she drew her hands over him and felt his body start to press against hers.

His fingers touched her, making her ready for his entrance. The tips slipped over her in circles. Round and round until her hips swayed in time with his hand's motion.

"Julia, be sure." His words came out in a rush between heavy breaths.

She didn't bother to answer with words. She lifted her

hips and used her hands on his waist to guide him. Then he was inside her, filling her. Her inner muscles pulsed and her body hugged his. When he pushed in, then pulled out, she gasped. The sweet dizziness hit her as the friction of their bodies had everything inside her tightening.

She felt primed and ready. Need spiraled inside her and the slide of his body over hers had her wrapping even closer around him. Heat mixed with desire, and every cell inside her sparked to life.

As his rhythm picked up speed, her head fell back. She couldn't get close enough or hold him tight enough. Her mouth opened on his neck. Her hips bucked and her muscles stiffened.

Then her body let go. The pulsing and shaking continued as light washed through her. The tremors went on and she tried to count the minutes but couldn't concentrate long enough to do it.

When she finally opened her eyes again, her chest rose and fell on rapid breaths. She was about to say his name when the tension over his shoulders tightened. She could feel his body shift and hear the soft grunts as his warm breath blew across her neck. It took another few seconds for his weight to fall heavier against her and even longer until his muscles appeared to loosen and drop.

"Wow." He made the word last for three syllables.

At least he could speak. She tried and a wheeze came out.

"You okay?" he asked, sounding as though he was sure the answer would be no.

"Understatement." She wanted to hold him but couldn't even move. Her muscles weighed a good hundred pounds each and her eyes started to close.

He lifted his head. "That sounds good."

"I'm mostly amazed we didn't break the cot. At one point it felt like it bent in half." She looked around and saw the clothing scattered all over the floor.

"We got lucky there." He lifted some of his weight off her as his body hovered over hers.

"I'd tell you to remind me to thank Holt for the condom, but that seems weird. It might freak him out. I don't want to do that, since I need to keep seeing him." It sounded weird even mentioning it, but she was grateful.

Cam laughed. "Yeah, even though we're on the same team, we don't share everything about our personal lives."

"That's good to know." She was just babbling now. She was willing to say anything to keep the closeness going.

"I need to check the outside and you need to rest."

But it looked as if that wasn't going to happen. The only good news was Cam seemed concerned about her feelings. She couldn't really ask for more than that.

"Is that your way of saying you have to get up?" she asked.

"Didn't want you to think I was getting up because of some anticommitment thing." He skimmed his fingertips along her collarbone, then kissed the trail he made.

Her vision blinked out. That was twice. She'd never had a man affect her the way he did. "You're not?"

"You mean running?"

She barely knew what they were talking about anymore. "Yeah."

"Not with you." He kissed her lips again, light and sweet. "I don't want to go anywhere else."

Now, that was worth remembering.

Chapter Ten

The alarm went off on Cam's watch at dawn, just as he stepped out onto the porch and into the chilly morning air. He wanted to head back to bed and wrap Julia in his arms, but work called. Literally.

The message on the watch was clear. People roamed nearby. Holt sent coordinates and photos. He was the only guy Cam knew who could give a briefing via watch.

He bolted for the door, ignoring the porch and its dangers. Opening the door, he caught Julia in the act of putting on her pants. She zipped, then froze.

"What happened?" The concern was right there in her voice.

"We need to move." He didn't have time to be more specific. He could fill in the details later. "Grab everything."

He went to work on the duffel bag, repacking the weapons Holt had provided and reaching for two more to carry on him. Now he had guns to go with his knives.

As he loaded up on ammunition, she stared. After a few seconds she broke eye contact and then went to work. They moved in silence. When he looked up again, she stood there in jeans and a blue shirt, the darkest outfit he'd ever seen her wear. He guessed it matched her mood. It sure fit his.

Her fingers clenched the strap of her backpack and he didn't see any sign of abandoned clothes or food. She'd gathered everything in record time.

"You're quick." He tried to make a joke, but it fell flat.

All the amusement and satisfaction that had played on her face even a half hour ago faded away now. Her lips stayed in a flat line and tension pulled around the corners of her eyes. She looked ten seconds away from blowing apart, but she didn't whine or complain.

"I had a feeling we weren't going to get to enjoy a lazy weekend morning today. Not after how the rest of our time together has gone. We think we're in the clear, men come, we run, people get shot."

"Julia—"

"A few die and then we start all over again," she said as she adjusted the weight over her shoulder.

"Someday soon this will be over. You'll wake up and things will be normal. We can probably even work in a shower. Go out for breakfast. Be somewhat normal." He didn't even know why he said it.

After this job he had to walk away and let her get back to her life. She had a job and friends. She didn't move around and live in motels or worse. She'd probably never had anyone threaten her or aim a gun right at her until he came along.

His life was nonstop action with short breaks of boredom. He liked keeping on the move. It suited who he was and how he was raised. Talking about mornings and lounging flew in the face of his reality. Even mentioning the options seemed unfair to her.

But he wasn't about to take it back. He knew it was

wrong—he was wrong—but now that he'd given the promise he would make it happen, even if the calm only lasted one night. There was just something about her and the idea of lounging around with her and getting through the day without a surprise or telling a lie that intrigued him.

She took two more steps and loomed right above him. "Now that we got that out of the way, are you ready to tell me what's going on? The whole packing-up-the-weapons thing was a little unnerving. Is that normal for you?"

"Yes." That wasn't really a lie. He checked the weapons every day as a security measure. Most days he also took them out and carried them to a job.

"Okay, then maybe nothing is happening and I imagined it." She sighed. "I've handled guns my whole life but usually on the range, not on my living room floor."

"No, you didn't imagine it. Holt says someone is headed this way." Cam stood up with the duffel bag in hand.

"Is the person we're worried about here Ray?"

"Not sure, but we're not waiting around to let him in for a chat." Cam worked at keeping his voice even. He could feel the tension coming off of her in waves. There was no need to add to whatever anxiety pinged around in her since the name *Ray* had worked its way into the conversation.

"There's nowhere else to hide."

"We'll be fine." But just in case he took out one of the guns and handed it to her. "As a last resort only."

She checked the gun and kept it tight in her hand. "Not to sound bloodthirsty, but if someone comes near me who is not you or your team, I'm shooting."

He loved that about her. "That's my girl."

He cut off conversation then. He needed her quiet and focused and hoped the finger over his lips telegraphed that. Since she followed without question, he wanted to believe he got the point across.

They'd made it two steps when he heard the crack. He backed up to protect her and felt only air behind him. Spinning around, he watched her body drop as the rotten wood beneath her splintered. Her leg slid down and she let out a shocked cry.

The urge to drop to his knees and lift her out almost overwhelmed him, but he had to be careful. Too much weight in one spot and they'd both be stuck hanging there.

"Are you okay?" he asked, though he wasn't convinced she was in a position to answer.

Her eyes were glazed with shock. "I think so, but I honestly can't feel much at the moment. I'm blaming that on surprise."

"Stay calm and very still." He said it as much to himself as to her.

Not that she was moving. She balanced there, half in a hole with one leg tucked beneath her and the other hanging out of sight. He spied her backpack and the strap where it had wrapped around her neck. He did slip to one knee then, careful not to put too much weight in one place.

He kept up the steady stream of conversation, hoping to keep her calm. "We need to get you out of there."

"No kidding." She tried to move her arm, but the strap had it pinned to her side.

"Here." With quick and efficient movements, he unwrapped the strap and lifted the bag from her shoulders. "Are you cut? Did it break the skin?"

She already had a swollen ankle. Early this morning

before she drifted off, he'd elevated it and packed it with ice before feeding her more painkillers. He'd thought it would help her walk, but now the injuries could be much worse.

She shook her head. "I don't feel any pain."

He wasn't convinced that was a good thing. "Do you feel anything?"

"Anxiety and mind-numbing fear." She put her hands on either side of her hips and pushed up. The move had her wrist crashing through another piece of wood. "Now I feel a little pain."

"Stop." He wanted to yell but kept his voice to a whisper. Holt and Shane might be close enough to create a diversion and lure whoever skulked around away, but most likely not. Cam refused to take the risk.

She just waited there, shaking her wrist. "That wasn't my best move."

"You think?" He pulled the board away that trapped her hand. The old wood crunched and crackled under his palms.

She yanked the arm out and rubbed her opposite hand up and down it. "Thanks."

They still had work to do. He glanced into the hole and saw the sharp edges of the broken planks digging into her leg. He knew she felt that. She covered the winces and didn't whine, but that had to hurt.

"Can you lift up at all?" He put his hands under her arms and tried to pull.

She shook her head. "Don't, stop. Okay, that will lead to slicing and cutting. I'm pretty sure."

He had to break more of the wood. Grab her before she slipped farther under the porch. "We can—"

The voice stopped him. Faint and male but there. A

steady chatter as if someone was answering questions. Cam only heard one person, but that was enough.

They had company, and he'd be willing to bet it was of the unwanted variety.

The color drained from her face as she grabbed for his hand. "Go. Leave and find help. Just give me weapons so I can scare them off."

"No way." He mostly mouthed the words, but he meant them as if he'd screamed them. He would not abandon her to whatever visitor was headed right for them. Her suggestion made him want to punch someone.

The voice got louder. The guy wasn't doing anything to cover his tracks. That could mean this amounted to nothing more than an innocent hike, but Cam doubted it, since the message on his watch kept flashing a warning for him to leave the area.

Anything they did now would make noise. Attract attention. There could be more out there. Too many gunmen and it wouldn't matter what his skill level was. He couldn't take on fifteen and promise survival.

That meant he needed an alternative plan. He looked at Julia again. "Do not move."

She glared at him over that comment.

He took the duffel bag and slid it behind her, half obscuring it from view and balancing it against the door. Her backpack went next. Then he took a large step back, making sure his foot hit a solid plank before going any farther.

The warped wood wobbled but stayed intact. Then Cam froze. He needed to figure out where the voice came from. It took two seconds to locate the noise. Back of the house and coming around to the front.

Taking cautious steps, Cam headed in the opposite

direction. The entire time he held eye contact with Julia, sending the silent signal that he would not go far.

He held up a finger as he moved, not more than a few inches at a time. His steps fell without making a sound. He slipped his gun out of its holster, then put it back in again. He needed this takedown to be quiet and simple.

He lifted one leg, then the other over the cracked railing at the side of the porch. It was a five-foot drop to the grass. No big deal, and the overgrown weeds should cover the sound of his landing.

When his feet hit the ground, he ducked down and waited. It didn't take long. A man walked around the opposite side of the building. He held a gun and a radio. That explained the one-sided conversation. He was reporting back. To where was the question.

He got to the bottom step of the porch and stopped. He shook his head as if he couldn't understand what he was seeing, and then a smile spread over his face. "Well, look who's here."

"Help me." Julia's voice shook.

Cam had to block the fear in her tone and the memory of her shocked face as her body fell in a whoosh. She needed him clear and focused. He would dig her out with his bare hands if he had to. He just had to get rid of this guy first. And that meant biding his time until the right moment, so Cam pulled back and continued to sneak a limited peek at the scene unfolding in front of him.

The guy's gaze toured over Julia, then traveled to the porch. When he glanced around the area, Cam pulled back and out of sight. He had to do some scanning of his own to make sure no one sneaked up behind him.

"Where is he?" the man asked in a rough tone. "You were with a man yesterday."

Cam tried to place this guy. He hadn't been at the ferry, but there was no question he moved around the island with Ray. They shared the same dark pants, dark shirt wardrobe.

"He took off for the ferry, leaving me here to wait." Julia sold it. She sounded convincing and scared at the same time.

Cam figured she probably was both.

The man unhooked the radio from his belt. Cam couldn't let him click that button. He tore around the side of the house and hit the guy just as he turned to follow the sound. The knock vibrated through Cam. This guy was not little, but the hit sent them both flying.

The grunt registered as their bodies crashed to the ground and the guy's gun tumbled away. Cam bounced on top of the guy's side, then scrambled. He had to grab the weapon first. Get to that radio.

But this one wasn't going quietly or easily. He shouted for help as he took to his knees and crawled in the dirt toward the weapon. Cam grabbed the guy's leg, then his shirt and pulled him closer. His face scraped against the rocky ground. Cam didn't care if the guy's skin peeled off.

Just as Cam moved to straddle his back, the guy threw an elbow and connected. Cam felt the shot to his toes but ignored the shuddering through his body. He lunged again. This time he put his full weight behind it as he reached for the gun by his ankle, since the other had gone missing in the fall.

Cam hit the guy in the center of his back and sent him sprawling in the dirt. He pressed a knee into his spine as he crawled over him. Without waiting another minute, Cam snaked his arm around the guy's throat.

The guy kicked out and pushed his weight back, which sent them rolling. But Cam didn't let up on the pressure. He wasn't aiming to make the guy pass out. He needed him gone as a threat. That meant holding and tightening the grip as the guy slapped and choked.

Then his body went limp. One minute Cam fought and held on. The next the other man's body slipped out of his hold, boneless and unmoving.

Still fueled from the fight and ready for battle, Cam sat back hard on his butt and held up his gun. He shifted around, ready to fire if anyone else came running, but the morning stayed quiet.

His gaze shot to Julia. "You okay?"

She shoved against the wood around her. "Get me out of here."

"Yes, ma'am." Cam checked the guy for a pulse and when he didn't find one went for his pockets. He came up empty there, but he got the radio, and that would help.

"Cam?"

He glanced up at her again. "Yeah?"

"Now."

He knew the look of a woman on the edge, and she hovered right there. Without another second of thought, he walked up to the porch. With the danger past, the noise didn't matter. Cam held one board after the other, breaking them as he made space to lift her out. When he ripped the third one out, her body bounced. He took that as a sign.

Reaching down, he dragged her out while his hands still shook. "You're okay."

She fell against his chest with her arms wrapped around his waist. "I thought he was going to gain the advantage and I'd have to watch him attack you."

Cam smiled into her hair. "Have a little faith."

She pulled back and looked up at him. "We need to leave."

"Yes." Ignoring the aches and pains that now held his body tight, he held up the radio. "But now we have this."

The corner of her mouth lifted. "Advantage us."

"Exactly."

RAY STOOD AT the outline of a wall near the main staging area of the old shipyard property. With supply low but demand high, Ray had come in to see what was happening. Instead of following the work production, he watched Ned shout into the radio with his voice rising with each sentence. Ray didn't know what was wrong, but something clearly was. Not a surprise, since after months of smooth drug production, things had started to break down.

First, one of the workers asked too many questions and had to quietly disappear. Then Rudy balked at running errands and started to call in reinforcement. He'd had to be put down, and they were almost too late.

Now Ray had to deal with Cameron Roth and his team. The same team that had him driving around in circles, chasing the wrong car. This Cameron turned out to be a bit smarter than Ray had originally thought. He'd thrown off the tail without trouble.

Tired of being ignored and having his time wasted, Ray walked over to Ned. With each step Ray tried to remember the name of the guy who seemed to be missing from his informal mental check-in.

"Where's your sidekick?" Ray decided that was good enough to get the point across.

Ned shook his head. "He's not checking in and I don't understand it, because he'd been giving me a play-by-play."

"You were just talking to him." Ray had heard the conversation as the other man fanned out, checking the area in and around the old shipyard.

Not that taking the lead on the search made up for losing sight of Cameron Roth and the woman. Ray didn't like losing and hated being made fun of even more. Now he had to sit through a meeting where the boss ranted and raved.

The only way to appease the guy was to catch someone. Grab the woman or one of the team members. Ray still wasn't sure how many lurked around, but he guessed at least two.

When Ned didn't offer any additional information, Ray raised his voice. "Start talking."

"Craig cut off." Ned shrugged. "He was talking and then just stopped."

The shrugging almost got Ned shot. If Ray could afford to lose more men he might have done it. At least he now had a name to go with the stupid face of the guy Ned had brought with him to the operation.

"I am familiar with the concept of being cut off." It was the incompetence Ray couldn't handle. With every passing hour, it became clearer that losing Bob would cost the operation something. "Where was Craig when you lost contact?"

"Scanning the area."

Ray ground his back teeth together. "Be more specific."

"Checking some of the small outbuildings on the edges of the shipyard property. Apparently the place is lined with them. Construction workers used to live there and now some hunters do during season."

Now, that sounded promising. The island had numerous seasonal and low-residency houses. Roth and the woman could be anywhere, but for some reason he sensed they'd stuck close. Though it was only a hunch, he played it.

"Show me on a map."

"It's not on a map. Locals talked about these construction trailers all along the border with—"

That was enough talking for Ray. Besides, it was time he ventured out. "Show me and stay off the radio just in case."

Chapter Eleven

Many more incidents like that and she'd have to cut off the leg. First the ankle and then the jolting fall through the porch. Julia knew she'd been lucky to sneak away with a few scrapes and little else after that one.

Cam stopped fiddling with the radio he'd lifted off the dead guy. The thing had been silent since almost right after they grabbed it.

"You still doing okay?" he asked without lifting his head.

He was being sweet and acting concerned, but if he asked one more time she was going to scream. And that would be a problem, since they were trying to be quiet and stick to whispers.

They'd walked away from the safety of the building, since it no longer seemed that safe with a dead guy on the front lawn. The walk took them out wide and farther into the trees. Except for a few wild animals and any stray hikers they might come across, they were alone.

She knew Cam planned to dump her off at the ferry once he made sure it was safe for her to get on board. She knew that was ridiculous.

"The abandoned shipyard." That was the right answer, but she had to convince him.

He stopped and stared at her. "Excuse me?"

At least she had his attention. "There's an abandoned shipyard not that far from here. Plenty of buildings and places to hide. We can go there and regroup."

He stood there for a few extra seconds and then started walking again. "You're going to the ferry."

Time to take a stand. And that was what she did. Stood there holding her backpack, trying not to think about the breakfast bar she'd put in there even though her stomach growled every two seconds. "I can't."

He glanced over to the space where she would have been had she kept moving and did a double take. He spun around to face her. "You can."

His single-minded focus on this point trumped any stubbornness she'd ever shown. She knew this came from a place of protecting her, but still. "Sandy made it clear the entire island knows about Rudy and us breaking out of jail. Even if the ferry crew thinks I was kidnapped, they'll still call the police."

Some of the tension over Cam's eyes eased. "I see you've thought this through."

"And that's the best-case scenario. If they think I'm an accomplice, I'll be arrested immediately." She couldn't even let her mind go to that place.

Forget about losing her job, which she would. Conservative offices did not like having their receptionist's photo splashed all over the news in association with a series of murders. This was way worse. It involved charges and lawyers and statements. She didn't even know what, if anything, she could say. For all she knew, the Corcoran Team's identity was top secret.

So many questions...

"The plan was to sneak you on board the ferry." When

she started to talk, Cam just talked louder. "Shane will go with you, act as your bodyguard and clear every space."

He wanted to pass her off to Shane? That bordered on insulting. "Too risky."

Cam swore under his breath. "You sound like Holt."

With that piece of information Julia felt secure in thinking she'd win this argument. She just had to get Cam there.

"What does *your boss* suggest?" She emphasized the job title, thinking that might move the conversation along.

"We lie low."

Now, that sounded familiar. "Ha!"

Cam shook his head. "Don't do that."

Fine, she'd be quiet about winning this argument, but they both knew she had. "The shipyard."

"The rain isn't letting up." He looked up into the trees. Rain fell, but the umbrella of branches covered them from most of the downpour. "We should be inside."

Not his most impressive stall, but she appreciated him trying to maneuver and analyze and think of ways to keep her safe. At heart, that was what this was. He had a singular focus in taking her out of harm's way. Usually she would agree to go. She was not the martyr type, but none of the solutions sounded all that great.

The only option that worked for her was one where she stayed with him. Attraction or not, she did trust him to keep her safe and she trusted almost no one.

"There are buildings at the shipyard," she said, pointing out what should be obvious.

"We're talking five outbuildings and a warehouse, not to mention the partial walls and rusted-out ship hulls." Cam listed off the hiding places on one hand. "No one has cleared any of it."

Just as she thought, he knew all about the location. Probably researched it before coming to the island. Despite his attempts to act disconnected, Cam struck her as the never-miss-a-briefing type. "Last time Holt picked a place, I fell through the floor."

The corner of Cam's mouth twitched. Looked as though he was trying to fight off a smile. "You make a good point."

"So?" She held out a hand and let the rain puddle there. "We're getting wet just standing here."

He let out a dramatic exhale. "How's your leg?"

She didn't see any reason to lie about that. If he planned to use her injury as an excuse, he would no matter what she said. "A throbbing mess."

"You're not convincing me we should walk."

"Are you going to steal another car?" The guy was an expert at hot-wiring on top of everything else.

"No, much more of that and the poor people on Calapan are going to start shooting each other if anyone goes near a car that's not theirs." He rubbed his face. "But fine."

Without another word he started walking. He'd switched directions and now they headed toward the shipyard. She half wondered if that had been the plan all along.

They'd gone a few steps with the relative quiet of the forest cocooning them. She'd spent so much of the past few hours on edge that it was hard to train her system to calm again. She tried a few deep breaths. That didn't help. She thought about slipping her hand into his...until he started talking.

"Tell me about Sandy." Cam's gaze roamed around them as he never lowered that protector shield.

Some part of her had seen this coming, but still she hadn't really braced for it. "Why?"

"Conversation."

She knew Cam had to research all the angles. He believed someone with power was in charge, and Sandy's house suggested he had some. Still, he'd helped raise her and that made her defenses click into place "Nope, not buying it. You're digging."

Cam shot her the side eye. "You have trust issues."

She had to accept that argument. She didn't trust easily, and there was a reason for that. "You should have had my father."

Cam shrugged. "I didn't have a father."

"What?" Her footsteps faltered and she kicked a piece of wood instead of stepping over it but managed to regain her balance.

"Raised in foster homes."

He casually dropped the piece of personal information. She guessed he didn't share that much very often, and part of her was humbled by the realization. "Cam, I'm sorry."

"Don't be."

"That explains your whole man-as-island thing." The way he held himself. The loyalty to his team and the absence of talk about anyone else. The drive to do the job right. Something about those features combined with his need to get things done on his own and without input pointed toward a loner upbringing.

"My what?"

"You strike me as a guy with few emotional commitments." She saw reflected in him the same way she led her life. Free from entanglements. Cutting off meant less pain.

"True."

"I can relate to that." But now that she'd met him she had to rethink her strategy. A part of her wanted to open up and share.

In such a short time he had her turned around and wanting things she'd never wanted before. All while they ran and ducked and tried not to get killed.

It was surreal and weird and kind of messed up. She couldn't explain it, and for the first time in her life she didn't try to. She just went with it.

"One more way we're compatible," he said. Before she could chime in, he glanced at his watch. "Interesting."

She was beginning to hate that word. Up on her tiptoes, she tried to look over his arm. "What is it?"

"Kreider."

She looked around, half expecting him to ride in with guns blazing. "Where?"

"Shane tagged his car with another tracker, and this one stayed on." Cam used his fingers to zoom out and make the map bigger.

"I have a feeling there's more to this story." Kreider riding to the grocery store or something equally innocent could not be the issue. She knew it would take more than that to grab Cam's attention and hold it.

"He's not far from here." Cam pointed to two dots, one green and one blue.

She assumed they were the blue dot and feared they were about to change course one more time. "Please tell me we're not going to go hunt him down."

Cam winced. "Okay."

"Yeah, that's what I thought." She slipped the bag off her shoulder and unzipped. Taking one granola bar, she handed the other to him. "Any chance we can get through the next hour without you having to kill someone?"

He eyed up the bar and then her. "I can't promise that."

THEY SLIPPED THROUGH the trees and around obvious trails and potential landmarks, getting from the construction trailer to the area near what looked like a storage shed. Forging a route close to the top of the hill risked their position but also gave them the advantage of elevation if it came down to a firefight.

He could also see most of the valley, including the police car parked right where the tracker said Kreider's vehicle would be. A car and a building. This had possibilities.

The whole time Cam kept sneaking peeks at Julia to check on that ankle. He doubted her reporting about being fine was accurate. She had a tight rein on her anxiety and was tamping down the pain.

Another thing to admire in the woman. As if he needed more in addition to her strength, that impressive face, those intense eyes and a mouth that drove him mad.

Julia lowered the binoculars and handed them back to him. "Are they in there?"

He took another turn scanning the area. "Don't know, since we missed seeing the car get here."

She let her arm fall against the ground. Not hard to do, as they were down on their stomachs, dropped low and out of sight. "Is that a statement about how I slow you down?"

"About the rain, actually." It no longer came down in sheets, but the downpour had slowed their progress. Now the air carried a mist.

He was soaked to the skin because he'd insisted she

wear his raincoat. The jacket dwarfed her, but she did look pretty cute with the wet hair and oversize hood. Even now she kept pushing it back off her head to get a better view.

Of what? was the question. There were no humans around. No sign of Kreider or his men. No guns. Nothing out here to see.

They'd basically followed a ring around the outskirts of the shipyard. The construction trailer in one spot. The storage shed in the next. There were garages and other outbuildings, all outlining the far edges of the property line. Not that anyone could see a line through the trees and overgrown grass.

"Kreider should be in there, but why? It's the middle of the day." Cam meant to keep the analysis to himself, but he voiced the words.

"I guess calling out for him is a bad idea." She patted her hands against the wet ground, ignoring water running over her palms.

"It's tempting."

She glanced up and the hood fell back. "Since the rain died down, we could sit here and watch the car and the shed. Basically, wait."

Not really his style. Cam hated stakeouts and did much better with action than hanging around. "I want the man outside and Ray next to him. That would let us wrap this up, or at least start asking the right questions. If those two are in some drug-running operation, we need to know."

"Your office can't use some fancy satellite or something with infrared to detect bodies inside?"

"That's not as easy as it sounds." Cam liked how she thought. Go big. He had an idea on that score. "But we can flush him out."

A familiar wariness washed over her. "How?"

"Explosion." He used his hands to highlight the word. "Boom."

Her gaze wandered over his face as her frown deepened. "Are you serious?"

"Most of the time, yes." Off the job, no. On the job, pretty much always, which was why being with her had him floundering. He joked, she gave him a hard time... they had lose-your-mind sex. Not his usual assignment.

"Let me get this straight." She wiped her hair out of her eyes. "You're going to blow up that building with people in it."

Probably a bit of an overstatement, but he liked the sound of it. Unfortunately, Holt would say no. "A small explosion next to the car. Set it on fire, that sort of thing."

"You don't have anything a bit more subtle? Maybe a rocket launcher." Her voice dripped with sarcasm.

"I don't really do subtle." But he would kill for a rocket launcher right about now.

"I'm starting to get that."

"The goal is to figure out how many men Kreider has and where they are. We blow something up and get their attention." The more Cam spelled it out, the more he liked it. "Holt and Shane can round up bodies from there. Then we can finally start asking questions, which is what we were sent here to do in the first place."

"Your team is around?" The jacket rustled as she looked behind her.

"Close by."

"And you're going to bring everyone running."

Now she was getting it. "That's the point."

"Including the people who want you dead."

"That's why I want to see their faces. I can't fight what

I can't see, and there is someone above Ray. I'm sure of it." Made sense to Cam, but from the he's-lost-his-mind stare she was sending him, he figured that might only run one way.

Rather than run through the details, he got up to his knees and reached for the bag. The rip of the zipper echoed around them as he drew it down and the soft rain began to fall again. He typed one word into his watch to communicate with Holt: diversion.

The response came back in a second: no fireworks.

Cam pretended he didn't see that. He wanted big but went small. He pulled out an explosive device. It resembled a stick of dynamite but wasn't. It consisted of an internal chamber housing the chemical substance and wires. He could use a trigger from a good distance away. There would be a crash and fire. Enough to bring anyone hiding out running, which was the point.

"If you trip with that thing, will you blow up?" She sounded more intrigued than concerned.

He wasn't sure how to take that. "I have to set it off, so no."

"I still want to go on record as doubting this plan."

He put the pieces together and lifted the device into his arms. "If we flush the right people out, we can end this right now and we can sleep in a warm bed tonight."

He left out the word *together*, but it was implied. From her smile he thought she got that.

She gestured toward the car. "Then what are you waiting for?"

"I thought so." Cam took off then. He slid down the hill on the side of his foot, winding through the trees and dropping to his stomach when there was nothing to block a direct line to seeing him. He could almost hear Holt swearing from a half mile away.

Cam crawled the last few feet. Pebbles crunched under his knees and something sharp dug into his thigh. The wet ground helped muffle the sound, but he couldn't go in using pure stealth. Not with an explosive device in his hands.

He had neared the front tire when the door banged open. Not knowing if he was made or just unlucky, he tucked the bomb against his chest and rolled under the car. Footsteps thumped around him. He heard the car door open and calculated how fast he'd have to move not to get crushed under the tires.

But the engine never turned over. One of the guy's legs stayed outside the car as if he was leaning in to grab something. Singing while he did it. Then he stepped back out and slammed the door.

Cam held his breath until he heard the building door shut again. He exhaled, trying to slow the sprint of his heartbeat. Let his head fall against the cool ground for a second. Then he thought about Julia on that hill and started moving again.

He shimmied back out and set up the device. Placed it close to the tire on the far side of the building. The explosion should blow the car and rock the house. Bring the singer and whoever else was in there running.

Two wires and he hooked it up and, ready to go, got to his feet. His palms stayed on the ground as he looked around for the best place to hide. He had just pushed up when he heard it. The pump of a rifle.

"Stand up nice and slow. Hands on your head." The man laughed as he talked.

"You are not supposed to be here, but unfortunately for you, you are," another one said.

Cam ignored the comment about his hands and turned around. One of the men looked familiar. Cam thought he remembered him from the ferry. The other, no. Neither was Ray and neither looked to be in charge.

He tucked the detonator in his hand, hiding it. He had to get out of the blast radius. If he didn't, he had to buy time for Holt and Shane to move in close enough to fire. But even with them on the scene, it might be too late. These two men were smart enough to put the car in front of them and the building behind. It was a good plan until the vehicle blew up, and that was about to happen.

Cam tried some guy talk while he put a map together in his mind. "Just out for a walk, boys."

"Nice try. We know who you are." The bigger one pointed to Cam with the end of his gun. "People are looking for you."

"Where's the woman?" the other one asked.

Confirmation. They were with Ray. Cam didn't know who else they were with, but he made that connection.

Cam shook his head. "Don't know what you're talking about."

"There." The guy pointed to the hill.

Cam almost hated to follow his gaze, but there she was, on the top of the hill. Standing. Was she waving her arms?

Anger rushed over him and he almost missed the opportunity Julia handed him. With the men's attention switched, Cam moved. He took a few lunging steps, then dived over a bush. His finger hit the button as he flew.

A crack sounded behind him and then a wall of heat smashed into his body. He fell to his stomach with his arms crossed over his head and listened as the world exploded into chaos behind him. Yelling and the crackle of fire. One explosion followed another, and chunks of car rained down around him.

He didn't know how much time had passed until the thunder of noise died down. When he lifted his head again, Julia hovered over him with fear shining in her eyes.

"Cameron?"

"I'm okay." He had no idea if that was true, but he rolled over and didn't spy blood, and all his limbs were there, so he took that as a good sign.

"We're going to talk about that stunt later," Holt said from somewhere above him. "Lucky for you Shane caught the one guy who was thrown before he could get up and run."

Cam assumed that meant there were just the two. "And the other?"

"Gone, as in dead." Holt looked down at Julia where she sat slumped over on her knees. "You go with Cam."

She shook her head but didn't say anything. The lack of response fueled Cam. This was not a woman who stayed quiet. He struggled first to his elbows as the adrenaline gave way to aches and pains. Then he sat up.

"You created a diversion." She'd risked her own safety, and the idea of that had him reeling. He was half furious and half drowning in his attraction to her.

She picked at something on the ground. "They were on a beer run."

"What?"

"The guy took beer out of the car, got as far as the porch, then turned again." She let out a ragged exhale. "I guess he sensed you were there."

"And you rescued me." The idea held him in awe. He was not in the habit of needing someone to ride in and save him.

She shrugged. "It was my turn."

He heard Holt moving around and looked his way. The place looked like a war zone. A flipped-over car and a fire raging up the side of the shed. One body on the ground and fire and debris everywhere.

Cam cleared his throat. "You get to pick where we go next."

She touched his sleeve. "Sandy's house."

That was not really what he had expected. "Really?"

"You smell."

RAY LOWERED HIS BINOCULARS.

The shed, the entire area was on fire. He had another man down and one caught. He'd almost gotten off a shot and taken the runner out, but then more men appeared. Good thing the guard didn't know anything. He was stationed out here, checking the boundaries. He hadn't even done a good job of that. Too busy drinking, apparently.

No, like every other man on the job, this one couldn't be traced back to the boss. Ray doubted the guy they caught could say much about him, either. But he could answer some questions, and that moved up the timeline to take the Corcoran Team out.

At least he had the information he needed. Corcoran didn't send one man to grab a witness. At least three wandered around out there, making his life difficult. Ray could dispose of three. While he was at it, he'd eliminate the woman, too.

The boss was not going to like this. Then again, the

boss wasn't going to be the boss for much longer, so Ray didn't care. It was all a time game now, and the countdown had started.

Chapter Twelve

Julia regretted her decision within an hour of getting to Sandy's house. She'd made him promise before they ever stepped on the property not to call the police. But that didn't mean Sandy greeted them with a smile. He grumbled and took verbal shots at Cam.

With Cam in the shower, she knew it was her turn. Still, she tried to avoid the moment by hiding in the kitchen. She leaned down with her elbows on the marble counter and paged through the news stories she'd called up on Sandy's laptop. She had one empty bottle of water next to her and was most of the way through a second. Once she had a hot meal she'd feel better.

But she had to live through the interrogation first.

"You can do better." Sandy set his coffee mug down with a hard clunk as he slid onto the bar stool across from her.

Julia didn't pretend to be confused or dance around the topic. "He's not a killer."

Cam was a lot of things. Lethal, determined, caring, stubborn and a heck of a kisser. He could be difficult and demanding, but she knew to her soul he was not a killer. Not in the sense Sandy meant.

But Sandy wouldn't let the subject go. "You're telling me he hasn't killed anyone since you've been together?"

"Not exactly." She couldn't really avoid the details. The news was all over the island. There was talk of instituting some form of martial law and keeping people in their houses until the police could search. Ferry service had stopped for all but essential services, and word was that more law-enforcement officials would be pouring in soon.

None of that was good news for Cam or his team. As outsiders they'd be tagged as perpetrators. And Cam hadn't exactly been subtle in fighting his way through the island. Add in a potential drug runner working somewhere on the island and disaster loomed.

"That's it. I've waited long enough." Sandy slipped his cell out of his back pocket.

"No!" She lunged over the stove top and reached for the phone.

"This is the best option. You need to trust me on this." He pulled it back just in time and glared at her. "What is wrong with you?"

She wondered the same thing. That phone came out and a furious fire roared to life in her brain. Instinctively she knew she had to protect Cam at all costs. "You promised."

"That was a mistake."

This couldn't happen. She'd grab Cam and run if needed, but she didn't want it to come down to that. Sandy would see that as her picking Cam over him. He was that type of man. A very black-and-white thinker, he put a high price on loyalty.

"I trust you, and if you…" She didn't want to threaten,

and she'd walked right to the edge. "You need to trust me back."

"I have a problem with him, not you," Sandy yelled as he pointed toward the hall.

The water had shut off and she waited for Cam to come running. When he didn't she filled in the piece that still didn't make any sense to her. "He's with me."

Sandy's mouth opened, then snapped shut again. He stuttered and shook his head—things that were very un-Sandy-like. "Oh, Julia."

Pity. Great. She hated that tone and the sad-eyed expression. He'd been shooting it her way for years. "Please don't look at me like that."

"At the very least agree that when he heads out, you'll stay behind with me. Behind locked gates and doors." He wrapped his fingers around the edge of the counter and leaned in. "That man is dangerous."

As far as she was concerned, he had it backward. "Right now this island is dangerous."

"Because of him." Sandy's knuckles turned white.

"He has put his body in front of mine and risked his own neck to save mine. He's played decoy and lured attackers away from me." She could keep listing but ticked off the highlights on her fingers instead. "Does that sound like a guy who will hurt me?"

Sandy leaned back on the bar stool. "Why is he on Calapan?"

She wanted to ignore the question or at least dodge it. But Sandy deserved more than a shove off. "He came here to interview a witness. Apparently there's some intel—"

"Intel?"

"—that someone is running drugs, serious drugs, off Calapan."

Finishing the sentence was easier than admitting she sounded like a television show. After a few days Cam had her sounding like him, and that wasn't necessarily a good thing, since she barely understood what he was talking about sometimes.

"How did an interview turn into a shoot-out?" Sandy asked.

She grabbed her water bottle because she needed something to occupy her hands. "Rudy was the witness and someone killed him."

"You keep ignoring how your man is at the center of all this."

She let the phrase *your man* slide by. She didn't hate it. Being linked to Cam didn't scare her or upset her.

"Someone in power is at the top of this. There's a man on the island pretending to be a police officer." She peeled down the corner of the label and heard a rip.

Sandy never broke eye contact with her. "You know that to be true?"

"Yes." Only because Cam and his team had told her, but she would not get knocked off track. The need to test Cam's trust kicked hard inside her, but she pushed it back. He didn't have anything to prove and she had to keep remembering that. "Is it possible Chief Kreider is involved?"

Sandy sighed at her. "I know you don't like him."

"He has connections and knows the island." She tore the label in half.

"You're taking on your boyfriend's paranoia."

"She's smarter than I am." Cam stepped up right behind her with his hands on her shoulders.

She noticed how he didn't correct Sandy about who he was to her. Like that, all the anxiety curling into a ball in her stomach disappeared in a flash. His voice had the power to do that to her.

She pressed a hand over his. "Cam."

He came around her side to stand directly in front of Sandy. "Is there something you want to ask me?"

"I'm worried about Julia," Sandy said before Cam finished the question.

Cam nodded. "So am I."

"I can get her off the island."

She listened to the verbal volleys until a migraine started to form over her eyes. "I'm sitting right here."

Silence flashed through the room. The refrigerator hummed and a clock ticked somewhere, but no one moved.

Finally Sandy stood up and put the cell back in his pocket. "You both look ready to drop."

Tension choking the room eased and Julia knew they'd avoided something pretty awful. At least for now. "We could use food and a good night's sleep."

Cam still didn't move. "Unless I need to worry about you calling the police the second I close my eyes."

"I'll agree not to call the police tonight if you agree not to run out into the rain with Julia," Sandy shot back.

She sighed at both of them...not that they were paying any attention to her. "I'm still right here."

Cam nodded. "Deal."

CAM HELD JULIA'S arms above her head and pushed into her one last time. Her head dropped back into the pillows, and her heels dug into the back of his legs. Watching her while she lost the last of her control was one of the sexiest things he'd ever seen.

She went wild, not holding back. Touching him, kissing him. And when her inner muscles grabbed on to him, his control snapped. His body bucked and the air rushed out of his lungs. Every muscle tightened until the last pulses moved through him. Then his bones turned to mush.

Desperate not to crush her, he rolled to the side and took her hand with him. Held it in his in the middle of his chest so they didn't break contact. He threw the other arm over his closed eyes and silently thanked Holt for handing him another condom back at the explosion scene. Cam had no idea how his friend knew, but he did. They didn't say a word. Just had a handoff.

Cam decided not to share that bit with Julia. She had enough on her mind without worrying about the team. She might not understand that the condom handoff meant acceptance. The Corcoran Team members were weird that way.

Cam's arm fell to the mattress. "I don't think this was what Sandy had in mind when he told us to go to bed."

"I'm a grown woman." Her legs shifted and a foot brushed up against his calf.

Cam wanted her to climb on top of him, but he'd need to build his strength back first. "No arguments here."

"I don't appreciate being talked about like I'm a child."

"Wait a second." At that tone, all surly and sharp, he lifted his head. "Am I in trouble for something?"

"Sandy is protective." She turned to her side and one arm snaked across Cam's stomach. "Overly so, and I don't always like the way he orders me around like I'm five."

Cam noticed, but he couldn't exactly get ticked off about the attitude. He had grabbed her in her father's house and dragged her into danger all over the island.

If the positions were reversed, Cam would have been skeptical. Might actually take out a gun and fire a shot to make sure she stayed safe.

The relationship with Sandy struck Cam as paternal. He knew she hadn't been close to her dad. She'd made that much clear. That could explain the tight hold on her. "Does he have kids?"

"Divorced a few times but no kids. He says he spent most of his younger business years making money and never at home."

"Now he's retired." Something about that fact caught in Cam's brain. A workaholic without a job, and Sandy was only about fifty.

"Which is weird." She rubbed her hand back and forth until her fingertips found Cam's exposed nipple. "He's not exactly the sit-around-the-house type."

Concentrating on the conversation became harder with each passing second, but Cam tried to stay engaged and ignore his resurging erection. He wanted to know about Sandy because something didn't feel quite right with the guy. "What does he do all day?"

"Count his money?"

"Me, too." Cam laughed at his own joke. "I think I have thirty-eight dollars."

"Dinner is on you when we get out of this." She stretched and her hand moved higher on his neck. Then she jerked and lifted herself up on her elbow. "Uh-oh. Did I scare you?"

He hadn't said anything, but his body went stiff. It was an involuntary reaction to the idea of commitment. His entire life had been about keeping free and being able to move. Except for the Corcoran Team, he'd never really believed in anything enough to commit to it.

He went with an answer that said nothing, because the idea of giving her the speech he'd delivered to others made him feel hollowed out inside. "I don't scare easily."

"But?"

Now was not the time. He had a prepared speech for this, but it clogged his throat and he couldn't figure out how to get it out. "You know I'm not the settle-down type, right? I go on missions and travel. I get shot at. A lot."

She leaned up on an elbow and stared down at him. "None of that is a surprise to me."

Nothing shook her. He'd never met a woman like her before, and the fact that he kept wanting to know more scared the crap out of him. "I'm just saying dating me is not easy."

She smiled. "Have you actually gone on dates? Like, at some point you found the time and strength to make it happen?"

Relief filled him at her amused tone. "Yes."

"And maybe one time in your life you've gone out with the same woman more than once?"

He wanted to laugh but went with an honest answer. "Yes."

"Do you see where I'm going with this?" She asked the question as if she were talking to a naughty child.

"You're telling me I'm overstating my dating issues."

"Yes." She slid over him, closing her eyes when the friction had them both groaning. "I'm not any different from the other women you've dated. You made it work with them, at least for a short time."

That was where she was wrong. That was the piece that had him both wanting to run and wanting to stay. "You're different."

She frowned at him. "Why?"

Cam thought about holding the truth back but let it fly. She'd earned his trust that much. "You matter."

"Well, that's pretty sexy." She leaned down and kissed his chin.

He moved his head to give her better access. "It's not a line."

She laughed and the sound vibrated through her. "That's what makes it so sexy."

Chapter Thirteen

Cam wandered through Sandy's house. He acted like a man who couldn't sleep, which was partially true. Julia had worn him out in the best possible way, but his mind kept churning. Something about this island, about the mystery surrounding Chief Kreider and the unanswered questions about Sandy, piqued Cam's innate need to investigate. Had his mind zipping away from Julia's warm body to something much more sinister.

The emergency call to Connor with Holt on the line didn't do anything to ease the concerns. Sandy had money but not the type Cam associated with this setup and the high-end, expensive security system that even Joel had trouble cracking. The situation made Cam wonder what the guy was hiding.

A workaholic who didn't work. Powerful and well-known in town. Had resources and was a hometown boy, so he knew every inch of the island. To Cam, eyeing Sandy made as much sense as checking out Chief Kreider.

One of those investigations would threaten what he had with Julia, even though he wasn't sure what that was. She talked about dating, and when she kissed him, every sensible promise he'd ever made to himself about stay-

ing unconnected and free while he did this job crashed
to his feet.

"You should leave."

At the sound of Sandy's voice, Cam turned around. It
wasn't a surprise that Sandy could sneak around without
making a noise. He seemed like the type, which was one
more reason Cam's alarm bells kept ringing. That and
the ninja security. Cam had spied two inside cameras—
one by the back door and one outside the closed office
door—and assumed they were recording every move.
It was the only reason he hadn't sneaked into the office
and looked around.

"I'm not going to hurt her." At least he was going to
do everything in his power to make sure no one else
touched her.

"Too late." Sandy kept walking until he stood in front
of the massive stone fireplace that divided the family
room from the sitting area on the other side. "She won't
say exactly how you two met, but if I had to guess I would
say you ran into her and then saw an opportunity."

Cam refused to lie about this point. If it ever came
down to criminal charges and him getting in trouble,
this bit of truth might save her from culpability. "You're
right."

"And you've been using her ever since."

That part he wouldn't cop to. "If you need to think so."

"Not even bothering to deny it?" Sandy shook his head
as he let out a harsh laugh. "I guess that's admirable."

"She was there. She knows what happened and what
I did." If the guy thought to blackmail or threaten, Cam
wanted him to know that tactic wouldn't work. He was
immune to that kind of pressure. "I didn't hide from her."

"But now she cares about you." Sandy leaned against

the armrest of the sprawling couch. "That makes her vulnerable and I don't want that for her."

Vulnerable was the last word Cam would use to describe Julia. She was, just like most people, but so many facets of her personality gave her strength that a very human vulnerability didn't weaken her at all in his eyes. "She's decent and compassionate."

"Interesting choice of description."

Sandy wasn't wrong. The words weren't strong enough, but Cam aimed for a different point. "She doesn't want me to get hurt while I figure out who's following us, which makes her a certain type of person. One I don't meet very often."

"We're saying the same thing."

Maybe they were. Cam wasn't sure, because Sandy lectured more than talked and getting to his point seemed to be a long journey. "I'm only here until I finish this assignment."

"I looked up the Corcoran Team." Sandy folded his arms across his chest. "You guys tend to get in the middle of a lot of trouble."

Not really possible. Except for a few cases, the group limited its internet presence and didn't advertise. Cases came to them through governments and corporations. Sometimes through connected individuals. But Connor worked miracles keeping the team and the members' individual names, as well as most of the details of their missions, out of the news.

Anything else would hamper their ability to move in and out and not be seen, which was usually how they operated. The bloodbath across Calapan was unusual and Cam knew Holt and Connor would demand explanations for every choice.

But it didn't hurt to see what Sandy did know. Possibly figure out how he knew it. Cam waded in. "Some people would say we solve trouble."

"They might," Sandy scoffed. "Not me."

The guy clamped down. It was as if he'd gone too far and showed his hand in admitting he'd checked the team out. Now he tried to pull back, all without showing one ounce of concern on his face.

Yeah, Cam didn't buy the caring-uncle routine for one second. This guy had skills and they came from somewhere.

"She'll forget you once you're gone, but you need to leave now while it's easier for her," Sandy said.

The comment sliced across Cam's senses. He hated every word and had to fight to keep his expression from changing. "She's an adult. She decides."

The last of Sandy's concern left his face. He stood up, looking ready to battle and much younger than fifty. "Be a man and do the right thing here."

Cam didn't even flinch. This guy did not scare him. And the fatherly advice rolled right off Cam. Maybe that was the one good part of never having one.

"We're leaving tomorrow morning." He didn't leave any room for question.

"You are." Sandy pointed toward the bedrooms. "She stays."

Now Cam saw it. The way Sandy stepped in and took over. Very paternal and borderline inappropriate even on the overprotective scale. "Does she know that? Julia does have a mind of her own and is old enough to make her own decision."

"She'll come to her senses."

Cam kept thinking the same thing. She'd wake up or

turn around and look at him and see what he saw when he looked in the mirror—a guy who did best on his own. "You can try to handle this however you want, but I'll let her decide."

"You'll see." Sandy nodded. "When the time comes she'll side with me."

JULIA ROLLED OVER and her hand hit a cool sheet instead of a warm male chest. She jackknifed into a sitting position and glanced around the room in time to see Cam walk back in from the hall.

"Why are you up?" She didn't bother whispering because she didn't think they had anything to hide.

Sandy had put them in two bedrooms. She'd vetoed that immediately and held her ground when he tried to explain that she needed sleep. She knew what she needed—Cam.

He jerked at the sound of her voice, then looked up at her. The frown came next. He made a face. Generally looked as though he was debating telling her the truth.

She knew then something bad had happened. "What?"

He hesitated for one more second before spitting it out. "The police are here."

She grabbed the sheet and held it to her chest. Until that moment she'd felt loose and comfortable, almost forgetting the horrors behind them and those yet in front of them. But the mention of police had her snapping back to reality.

Still, she didn't want to believe Sandy had betrayed her that way. "That's not possible."

"There's one police car outside. It's sitting at the end of the driveway."

Her heart crashed inside her chest. "You saw it?"

His expression stayed blank. "I'm guessing."

That didn't make any sense. She'd been with him non-stop and he didn't guess. He reasoned things out, listened to his team, researched the intel. Random guessing seemed odd…along with almost everything else that was happening on Calapan. "I don't understand."

Cam sat down on the side of the bed with his hand on the comforter covering her thigh. "Sandy wants me gone."

That was not news. She'd survived the earlier testosterone battle but knew that had only been round one. Looked as though they were at it again. "I'll talk to him."

"It's too late." Cam got up and went to the end of the bed. He had his jeans on and tucked in his T-shirt. "I need to sneak out."

"We are not having this discussion again. You go, I go." Even though the idea of getting out of that warm bed and stepping out into the wet dark night made her want to scream.

He froze in the act of putting a sweater on. "Julia, this is—"

"No, not again." She slipped over the usual arguments and zoomed right to the heart of what drove her. "I am sleeping with you because I care about you. Do you really think I'd let you wander off without me, especially if the police are looking to frame you?"

Cam dragged his sweater down his torso as his eyes grew soft. "Sandy will make sure no one hurts you."

"So will you." She stood up and moved to stand in front of him.

"No."

"I will follow you." Her hands went to his waist as she willed him to finally get it. She trusted him and would not leave him. "You know I will. Imagine the danger I can get into."

He sighed hard enough to blow her hair. "Get dressed."

She was already in her pants and searching for a shirt to go under his raincoat. By the time she stepped into the oversize bathroom a few minutes later, he stood there waiting by the alarm pad. Eyed it up and then looked to her.

The red light held steady. That meant the place was locked down, which made sense, as it was nighttime and normal people should be sleeping. She decided not to point that out and hoped she didn't fall asleep in the middle of their big escape.

She punched in the number on the keypad, but nothing happened. The alarm box beeped, but the light did not turn green. She tried again and got the same result, which made no sense.

She glanced over her shoulder at Cam. "The code isn't working."

"He changed it." Cam leaned back against the wall.

His comment made it sound as if Sandy had locked them in, but that couldn't be right. "Why?"

"He doesn't want us to get away this time."

Cam had broken into full-blown paranoia. She knew Sandy could be demanding and a whole host of other annoying things, but he didn't live in a prison and had never expected her to do so.

"What does that mean?" she asked. "You're being cryptic and now isn't the time."

"We need another way out. One that won't trip the alarms." Cam aimed his intense stare at her and did not let up. "Think."

"We can't just walk out, because the red light means the doors are locked and we'd need the override code."

"He has a system that locks him in? That's unbelievable." Cam shook his head. "Okay, any other ideas?"

The answer popped into her head immediately. "The balcony off his bedroom. He likes fresh air and keeps one of them open. He usually locks it out of the security system."

"This should be fun." Cam opened the door to the hallway just a fraction and looked out.

"We can take the back stairway, but he could be up there."

"I can't believe we're going up to go out." Cam went down on one knee in front of the duffel bag and loaded up with weapons.

Looked to her as if he planned on taking on an entire army before they broke free of the lawn. When the knife flashed and then disappeared by his side, her stomach rolled. "You're the one who insists we leave."

"And I'm right about that." He took her hand and brought her along behind him. "No talking."

As if she needed that warning. She thought all of this sounded overboard and odd, but the determination in his voice and on his face was not a joke. Neither was the sound of male voices coming from the front of the house.

Sandy was talking to...Kreider. Julia picked up the voice and double-timed the walk down the hall and around to the kitchen before the panic and confusion buzzing around her brain could catch up to her.

Cam pushed her back and out of the way when they got to the hallway that led to the foyer. If they could clear this they could get out without Kreider moving in. Never mind the fact that they'd have to rappel down the side of the house instead of just walking outside. She assumed Cam had a plan for that.

They waited. Stood there as Sandy talked about Cam being in the house and his concerns. Julia felt her temper build and boil, then explode in a flash before her eyes. Sandy had lied to her, and the reality of that burned through her, leaving her feeling raw.

One more peek and then Cam crossed to the other side in one giant yet quiet step. He held up a hand, keeping her back, then after a few seconds gestured for her to make a run. The plush carpet covered the noise of her footsteps and they stepped with caution as they walked upstairs.

She knew the floor creaked somewhere at the top of the steps and tried to circle around the general spot. But going into Sandy's bedroom for any reason felt weird. Not that she had a choice right now. Cam stood in the middle of the upstairs hall and held out his hands as if to ask for directions. She blocked out the violation and her anger at Sandy's bullying and moved toward the big double doors to the left.

Once she was inside, Cam frowned. She understood why. The bedroom was bigger than most houses and nicer than most hotel suites. It spanned almost half of this floor. The huge bed, still made, the sofa and desk. A wall of bookcases.

Cam hesitated at the desk. Brushed his fingertips over the handle to the top drawer but then shook his head.

She had no idea what was going through his head but guessed it had something to do with violating Sandy's privacy. She couldn't go there and snapped her fingers at him to let him know that.

With a nod Cam walked straight past her to the French doors to the balcony. One side was open and he slipped through. She could smell the rain and feel the breeze as it kicked up. They both stood at the railing and stared down the straight drop.

"Well?" She half mouthed and half whispered the word.

If he pulled a rope out of the pocket of his pants, she might lose it. But that wasn't what happened. He went to the bed and stripped it. The bedding rustled and the mattress bounced. Silk sheet slid over silk sheet with a strange, almost zipper-like, sound. Then he had them off and tied together and held them up as though he'd done a good thing.

She was pretty sure he'd lost his mind. "Are you kidding?"

He shrugged. "You can stay."

It was a dare and she refused to be baited. "Fine. You go first and wait for me to get down."

They went back out to the balcony and he dropped the makeshift rope. One end fell into the night and he secured the other to the marble column on the balcony. A tug and a pull and he looked ready to go.

"Hug the wall. Do not swing in front of the window." Cam glanced over the side. "I'll get down there and then hold it taut for you so it's easier to rappel."

"Fine." Except this was anything but fine. Growing up in Calapan with the mountains and steep trails heights didn't scare her. Falling to her death kind of did.

He slipped over the wall and was gone. No preparation or goodbyes. She was so fascinated watching the top of his head and the sure hand over hand as he scooted down that she almost missed the sound of footsteps echoing nearby. Her gaze shot to the closed door and she sensed she had only minutes to act.

She didn't wait for Cam to land. She pulled on the sheet and he looked up. Then she went over. He must have gotten the message, because he jumped the rest of the way and held the sheets steady for her.

She heard a sound above her head and a shout. The backyard flooded with light and for a second she stopped. Just hung there. With the plan imploding she did the only thing that made sense. She let go and closed her eyes, hoping Cam would have the sense and strength to catch her.

Her body jolted as it fell into his arms. One minute she snuggled up tight to his chest, and the next her feet hit the ground.

They took off running while male voices yelled from above.

She guided them around the patio furniture and pool, up the hill to the fence gate leading to the woods behind. The knob didn't move when she tried to turn it.

"Hold on." Cam lifted his foot and slammed his heel right by the lock.

The wood splintered and Cam kicked the pieces to the side. She didn't stop to ask questions. She ran until her chest ached and her throat burned. When she finally stopped she panted hard enough to bend her body over double.

Cam was right there with a hand on her lower back. Caressing, soothing.

He said something, but she ignored it to go with her own question as she glanced up. "Now what?"

He didn't hesitate. "The shipyard."

Chapter Fourteen

The sky turned a purplish pink right before the sun rose. The rain had stopped and the breeze died down, suggesting a normal summer day loomed before them. Cam welcomed some sense of calm, though he guessed it wouldn't last.

His gaze traveled to Julia where she sat on the trunk of a fallen tree. She tapped the toes of her shoes together and stared at the ground. Didn't make a sound as she tucked her hands between her thighs.

He knew the quiet wasn't a good sign. Julia liked to talk. Even through danger, she kept up a running commentary and asked questions. Now she sat stiff without making a sound, only rocking now and then.

"What do you know about Sandy's business?" He'd tried getting an answer several ways already without any real success. Any discussion on this topic seemed to shut her down. But he needed the intel, so this time he raced directly toward the point. "The actual source of his income and business."

Tap, tap, tap. "I already told you."

During the hike from Sandy's house, including the short-term borrowing of yet another car to get them most of the way to the shipyard area and the few hours of rest until morning, she'd shut down. He asked her about Sandy's money and his family and could see the wariness fall over her eyes. Instead of asking questions, she'd spent the drive staring out the window and offering directions in a flat tone.

She was smart enough to know why he was asking all about Sandy. Cam didn't have to explain. That didn't worry him. He wasn't looking to keep his concerns some big secret. But he didn't like the silence and lack of eye contact.

Cam tried again. "He's connected and wealthy and knows the island."

"That description fits a lot of people on Calapan."

He sat down next to her, hoping that closeness would help bridge the gap forming between them. "Then direct me to one of them. Tell me where to look and I'll have Connor and the rest of the team back in Annapolis start working."

When his leg touched hers, she shifted. "I don't live here anymore."

"Julia, come on." Cam inhaled, trying to wrestle the adrenaline pumping through him back under control. "I get that you're angry with me."

She slipped her hands out from between her legs and folded them on her lap. "I'm too busy trying not to be shot to be angry."

Could have fooled him. "I don't want Sandy to be involved."

She looked at him then. Slow and with a deliberate shift that highlighted that anger she claimed not to have, she stared at Cam. "You sure?"

Tension rolled off her and plowed into him. Gone was the soft woman from bed and the joking one from the trail. A certain seriousness had fallen over her and tightened her expression to the point of breaking.

This went beyond his questions about Sandy. Had to. The reaction was way out of proportion to his prodding. "What does that mean?"

Her head fell to the side, and her hair fell over her shoulder. "You don't like him."

There was no way for Cam to hide that, so he didn't try. Didn't hold back on his frustration, either. She actually sat there and accused him of getting an innocent man in trouble. "You think I'd set the guy up?"

She shrugged. "As you keep reminding me, I don't really know you that well."

Then it hit him. She was purposely picking a fight. The mix of exhaustion and frustration and feeling out of control had crept up on her and she'd come out fighting. He got it because he did the same thing now and then. But thinking he knew what was going on inside her and accepting being on the receiving end were two different things. She wasn't the only one looking for a way to control the situation.

Instead of yelling or reasoning with her, he stated a fact. "You're determined to be ticked off."

She stood up and whipped around to face him. The red stain on her cheeks suggested the anger had blown up on her. "He helped raise me. When my father was too drunk or too uninterested, Sandy stepped up."

"I get that."

"He was there for me. I know you don't get what that's like because of your upbringing, but he was."

The verbal shot landed right to his gut, and the last hold on his control broke. "Which explains why you came to the island and didn't bother to tell him."

As soon as Cam said the words he regretted them. She didn't do this work. It made sense for her to feel ripped apart and shredded. He didn't have an excuse.

When he started to talk she held up a hand to cut him off. "Stop talking."

"I overstepped." That qualified as a vast understatement, but right now it was all he could offer. After they solved the drug issue and got her to safety, he'd hold her and apologize and try to fix the part of the damage he'd inflicted.

Fury continued to vibrate off her, and those eyes stayed wild. She backed away from him and kept going until she moved right out of touching range.

"He was the first man I truly trusted," she said in a shaky voice.

The look, the pain all cut into him and he had to sit there and take them. "Julia, I—"

"Him, then you."

Her words hung there. The import of what she meant hit him a second later. That hollowed-out feeling in his chest came back and his mind blanked as he searched for the right words to say.

"Lovers' quarrel?" A man stepped out from the ruin off to their left of the half wall of what used to be a building. He held a gun and walked quickly as he moved right toward Julia. "That's a shame."

Cam reached out to grab her, but the effort came too late. In her need to get away from him she'd strayed a bit too far and the attacker, some guy Cam had never seen before, nabbed her first. He had his arm wrapped around her throat as he dragged her a few more feet away with a gun pointed at her head.

"This isn't your business." Cam stood up and closed

the gap between them. He had guns at his side and back and ankle. A few more knives rounded out his weapons inventory.

"You're on my property." The man dropped that verbal bomb without offering more.

Cam didn't believe it for a second. This guy had *underling* written all over him. He followed orders. He'd just happened to be lucky enough to stumble across them.

But Cam needed to confirm. "You own a shipyard?"

"My boss does."

Julia grasped at the arm confining her. Fingernails dug into the guy's jacket as her feet scraped against the ground. The guy had her in a headlock that almost lifted her off the ground and her panic filled the air.

Cam couldn't look at her. Couldn't see the pleading in her eyes. Not if he wanted to get through the next few minutes.

He pitched his voice lower and struggled to keep it even. "Then go get him and we'll work this out."

"Nice try, Mr. Roth."

Julia let out a soft sound and the attacker put his cheek against hers. "Yes, I know who you are, and you two have some lives to answer for."

She pushed the arm lower and lifted her head. "It was self-defense."

Cam didn't want her talking or moving. She needed to stay still while he stalled for an opening.

"I'm doing you a favor. You sounded pretty angry with your boyfriend, and now I'll get rid of him for you." The attacker laughed. "Then you can thank me."

She inhaled loudly enough to fill the quiet space. "No."

The attacker looked back at Cam. "Weapons on the ground or I start cutting her."

That was not going to happen. Not to her and not all of his weapons. Cam pulled out the gun on his side and held it up so both hands were in the air. "Let's stay calm."

"On the ground." The attacker used his chin to gesture toward Cam's gun. "Do it now."

She tightened her hold on the guy's arm. "Cam—"

He looked at her then. Focused all his attention on her and tried to send the silent message to hang on. "You're going to be fine."

And she would be. He'd promised her and that was back when she was an innocent woman he'd dragged with him on the run. Now she was more, so much more.

"You shouldn't lie to your woman." The attacker turned his head to look at Julia's face. "But maybe you won't mind seeing your boyfriend die."

Cam could see her hands shake and the disgust when she closed her eyes and tried to turn and put some room between her body and the man holding her. Terror or something close moved through her.

Cam could see it and wanted her attacker's focus back on him. "What's the next play here?"

"I have the authority to kill you." The attacker said the phrase with all the enthusiasm some people used to order breakfast.

Cam suspected that was true. He amounted to a nuisance, but he could be valuable and now he had to convince this guy of that fact. "But you should take me in."

"You don't make the rules."

"You don't, either." Cam took another step. "That's the problem, right? Men are ordering you around and you're sick of it."

"Be quiet." The guy snapped out the order as he jerked the arm holding Julia.

She choked and stumbled but stayed on her feet. When Cam took a step forward she waved off the concern. "I'm okay."

"For now." The attacker gestured for Cam to move. "Walk."

He'd done a quick look around when they got there. Hadn't seen footprints or signs of life. He had no idea if he'd missed something. "Where?"

"Through there." He used the gun to point to the doorway near the ruin where he'd appeared earlier. "And remember I have a knife to her throat, so don't try anything."

The guy was so busy talking and pointing that he created opportunities. Just what Cam expected from an amateur.

He waited for the next break in eye contact to drop his hands and slip the gun out of his waistband and into the pocket away from the attacker, then lifted them again. "I don't want her hurt."

"Hear that? You're in here cackling at him and he's trying to protect you." The attacker pulled her back against him. "Nothing to say?"

Fury burned through Cam and he almost went for his nearest weapon. "Don't touch her."

"You don't make the rules."

"I will lunge for you and make it hurt." Cam delivered the promise. "Snap your neck."

Something that looked like worry passed through the attacker's eyes before he nodded toward the entryway again. "Move."

Cam memorized every step and every piece of grass as he walked. The attacker took them through the ruins of one building, down a long grassy area to a small hill.

From there Cam could see the water beyond. Caught the scent of fish.

Between them and the shoreline were rusted-out carcasses of old ships and a series of buildings, most of them missing walls or a roof or both. One long narrow building looked mostly intact except for the blown-out windows and graffiti splattered over every smooth surface.

And the trucks. Two of them, both with their back doors open. There weren't any people working or moving around, but boxes littered the ground in front of the delivery vehicles as if this was the stuff left over after loading the good stuff. Made sense, since the bodies found around the island had drawn the attention of the media and law enforcement. Running the drug operation out of here—and suddenly Cam knew this was the right location—would be too risky right now.

Cam started down the slope. He made sure to keep his body as even with the attacker as possible. Out in front the guy might see the weapons, and Cam needed those.

The wet grass had his shoes slipping. The attacker had it harder, as he had to balance two people. Cam didn't help, because he was counting on a fall. When they got more than halfway down without incident, Cam started to rethink his strategy.

He glanced over at Julia. The attacker had her body bumping against his as her feet slid and ankles turned underneath her. Cam wondered about her injury and was about to look away to scan the area when she met his stare. Intense and determined, she glared as if willing him to understand, then her attention went to her feet. She repeated the action two more times.

A signal. He wasn't 100 percent sure of her plan, but he knew it included a fall. He answered with a short nod as the hand farthest away from the attacker dipped. He knew he'd have to grab and turn and shoot and do it all while gravity dragged him down the hill. Not the most convenient shot, but Julia had planned this, which meant she intended to duck and roll.

Good woman.

She took one more step and then her ankle turned. This time her knees buckled and her weight pulled the attacker down. He tried to catch her, but she was slipping and Cam was moving. The second she cleared the attacker's torso, Cam jumped over her body and slammed into the man, throwing him to the ground.

The man tumbled backward and momentum took Cam flying with him. They somersaulted and Cam lost hold of his gun. They rolled as he punched. He made a grab for the grass but couldn't stop the free fall.

They spun and when they landed the attacker ended up on top and took advantage. He punched Cam in the side, then did it again. Cam bucked his hips and the guy lost his balance. Cam slammed the guy into the ground on his side, then did a frantic visual search for his gun. Any gun.

An elbow crashed into his jaw, and his head shot back. Cam would've sworn he saw stars, but he blinked them out. He had to stay conscious. Had to win this one.

He saw a gun in the grass right in front of them as the attacker started crawling for it. Cam reached for the one by his ankle. Had it out and was about to aim when legs came into view. Julia's legs.

She stood just out of reach and held a gun. Had it pointed at the attacker's head. "I dare you to move."

The guy froze and looked up. He looked ready to go

for her legs when Cam shoved his weapon into the back of the guy's skull. "You heard her."

"It's tempting to tie something around his neck so he knows how it feels." Julia's chest rose and fell and her words came out choppy and disconnected, but the gun made her point.

Cam scrambled to his feet and put a heel in the middle of the guy's back before he could lift himself up. "You upset the lady."

He spit into the grass by her shoe. "Like I care."

Cam wrenched the guy's arms behind his back and held them with one of the last two zip ties he had in his pants pocket. Then he leaned down to make sure the guy could hear him. "You should, because now it's my turn to threaten you."

Chapter Fifteen

Julia leaned against what was once a wall of some building and rubbed her neck. She couldn't get the sick feel of this guy's beefy hands out of her head. The smell of his sweat and the sense of fear that wound around him and her. It all rushed back on her until she had to look away.

Even though he sat in a chair with his arms tied behind his back and one leg fastened to the chair, she waited for him to jump up and grab her again. She knew it was crazy and that Cam would shoot the guy first, but still.

Cam.

She'd pushed and picked at him because he'd targeted the one piece of her childhood that had always felt safe—Sandy. She believed in him and she believed in Cam and in one swift move Cam was trying to rob her of all of that.

"What's your name?" Cam stood in front of the attacker with both a gun and a knife in his hands.

The question had her attention zipping back to him. Despite the trickle of blood by his hairline, he looked totally in control.

He'd picked this building because it had walls and some protection, or so he'd said. It probably once consisted of workers' stations lining the long rectangular space. Now the plants had moved in. They grew up the walls and through the broken windowpanes. Grass sprinkled where the floor should be.

The entire place had a spooky, abandoned feel to it. This close to the water she could hear the waves splash. Every now and then a loud creak from the shift of some piece of metal out there in the ship graveyard would break the stillness.

She wanted to leave, but the attacker was not making that easy.

He shook his head and spit for what seemed like the fifth time. "I'm not saying anything."

"This is an easy one." Cam pocketed his gun but kept the knife out. "The questions will get harder."

She pushed off from the wall and joined them. Cam had contacted his team and they were on the way. The attacker couldn't know that. The watch Cam wore looked like any other dive watch, but it kept a line of communication open with Holt and Shane that just might save them all.

She stared down at the man who had terrified her enough a few minutes ago to steal her ability to speak. "Tell him."

"Shut up," the guy shot back.

"Hey." Cam smacked the guy in the side of the head. "You don't get to talk to her like that."

The attacker's gaze switched from Cam to her. "So the fight was a fake. You were pretending to be ticked off." He shook his head. "I should have known from the topic. A dumb thing to fight over."

Well, that was embarrassing. She cleared her throat to let Cam know she planned to chime in before he could. "Yeah."

The attacker's gaze switched to Cam. "Who are you?

I know your name, but what or who has you killing men across the island?"

"I'm someone you should listen to." Cam managed to look and sound bored. "Your name. Now."

"Ned."

Julia wasn't sure what good knowing did. She actually didn't want him to have a name. That way she could think of him as a nameless attacker and not an actual person.

Cam played with his knife. Looked as though he wasn't even interested in anything Ned did or said. "Okay, Ned. Tell me about Ray Miner."

Ned frowned. "How do you—"

"You should assume I have access to information, weapons and resources." Cam grabbed the only other intact chair and put it in front of Ned. "Ray Miner."

"Second to the boss."

A wave of excitement hit Julia. The guy kept coughing up information. The more they collected, the closer Cam would get to solving the case. And then he'd leave… That burst of excitement fizzled out as quickly as it came.

Cam put one foot on the seat of the chair. It wobbled but didn't disintegrate. "Who is the boss?"

"I don't know."

Cam didn't even blink as he balanced his arm on his knee and leaned in closer to the guy. "Try again."

"You can ask it a hundred times and the answer will be the same." The blade flashed and a line with bubbles of blood showed up on Ned's cheek, causing him to duck his head and flinch. "Ouch."

Cam let out a long sigh. "It only gets more painful from here."

She hadn't seen this side of him since those first couple minutes after he stormed into her dad's house.

Controlled with a deadly calm to his voice. He showed off his weapons, and everything about the way he held his body suggested he would use them.

Ned must have felt the power shift, too, because he started talking. "I dealt with Ray. He hired me."

"Where is he now?" Cam asked.

"Here." Ned looked around, moved his head from side to side.

Her heart slammed to a stop. "What?"

The question brought Ned's attention to her. He no longer looked angry. If anything he seemed pleased with himself. Certainly not scared. "He's on the grounds somewhere."

Cam didn't let up. His intensity still held the room captive. "What's happening at the shipyard?"

Julia found herself leaning in. This was the question she wanted answered. After years of nothing happening here, of all the decay and loss, it sounded as if someone had stepped in and opened a business. Drugs instead of ships, a terrible exchange.

Ned broke eye contact to stare at the floor. "I'm done talking."

She didn't know if it was guilt or his way of taking responsibility, but she wanted everything clear. If he wouldn't say the word, she would. "Drugs."

Cam smiled as he shot her a quick glance. "He thinks we don't know."

Ned's head shot up. "You're guessing."

"Wrong." Cam made a show of exhaling as he dropped his foot and moved the chair out of the zone between them. "You're supplying a new hybrid drug that has the nasty side effect of stopping some people's hearts."

The information screeched through Julia's brain. She

knew about the witness…poor Rudy. But Cam knew more details. He'd had a specific assignment—come to the island, talk to the police chief, then go fetch a witness, who happened to be Rudy. But now and then he'd let some other detail slip, which made her wonder what else he knew but wasn't saying.

As soon as the thought moved through her head, she saw Sandy's face. Now Cam had her doubting a man she always trusted.

"People shouldn't use drugs if they can't handle them." Ned delivered that gem.

He wasn't wrong, but hearing life advice from him made Julia's back teeth slam together.

"You have law enforcement on edge from Canada down to Mexico," Cam said.

Ned answered that with a feral smile. "Which should tell you about the power you're dealing with here."

"Whatever." Cam didn't look or sound impressed. "Where are the drugs?"

"Not talking."

She grew weary of running into wall after wall. They'd make progress and then lose ground. All she wanted was a firm mattress and a few hours rolling around in the sheets with Cam. They could talk and argue and anything else he wanted so long as they broke free of the mess that had bogged them down for days.

And this guy was the perfect place to start. "Your boss is going to think you talked, so you may as well cough up something and make it easier on yourself."

Cam shrugged. "She's right."

"He won't believe you." Ned said the right words, but his tone didn't match. Didn't sound sure.

"I am very persuasive." Cam brought the blade in front of Ned's face. "You want me to show you?"

"You won't—"

"Watch me." Cam held the knife right there. "See, you touched her and no one touches her without her permission."

She smiled at that. To think she ever doubted him.

RAY LOWERED THE rifle and watched Ned's face. From his position a solid three hundred yards away, Ray could see his targets walking around and his man sitting. He guessed they were having a conversation and that it wasn't a willing one on Ned's part.

The guy deserved it. Ray had watched Cam grab the advantage. He'd gotten the drop on Ned with the woman's help. It was an embarrassment for someone paid as well as Ned was. So was the fact that they all now sat there, chatting like old friends.

The talking was the problem. Sharing information couldn't happen. Ned knew about pieces of the operation and how they had started loading up trucks yesterday thanks to the news of incoming law enforcement to investigate all the murders. He didn't make the product, but he understood what it was and how lucrative it had turned out to be.

Ray had known Cameron Roth was on his way to the island to talk with someone. Enter Rudy, a onetime decent employee turned scared. Ray got to Rudy just in time and got him to crack. Killing him after actually came as a relief.

That had left the task of erasing the concerns Rudy had raised. Ray had arranged to play the role of police chief and stall Cameron's meeting with Rudy since the guy was already dead anyway. Ray's men handled the fake witness handoff.

The original plan had been to step in and eliminate Cameron before he caused trouble. To limit the disruption in production while they set him up and cleared the slate. But Cameron must have sensed trouble. First came the gunfire, then Cameron took off. And that woman kept popping up. The combination had the plan quickly falling apart.

The explanations to the boss all fell to Ray. Bigger for him, Cameron and his crew had ruined Ray's plans to make a move on the business. But overtaking anyone now that the equipment and crew were spread out and set to start leaving the island in shifts would be impossible. Ray had to wait. Double back and let the business reset before he moved in.

But he could kill Cameron Roth now. Just for fun.

Ray lifted his rifle to do just that. Would have blown the guy away, but he had company. Two men walked up. Since Roth didn't panic and the woman's body language suggested she was pleased, Ray assumed this was the rest of the group. These were the men of the Corcoran Team, at least the ones in town. If Ray wanted to go after the others, he'd have to travel to do it.

Tempting.

Now they had a squad of people to ask questions of. People everywhere who could pull details out of Ned and then put them together in a coherent way. Ned might not have all the pieces, but this team had the ability to bridge some of the mental gaps.

That left one choice. Not the one he wanted to make, but the right one.

It wasn't that he cared all that much for Ned, because

he didn't. The guy laughed at the wrong times and always seemed to be a step behind when talking tactics. But he could shoot and his size intimidated, so not having him on the payroll would be a loss.

Ray raised his rifle again. While it was tempting to unload and shoot them all, the problem of keeping the woman alive still lingered. The boss was already furious about having his trade interrupted. Having a stray bullet nick the one person he wanted alive in this thing would borrow trouble, and for now Ray was not the boss.

He looked again. Using the well of patience he kept for this sort of situation, he aimed. Lay there and watched. When the people cleared out of the way, he sighted on Ned's forehead...and fired.

Chapter Sixteen

Holt and Shane arrived before Cam could use the knife. Probably a good thing. Cam turned to welcome them to the strange party just as he heard the crack. The constant stream of noise around the shipyard as the place settled muffled the sound. The building creaked and groaned but somehow stayed up. But this was different. More focused and familiar.

He jumped in front of Julia. Thought about bringing her to the ground so he could cover her but stopped when she dived into his chest and cuddled there. Wrapping around her, he got her to the wall so her back would be protected by the wall while his body took care of the front.

Holt and Shane must have heard the sound, too, because they both turned and dropped. Holt headed for the wall directly across from Cam. The lack of furniture and firm structure made it hard to take cover. The few desks and random chairs bordered on sawdust thanks to the exposure to the elements and lack of use. Not exactly the best shields.

"That was—" Then Cam saw it. The noise had been a shot. No mistake about that now. And someone with some skill had fired it, because it'd connected to its target. "Damn."

Julia lifted her head. "What?"

Holt was the one to swear this time. He let out a string, then dropped to his knees next to Ned's body. The man's head tipped forward and blood dripped from somewhere. When Holt moved it back, Ned's eyes were closed. The only true sign of trouble was the tiny hole marring his forehead.

Cam moved Julia then. He hustled her over next to an old heater. When he ducked he brought her with him. Tucked her in front of him, tight against the wall. She mumbled something, but he couldn't hear her as Shane and Holt scurried around for better cover.

It took another few seconds to realize that in the chaos only one shot had sounded. Yeah, there could be more. The shooter could be waiting and excited to take them out one by one.

The mumbling near the side of his head finally caught his attention. He leaned in until Julia's mouth tickled his ear.

"What did you say?" he asked her.

He expected her to scream or confirm her hatred for Calapan. Both seemed fair to him at the moment. Instead, she whispered one word against the tip of his ear. "Sorry."

At first the sentiment didn't compute. She'd been both a good sport and a huge help just about from the first time they met. Her ability to stay calm in the face of terror amazed him. Which made her flat comment and dead eyes even more of a concern.

He lowered his head so only she could hear. "For what?"

"Doubting you."

The Sandy thing.

Cam knew that would come up again. That they'd churn through that topic a few times before coming to any sort of agreement.

And, man, he wanted to kiss her. Right here in the middle of danger and in front of his team. That was what she did to him. Took all of his caution and blew it away. Replaced his common sense with a blinding need for her.

No question hearing her wonder earlier about his motivations had dug into him. He was equally sure that her moment of uncertainty made sense. Sandy had been in her life forever. Cam had been in it for about forty-eight hours. Even for people without trust issues, blind faith was a rough call.

Cam saw Holt stand up and Shane unfold his body from where he'd slipped in behind Ned's chair and waited. Cam watched each move, knowing there was so much more for them to get through this morning, including knocking out a random shooter.

But he needed her to know one thing first. "You were great."

She glanced up then. "I was angry."

"That looks hot on you."

"Cam." Holt's voice carried across the open space. "This guy is out of the picture. Nothing more we can get from him."

Which was a shame. Cam truly believed Ned would have coughed up some more details. He wasn't the loyal type that rode his information to the grave. He would have been a good but reluctant source of intel.

That was probably an excuse for why he was no longer breathing. The guy couldn't be a threat if he didn't open his mouth. "Someone didn't want him to talk."

Holt looked at Julia and she froze. "Should I know who?" she asked.

Shane didn't wait for an answer to that one. "Did he say anything valuable?"

"Confirmed the drug operation and Ray Miner's role but didn't know anyone above Ray, only that someone was." That grated against Cam's nerves. The men were out here producing and transporting. On an island and away from everyone else. He didn't understand how the boss kept his identity a secret.

The success made Cam think Ned might have actually met the man in charge and didn't know it. If the guy who ran the operation was connected and well-known, which they all seemed to agree on, he'd have to be careful as he moved around.

Holt stood with the binoculars in his hands and looked into the open greenery, following what he thought was the trajectory of the shot. "I'm thinking whoever he is can shoot a gun with pretty good accuracy."

"I doubt the boss does any of the dirty work," Shane said.

"Then it should be easy to flush him out." Cam agreed, but they felt so close to figuring out this conspiracy that he wanted it disbanded and the members spread in different jails. "Create a problem and have him come running."

"A problem like how we keep killing his men?" Julia asked in an amused voice.

Cam settled on one point—she'd said *we*, and he believed she actually viewed the situation that way. She put her body in as a team member's.

He didn't hate that comparison.

"Why are you walking around?" Julia hadn't left her

safe spot next to the wall. She stood there, anchored and not moving. "The shooter could still be up there."

Shane shook his head. "He's long gone."

"How do you know that?" She glanced up at the spot where Holt had just been looking. "He could be waiting, just like he's been doing all day."

Cam knew the answer to that, but he wasn't sure telling her would ease her worry. He debated. Went back and forth and then spelled it out. "He wanted Ned here."

"If he wanted the rest of us, we'd be dead." Shane took a second to go over to her. He patted her shoulder, and from the way she flinched after each pat, Cam guessed Shane wasn't clear on how much force he used.

"Is that supposed to be comforting?" She rubbed the spot where he'd knocked against her with his palm.

Cam thought she was probably talking about the words and not the awkward bonding moment. "Poor Shane."

"No kidding," Holt whispered.

She left the sanctuary of the wall and joined them closer to the middle of the room, or warehouse floor or whatever it was. "It's scary to me that you're the best with people of the three of you."

"We used to have a fourth team member. A woman." Cam smiled when he thought about Erica. She'd been recently divorced and a sharpshooter. She could nail a target from distances that left others gawking. "She played the role of human-emotion interpreter."

Julia tried to ask a question and stumbled. She got it out the second time. "What happened to her?"

The confusion made sense. A lot of times people didn't think about women being lethal. Erica was, even though she looked as if she made a fortune in tips tending bar.

"Assignment with a bodyguard agency. She loves it, so I'm thinking we've lost her forever."

"Then I'll take over the female role." Julia pulled up straight and stared them all down. "For now."

Holt glanced over at Shane. "She's bossy."

Cam nodded. "I still like it."

"I'm thinking the only person she cares about here is Cam," Holt added.

"Enough." Cam seriously considered banging their heads together. "She is in the room and capable of talking."

Julia saved her smile for Holt and Shane. "You two are growing on me."

RAY LOOKED AT the message on his phone. It wasn't like the boss to leave a trail of any sort. Not that any phone they used could trace back to the guy. He was careful and he knew how traces worked. No way would he let something as simple as a phone trip him up.

But the words crawled across the screen and Ray could not ignore them. He had to drive out past that falling-down farmhouse and all the outbuildings on the shipyard property. He'd cleared the men out in an attempt to restore the shipyard and not raise questions. Some of the men carried loads on trucks and had coordinates for safe houses.

Everything had been split up so no one would benefit by going rogue and trying to smuggle the contents out on their own. Not that they could or that the boss would tolerate the loss anyway. All anyone had to do was ask Rudy. The boss demanded loyalty and got it.

And what the boss wanted mattered…for now. Because according to his message, he'd be there in a few minutes and he had a plan.

Chapter Seventeen

They all stood around while Holt and Connor, the one she'd never met and still only saw via a tiny screen, had some sort of virtual meeting. They talked facial recognition and drugs and something about trucks. Julia had trouble keeping up because she could barely hold her eyes open.

The danger hadn't passed, but it sounded as if the drugs were on the move, which should mean the people connected to the drugs were looking for a way out. That seemed like good news to her, even though the Corcoran guys looked ticked off that they couldn't capture someone to take to the police.

She balanced her hands behind her on what used to be a windowsill and watched Cam approach. That sure walk was back in place and his newest round of aches and bruises had been cleaned up in about two seconds by Shane. She guessed injuries suggested weakness, so these guys willed the pain away.

"Hey." That was all she had left. A simple greeting. Not even a full sentence.

Cam stood next to her and scanned the room as Shane and Holt moved around, with Shane taking photos and Holt talking to his watch.

For some reason none of it struck her as weird. Shooting, killing and chitchatting via watch seemed normal. The fact that people out there still wanted Cam dead and her captured didn't even register anymore.

Cam pressed in close enough for his body to touch hers from arm to thigh. "Any chance I can talk you into taking one of those ferries today?"

He just kept playing this refrain. Each time it got a little more tempting to say yes and demand he go with her. She was on a leave of absence and had a little time left, but this wasn't exactly her idea of a vacation. "Are they running?"

Cam crossed one ankle over the other and continued to stand there. "Connor is working on it."

She looked at Cam and saw competence. She'd heard about Connor and wondered if the guy was even human. He seemed to be able to pull off any errand or favor. He might be the leader of the team, but it sounded more as though he should lead the country.

"I have to meet your big boss." Though she'd be tempted to give him a bill for all the therapy she feared she'd need in the future thanks to this operation of his.

"You'd like him." Cam smiled. "You'd probably like his wife even more."

His...wife... "He's married?"

Cam winced. "Yeah."

For some reason that information stopped her. After the "no commitments" lecture from Cam and the lack of rings on Shane and Holt, she'd assumed the whole team had a hands-off policy. The reference to a wife blew that idea.

"I guess that means *he* found time to date at some point." And only Cam hid behind that crazy excuse.

She was joking, but the thought of that and his pledge and his strange insistence that going out with him could only be a one-off thing started an ache in the center of her chest.

He closed one eye as if he were thinking of the comment only. "I'm impressed with your ability to fall back on an argument from earlier as if we never finished that conversation."

"And win it in a landslide." She wanted that clear. She made her point and kept making it.

He nodded. "That, too."

She thought about picking at that topic a little more. She could demand an answer about the next time they saw each other, ensuring that there would be a next time. When the idea of something happening between them past tomorrow rose, he panicked. Got all twitchy and started shifting around. It was cute…and a little insulting. Here she was, so in tune to him that she could sense his moods, and he dwelled in this fear that she would start demanding things.

Looked as though she was not the only one with a trust issue.

Wading through the personal, she went right to the workday stuff. "What happens now?"

"Connor called in law enforcement. Some are on the way to the island and others have arrived but are stationed at the ferry, watching the docks and any way on and off the island by water. Ray thinks he has control of the boats, but he doesn't. If those trucks move, we should get them."

She tried to imagine how the privacy-protecting citizens of Calapan would take being infiltrated by law-enforcement types. Then a bigger question popped into her mind. "Are these law-enforcement folks going to make the murder charges against you go away?"

"Unless I tick off Connor."

She laughed then and all three of the men stared at her. "So probably not, then."

"Call is almost over." Shane walked up, already talking. "Connor is searching for more information on Ned."

"How does that help?" she asked because she honestly didn't know. The guy was dead and for her that ended the line of questioning. But what did she know?

"If we know about him, we might be able to find a string and trace it back to the leader of this drug show." Shane didn't name a name or tag Sandy as a possible suspect. He just laid the facts out and then walked away.

Not the chattiest guy she'd ever met.

She leaned into Cam. When he didn't push back or show any signs of feeling uncomfortable with the innocuous touching, she put her head on his shoulder. "Your job is exhausting."

"We rest eventually."

Shane spun around and stared at Cam. "Heads up. We have company."

"How does he know that?" The guy had just been standing there.

"He's spooky like that." Cam stood up and took her along with him. "Who?"

No one answered, but the room seemed to spin with sudden motion. They could scatter, but it would be too easy for someone to see them and follow the weakest link, which she feared was her.

Cam, Holt and Shane all stood with weapons. They formed a barricade of sorts by standing in a line. To her that made them targets, and none of them raced around to hide. But they did stand in front of her. She had to go up on tiptoes to see what was happening in front of her.

Cam's voice broke into the quiet. "We need to find better assignments from now on. Stick the Annapolis guys with the drug stuff."

A second later Chief Kreider showed up at the far end of the long room. He held a gun but didn't have any men with him. None that she could see, but they could just be off waiting somewhere. Totally possible and a little creepy.

"You can start thinking about that new job right now." Kreider aimed his weapon at Cam, clearly ignoring the fact that he was outnumbered by a decent margin. "Hands in the air. All of you."

None of them moved. Julia looked around and Holt and Cam wore similar expressions of disbelief. Shane whistled. Actually whistled. They didn't appear ruffled or impressed with Kreider's big show. She didn't like the guy either, but a gun was a gun.

"Maybe we should all stay calm." That applied to her as much as them, but she felt the need to say it.

The chief didn't take his eyes off Cam. "Ms. White, you are in no position to demand anything, but you would be wise to step on out here and come to me."

Cam's arm shot out. "No. She stays with me. Always."

Something about the way he said it had those nerves jumping around in her stomach calming just a bit. The urge to run and throw up still tried to overtake her, but she beat it back and focused on Kreider. The man hadn't changed in years. Still grumpy and demanding and generally hating women.

"Tell your friends to drop their weapons and get on

the ground or I will open fire." Kreider talked to her as if they got along.

She couldn't think of one time when he'd sided with her or helped her. He was too busy protecting his old friends to actually do anything to keep Calapan a place where people would want to live. The drug issue was only the example of his inability to do his job.

Holt frowned. "No one is threatening you. What would justify the use of force against any of us?"

"The dead men all over Calapan Island."

She had to admit Kreider had a point. Even if he wasn't guilty on the drug charge—and she was not ready to say that yet—he couldn't let Rudy's death and those of the others pass without any discussion.

But for a man who had supposedly been tracking them for days, it sure had taken him a long time to find them. Made her wonder why now. "Why are you here?"

Kreider barely spared her a glance. "You're not the one asking questions."

"What about me?" A strong male voice echoed down the other end of the room.

Another man in uniform walked into the building from the opposite end. They were surrounded by law enforcement, even though this second one wasn't real. He hadn't been real police when he shot at Cam and chased him to her father's house. Hadn't been real police when he brought two of his goons into Dad's house and scared her.

"Ray Miner. You and Chief Kreider are quite the pair." Cam made a face. "It's like the worst welcome party ever."

Kreider crowded in toward the still body in the chair, and the men parted to let him pass. Kreider did a check of the pulse, then called it in on his radio as a murder.

Never asked for backup or explained what was happening. An interesting choice for someone who was supposed to be keeping the whole town safe.

Then he turned back to Cam. "What a surprise, Roth. I find you and end up tripping over another dead body."

Cam nodded in Ray's direction. "And you brought a fake law-enforcement official to this unwanted meeting. Good call."

"Again with that argument." Kreider shook his head. "Miner here is legitimate. I called and checked his references myself."

"What did you use for verification? Because it's wrong," Shane said.

But Cam was already off and running. "You can't be this bad at your job. You just can't."

Every word sliced through her. The Corcoran men were tough and ready for almost anything, but their guns weren't up, and bad-mouthing a police officer was never a good idea. On the tiny island of Calapan it was really bad.

"Can we all put the weapons away and talk this over?" She hoped Cam would ignore the *all* part and keep one on him just in case.

"My weapons stay with me," Shane said.

"I don't think so." Ray approached Holt first. "Weapons on the floor or Ms. White will pay the price."

Cam glanced at Holt before returning his attention to Ray. "For the record, that doesn't make you sound legitimate even with the uniform."

She knew that look. There was a plan in motion. She didn't know what or how she could help, but she sensed motion coming.

She did what she could to stall for time. "Wouldn't just talking, without the weapons, be a better use of our time?"

Kreider ignored her and started his own conversation. "Why are you all here? This is private property."

"Are you afraid the corporation will get upset?" Cam asked.

Kreider frowned at him. "Last I checked, an individual owned the property."

She listened, fascinated, as the team picked up pieces of information without a full-on interrogation. Just went to prove that most people liked to pass on what they knew. They talked and shared and made a mess of everything.

"We came to town for a meeting with Rudy, who is now dead, but we know there is a drug problem here." Cam held out his arms. "That's why we're here. We needed to find the operation, and now we have."

"I checked the grounds and there's nothing here," Ray said.

Kreider looked up and down the room. "Yeah, Roth. You see something I don't?"

"It's mostly been cleaned out," she said.

She hated that part. After all they'd been through, it only seemed fair that they would get to the end of the chase and find a room full of something and be able to point to it as proof of her innocence.

Ray chuckled. "Convenient."

"Not really," Cam said as he folded his arms in front of him.

Something in the way he moved suggested Ray was getting twitchy. He widened his stance and pulled out a zip tie. "This is the last time we're telling you to get on the floor."

"Or?" Holt asked.

That tone. Those expressions. She was prepared to

dive out of the line of battle if it came to that. "Maybe if we went with fewer threats."

"Swab the walls and floor. Check the buildings and those trucks outside. You'll find the evidence of a drug lab." Cam's gaze did a quick bounce to Ray before coming back to settle on Kreider. "We have nothing to hide."

Ray shook his head. "I'm taking you all in, including the woman."

"Hold up." Kreider held out a hand. "They're mine."

"Actually, gentlemen—" Holt's husky voice cut through the arguing "—we're not going anywhere."

"I'm tired of this." Ray raised the gun and fired.

Kreider hit the floor and the team pulled their weapons. She was the only one without a gun in her hand, but she barely noticed. The shock of seeing the chief fall back, just wither and slide, echoed in her head.

By the time she looked up again, Ray had one gun on the men and one aimed at her. She shifted and the barrel followed.

Ray's smile turned feral. "Now are you all ready to listen?"

"You just killed your boss?" Cam asked.

"I think we can both agree I'll make a better boss." Ray kicked Kreider's foot. "I managed to trick him and most of this dumpy island into thinking I was a police officer."

"Why?" Julia wasn't even sure what question she was asking. Why do this, why the killing and the lying? Why use poor Calapan as his stomping grounds?

"I'm stronger, smarter. More efficient."

When he went with his ego she wasn't sure how to respond. She glanced at Cam and he shook his head. Slight but she saw it.

"So this was all you." Cam shifted his stance. The move put him closer to her. "The setup and production, all you?"

"Yes."

Cam's eyes narrowed. "Transportation and break-down."

Ray waved off the question. "We're done talking."

"It's four against one," Shane pointed out.

She liked those odds. She'd seen what Cam could do when he was on the one side, and she thought this had to be better.

"Not really because, first, I'm not alone." Ray continued to aim a gun at her. "And second, anyone comes near me or if I feel even a twinge from a muscle cramp, I will assume you are at fault and punish the woman."

The whole feeling-better thing gave way to waves of nausea. "Why do you want me?"

"I'm going to have to insist you all disarm…unless you want to hear her scream."

Cam held up his hands. "Fine. You win this round."

"What are you doing?" The shock came through in Shane's voice.

She wondered the same thing. There were three of them. Even if reinforcements lingered out on the property somewhere, these guys had the advantage.

Cam glanced at Shane. "I won't let him hurt her. We're fine without them."

"That's sweet." Ray waved his weapon. "All the guns. Now."

She heard a series of clicks and thuds as they took off the firepower. Holt and Cam wore three guns each. Shane unpacked for what felt like forever. By the time they were done, the area in front of them was littered with weapons.

"Come here." Ray pointed at her.

She didn't move, but Cam clamped a hand over her arm anyway. "She stays with me."

"I'm afraid not." Ray used the side of his foot to move the guns. Shifted them out of the direct reach of the Corcoran men. "You see, I have a need for her."

Her stomach flopped. "What does that mean?"

"You're useful." He reached for her. "Be grateful."

Everything happened so fast after that. She shrank back from his touch at the same time Shane kicked Ray in the hand. Bodies moved and she tried to keep track of Ray's gun, but she lost sight when Holt and Shane moved in.

She heard a yell akin to a battle cry. She wanted to close her eyes and hide, but she watched. Saw Cam let his knife fly and Ray squealed when it sliced through his shooting hand. The gun dropped and Shane jumped on it as Holt tackled Ray to the floor.

When the chaos calmed, Holt had Ray pinned, but he didn't notice. He was too busy rolling to his side as he cradled his hand.

Then Cam's face appeared in front of her. "Are you okay?"

She tried to draw enough air into her lungs to breathe. "That was the plan?"

Cam shot her a smile. "He only asked for the guns."

"And we wanted him alive." Holt stood and pulled Ray up beside him.

He was cursing and trying to roll into a ball. "You will all pay."

He sounded wild and out of control. His words slurred and the blood continued to flow. The guy needed medical help and a prison cell. She didn't think the order mattered.

While Holt and Shane dragged him out, she tried to reboot her brain. She felt raw and exposed and not prepared to do anything but slide to the floor in a heap.

Cam's arms came around her. "It's going to be okay."

She said the first thing that came into her mind. "I want to see Sandy."

Cam's shoulders stiffened, but he placed a gentle kiss in her hair. "Me, too."

Chapter Eighteen

Two hours later Ray was in the hospital with Holt by his side. He hadn't started talking, but it was only a matter of time. Finding the trucks took a little longer. Kreider or Ray or whoever had played that one smart, which ticked Cam off. Didn't try to remove the trucks from the island. Just hid them and waited.

No doubt about it, someone with smarts led this drug ring. Cam still didn't believe it was Kreider.

Sandy let the refrigerator door close and turned around to the counter with a water in each hand. He handed one to Julia and Cam took the other.

"Kreider's a drug dealer?" Sandy shook his head as he twisted off the cap to his bottle.

"Was." Julia shivered. "He's not anything now."

Cam slipped his hand over her leg and gave her knee a squeeze. She'd been thrown around and injured, so he almost hated to touch her. Except for the other part of him that was desperate to touch her.

Sandy continued as if she never spoke. "Either way, it doesn't really make sense."

Cam didn't think so, either. He sat on the bar stool in Sandy's kitchen and tried to make the pieces fit together, but they wouldn't. Nothing in Kreider's demeanor suggested he'd worked with Ray in the drug trade. Kreider had acted as if he thought the other man was a legitimate law-enforcement officer.

There was no evidence in Kreider's finances or history to support his being some drug kingpin. Even though he wasn't the greatest police chief, everyone agreed he worked long hours. He liked to hang out in his uniform and visit with people. That hardly left a lot of time to run up to the shipyard and oversee production.

And then there was the comment about the ownership of the shipyard now. Connor and Joel were working on that pile of shell companies and business names right now, but Cam thought he could find the answer in a much easier way. "Who purchased the shipyard from you?"

Sandy slowly lowered the water bottle. "Excuse me?"

"Julia told me a company bought it and then ran it into the ground." If they knew who, maybe they could trace the whole thing back to Kreider and put it to bed.

Until then, as far as Cam was concerned, the case was not over. Many of the people who could explain were dead. Kreider was supposed to be the boss, but no matter how many times Cam turned that over in his head he couldn't make sense of it.

Julia finished off the bottle and clunked the plastic container against the counter. "It was a Canadian outfit. I remember that much from my father's complaining."

Cam didn't want to go down that road and open up those memories again. She'd already made it clear she hadn't trusted her dad. Anything that raised his name or even for an instant made her tie him to her father was a no-go for Cam.

"Do you remember the name?" he asked Sandy.

"It doesn't matter, because it was sold again." Sandy

went back to the refrigerator. This time he pulled out a plate of food with foil over the top. "Hungry?"

The whole scene struck Cam as surreal. Julia was out of it, almost comatose. She'd been through threats and pain and shootings and fires. She needed to recuperate for more than a few hours to be back on track.

And Sandy didn't seem to care about any of it. A civic leader who didn't have a single reaction to the idea of drug runners taking over the business he had once nurtured and built. Not when he was hungry.

The ticking at the back of Cam's neck kicked up again. Nothing had felt right about this assignment since he walked onto the island. The supposed resolution of the case being the biggest question mark for him.

"I need to head over to the clinic." The words came out before Cam could even think them through.

She stopped in the middle of reaching over to steal his water bottle. "Why?"

"Ray Miner is awake and talking." In truth he was awake and staring at the ceiling. He insisted he was the boss and it was his operation now that Kreider was gone. He implicated the dead man and then clammed up.

It was too convenient. Though it didn't make much sense to Cam that a man with Ray's ego would take part of the fall for anyone else. It was possible his hubris drove him to claim more responsibility than he had. His personality might just not let him be seen as a simple employee. Either way, he was going to prison, which was a good thing for everyone.

"That's good, right?" Julia shook her head as the memories played across her face. "That guy should not be out among people."

Cam wanted to stay and comfort her. Guilt smacked

into him at the thought of opening this door with her one more time after she'd been so clear and so broken when he broached it before.

But Cam kept playing the role. If Ray really was the boss, no harm could come from this. But if he wasn't, this might draw the real boss out. "He's not happy with how things ended for him. Apparently he thought he should be the boss, and that bitterness should work for us."

Cam stared at Sandy until he finally piped up with a response. "Good."

"I'll go with you." Julia slid off the bar stool.

"You need to stay here and get some rest." He was deadly serious about this. There wouldn't be an argument or a battle. He was winning this round. If Sandy made a move on Ray, she should be here, out of the fray. "She injured her ankle."

Sandy frowned. "What?"

"It's fine."

Before she could downplay it, he made it clear she was not okay. "You should stay off it. I'll be gone for a few hours, and then we can figure out what's happening with the ferries and return to Seattle."

The remaining light left her eyes. "Cam, I'm not ready to talk about that yet."

He wasn't, either. The idea of leaving her, of walking away and letting some other man get to know her, made Cam want to rip Sandy's expensive house down stone by stone.

"I was thinking I could use a break and some time in Seattle. Thought you might have some ideas on how I could spend that time." Though if his hunch was right she was never going to want to see him again.

He pushed that thought away and concentrated on getting through the next hour and the assignment he'd given himself. He kissed her on the forehead. "I'll step out and be back."

"Let us know what's happening," Sandy said in his usual voice.

That wasn't going to happen, but it was time to plant as many seeds as possible. "Do I need to know anything for the alarm system to get back in?"

The older man didn't say anything. Didn't offer up a number or a detailed account of how to get around the system. Enough time passed that Julia noticed. She joined Cam in looking at Sandy while the answer came to him.

Julia glared at him. "Sandy?"

"I don't like giving it away," he said.

This guy had an obsession and Cam thought he knew why. "Understandable, but I don't like sleeping on the porch."

Sandy took a piece of paper out of one of the drawers and wrote a number on it. "Here."

Cam wasn't convinced whatever was written on that paper would do anything. But for Julia he would try. Try and hope he was wrong so they could avoid talking about this topic ever again.

A SHORT TIME later Cam pulled into the clinic's parking lot and went inside. There were people lined up against all the walls. The coughing echoed through the space until Cam was sure he'd come back out of the building with a disease.

He flashed his ID downstairs and then again on the assigned floor to get by the guards Connor had set up. After calling, Holt met him in the hall.

They walked side by side, but Holt started talking. "I thought you'd be in bed."

"I'm not tired. Too wound up." The exhaustion would hit him but it hadn't yet.

Holt chuckled. "I didn't mean sleeping."

Since the guy had handed him a box of condoms this last time, Cam knew Holt was on top of this subject. But Cam wasn't in the mood to talk about anything personal. "Is he talking?"

Holt didn't pretend not to understand. "No."

"I need him to."

"Yeah, well." Holt shrugged. "We all want that."

Looked as if he needed to spell this out a bit more. He was trying to remain vague in case they got questions. He didn't want trouble to roll over to Holt. "No, I need people to think he's talking. Naming names."

"Why?"

Damn, he was going to insist on details. That was probably fair, since for this to work Cam needed the assistance of the guards and some of the staff. "You know why."

Holt's eyes narrowed but a spark of understanding showed in his eyes. "You sure."

"I think so." The longer Cam thought about it the more clear the idea of Sandy being in the middle of this mess became.

Holt let out a low whistle. "This is a dangerous game for you."

Cam didn't care about the physical danger, but he knew that wasn't what Holt was talking about. He referred to how this could rip him and Julia apart. They'd had such a fragile relationship so far. The sex was great, but they both tiptoed around more and threw up trust concerns now and then.

Hell, Cam didn't know what he wanted with her or even what he could handle. He just knew that the idea of not seeing her after being in this intense relationship with her would crush something inside him. In a short time she had wrapped her life around his and he didn't know how to break them apart again…or if he even wanted to.

If he removed her, took her face and that body out of the equation, forgot all about her strength and the comfort in being with her and boiled her down to this person he was not connected to, the lingering question about Sandy would remain.

That meant he couldn't let this drop. Cam knew he had to dig and poke and risk her wrath. "But if I'm right about—"

Holt was already shaking his head. "You still lose because Julia is going to be furious. I was there when we delivered you guys to Sandy's house a short time ago. They have a connection." Cam had seen that, too. A pseudo father-daughter bond.

A genuineness of affection behind the gruff exterior. Still, Cam said, "Something is not right."

"Could you be jealous?" Holt said the words carefully, hesitating over each one.

The delivery didn't stop the rush of angry heat that breezed through Cam. "Julia isn't involved with the guy."

"I meant emotionally."

"That doesn't really sound like something I'd know about." But now he did. He got the idea of a connection. He'd experienced the sensation of having someone else's happiness mean more than anything—his needs, the job and everything else.

"You're not you when you're with her."

Cam knew exactly what his friend meant and dodged the comment. "It's only been a few days."

"It's about intensity, not actual time together."

"I know." But the words sounded weird coming from Holt. He was this big bruiser of a guy who had never had a serious girlfriend so long as Cam had known him. And here he was, talking about romance in a way that sounded like poetry.

Holt exhaled. "She's going to hate you."

"I know that, too." That was the part that kept stopping him even though he knew it was selfish. She needed him to do that right thing even when doing the wrong thing was too easy.

"Is this worth losing her? I can play the bad guy. If I'm wrong it won't matter." Leave it to Holt to offer.

But that was never going to work.

"If I can't live with myself, we don't have a future anyway." That was the closest Cam could get to admitting she might mean something. That if they made it through the fallout with Sandy, she might.

Holt made a hissing sound between his teeth. "You're stuck."

"Yeah, I know."

Chapter Nineteen

Julia sat curled up on the edge of the sofa in Sandy's impressive family room. The bed called to her, but she wanted to stay up until Cam got back. Something about the idea of snuggling under the covers with him sounded so good. After all they'd endured and survived, she wanted to touch him and kiss him and feel his heat. But he had to get back here first.

Sandy had gone into his home office over an hour ago. She hadn't heard a word since. She thought he'd come out and talk to her, maybe take her mind off everything. Even with Ray caught and Kreider gone, the path of destruction cut through Calapan was hard to ignore. Shattered lives and so many questions.

She got up and walked into the kitchen, thinking a second snack wouldn't be totally out of line. On the way in, the alarm panel in the dining room caught her attention. The red light beamed at her. If she was going to stay here a few days—and that was the plan in light of the questions she needed to answer—she needed to be able to come and go. That meant knowing the security codes. The one she had didn't work, which meant she didn't have access.

With her mind in a whirl she knew the chances of

her forgetting were pretty high. She decided to fix the problem now before she was standing out there one day in a rainstorm.

She dumped off the coffee mug and empty water bottle and made her way to the front door. She just wanted to double-check. The alarm pad was all lit up, but the only light that flashed was red. No green light here either, which made sense in light of a drug ring being run right under their noses.

Her feet padded against the hardwood as she went back to Sandy's office. She hated to disturb him, although Cam had raised a good question about Sandy not actually having any work right now.

Still, she was respectful. She held the knob in one hand as she knocked with the other. No one answered. Since she'd seen him go in an hour ago and since there was not a door in and out of there other than the main one into the hall, he had to be in there.

She looked at the knob and knocked again. She'd never burst into this room. She viewed this as his private space and didn't violate that sanctuary.

But something pulled hard at her tonight. She wanted to peek in and see what he did when he was alone and when he worked.

Inhaling a deep breath, she twisted the knob and pushed the door open. She saw the empty chair and the walls lined with bookshelves. But no Sandy. She tried to remember if she'd dozed off and maybe missed him. She doubted it.

She went to the house intercom system and called for him. Nothing there, either.

As she stood there she felt the walls close in. It was an odd sensation and not one based in reality, but she knew the red light meant no way out. She'd have to break a window or risk the alarm. The latter wouldn't be too bad except that the new system actually didn't let you accidentally set off the alarm. If the system was on and you didn't have the code, you were trapped in that room.

That suddenly seemed like a terrible idea. So did the thoughts going through her mind about Sandy's desk. It was right there. She could look through some of the paperwork, if only to let Cam know his initial suspicions were truly wrong.

And she might be able to clear up some of those questions about the shipyard's ownership. She couldn't believe Sandy didn't know. He was a man who knew everything down to the penny. But then, nothing had been normal about the past few days. They all wanted this episode over, except her, who wanted the part with Cam to linger.

She sat down in the oversize chair and was immediately transported back to being a kid. She'd sit in his chair and spin, pretending she was on an amusement park ride. She shifted the seat from side to side and opened the top drawer. The move felt so naughty she only got it out far enough to stare at the pens sitting in the tray.

That was enough. Snooping was not her style. If Cam needed proof or wanted to talk to Sandy, he could. She was not going to get in the middle of that.

She walked back to the alarm keypad by the front door. She entered the code and tried a few variations. By the fifth time she had the nerves in her belly jumping around in a chaotic frenzy.

People could talk about being comfortable at home and not wanting to leave. She got that. But being locked in made her twitchy. If Cam needed her, she couldn't get there…and that realization set something spinning inside her.

She went back into the family room and picked up the phone. Cam might jump to the wrong conclusions, but he might have a way to get out other than through an upstairs balcony. When she lifted the receiver she didn't hear anything on the other end. No dial tone. She hung up and tried again. Then another time.

By the time she slammed down the phone the last time, she was near frantic. She couldn't control her breathing or her thoughts. She started jumping to bigger conclusions than Cam had. Then she remembered her cell. She'd left it on the kitchen counter.

She raced back to the kitchen because plain walking no longer seemed fast enough. She stepped into the doorway and stopped. Sandy had cleaned off the counter after they ate, and the phone was gone.

She pulled open drawers and looked on every flat surface. She made a run in the bedroom to see if he'd thrown it on the bed. No luck.

She stood in the middle of the hall and thought it all through. No cell, no landline, no alarm code. No way out.

Maybe Cam wasn't so paranoid after all.

CAM TRIED JULIA'S cell for the third time. The phone rang and she didn't pick up. He wanted to write it off to her being tired and crawling into bed. Maybe she was so wiped out she'd turned off the sound.

There were a lot of reasonable possibilities. He kept dwelling on the awful, like that something had happened to her and she couldn't get to the phone.

The clinic floor was quiet, just as planned. They had the world thinking Ray was on the second floor. He was really on the third. They'd cleared patients out except for a few who couldn't or refused to be moved.

"What's wrong with you?" Holt came up beside him and leaned against the wall in the visitors' lounge.

Cam tried to keep the panic out of his voice. The anxiety whipping through him was enough to deal with. "I can't reach her."

Holt made a sound, something like a humph. "Maybe she needs a break."

"Didn't seem like it." If anything, she'd been trying to get him to commit to something. She'd been pretty unimpressed with his schedule and the danger aspects, probably because he was dragging her through the middle of danger at the time.

"Is your head in this?" Holt asked as he checked his watch.

"Yes."

Holt nodded and didn't say anything else on that topic. That was Holt's style. He didn't browbeat. He treated everyone like a grown-up, which was quite refreshing. That wasn't to say he didn't butt in, because he did. But had an innate sense of when to back down, and he used it now.

There was a broader principle at work. They had an understanding on the team: if you couldn't go for the job, for whatever reason, you spoke up. You did not put the other team members in danger. Cam knew the rule and lived by it. He spent almost every day with Holt and Shane. There was no way he was going to put them in a position of having to pick up for him.

And if he was right and Sandy presented a danger, then he needed to figure this out right now. The longer Julia spent in his house, trusting him while he did whatever he was doing, the worse the end could be. And one day he might decide that she knew too much or knew the wrong people, and then Cam didn't want to think what would happen.

But the worst part was they might get this close and not be able to finish this off. That was the line that Holt kept repeating, and he said a version of it here again. "He might not even show."

"He will." Cam knew that Holt, who was usually right about these things—about most things, except women—had this part wrong. Sandy's personality would not let him stay at home. If he thought he could fix this and save his reputation and all he'd built, he would. A guy who lived in that kind of house liked to send a personal message and would not be content to let that message flash about him being a drug dealer.

"Yeah, I think so, too." Holt looked down at his feet. "How are you going to explain that to her?"

Cam had run through the various options numerous times. It all came down to the same thing. He would have to pull her aside and tell her that the first man she'd ever trusted—one of the few she'd ever trusted—had violated that trust in a serious way. He had no idea how she'd recover from that.

So, for now, he dodged. "I can only handle one disaster at a time."

"That's not true, but I'll let you get away with that excuse."

THE CLINIC HALLWAYS were quiet except for the occasional squawk over the speakers. Emergencies requiring serious care were flown to Seattle. The clinic served all the other needs of the community. Tonight it also acted as the scene for a setup.

Cam stood in the bathroom of Ray's reported room. Back at the house Cam had made sure to give the information to Julia in an offhanded way and she'd repeated it in front of Sandy. Cam had witnessed that part.

With the silence coming from Sandy's house, Cam wanted to send Holt over, but they needed all three of them there. Cam went back and forth between wanting Sandy to show up and not. He believed to his bones the older man had some side business going on. One that wasn't legal. He'd love to be wrong, but he didn't think he was.

A long and painful hour passed with no signs of anything. The world outside the clinic had morphed into night and stretched into the early hours of the morning. The sky remained a dark gray, signaling another rainy day tomorrow.

Cam leaned his head back against the wall. He was about to call this off and check on Julia when he heard the footsteps. Not sneakers. These were dress shoes. If he guessed right, expensive black dress shoes that he'd already seen.

Whoever it was got by the guard, which was part of the plan. The guy was to sit there but get up for food and drinks. Set a pattern of not being great about being at the door. It didn't matter, since Ray wasn't on this floor. The real guard had strict orders, and after the way the guy got all wide-eyed and panic-stricken talking to Holt, Cam doubted that guard would mess up.

The footsteps grew louder and there was a muffled sound that Cam now associated with the door opening and closing. The sound of the privacy curtain being peeled back and the way the rings clanked against the bar suggested the guy was moving around. If he came into the bathroom he'd see cabinets and not Cam hiding inside. Out there he'd see a man with Ray's coloring sleeping on his stomach and all bandaged around the shoulder and stomach.

The Ray part was tougher to pull off. If Sandy bent down and looked in close, he'd see that the face smashed in the pillow did not belong to Ray. The hope was that he'd buy the room and the clinic and try to do the job fast.

Cam looked out of the crack in the door to the room beyond. Sandy walked around wearing doctor's scrubs. It was a nice but unnecessary touch. They'd already covered that with the guard. But now when nurses and other people on the hall ignored him, it wouldn't seem so odd.

Sandy slipped around the bed toward the headboard and the beeping equipment. Nothing was actually connected to Shane as he played Ray, but Sandy didn't need to know that. When Sandy took out a syringe and started filling the tubes he thought led into Ray, Cam felt sick. He didn't even know if Julia would believe him despite the other witnesses.

Cam slid out as Sandy finished. When he turned to leave he almost walked right into Cam.

Cam held his gun steady. "You're a doctor now?"

"I was… There was… Just checking on him." Sandy stumbled his way through a sentence that made no sense in light of who he was and his professed lack of knowledge about Ray Miner and who he was.

"Do you need him to come back to work at the drug-producing plant? Must be hard to find people loyal enough to do that." Cam almost spat. The guy made him sick.

Sandy was one of those. He had everything and greed pulled at him until he went out and earned more. And not the legal way. No, he had to move drugs. Cam would bet he was a guy who found drug use to be disgusting yet had no problem pushing it to kids and getting rich off them.

"What?"

Sandy was playing dumb and Cam refused to buy it. The blank stare and confusion. He was acting to the wrong audience. "It's over."

"I don't know what you think you have, but—"

Cam could almost see the wheels turning in the guy's head. He was searching for a reasonable explanation and kept coming up blank. Cam almost wished Sandy would come forward and admit it, not hide behind the money he earned from illegal drugs. Just own his behavior.

"You're a drug dealer and murderer." Cam had some other choice words for him but led with those two.

Sandy starting shaking his head. "You're passing your mess off on me."

"Why do this? Why drugs? I hear it's a huge operation with great stuff." Cam had promised he wouldn't ask, but the question came out.

He'd heard so many excuses and justifications over the years, most of them not true, that he no longer cared. The fact was, people committed these crimes and then acted shocked when caught. Sandy was the type to play the victim. Poor little millionaire got bored or was in the right place or whatever.

Cam worked his butt off in his job and paid the bills. He didn't expect a handout and he sure didn't understand people who had it all and threw it away in the search for *just a little bit more.*

Something came over Sandy. The fake fear in his eyes

faded. Now he looked tall and in charge and every bit the crime boss. "Moving the drugs is easy. Growing them is easy. And if you're really good and have the open land, it can be very lucrative." He smiled. "Or so I hear. I don't have personal experience, of course."

"Right." Cam was done playing this game. "Step away from the bed."

"Or I could shoot the person in here." Sandy brought out a gun that had been tucked into the waist of his pants. "Does this person mean anything to you? Actually, it doesn't matter, because you're one of those people who believes in others. Very tiresome."

Sandy brought the gun around and aimed it at the person in the bed.

Cam shook his head. "I wouldn't do that. He gets upset very easily."

"Why do I care?"

"Because he has a grenade." Cam said the code word for Shane to move.

He did not waste time. He brought his arm out from under him with the blade arcing through the air. Just as Sandy turned and aimed again, Shane stabbed his knife into Sandy's thigh.

The man dropped his gun and let it clank against the floor. He let out an awful scream, one that was almost inhuman in its piercing squeal. Then he bent over, holding the wound.

Real doctors came running and Holt slipped into the room. When Shane sat up, he looked down and watched Sandy make demands about his leg and a scar. After ripping the fake tubes out, he came to stand with Holt and Cam.

Sandy rocked back and forth on the floor while Holt

grabbed the discarded gun and a nurse tried to stop the bleeding. "You think you won, but I'll beat this."

The guy fought to the end. Cam guessed a part of him should admire that, but it was hard to after hearing that squeal. "Good luck wasting your money doing that."

Sandy's head whipped up and he pinned Cam with an intense stare. "And in the meantime you lose Julia."

"She loves you." Cam wasn't clear why at the moment. "Why would you do this to her?"

Sandy's rage spilled out of him now. There was nothing fatherly or caring about the guy huddled on the floor in a sitting position. "I am convenient to her. I did everything for her and she left. She was as useless as her father and look what happened to him."

Cam remembered the story. "He fell."

"Fell. Sure." Sandy laughed.

Everything inside Cam went cold. He heard Holt swear under his breath and saw Shane take a step back while he shook his head. "You're saying that you—"

"You might want to get to my house." Sandy clenched his teeth as the nurse continued to work on his leg. "No phone. No way out. Julia could be on the edge right now."

Cam imagined her trying to get out of the house. All frantic and confused and winding up. "Why would you do that?"

"Because for once I needed her to listen and do what she was told."

The comment was so cold, so awful, that Cam knew he couldn't repeat it. Sandy had belittled her and expressed disappointment. And unless Cam misheard, Sandy had also admitted to doing something to Julia's drunken father.

"So you hate women," Shane said.

Sandy scoffed. "I hate weakness, and she and her father are all about weakness."

"That's where you're wrong." Right there was where Cam wrote the guy off. He couldn't speak to Julia's father, but he did know all about her. "She's stronger than both of us."

Chapter Twenty

Julia couldn't take the confinement one more second. She stood at the bank of glass doors that ran along the back of the house and stared into the lit yard beyond. The security lights plunged the patio and pool into a burst of white. She wasn't much of a swimmer, but right now she wanted to run out there and jump in. Cold or not, didn't matter.

Her insides jumped and tingled. Every nerve seemed to be on fire or ready to burst. She'd never thought of herself as nervous or anxious, but being locked in, penned against her will and unable to contact anyone, had her walking around and dreaming up crazy ways to get out.

She'd paced so much she'd broken out in a sweat. The landline phone lay on the floor. No dial tone. A laptop was open and the television was on. Nothing got her access to the world beyond the walls. It didn't even matter that these were pretty well-decorated walls. Prison was prison.

Her footsteps thundered as she ran up to Sandy's bedroom again. She'd made this journey twice already. She'd seen how Cam got them out. Just tie the sheets and jump. But without him here she didn't trust herself to go. She did trust Cam.

He'd been right about Sandy. She didn't know what

was going on, but what was happening now was so odd. She couldn't wrap her brain around it. Didn't believe she'd be okay without him.

She heard a pounding. At first she thought it was wishful thinking or her brain playing tricks. Then the doorbell began to ring. Over and over. Chiming until she felt it inside her head.

She ran downstairs, looking first at the front door. As soon as she appeared in the small window next to the double door, Shane waved and pointed toward the back of the house.

She should have been angry, but all she felt was relief. It almost knocked the legs out from under her. She spun around on her heel and got to the glass doors again. Holt and Cam stood out there, looking as if they were locked in deep thought. Holt held a gun but Cam shook his head.

Cam glanced up and smiled. A warmth filled her when she saw that face. He was fine and here and everything would be okay. Even if she never got out of this house again.

"The alarm is in shutdown." She yelled the words because she knew the glass would muffle them.

For some reason he seemed to know. He nodded and bent down. When he stood up again he had a planter in his arms, and not a small one. This thing could break glass and bones.

The first hit bounced off the glass, but her belief never wavered. He might talk about not caring about a woman and keeping things light, but that look of determination did not say acquaintance to her. The second hit landed square against the glass and a huge cracking sound split the night. She waited for the glass to fall. He stood on the other side looking as if he was trying to will it to fall.

Finally he motioned her back and lifted his leg. As Holt yelled something, Cam kicked. The glass exploded. It shattered into pieces, breaking off into slivers as it crashed over the dining room table and pinged in what looked like a million tiny cubes against the hardwood floor.

Then he was there. He had her wrapped in his arms and was kissing her hair. He said something about trust, but she didn't hear it. Couldn't hear anything over the frantic beating of her heart.

The night was a blur, but he was solid. She ran her hands over him and tugged him in close. Her last thought was relief.

Then the world went dark.

CAM SAT BY Julia's bedside at the clinic and willed her to wake up. The doctor had chalked her reaction up to anxiety and shock. Cam didn't like either answer. Also hated that she still hadn't opened her eyes.

He put her hand between both of his and rubbed. The heat had slowly returned to her body. When she first passed out she'd felt like ice. Her skin had actually been cold to the touch.

"How are we doing?" Holt asked as he opened the door and came in.

Shane followed. "Looks like she's not ready to wake up yet."

The doctor had said the same thing. Cam now hated that phrase.

He glanced at her, saw her hair on the white pillow and the slow rise and fall of her chest. "Apparently."

Shane walked around the bed, looking at her. Whatever he was looking for he must have found, because he stopped at the end of her bed and stood there. "What are you going to tell her when she wakes up?"

Cam had walked through that in his mind. Over and over. He could soft-pedal it all and fill in blanks. But that wouldn't be fair. She'd been strong and right by his side throughout the entire ordeal. He owed her as much information as he could give her and a shoulder to cry on when the disappointment about Sandy hit.

"The truth." He'd mess up if he tried to do anything else, anyway.

"Smart." Holt nodded. "But that's a rough story. Her uncle—"

"They weren't blood related." For some reason, that mattered to Cam. He didn't want her tied to Sandy any more than she was.

"I don't think that will be a comfort, since he ran drugs, killed, scared her on purpose, tried to kill you and possibly killed her father."

Man, that list. Cam ran through it in his head, but hearing it out loud sounded so much worse. And that wasn't even all of it. He knew it would get worse over the next few days as they gathered more information on the choices Sandy had made. Then came the criminal part. No way would that man go down easy.

But that wasn't even the biggest problem of all. Julia's feelings for him were. "She loved him."

Shane snorted. "Well, her taste in men stinks."

"Thanks." Since that actually made Cam smile, he didn't bother to shoot an insult right back at his teammate.

Holt looked over at him. "I guess this means you're off the market."

"Was I ever on it?" Cam kept his dating life light. It had been a good system until he met Julia.

"You were single." Holt shrugged as a smile tugged at the corner of his mouth. "Fight it all you want, but I saw the look on your face. You want her."

The knee-jerk reaction to deny and minimize had faded. When Holt delivered his assessment, Cam could only agree. "I do."

Shane put a hand on Cam's shoulder. "Then don't mess it up."

That seemed simple enough. Maybe too simple. "That's your advice?"

"Hey, it's good advice." Shane walked toward the door.

"Call us if you need a ride," Holt said as he joined Shane. "Otherwise, Connor said you should take some time off."

"He's a hopeless romantic." Cam had never thought he'd say that about a six-foot-something bruiser who could shoot and run and do anything Corcoran needed. But Cam did admire Connor's ability to balance his marriage and the work. He wasn't the only one. The entire Annapolis office was paired off.

They'd all survived dating. Maybe he could, too. He rubbed a thumb over the back of Julia's hand. Maybe it just depended on the partner.

"I'm thinking all of you have marriage fever." Holt sounded disgusted by the possibility.

Shane touched his chest. "Except me."

Holt nodded. "Right, except me and Shane."

Cam remembered saying something similar and thinking it was brilliant. Now he knew better. "Your time will come."

Holt's smile fell. "Don't come back with that attitude."

JULIA CAME AWAKE in bursts. She'd wake up and try to open her eyes, then drift again. Every time she thought she'd reached the surface, she would feel a hand in hers or the brush of fingers through her hair. It was that loving touch that had her keep trying. She craved it.

On the last swim to the top she heard her name spoken in a deep, husky voice. She knew that voice, which meant she knew that hand. Using all her energy, she opened her eyes. The light flooded in and had her blinking. She wanted to lift her hand to block it, but her muscles weighed too much to lift.

"Hey there." Cam leaned in farther as she woke up.

"What happened?" She remembered being in the house and the sense of desperation. Then there was glass everywhere. She didn't even know what had happened to Sandy and why he'd locked the house down.

"Sandy set the security system and you couldn't get out." Cam kept up the gentle caress of his fingertips against the back of her hand. "The doctor said that shock along with being dehydrated was too much for your system."

"Am I okay?"

"Yes." He leaned down and kissed her forehead. "You need rest, which is what I think I said to you about a hundred times."

She wanted to roll her eyes, but it hurt to move her head. "I'm not weak."

"Of course not." His head pulled back. "Is that what you thought I was saying?"

She thought back to all he'd told her. He'd praised her. She didn't remember the word *weak* or any other negative word. He wasn't her father or like any man she'd ever dated. "I just wanted you to know."

He raised their joined hands to his mouth and kissed her fingers. "I know."

She knew she should close her eyes and drift off. Him being there made her feel safe, but there were so many questions spinning in her head. She started with the obvious one. "Sandy was involved, wasn't he?"

A flash of pain crossed over Cam's face. She knew then that he was trying to hold that back and protect her. But she'd already guessed the truth. The second she'd looked for her cell and found it gone and then couldn't get out of the house, her mind had gone from thinking Sandy was being overprotective to knowing he was hiding something.

Part of her wanted to believe he'd done it because he hadn't thought Cam safe. But she knew that wasn't it. Sandy had become secretive, and that security system kept growing to include new and scary features. When she'd stopped visiting, his mood had turned surly.

Cam continued to hold her hand in his. "We think Sandy is the drug runner, Julia. The boss. In charge of it all."

She closed her eyes and tried to let those words sink in. "I can't imagine him doing it."

She'd never known him to use drugs or even alcohol. He'd shamed her father repeatedly on the alcohol issue. It made her wonder if dealing was his way of proving he was stronger and everyone else was weaker. That did fit with his personality.

"He pretty much admitted it to me and the team." Cam exhaled. "He got caught up in telling us how great he was and started talking about this."

"I bet he's trying to back off of that admission now." The thought of Sandy in prison made her mind rebel. The guy liked comfort. Big-time comfort. Thinking about him in a uniform with set mealtimes… What had he been thinking?

"We set him up at the hospital and he took the bait. Came to the clinic to kill Ray, the one guy who could finger him, but it was really Shane in the bed."

The body blows kept coming. That was not the man she knew. Watching who he was unwind in front of her made her wonder if she knew anything about men.

She glanced up at the only other man who had meant so much to her. She lay there waiting for Cam to deliver the news that he was off to a new assignment or going to live under a new name. There was an automatic finality that came with being with him.

"You can just tell me." She braced for the pain that would come when he uttered the words. "You don't have to be careful with your words or worry about my feelings."

Instead, he frowned at her. "What?"

"That you're leaving. How you hate commitment."

"When did I say that?"

"You've said it before and I want you to know I'm ready for the speech." But she wasn't. She totally wasn't.

"Do you want me to go?" He laid her hand against the bed but kept his over it.

"No." She practically screamed the answer. A nurse walking by in the hallway did a double take.

He shot her that sexy dimpled smile. "Then why are you trying to get me to say something I don't want to say?"

Her brain kept misfiring. She had no idea what they were talking about or how they'd gotten here from where they were the last time they'd discussed this subject. "But you—"

"Julia, I wasn't kidding when I told you I felt something I'd never felt before. I haven't had wild love affairs or had the benefit of growing up in a big family and watching my siblings pair off." He switched seats so that he sat on the edge of her bed. "I want you."

"A date." It felt risky to even put that out there knowing how he felt about the subject.

"I'm hoping for a lot of dates." His eyes gleamed. "See, I'm falling for you and it seems to me when that happens, two people should spend a lot of time together."

She couldn't figure out how to open her mouth to speak.

"Let's try this." He lowered his head and took her mouth with his. The dragging kiss had her remembering every touch and wanting so many more.

When he lifted his head again, her body sparked to life. This time she grabbed his hand and pressed it right between her breasts. "That falling thing?"

"Yeah?"

Oh, that smile. "You're not falling alone."

Falling, fell. They could use whatever words he wanted. She just knew she thought about him all the time, even when he was right beside her. Something about him—the charm or maybe the bossiness—had gotten under her skin from the beginning.

He turned his hand to trace a line along her collarbone. "In the interests of disclosure, my world is about danger and secrets and—"

"I've known that from day one. Literally." He'd busted into the house and nothing had ever been the same.

"True." His expression grew serious. "I want to give us a chance. A real chance."

She was in for that. She could give him as long as he needed. She'd waited. "So long as we give it a nice long chance."

He nuzzled her nose with his. "Months and months."

She grabbed his face and held it in front of her. "No more informal dating."

He gave her a quick kiss on the cheek. "Not with you."

"I knew I liked you from the beginning." She wrapped her arms around his neck and brought him in closer.

His laugh had someone outside the door hesitating for a second. The person stood there and then moved on.

"Now be honest," he said with a smile. "You didn't like me all that much for a long while."

That was probably fair. The beginning part, anyway. The fear had come first and quickly dissipated. The driving need and blinding attraction had seemed to settle in and refuse to go, even after they'd slept together. "But the second I got to know you, I was hooked."

He leaned down, almost climbed into bed with her. "And I plan to keep you that way."

She rubbed her hand up his arm. "I like your style, Cameron Roth."

"And I like everything about you, Julia White."

"Then let's get me out of here and to that hotel you promised."

He winked at her. "Done."

Chapter Twenty-One

Holt and Shane sat down in the bar nearest to the clinic. Watching Cam fall deserved a beer. Maybe a bottle of gin. The good thing about this island was they had plenty of those. Seemed something about the cool, wet air got people drinking.

Law enforcement had swooped in and started investigating everything. It looked as though Sandy was in big trouble going forward. Ray hadn't rolled, but Shane and Holt had a bet he would.

Neither Ray nor Sandy was the type to thrive in prison. They both had skills, but their egos were problematic. The prosecutor was already offering a deal for testimony. Ray would be dumb not to take it.

Shane lifted his beer in salute. "We lost another one."

"And Cam." Holt felt he should say a prayer or something. "He was pretty clear that he was out when it came to the long-term-girlfriend thing."

"That vow lasted all of four seconds after he met Julia."

"She is hot." Holt had to be fair about that. She was off-the-charts pretty and probably way out of Cam's league, or at least that was what Holt planned to tell him all the time.

"And she didn't spook when guys died in front of her. She held on." Shane nodded. "Yeah, you're right. She is hot."

"It's like a disease in the office." Holt touched his chest because the idea of hooking up and getting married gave him pain. "Any chance there's a vaccine?"

"I'd ask, but then I'd accidentally insult one of them."

Made sense, since the *entire* office was now taken except for him and Shane. Connor and his wife had been estranged, but the rest of them had found women and in record time went from confirmed bachelors making fun of the married agents to one of them. The traveling team had vowed to stay out of the fray, but now that deal was busted, as well.

Shane lifted his half-empty glass. "I'm going to need another one."

"What if Ms. Right is here tonight?" Holt looked around, scanned one table after the other. But he never saw what the others did. He got pretty. He liked smart and resourceful.

"If the right woman comes in, I'll know because she'll buy me a beer." Shane stared at the door. When it remained closed and he didn't have a new beer in front of him, he shrugged.

That was the Shane Holt loved and admired. "Romantic."

"We need a new pact," Shane said. "Except…"

Holt knew this was going to be bad. "What?"

"I bet you're next."

"Double or nothing." Holt was willing to hand over his house to win that one.

"We'll see." Shane downed the last of the glass. "We'll see."

* * * * *

**"How did you know my name?"
she demanded.**

He stood, forcing himself to relax, or at least to look as if he didn't have all these turbulent emotions fighting it out in his gut. "Hello, Abby," he said softly. "I'm Michael Dance."

"I don't know a Michael Dance," she said.

"No, you probably don't remember me. It's been a while. Five years."

She searched his face, panic behind her eyes. He wanted to reach out, to reassure her. But he remained frozen, immobile. "You knew me in Afghanistan?" she asked. "I don't remember."

"There's no reason you should," he said. "The last time I saw you, you were pretty out of it. Technically, you were dead—for a while, at least."

He'd been the one to bring her back to life, massaging her heart and breathing into her ravaged mouth until her heart beat again and she sucked in oxygen on her own. He'd saved her life, and in that moment forged a connection he'd never been quite able to sever.

THE GUARDIAN

BY
CINDI MYERS

Published in Great Britain 2015
by Mills & Boon, an imprint of Harlequin (UK) Limited,
Eton House, 18-24 Paradise Road, Richmond, Surrey, TW9 1SR

© 2015 Cynthia Myers

ISBN: 978-0-263-25309-2

46-0615

Harlequin (UK) Limited's policy is to use papers that are natural, renewable and recyclable products and made from wood grown in sustainable forests. The logging and manufacturing processes conform to the legal environmental regulations of the country of origin.

Printed and bound in Spain
by CPI, Barcelona

Cindi Myers is an author of more than fifty novels. When she's not crafting new romance plots, she enjoys skiing, gardening, cooking, crafting and daydreaming. A lover of small-town life, she lives with her husband and two spoiled dogs in the Colorado mountains.

For Katie

Chapter One

Abby Stewart was not lost. Maybe she'd wandered a little off her planned route, but she wasn't lost.

She was a scientist and a decorated war veteran. She had GPS and maps and a good sense of direction. So she couldn't be lost. But standing in the middle of nowhere in the Colorado wilderness did have her a little disoriented, she could admit. The problem was, the terrain around Black Canyon of the Gunnison National Park tended to all look the same after a while: thousands of acres of rugged, roadless wilderness covered in piñon forests, and scrubby desert set against a backdrop of spectacular mountain views. People did get lost out here every year.

But Abby wasn't one of them, she reminded herself again. She took a deep breath and consulted her handheld GPS. There was the shallow draw she'd just passed, and to the west were the foothills of the Cimarron Mountains. And there was her location now. The display showed she'd hiked three miles from her car. All she had to do was head northeast and she'd eventually make it back to her parking spot and the red dirt two-track she'd driven in on. Feeling more reassured, she returned the GPS unit to her backpack and scanned the landscape around her. To a casual observer, the place probably looked pretty desolate—a high plateau of scrubby grass, cactus and stunted juniper. But to Abby, who was on her way to earning a master's degree in environmental science, the Black Canyon of the Gunnison was a treasure trove of more than eight hundred plant species, including the handful she was focusing on in her research.

Her anxiety over temporarily losing her bearings vanished as she focused on a gray-green clump of vegetation in the shadow of a misshapen piñon. She bent over, peering closer, and a surge of triumph filled her. *Yes!* A terrific specimen of *Lomatium concinnum*— desert parsley to the layman. Number four on the list of species she needed to collect for her research. She knelt and slipped off her pack and quickly took out a digital camera, small trowel and collecting bag.

Intent on photographing the parsley in place, then carefully digging it up, leaving as much of the root system intact as possible, she missed the sounds of approaching footsteps until they were almost on her. A branch crackled and she started, heart pounding. She peered into the dense underbrush in front of her, in the direction of the sound, and heard a shuffling noise— the muffled swish of fabric rubbing against the brush. Whoever this was wasn't trying to be particularly quiet, but what were they doing out here, literally in the middle of nowhere?

In the week Abby had been camped in the area she'd seen fewer than a dozen other people since checking in at the park ranger station, and all of those had been in the campground or along the paved road. Here in the backcountry she'd imagined herself completely alone.

Stealthily, she slid the Sig Sauer from the holster at her side. She'd told the few friends who'd asked about the gun that she carried it to deal with snakes and other wildlife she might encounter in the backcountry, but the truth was, ever since her stint in Afghanistan, she felt safer armed when she went out alone. Flashes of unsettling memories crowded her mind as she drew the weapon; suddenly, she was back in Kandahar, stalking insurgents who'd just wiped out half her patrol group. As a woman, she'd often been tasked with going into the homes of locals to question the women there with the aid of an interpreter. Every time she stepped into one of those homes, she wondered if she'd come out alive. This scene had the same sense of being cut off from the rest of the world, the same sense of paranoia and danger.

Heart racing, she struggled to control her breathing and to push the memories away. She wasn't in Afghanistan. She was in Colorado. In a national park. She was safe. This was probably just another hiker, someone else who appreciated the solitude and peace of the wilderness. She inched forward and pushed aside the feathery, aromatic branches of a piñon.

A small, dark woman bent over the ground, deftly pulling up plants and stuffing them into the pockets of her full skirt. Dandelions, Abby noted. A popular edible wild green. She replaced the gun in its holster and stood. "Hello," she said.

The woman jumped and dropped a handful of dandelions. She turned, as if to run. "Wait!" Abby called. "I'm sorry. I didn't mean to frighten you." She retrieved the plants and held them out to the woman. She was young, barely out of her teens, and very beautiful. Her skin was the rich brown of toffee, and she had high cheekbones, a rosebud mouth and large black eyes framed by lacy lashes. She wore a loose blue blouse, a long, full skirt and leather sandals, with a plaid shawl draped across her body.

She came forward and hesitantly accepted the dandelions from Abby. *"Gracias,"* she said, her voice just above a whisper.

Latina, Abby thought. A large community of Mexican immigrants lived in the area. She searched her mind for what schoolgirl Spanish she could recall. *"Habla inglés?"*

The woman shook her head and wrapped her arms around what Abby had first assumed to be a bag for storing the plants she collected, but she now realized was a swaddled infant, cradled close to the woman's torso with a sling made from the red, blue and green shawl. "You have a baby!" Abby smiled. "A *niño*," she added.

The woman held the baby closer and stared at Abby, eyes wide with fear.

Maybe she was an illegal, afraid Abby would report her to the authorities. "Don't worry," Abby said, unable to remember the Spanish words. "I'm looking for plants, like you." She broke a stem from the desert parsley and held it out. *"Donde esta este?"* she asked. *Where is this?*

The woman eyed Abby warily, but stepped forward to study the plant. She nodded. *"Si. Yo conozco."*

"You know this plant? Can you show me where to find more? *Donde esta?*"

The woman looked around, then motioned Abby to follow her. Abby did so, excitement growing. So far, specimens of *Lomatium* had been rare. Having more plants to study would be a tremendous find.

The woman moved rapidly over the rough ground despite her long skirts and the burden of the baby. Her black hair swung behind her in a ponytail that reached almost to her waist. Where did she live? The closest homes were miles from here, and the only road into this section of the park was the one Abby had come in on. Was she collecting the dandelions because she had an interest in wild food—or because it was the only thing she had to eat?

The woman stopped abruptly beside a large rock and looked down at the ground. Desert parsley spread out for several feet in every direction—the most specimens Abby had ever seen. Her smile widened. "That's wonderful. Thank you so much. *Muchas gracias.*" She clasped the woman's hand and shook it. The woman offered a shy smile.

"*Mi nombre es* Abby."

"*Soy* Mariposa," the woman said.

Mariposa. Butterfly. Her name was butterfly? "*Y su niño?*" Abby nodded to the baby.

Mariposa smiled and folded back the blanket to reveal a tiny dark-haired infant. "*Es una niña,*" she said. "Angelique."

"Angelique," Abby repeated. A little angel.

"*Usted ha cido harido.*" Mariposa lightly touched the side of Abby's face.

Abby flinched. Not because the touch was painful, but because she didn't like being reminded of the scar there. Multiple surgeries and time had faded the wound made by shrapnel from a roadside bomb, but the puckered white gash that ran from just above her left ear to midcheekbone would never be entirely gone. She wore her hair long and brushed forward to hide the worst of the scar, but alone in the wilderness on this warm day she'd clipped her hair back to keep it out of the way while she worked. She had no idea what the Spanish words Mariposa had spoken meant, but she was sure they were in reference to this disfigurement. *"Es no importante,"* she said, shaking her head.

She turned away, the profile of her good side to the woman, and spotted a delicate white flower. The three round petals blushed a deep purplish pink near their center. Half a dozen similar blooms rose nearby on slender, leafless stems. Abby knelt and slipped off her backpack and took out her trowel. She deftly dug up one of the flowers, revealing a fat white bulb. She brushed the dirt from the bulb and handed the plant to the woman. *"Este es comer. Bueno."* Her paltry Spanish frustrated her. "It's good to eat," she said, as if the English would make any more sense to her new friend.

Mariposa stroked the velvety petal of the flower and nodded. "It's called a mariposa lily," Abby said. *"Su nombre es Mariposa tambien."*

Mariposa nodded, then knelt and began digging up a second lily. Maybe she was just humoring Abby—or maybe she really needed the food. Abby hoped it was the former. As much as her studies had taught her about wild plants, she'd hate to have to depend on them for survival.

She turned to her pack once more and took out another collection bag, then remembered the energy bars stashed on the opposite side of the pack. They weren't much, but she'd give them to Mariposa. They'd at least be a change from roots. She found three bars and pressed them into the woman's hands. *"Por usted,"* she said.

"Gracias." Mariposa slipped the bars into the pocket of her skirt, then watched as Abby took out the camera and photographed the parsley plants. On impulse, she turned and aimed the camera at Mariposa. *Click.* And there she was, captured on the screen of the camera, face solemn but still very beautiful.

"You don't mind, do you?" Abby asked. She turned the camera so that the woman could see the picture.

Mariposa squinted at the image, but said nothing.

For a few minutes, the two women worked side by side, Mariposa digging lilies and Abby collecting more specimens of parsley. Though Abby usually preferred to work alone, it was nice being with Mariposa. She only wished she spoke better Spanish or Mariposa knew English, so she could find out more about where her new friend was from and why she was here in such a remote location.

Though the army had trained Abby to always be attuned to changes in the landscape around her, she must have gotten rusty since her return to civilian life. Mariposa was the first to stiffen and look toward the brush to the right of the women.

Abby heard the movements a second later—a group of people moving through the brush toward them, their voices carrying in the still air, though they were still some distance away.

She was about to ask Mariposa if she knew these newcomers when the young woman took off running. Her sudden departure startled Abby so much she didn't immediately react. She stared after the young woman, trying to make sense of what she was seeing.

Mariposa ran with her skirt held up, legs lifted high, in the opposite direction of the approaching strangers, stumbling over the uneven terrain as if her life depended on it. Abby debated running after her, but what would that do but frighten the woman more? She watched the fleeing figure until she'd disappeared over a slight rise, then glanced back toward the voices. They were getting louder, moving closer at a rapid pace.

Abby slipped on the pack and unholstered the weapon once more, then settled into the shade of a boulder to wait.

The group moved steadily toward her. All men, from the sound of them. The uneven terrain and stubby trees blocked them from view, but their voices carried easily in the stillness. They weren't attempting stealth; instead, they shouted and crashed through the underbrush with a great crackling of breaking twigs and branches. As they neared she thought she heard both English and Spanish. They seemed to be searching for someone, shouting, "Come out!" and, "Where is he?"

Or were they saying, "Where is *she*?" Were they looking for Mariposa? Why?

The first gunshots sent a jolt of adrenaline to her heart. She gripped the pistol more tightly and hunkered down closer to the boulder. For a moment she was back in Afghanistan, pinned down by enemy fire, unable to fight back. She closed her eyes and clenched her teeth, fighting for calm. She wasn't over there anymore. She was in the United States. No one was shooting at her. She was safe.

A second rapid burst of gunfire shattered the air, and Abby bit down on her lip so hard she tasted blood. Then everything went still. The echo of the concussion reverberated in the air, ringing in her ears. She couldn't hear the men anymore, though whether because they were silent or because she was momentarily deaf, she didn't know. She opened her eyes and reached into the pocket of her jeans to grip the small ceramic figure of a rabbit she kept there. She'd awoken in the field hospital with it clutched in her hand; she had no idea who had put the rabbit there, but ever since, she'd kept it as a kind of good-luck charm. The familiar feel of its smooth sides and little pointed ears calmed her. She was safe. She was all right.

The voices drifted to her once more, less agitated now, and receding. They gradually faded altogether, until everything around her was silent once more.

She waited a full ten minutes behind the boulder, clutching the pistol in both hands, every muscle tensed and poised to defend herself. After the clock on her phone told her the time she'd allotted had passed, she stood and scanned the wilderness around her. Nothing. No men, no Mariposa, no dust clouds marking the trail of a vehicle. The landscape was as still as a painting, not even a breeze stirring the leaves of the stunted trees.

Still shaky from the adrenaline rush, she holstered the pistol and settled the backpack more firmly on her shoulder. She could return to her car, but would that increase her chances of running into the men? Maybe it would be better to remain here for a while longer. She'd go about her business and give the men time to move farther away.

She returned to the parsley plants. Digging up the specimen calmed her further. She cradled the uprooted plant in her fingers and slid it into the plastic collection bag, then labeled the bag with the date, time and GPS coordinates where she'd found it, and stowed it in her pack. Then she stood and stretched. Her muscles ached from tension. Time to head back to camp. She'd clean up, then stop by the ranger station and report the men and the shooting—but not Mariposa. She had no desire to betray the woman's secrets, whatever they were.

She checked her GPS to orient herself, then turned southwest, in the direction of her car and the road. She had no trail to follow, only paths made by animals and the red line on the GPS unit that marked her route into this area. On patrol in Kandahar she'd used similar GPS units, but just as often she'd relied on the memory of landmarks or even the positioning of stars. Nothing over there had ever felt familiar to her, but she'd learned to accept the unfamiliarity, until the day that roadside bomb had almost taken everything away.

She picked her way carefully through the rough landscape, around clumps of prickly pear cactus and desert willows, past sagebrush and Mormon tea and dozens of other plants she identified out of long habit. She kept her eyes focused down, hoping to spot one of the other coveted species on her list. All the plants were considered rare in the area, and all held promise of medical uses. The research she was doing now might one day lead to cultivation of these species to treat cancer or Parkinson's or some other crippling disease.

So focused was she on cataloging the plants around her that she didn't see the fallen branch until she'd stumbled over it. Cursing her own clumsiness, she straightened and looked back at the offending obstacle. It stuck out from beneath a clump of rabbitbrush, dark brown and as big around as a man's arm. What kind of a tree would that be, the bark such a dark color—and out here in an area where large trees were rare?

She bent to look closer and cold horror swept over

her. She hadn't fallen over a branch at all. The thing that had tripped her was a man. He lay sprawled on the ground, arms outstretched, lifeless eyes staring up at her, long past seeing anything.

Chapter Two

Lieutenant Michael Dance had a low tolerance for meetings. As much as they were necessary to do his job, he endured them. But he'd wasted too many hours sitting in conference rooms, listening to other people drone on about things he didn't consider important. He preferred to be out in the field, doing real work that counted.

The person who'd called this meeting, however, was his boss, Captain Graham Ellison, aka "G-Man." Though Graham was with the FBI and Dance worked for Customs and Border Protection, Graham headed up the interagency task force charged with maintaining law and order on this vast swath of public land in southwest Colorado. And in their short acquaintance, Graham struck Michael as being someone worth listening to.

"National park rangers found an abandoned vehicle at the Dragon Point overlook yesterday," Graham said. A burly guy with the thick neck and wide shoulders of a linebacker and the short-cropped hair and erect stance of ex-military, Graham spoke softly, like many big men. His very presence commanded attention, so he didn't need to raise his voice. "The Montrose County sheriff's office has identified it as belonging to a Lauren Starling of Denver. Ms. Starling failed to show for work this morning, so they've asked us to keep an eye out. Here's a picture."

He passed around a glossy eight-by-ten photograph. Michael studied the studio head shot of a thirtysomething blonde with shoulder-length curls, violet-blue eyes and a dazzling white smile. She looked directly at the camera, beautiful and confident. "Do they think she was out here alone?" he asked, as he passed the photo on to the man next to him, Randall Knightbridge, with the Bureau of Land Management.

"They don't know," Graham said. "Right now they're just asking us to keep an eye out for her."

"Hey, I know this chick," Randall said.

Everyone turned to stare. The BLM ranger was the youngest member of the task force, in his late twenties and an acknowledged geek. He could rattle off the plots of half a dozen paranormal series on television, played lacrosse in his spare time and wore long-sleeved uniform shirts year-round to hide the colorful tattoos that decorated both arms. He didn't have a rep as a ladies' man, so what was he doing knowing a glamour girl like the one in the picture?

"I mean, I don't know her personally," he corrected, as if reading Michael's thoughts. "But I've seen her on TV. She does the news on channel nine in Denver."

"You're right." Simon Woolridge, with Immigration and Customs Enforcement, grabbed the picture and gave it a second look. "I knew she looked familiar."

"Like one of your ex-wives," quipped Lance Carpenter, a Montrose County sheriff's deputy.

"Lauren Starling is the evening news anchor for channel nine," Graham confirmed. "Her high profile is one reason this case is getting special attention from everyone involved."

"When did she go missing?" Marco Cruz, an agent with the DEA, asked.

"The Denver police aren't treating it as a missing person case yet," Graham said. "The car was simply parked at the overlook. There were no signs of a struggle. She took a week's vacation and didn't tell anyone where she was going. Nothing significant is missing from her apartment. That's all the information I have at the moment."

"Are they thinking suicide?" asked Carmen Redhorse, the only female member of the task force. Petite and dark haired, Carmen worked with the Colorado Bureau of Investigation.

No one looked surprised at her suggestion of suicide. Unfortunately, the deep canyon and steep drop-offs of Black Canyon of the Gunnison National Park were popular places for the despondent to end it all. Four or five people committed suicide in the park each year.

"There's no note," Graham said. "The Denver police are on the case right now. They've simply asked us to keep an eye on things. If you see anything suspicious, we'll pass it on to the local authorities." He consulted the clipboard in his hand. "On to more pressing matters. State police impounded a truck carrying a hundred pounds of fresh marijuana bud at a truck stop in Gunnison last night. The pot was concealed inside a load of coffee, but the drug dogs picked up the scent, no problem."

"When will these rubes learn they can't fool a dog's nose?" Randall leaned down to pet his Belgian Malinois, Lotte, who'd stretched out beneath his chair. She thumped the floor twice with her plume of a tail, but didn't raise her head.

"The logbook indicates the truck passed through this area," Graham continued. "That's the second shipment that's been waylaid in as many months, and another indication that there's an active growing operation in the area. We know from experience that public lands are prime targets for illegal growers."

"Free land, away from people, limited law enforcement presence." Carmen ticked off the reasons wilderness areas presented such a temptation to drug runners. "I read the first national parks had problems with bootleggers. Now it's pot and meth."

Graham turned to the large map of the area that covered most of one wall of the trailer that served as task force headquarters. "We're going to be flying more surveillance this week, trying to locate the growing fields. We'll be concentrating on the Gunnison Gorge just west of the park boundaries. The counters we laid last week show increased vehicle traffic on the roads in that area."

In addition to the more than thirty thousand acres within the national park, the task force was charged with controlling crime within the almost sixty-three thousand acres of the Gunnison Gorge National Conservation Area and the forty-three thousand acres of the Curecanti National Recreation Area. It was a ridiculous amount of land for a few people to patrol, much of it almost inaccessible, roadless wilderness. In recent years, drug cartels had taken advantage of short-staffed park service to cultivate thousands of acres of public land. They dug irrigation canals, built fences and destroyed priceless artifacts with impunity. This task force was an attempt to stop them.

A pretty feeble attempt, Michael thought. He thumbed a butterscotch Life Saver from the roll he kept in his pocket and popped it into his mouth. They were wasting time sitting around talking about the problem, instead of being out there doing something about it.

"If we want to find the crops, look for the people who take care of the crops," Simon said.

"You mean the people who plant the weed?" Randall asked.

"The people who plant it and water it and weed it and guard it from predators—both animal and human," Simon said. "Illegals, most likely, shipped in for that purpose. We find them and put pressure on them, we can find the person behind this. The money man."

Here was something Michael knew about. "Human trafficking in Colorado is up twenty percent this year," he said. "Some sources suggest a lot of victims who end up in Denver come from this area. We could be looking at a pipeline for more than drugs."

"So the guys in charge of drugs offer a free pass into the country to people who will work for them?" Lance asked.

"More likely they work with coyotes who charge people to bring them into the country, but instead of going to their cousin in Fort Collins or their aunt in Laramie, they end up prisoners of this drug cartel," Michael said. "And once they've worked the fields for a while or learned to cook up meth or whatever the drug lords need them to do, they take the women and the younger men to Denver and turn them out as prostitutes. It's slavery on a scale people have no idea even exists anymore."

"So in addition to drugs, we may be dealing with human trafficking," Carmen said.

"We don't know that." Simon's voice was dismissive. "It's only speculation. We do know that if these people have workers, they're probably illegals. Deport the workforce and you can cripple an operation. At least temporarily."

"Only until they bring in the next load of workers." Michael glared at the man across the conference table. "Rounding up people and deporting them solves nothing. And you miss the chance to break up the trafficking pipeline."

"End the drug operation and you remove the reason they have to bring in people," Simon countered.

"Right. And now they take them straight to Denver, where no one even notices what's going on."

"Back to the discussion at hand." Graham cut them off. He gave each of them a stern look. "As a task force, our job is to address all serious crime in this region, whether it's human trafficking or drugs or money laundering or murder. But I don't have to tell you that in this time of budget cuts, we have to be able to show the politicians are getting their money's worth. A high-profile case could do a lot to assure we all get to keep working."

And drugs were worth more to federal coffers than people, Michael thought grimly. The law allowed the Feds to seize any and all property involved in drug crimes, from cash and cars to mansions.

"Tomorrow we'll begin five days of aerial patrols, focused on these sectors." Graham indicated half a dozen spots on the map. "These are fairly level spots with access to water, remote, but possible to reach in four-wheel-drive vehicles."

"What about the private property in the area?" Michael asked. Several white spots on the map, some completely surrounded by federal land, indicated acreage owned by private individuals.

"Private property could provide an access point for the drug runners, so we'll be looking at that. Most of the private land is unoccupied," Graham said.

"Except for Prentice's fortress," Simon said.

Michael didn't ask the obvious question. If he waited, someone would explain this mystery to the new guy; if not, he'd find out what he needed to know on his own.

"Richard Prentice owns the land here." Graham pointed to a white square closest to the park—almost on the canyon rim. "He's built a compound there with several houses, stables, a gated entrance, et cetera."

"But before that, he tried to blackmail the government into buying the place at an exorbitant price," Carmen said. "He threatened to build this giant triple-X theater with huge neon signs practically at the park entrance." Her lip curled in disgust.

"He's had success with those kinds of tactics before," Graham said. "He threatened to blow up a historic building over near Ouray until a conservation group raised the money to buy the place from him."

"At an inflated price," Carmen said. "That's how he operates. If he can figure out a way to exploit a situation for money, he will."

"But the government didn't bite this time?" Michael asked.

"No," Lance said. "And the county fought back by passing an ordinance prohibiting sexually oriented businesses. He built a mansion instead, and spends his time filing harassment complaints every time we drive by or fly over."

"So do we think he has anything to do with the crime wave around here?" Michael asked. Greed and a lust for power were motivation enough for all manner of misdeeds.

Graham shook his head. "Prentice likes to thumb his nose at the government, but we have no reason to suspect he's guilty of any felonies."

"Which doesn't mean he isn't guilty," Carmen said. "Just that we can't prove it—yet."

Michael studied the map again. First chance he got, he'd check out this Prentice guy.

"Next on the list." Graham scanned the clipboard again, but before he could continue, a knock sounded on the door.

"Come in," Graham called.

The door opened and a woman stood on the threshold, eyes wide with surprise. A fall of long honey-blond hair obscured most of her face, but she appeared young, and pretty, with dark eyes and a well-shaped nose and chin. She wore canvas cargo pants, hiking boots and a long-sleeved canvas shirt, open at the throat to reveal a black tank top trimmed in lace, and a hint of tanned cleavage. Michael's gaze locked on the holstered weapon at her side—a .40-caliber Sig Sauer. He had one like it at his hip. So was she some kind of law enforcement? A new member of the team no one had mentioned?

"I, uh, I didn't mean to interrupt," she said. "I was looking for the park rangers. Their office was closed, and I saw the cars over here…"

"The park rangers go home at four," Graham said.

"They'll be in at nine in the morning if you need help with camping permits or something."

Her eyes narrowed, focused on the tan uniforms, then on the name badge pinned to Graham's shirt pocket. "Captain Ellison. Are you a law enforcement officer?"

"Yes. Can I help you?"

She pressed her lips together, as if debating her next move, then nodded. "I need to report a crime. A murder."

The temperature in the room dropped several degrees, Michael was sure, and the group around the table leaned forward, all eyes—including the dog's—focused on the petite woman in the doorway.

"Why don't you come in and give us a few more details." Graham motioned the woman forward.

As she moved past him, Michael caught the scents of wood smoke and sweat and something lighter and more feminine—a floral perfume or shampoo. An awareness stirred in his gut, a sense of familiarity, and the hair rose on the back of his neck. Where had he seen this woman before?

"I'm a biologist," she said, speaking primarily to Graham, but casting nervous glances at the rest of them. "Or rather, I'm working on my master's degree in biology. I'm studying several plant species found in the park for my thesis. I was out collecting specimens this morning when I heard people approaching. They were shouting in English and in Spanish, and they appeared to be searching for someone."

"Did you get close to them?" Simon asked. "Did you talk to them?"

She shook her head. As she did so, her hair swung

away from her face, revealing a jagged scar diagonally bisecting one cheek. The scar was bizarrely out of place on such a beautiful face, like a crack in an otherwise pristine china plate. Michael's gut tightened, and he struggled to control his breathing. He was sure he knew her now, but maybe his mind was playing tricks on him. Post-traumatic stress throwing up some new, bizarre symptom.

"They were some distance away—maybe two hundred yards," she continued. "I hid behind a large boulder and waited for them to leave."

"Why did you do that?" Simon asked.

"Because she's smart," Carmen said. "A woman alone in the middle of nowhere sees a group of rowdy men? Of course she hides."

Simon flushed, like a kid who's been reprimanded. "She looks as though she can take care of herself." He nodded to the weapon at her side. "You got a permit for that thing?"

"Yes." She turned away from him. "I couldn't see what they were doing—the terrain is rough out there. But I heard gunshots. Then they quieted down and left."

"You're sure they were gunshots?" Graham asked.

She nodded. "I was in the army, stationed in Kandahar. I know what gunfire sounds like. This was a semi-automatic. A rifle, not a handgun."

Michael gripped the underside of the conference table until his fingers ached. This was no trick of a war-stressed mind. This was *her*—the woman who'd lingered in the back of his mind for the better part of five years. The one he could never forget.

"All right." Graham leaned against the table, his pose deceptively casual. "What happened next?"

"I waited ten minutes to make sure they were gone, then I resumed collecting the specimens I'd come for. I headed back toward the road where I'd parked my car. I had walked less than half a mile when I stumbled over something." Her face paled and she swallowed hard, her lips pressed tightly together, holding in emotion. "It was a body," she said softly. Then, in a stronger voice, "A young man. Latino. He'd been shot in the chest."

"He was dead?" Randall asked.

"Oh, yes. But not for long. The body was still warm."

"So you think the men you heard shot him." Simon couldn't keep quiet long. Clearly, he liked playing the role of interrogator.

"It's your job to decide that, not mine," the woman said, a sharp edge to her voice. Good for her, Michael thought. Put Simon in his place.

"Can you show us where the body is?" Graham asked.

She nodded. "I think so. I was collecting specimens near there and I made note of the GPS coordinates. I should have noted the coordinates for the body, too, but seeing it out there was such a shock..." She looked down at the floor, hair falling forward to obscure her face once more. But Michael didn't need the visual confirmation anymore. This was *her*. And to think he'd thought he'd never see her again.

What were the odds that he'd run into her now—in this place half a world away from where they'd last met? Then again, his mother always said everything happened for a reason. Michael told himself he didn't believe in that kind of divine interference—in fate. But maybe some of his mother's superstition had rubbed off on him.

"We'll want a full statement from you later." Graham pulled out a pen and turned to a fresh sheet on his clipboard. "Right now, if you'll just give me your name and tell me where you're camped."

"Abigail Stewart."

Only when the others turned toward him did Michael realize he'd spoken out loud. Abby stared at him, too, her mouth half-open, a red stain coloring her previously pale cheeks. "How did you know my name?" she demanded.

He stood, forcing himself to relax, or at least to look as if he didn't have all these turbulent emotions fighting it out in his gut. "Hello, Abby," he said softly. "I'm Michael Dance."

"I don't know a Michael Dance," she said.

"No, you probably don't remember me. It's been a while. Five years."

She searched his face, panic behind her eyes. He wanted to reach out, to reassure her. But he remained frozen, immobile.

"You knew me in Afghanistan?" she asked. "I don't remember."

"There's no reason you should," he said. "The last time I saw you, you were pretty out of it. Technically, you were dead—for a while, at least."

He'd been the one to bring her back to life, massaging her heart and breathing in her ravaged mouth until her heart beat again and she'd sucked in oxygen on her own. He'd saved her life, and in that moment forged a connection he'd never been quite able to sever.

Chapter Three

Having a total stranger announce to a bunch of other strangers that you'd come back from the dead didn't rank high on Abby's list of experiences she wanted to repeat—or to ever have in the first place. From the moment she'd entered the trailer parked alongside the park ranger's office, she'd felt the tall, dark-haired officer's gaze fixed on her. She couldn't decide if he was rude or just overly intense; she hadn't spent a lot of time around law-enforcement types, so what did she know?

And what did she care? Except that the agent—Michael Dance—had made her care. He knew things about her she didn't. He knew what had happened in the hours and days she'd lost to unconsciousness and trauma. That he'd seen her ripped open and clinging to life by a thread felt so personal and intimate. She both resented him and wanted to know more.

As for Michael Dance, he seemed content to keep staring at her, and when she'd agreed to take the officers to the body she'd found, he'd slipped up beside her and insisted she ride with him.

"You could ride with me and Graham if you'd rather," Carmen, the only other woman in the room, offered, perhaps sensing Abby's unease.

"No, that's all right. I can ride with Lieutenant Dance." Alone in a vehicle, maybe she could ask him some of the questions that troubled her.

But now, as they cruised along the paved South Rim Road through the park, she felt tongue-tied and awkward.

He took a roll of Life Savers from the pocket of his uniform shirt and held it out to her. "Want one?"

"Okay." She took one of the butterscotch candies, then he did the same and returned the roll to his pocket.

"I'm addicted," he said. "I quit smoking last year and took up the candy as a substitute."

"Good for you for quitting," she said. "I knew a lot of soldiers who smoked, but I never took it up."

"Smart woman." He settled back in the driver's seat, gaze fixed on the curving ribbon of blacktop that skirted the park's main attraction—the deep, narrow Black Canyon.

Abby tried to relax, too, but curiosity needled her, overcoming her natural shyness. "How do you possibly remember me after all this time?" she blurted. "It's been years, and you must have only seen me for a few hours, at most." Had he been an orderly in the field hospital, a medic or a pilot, or simply a grunt tasked with transporting the wounded?

"I was a PJ. We saw hundreds of casualties during my tour—but you were the only woman. And you were my first save. It made an impression."

PJs—pararescuers—were bona fide superheroes. Members of the US Air Force's rescue squadron swooped into the thick of danger in Pave Hawk helicopters, often under heavy enemy fire, to snatch wounded soldiers from almost certain death. They performed critical lifesaving procedures in the air, long before their patients reached the doctors at field hospitals. Abby remembered none of this, but she'd seen a special on TV and watched with sick fascination, trying to imagine what it was like when she was the patient, being patched together by young men she'd likely never see again.

"I...I don't know what to say." She plucked at the seat belt harness, feeling trapped as much by her own emotions as by the confining cloth strap. "Thank you doesn't seem like enough."

"I was glad you made it. We lost too many soldiers over there, but losing a woman would have been worse. I know it shouldn't be that way, but it was—I won't lie."

She nodded. Though women weren't authorized for combat roles back then, the army needed female soldiers to interrogate native women and to fill a variety of noncombat roles, from resupply to repairing equipment that constantly broke down. Women soldiers stood guard and went on patrol, and sometimes got caught up in battles, in a war with no clearly defined front line, where every peasant could be friend or foe. But for all the roles they filled, women made up only about 10 percent of the ground forces in Afghanistan. As a female soldier, Abby hadn't wanted to stand out from her fellow grunts, but she couldn't help it.

"I still can't believe you remembered my name," she said.

He winced. "I made it a point to remember it. Later, I tried to look you up—just to see how you were doing. I'm not a stalker or anything. I just wanted to know."

"But you didn't find me?"

"I found out you'd gotten transferred stateside, but that was about it." He adjusted his grip on the steering wheel of the FJ Cruiser he drove. A second Cruiser followed a few car lengths behind, with Graham and Carmen; for all Abby knew half a dozen other vehicles full of more law-enforcement agents came after that. "But now I know. You look good. I'm glad."

She resisted the urge to touch the scar. "Thanks for not qualifying the compliment."

He frowned. "I don't get it."

"Thanks for not saying, 'You look good, considering what you've been through.'"

"People really tell you that?"

"Sometimes. I also get 'That scar is hardly noticeable,' which I know is a lie, since if it was so unnoticeable, why are they bothering to point it out?" Had she really just said that? To this guy she didn't even know? She didn't talk about this stuff with anybody. Not even the therapist the Army had sent her to. Waste of money, that.

"So you're studying botany?" Maybe sensing her uneasiness, he smoothly changed the subject.

"Environmental science. And to answer your next question, which I know from experience is, 'What do you do with a master's degree in environmental science?' I'll probably end up teaching ungrateful undergrads somewhere. But all that is just to support the research I want to do into developing medicines from plants."

"You mean, like herbal remedies and stuff?"

"I mean, like cancer drugs and medicine to cure Parkinson's or diabetes. Plants are a tremendous resource we've scarcely begun to explore."

"So there are plants in this park that can cure diseases?" He motioned to the scrubby landscape around them.

"This might look like desert to you, but there are

hundreds of plants within the park and surrounding public lands. It's the perfect place for my research."

"A big change from the war," he said.

"Everything is a big change from the war," she said. "Didn't you feel it, after you came home? That sense of not knowing what to do next? Of being a little out of place? Or was that just me?"

"It wasn't just you," he said. "Every day over there you had a mission—a purpose. Life over here isn't like that." He stared at the road ahead for a long moment, then added, "I thought about going back to school after I got out, but sitting in a classroom all day—that wasn't for me."

She shifted toward him, feeling more comfortable scrutinizing him for a change. He was good-looking—no doubt about that—with dark eyes and olive skin and a hawk nose and square chin. His broad shoulders filled out his short-sleeved tan shirt nicely, and slim-fit khakis showed off muscular thighs. "How did you end up working for border patrol?"

"They were at a job fair for veterans and it looked like interesting work. It was a lot of independent work, outdoors. I liked that."

She nodded. She understood that desire to be outdoors and alone, away from other people. After the noise, chaos and crowds of the war, the wilderness felt healing.

"It's great that you found work that's important," he said. "I mean, what you're doing could make a big difference in peoples' lives someday."

"Someday, maybe. But yeah, I do feel as though it's important work. Don't you think what you're doing is important?"

"Sometimes I do. Sometimes I'm not so sure." He checked his mirrors and crunched down on the candy. "You said this guy you found is Mexican?" he asked.

Back to the reason she was here. Guess they couldn't avoid that subject forever. "Well, Latino. He had dark hair and brown skin—like you."

"My mom is from Mexico. My dad's from Denver."

"Do you speak Spanish?"

"I do. Comes in handy on the job sometimes."

"Do you run into a lot of people from Mexico in the park?" she asked, thinking of Mariposa and Angelique.

"Some." He slowed as they reached the end of the paved road and bumped onto a rougher gravel surface. "How much farther from here?" he asked.

She checked her GPS. "About nine miles."

"You weren't kidding—remote."

"The best specimens are usually where they haven't been disturbed by people or grazing animals."

"Right. You haven't seen anything else suspicious while you were out and about this week, have you?"

She stiffened, again thinking of the Mexican woman and child. "What do you mean, suspicious?"

"A bunch of marijuana plants, for instance? Or a portable meth lab?"

"No. Should I have seen those things?"

"Probably not, if you want to stay safe."

"Is that why border patrol and the FBI and BLM and who knows who else are meeting in a trailer at park headquarters?" she asked. "To go after drugs in the park?"

The seat creaked as he shifted his weight. "We're an interagency task force formed to address rising crime in the park and surrounding lands—much of it drug related." He cut his eyes to her. "Just be careful out there. Good idea to carry that Sig."

"When I applied for my backcountry permit at the ranger station, they told me to watch out for snakes. No one said anything about drug dealers or murderers."

"Most tourists will never know they're there. And how many people who visit the park ever step off the main road or popular trails?"

"Not many," she said. "I almost never see anyone when I'm out in the backcountry." Which had made her encounter with Mariposa all the more remarkable. "If I do see anything suspicious, I'll stay far away," she said. "All I want to do is collect some plant specimens and get back to my research."

They both fell silent as the Cruiser bumped over the rutted, sometimes muddy road. Though it was already early June, most of the usually dry arroyos trickled with snowmelt, and grass that would later turn a papery brown looked green and lush. Abby spotted several small herds of deer grazing in the distance, and a cluster of pronghorn antelope that exploded into life as the vehicles trundled past, bouncing away in stiff-legged leaps.

Finally her GPS indicated they were near the area where she'd found the body. "Pull over anywhere," she said. "We'll have to walk in from here."

Michael stopped the Cruiser alongside the road and Graham slid his vehicle in behind them. The officers opened up the backs of the Cruisers and pulled out packs, canteens and, in Graham's case, a semiautomatic rifle. They were going in loaded for bear, she supposed in case they ran into any of the bad guys.

Graham indicated she should lead the way. GPS in

hand, she set out walking. The officers fell in behind in classic patrol formation. Abby's heart raced. She slipped her hand into the front pocket of her jeans and wrapped it around the rabbit charm. *Nothing to worry about*, she reminded herself. *You're in Colorado. In a national park. No snipers here.*

But of course, the dead man she'd found earlier reminded her that the serene landscape was not as safe as it seemed.

They walked for an hour before they came to the patch of desert parsley she'd harvested earlier. She noted the freshly turned earth where she'd dug up her specimen. "There's the boulder I hid behind." She pointed to the large rock, then walked over to it, trying to remember everything she'd done in those moments before she discovered the body. "I started walking this way."

She led the way, the other three moving silently behind her. A few minutes later she spotted the pink bandanna she'd left tied to the branch of a piñon. "There." She pointed. "The body is by that tree."

She stopped and let the three officers move past.

She watched from a distance as they surveyed the body. Carmen took a number of photographs, then they fanned out, searching the ground—for clues, she supposed. She stood in the shade of the piñon, wishing she were anywhere else. She'd thought she'd put killing and bodies behind her when she left Afghanistan. The wilderness was supposed to be a place of peace, not violence.

Michael returned to her side. "You doing okay?" he asked.

She nodded. "I'll be fine."

She felt his gaze on her, but he didn't press, for which

she was grateful. "Which direction did the men you saw come from?" he asked after a moment.

"From over there, near that wash." She nodded in the direction of the shallow depression in the terrain.

Graham joined them. "We'll need to seal off this area and send a team out to collect evidence."

"We need to figure out where he came from," Michael said. "There might be a camp somewhere nearby."

"Where are you camped, Ms. Stewart?" Graham asked.

"I'm in the South Rim Campground."

"Let us know if you decide to move into town or return to your home, in case we have questions," Graham said.

"I'd planned to stay here for another week to ten days," she said. "I've only just begun collecting the specimens I need."

"This part of the park will be off-limits to the public for most of that time, I'm afraid," Graham said. "Until we determine it's safe."

He was going to close the backcountry? "That really isn't acceptable," she said. "I'm not some naive tourist, stumbling around, but I really need to collect these specimens to complete my research."

"You'll have to find them somewhere else. Until I decide it's safe, this section of the park is closed."

The three officers studied her, expressions impassive, implacable. She turned away, and her gaze fell on the body on the ground. All she could see was the feet, but they lay there with the stillness of a mannequin. Lifeless, a cruel joke played out in the desert.

She hated having her plans thwarted, but she knew Graham and the others were right. Until they knew who had killed this man and why, they had to err on the side of caution. "Fine. There are other places in the back-country where I can look for specimens."

"Let us know…"

But Graham never finished the sentence. Bark exploded from the trunk of a tree beside her. "Get down!" Michael yelled, and shoved her to the ground as bullets whistled over their heads.

Chapter Four

In the silence that followed the burst of gunfire, the drum of Michael's pulse in his ears was so loud he was sure everyone could hear it. He slowed his breathing and strained his ears, alert for any clue about the shooter. Beneath him, Abby shifted, and he became aware of her ragged breathing. She shoved and he realized he was crushing her. Better crushed than shot, he thought, but he eased up a fraction of an inch, putting more of his weight on his hands, braced on the ground beneath his shoulders, and his knees, straddled on either side of her.

They lay in a depression in the ground, a shallow wash pocked with rocks and low scrub and a few stunted piñons. Turning his head, Michael spotted Graham and Carmen about five feet away. His eyes met Graham's. The supervisor looked angry enough to chew nails.

"Who's shooting at us?" Abby whispered, her voice so low he wondered at first if he'd imagined the question.

"Sniper," Graham answered. "I make his hide site about three hundred yards to the south, on that slight rise."

Michael turned his head, but he couldn't see anything except grass and dirt and the trunk of a piñon. They were too exposed here for him to even lift his head.

"He must be wearing a ghillie suit," Carmen said. "I can't see a thing." Michael turned back to look at her and realized she was half sitting behind a boulder. She'd pulled binoculars from her pack and was scanning the area.

"What's someone out here doing with a ghillie suit?" Abby asked.

Michael had been wondering the same thing. In a training course he'd taken, he'd seen men in the cumbersome camouflage suits covered with twigs and leaves so that when the wearer froze, he blended in completely with the surrounding landscape. It wasn't something you could pick up at your local outdoor supplier.

"They could have stolen one from the military, or made their own," Graham said. "These drug operations spare no expense to protect their business. That sniper rifle he's got is probably military issue, or close to it."

Graham shifted, reaching for his radio; the movement was enough to draw another blast of gunfire, bullets spitting into the dirt in front of them. Abby flinched, jolting against Michael. "Are you okay?" he whispered.

"Just a rock on my cheek. It's nothing."

More gunfire exploded, this time to their right. From her vantage point behind the boulder, Carmen had returned fire. "He's too far away," she said, lowering the weapon.

"Ranger Two, this is Ranger One, do you copy?" Graham had used the distraction to retrieve the radio from his utility belt and key the mike.

"Ranger Two. I copy." Simon's voice crackled through the static.

"We're pinned down by a sniper in the backcountry." He recited the GPS coordinates Abby had given them for her plant find. "Looks like one shooter. His hide site is approximately three hundred yards south of our position. He's on a small rise, maybe wearing a ghillie suit."

"We're on it. We'll try to come in behind him."

"Roger that. Over." Graham laid the radio on the ground beside his head. "Now we wait," he said.

Michael tried to ignore the cramping in his arms. If he let up, he'd crush Abby again, but any movement was liable to draw the sniper's fire. "Sorry," he said to her. "I know this isn't the most comfortable position."

She didn't answer. Instead, she started to tremble, tremors running through her body into his. She made a muffled sound, almost like…sobbing.

The sound tore at him. The sight of the dead man hadn't moved him, and while the sniper's fire got his adrenaline pumping, it didn't shake him the way Abby's sorrow did. "Hey." He slid one hand to her shoulder and turned his head so that his mouth was next to her ear. He spoke softly, not wanting the others to hear. "It's okay," he said. "Our team is good. They'll nail this guy."

She tensed, her fingers digging into the dirt beneath them. Her breathing was ragged, and he could sense panic rising off her in waves. Was she having some kind of flashback? How could he help her—comfort her?

He'd been shot at plenty of times as a PJ, but they always had the Pave Hawks to swoop them out of danger. He'd always been too focused on the mission, on saving lives, to worry much about his own. It must have been worse for troops on the ground, like her.

He tried to lift more of his weight off her. "Hey," he said again. "Abby, talk to me. You're going to be okay."

She sucked in a ragged breath, her body rising and falling beneath him. "I hate this," she said after a minute.

"I hate it, too." The words sounded lame, even to him, but he'd say anything to keep her talking. "But you'll be okay. The cavalry is on its way."

The muscles of her cheek against his shifted; he hoped she was smiling at his lame joke. "This is probably the last thing you expected when you came out here to dig plants," he said.

"Yeah." The shaking wasn't as violent now—only a tremor shuddering through her every now and then. Her hands had relaxed, no longer gripping the dirt. He resisted the urge to smooth his hand along her back; she might take it the wrong way. As it was, he was becoming all too aware of the feel of her body beneath his, the side of her breast nestled beside his arm, the soft curve of her backside against his groin.

"This is just a little too familiar," she said.

He realized she wasn't talking about the feel of their bodies pressed together. "You've been pinned down by a sniper before?"

"Oh, yeah. That was the thing about being over there—the unpredictability of it all—not knowing when an IED would explode or a sniper would fire, not knowing who you could trust."

You can trust me, he wanted to say. But he didn't. Trusting him didn't change the fact that there was somebody they couldn't see determined to kill them if they so much as lifted their heads. He hadn't done a very good job so far of protecting her. The best he could hope for was to provide a distraction. "Have you always been interested in plants?" he asked. "Did you always plan to study biology?"

"I was going to be a television news anchor," she said. "Or a model. This scar on my face put an end to that."

Only a deaf man would miss the bitterness in her words. She was certainly pretty enough to be a model— but she probably didn't want to hear that, either. He tried once more to get the conversation back on track. "What you're doing now—finding plants that could cure cancer. That sounds a lot more rewarding."

"Yeah." She fell silent again. Okay, so she didn't want to talk. At least she'd stopped shaking.

"Mostly, I like the solitude," she said after a moment. "It's so peaceful out here. Usually."

"Yeah. Usually it is. You just got lucky."

She actually chuckled then—the sound made him feel about ten feet tall, as if he'd done something a lot more heroic than make lame jokes.

"Why do you think he's shooting at us?" she asked. "Is it because we found the dead man?"

"I doubt it's that. My guess is the dead guy's an illegal. He won't have any ID on him, or anything to tie him to anyone or anything. Most likely the sniper is protecting something. A meth lab or something like that."

"But doesn't firing at us give away the fact that there's something out here worth protecting?"

"Yeah, but it keeps us from getting too close and buys them time to move the operation. When we finally make it out to investigate, whatever is going on will be long gone."

"What happens after that?"

"We have a starting place for our search. From there we try to track them to their new location."

"Like in the war," she said.

"Yeah. A lot like in the war."

"Just my dumb luck that I come out here to get away from all that and end up in the middle of it. Do you ever feel that way?" she asked.

"Yeah," he said. "I thought my job would mostly be inspecting shipments and checking passports— looking for drugs and illegals, for sure. I knew I'd carry a weapon, but I didn't expect to ever have to use it. But then I think, maybe I'm exactly where I'm supposed to be. Maybe my military training can help me put an end to some of the violence, at least."

"Do you really believe that?" she asked. "That things happen for a reason?"

"Yeah. I mean, don't you think it's more than coincidence that we met up again after all this time?" Five years in which he'd never really forgotten about her. "I mean, what are the odds?"

"That's why it's called a coincidence," she said. "It's random. Just like me ending up out here in the middle of your little drug war. It's the way life works, but it doesn't mean anything."

MICHAEL DIDN'T SAY anything after Abby shot down his theory that the two of them were meant to meet up again. Well, sorry, but she didn't believe in fate. She wasn't meant to be flat on her stomach, squashed by some big guy in fatigues while another guy took pot-shots at her, any more than she was meant to disappoint her family by becoming a recluse who wandered the desert in search of rare plants. Life was life. Things happened and you rolled with the punches. She liked looking for plants in the desert, and she hoped the work she did now would help somebody else someday. But that didn't mean she'd been guided by fate. She made her own choices and accepted the consequences.

She closed her eyes, thinking she might as well catch a nap while she waited for whatever Michael's partners were doing out there. But closing her eyes was a mistake. As soon as her eyelids descended, she was back in Kandahar, pinned down by a sniper, her face in the dirt just like it was now. Only back then, there had been no cavalry to come to the rescue—the rest of her unit had been pinned down by enemy fire or already wiped out. For six hours she'd lain there with her face in the dirt while the guy next to her silently bled out and the guy on her other side freaked out, sobbing like a baby until every nerve in her was raw. In the end, the shooter must have decided they were all dead and moved on. Her own company thought the same thing—she woke up with two men slinging her onto a stretcher and someone shouting, "Hey, we've got a live one here!"

She opened her eyes again. Time to think about something else. Mariposa. Where were she and Angelique right now? Was she safe? Was she somehow mixed up in whatever illegal operation the sniper was protecting? What was she—somebody's wife or girlfriend, along for the ride, in over her head now? Was she as surprised by the violence that intruded on such peaceful surroundings as Abby was?

"When you were out here before, collecting your plants, did you see anybody else?" Michael asked. "Besides the men who were after our dead guy?"

What was he, a mind reader or something? "No, I didn't see anybody," she lied.

"No other hikers or campers?"

"I saw two hikers three days ago. They were tourists from Australia. And I pass people on the roads and see campers in the campground."

"That's it?"

"Why? Don't you believe me?"

"In interrogation training, they tell you that if you ask the same question in several different ways, you sometimes get different answers."

"So now you're interrogating me?" What she wouldn't give to be able to look him in the eye when she spoke. Instead, she was forced to address the ground while he lay on top of her. She appreciated that he was doing his best to hold himself off her, but still, the guy was big and solid. An easy one hundred and eighty pounds.

"It's a harsh word for questioning," he said. "A lot of law enforcement is just asking the right questions, of victims, or witnesses, or suspects."

"Well, you're not going to get different answers from me." She saw no reason to betray Mariposa to him. "Do you think you could just slide off me?" she asked.

"I don't think we'd better risk it. Movement seems to set off our shooter."

"Why did you throw yourself on top of me in the first place?"

"I'm trained to protect civilians. And I don't care how politically incorrect it is, my instincts are to keep women and children out of harm's way."

"How chivalrous of you." She hesitated, then added, "But thanks, all the same." The one thing she'd missed about the military was that sense that her buddies had her back.

"You're welcome. Sorry we couldn't have gotten re-acquainted under better circumstances."

"Now that he's not actually shooting at us and we're just waiting, it's pretty boring," she said. "Like most of the time in the war."

"Are all our conversations going to come back to that?" he asked.

"Does it bother you, talking about the war?"

"Not really. I thought it bothered you."

"Sometimes it does," she admitted. When other people asked about her experiences in Afghanistan, she deflected the questions or changed the subject. "It's easier with you. You were over there. You understand."

"I guess I do relate to what you went through. A little bit anyway."

The radio's crackle made them both flinch. Abby turned her head toward the sound. Graham keyed the mike. "What have you got?" he asked.

"All clear here." One of the team members—maybe the sour-faced guy, Simon—said.

"No sign of the shooter?" Graham asked.

"Somebody was here, all right. There's broken brush and we found some shell casings. Looks like a .300 Win Mag. The dirt's a little scuffed up, but the ground's too hard to leave much of an impression."

"Get Randall and Lotte on it."

"They're here. The dog picked up a scent, but it died at the road. We found some tire tracks that look like a truck. We figure someone was waiting to pick up our guy. We never saw signs of a vehicle, so he probably left not long after he fired the last shots at y'all."

Graham swore under his breath and shoved up onto his knees. No gunshots split the air. Abby let out the breath she hadn't even realized she'd been holding.

Michael rolled off her and popped to his feet, then reached out a hand to help her up. She let him pull her up, her limbs stiff and sore from so long being prone. Clearly, she wasn't in as good a shape as she'd thought. "You're bleeding," he said, and gently touched the side of her face.

She flinched as his fingers brushed against the scar, but then she felt the stickiness of already drying blood. "A rock ricocheted off the ground," she said. "It's nothing."

"Here." He handed her a black bandanna, then offered a bottle of water. "You should clean it up."

Head down, she accepted the water and dampened the bandanna. The square of cloth was clean and crisp, like something a businessman would carry tucked into his pocket. She turned her back to the others as she cleaned off the blood and dirt from the side of her face.

"Let me have a look." Michael moved around in front of her. "You may need stitches."

"It's nothing." She tried once more to turn away, but he put his hand on her shoulder and took her chin in his other hand. "It's okay," he said softly. "I promise I don't faint at the sight of blood."

The teasing quality of the words almost made her smile. If anyone had seen her at her worst, it had been this guy. She had no idea what she'd looked like when the PJs had hauled her onto that helicopter, but the doctors had told her the shrapnel from the IED had torn through the side of her face, narrowly missing her eye.

As much as she hated the scar, it was nothing compared to how she might have ended up.

She let him lift her chin and study the side of her face.

"It's just a little cut, pretty shallow. When we get back to the truck I'll get a bandage for it."

"Thanks." She turned away and combed her hair down to cover the side of her face again.

"Get Marco to help you with recon," Graham said. "I'll notify the park rangers that the backcountry is closed indefinitely. No more permits, and they'll need to round up anyone out with a permit now. Over."

"You mean just the backcountry within the park, right?" Abby asked.

"I mean all the park, the recreation area and Gunnison Gorge. If these people have a sniper looking after their interests, they have some real money and muscle behind it. Until we know the scope of their operation, we can't risk the safety of the public."

"You can't expect to keep people out of an area that large," she said.

"We can't prevent all unauthorized access, but we can stop issuing permits and close all the roads leading into the area. I'm sorry, but that means you won't be able to continue your research in the area."

His tone of command left little room for argument. He looked past her to Michael. "Take her back to headquarters, then meet up with Simon and the others. Ms. Stewart, we may have more questions for you later."

She doubted she'd have any useful answers, but she only nodded and turned to follow Michael back to the Cruiser. By the time they reached the vehicle, she was fuming.

"Sorry about your research," Michael said as he started the truck. "Maybe you can come back and finish up next summer. Hopefully, things will have calmed down by then."

"I don't have next summer," she said. "My grant is for this summer. Next summer I'll have to find a job and start paying off my student loans."

"Is there someplace else you can research—another park, or another part of the state?"

"My grant is to explore this area. Shifting my focus requires a new grant application. Your commander is overreacting. He doesn't have to close off all one hundred and thirty thousand acres of public land. That's ridiculous."

"Can you blame him? He's already under the gun from politicians who think this task force is a waste of money—can you imagine the fallout if some tourist gets taken out by a sniper? We've already got one murder on our hands. Your plants will still be there when this investigation is over."

"Don't patronize me."

"I'm not patronizing. I'm just trying to get you to calm down."

His words only made her more furious. She did not need to calm down. She'd just been shot at and forced to lie on her stomach on the ground for over an hour, and suffered the humiliation of almost flaking out in front of a bunch of strangers—if she didn't give vent to the tornado of emotions inside of her she might explode. "Shut up," she said. "Whatever you have to say, I don't want to hear it."

He glared at her for a long moment, then turned his attention to the road. The truck rocketed forward, bouncing over the rough two-track so that she had to grip the handle mounted at the top of the door to steady herself. Dust boiled up behind them, and rocks pinged against the undercarriage like BBs. She clenched her jaw to keep from shouting at him to slow down and not be so reckless. But that was what he wanted from her— another reaction. She wouldn't give him the satisfaction.

She'd already let him affect her emotions too much, his combination of brashness and consideration, strength and tenderness, touching vulnerable places inside her she hadn't let anyone see. She never talked about the war with anyone, and yet she'd confided in him. She didn't willingly let others see her scars, but she'd turned her face up to him with only a moment's hesitation. She didn't like how open and undefended he made her feel, with all his talk of fate and meaning behind what had to be only coincidence.

After a few miles, he slowed down enough that she could relax back in the seat. She hugged her arms across her chest and stared out at the landscape. Most people probably thought the land was ugly, with its scraggly vegetation and covering of rock and thin dirt. The real treasure lay beneath eye level, in the startlingly deep, narrow canyon that cut a jagged swatch through the high desert, its walls painted in shades of red and orange and gray. People long ago had dubbed it the Black Canyon, since sunlight seldom reached its depths. The silvery ribbon of the Gunnison River rushed through the bottom of the canyon, nurturing lush growth along its rocky banks, creating a world of color and moisture far below the parched landscape above.

But that stark desert held as much interest for Abby as the canyon below. She'd enjoyed discovering the secrets of the twisted piñons and miniature wildflowers, learning about the deer, rabbits, foxes and other wildlife that thrived there. She thought of herself like them—someone who had learned to survive amid bareness, to find the beauty in hardship.

They pulled up in front of headquarters. Her car was the only one in the lot now. She unsnapped her seat belt and her hand was on the door when Michael spoke. "Look. It isn't safe for you to go into the backcountry by yourself, but what if I went with you? You can look for your plants while I patrol. I can square it with Graham."

She could only imagine the pushback he'd get from his supervisor when he made that suggestion. Captain Graham Ellison struck her as a man who wasn't into bending the rules. "Why would you do that?"

He shrugged. "I kind of feel responsible for you."

Wrong answer. She didn't want anyone—she especially didn't want this man—to be responsible for her. She was responsible for herself. She climbed out of the truck and turned to face him. "I get that you saved my life," she said. "And I'm grateful for that. But that doesn't give you any kind of special claim on me."

He held up both hands. "I'm not making any claim on you. I'm just trying to help."

"I don't need your help. Thanks anyway." She turned and stalked away, though she could feel his gaze burning into her all the way to her car.

Chapter Five

"We got nothing." Simon slapped a thin file folder onto the conference room table and sank into a chair, a look of disgust on his face.

Graham, seated at the head of the table, frowned and reached for the folder. "What do you mean, you've got nothing?" he said. "We've got a dead body. We've got shell casings from a gun—tire tracks. All of that must lead to something." He leveled his stern gaze on the others around the table. Michael unwrapped another Life Saver and popped it into his mouth. Already, this meeting was off to a bad start. Twenty-four hours in and they had no more to go on than they had when Abby had walked into their office yesterday afternoon.

"It leads nowhere," Simon said. "The man had no ID. His fingerprints aren't in any database. We sent in DNA, but I doubt it will come up with anything—he's obviously an illegal. We're not even sure where he's from. Could be Mexico, Central America, South America…" He shook his head.

"Where he's from may not be important," Graham said, tapping the file, which he hadn't bothered to open. "I want to know why he was shot in the middle of nowhere like that, and who shot him."

"Somebody wanted to shut him up."

All heads turned toward Marco, who had spoken. "Shut him up why?" Graham asked.

"I think he was trying to escape and they silenced him," Marco said.

"Why not bring him back?" Randall asked. "If our theory is these illegals are brought here to work in some drug operation, why lose a good worker?"

"A man who wants to get away badly enough to take off across the wilderness on foot isn't a good worker," Marco said.

"With this level of security, I'd say we're definitely looking at a drug operation," Simon said. "So why can't we find it?"

"If it's meth, it could be in a little trailer camouflaged on the back of beyond," Michael said. "Even if it's a grow op, they can hide acres of the stuff in remote canyons."

"Our aerial patrols haven't spotted anything suspicious." Graham's chair creaked as he leaned back in it. "Did Lotte pick up any scent?"

The Belgian Malinois raised her head, alert. Randall dropped his hand to idly stroke her head. "She worked for a couple of hours yesterday, but none of the trails she picked up led to anything."

"What about Abby Stewart?"

Michael realized Graham had addressed him. "What about her?" he asked.

"She's the one who found the body, and she was with us when the sniper fired," Graham said. "What's her link to all this?"

"She was in the wrong place at the wrong time," Michael said. "No link."

"What do we know about her?" Simon asked. "Is she really who she says she is?"

"She's who I say she is." Michael tried to suppress his annoyance and failed. "I knew her in Afghanistan. She was wounded over there, came home to recuperate and now she's a student at University of Colorado, earning her master's in biology."

"Her story checks out," Carmen said. "She came to the park five days ago and requested a backcountry permit. The park rangers told me she goes out every morning and comes back in the evening with her notebooks, pack and specimens she's collected."

"She could be meeting with anyone in that time," Simon said.

"You checked her out?" Michael's stomach churned, as if he'd been the subject of their snooping.

"We check everyone out," Graham said. "How was she when she left you yesterday?"

She'd been furious with him. If looks could kill, he'd be seriously wounded right now. "She was upset about not being able to continue her research," he said. "She has a grant that runs out at the end of the summer."

"What's she researching anyway?" Randall asked.

"Plants that grow in this area that have medicinal purposes," Michael said. "She says stuff that grows out there could be used to treat or cure cancer and other diseases."

"Sounds like a good excuse to spend time in the backcountry," Simon said. "Maybe the plant she's really interested in is marijuana."

"There are a lot of plants that have medicinal uses," Carmen said. "My people have known that for centuries. You palefaces are just now figuring it out."

Simon ignored the dig and leaned across the table toward Michael. "Even if she's not involved with our killers, that sniper saw her with us yesterday. He'll report that to his handlers."

"If they think she witnessed something out there, they'll want to shut her up, too," Marco said.

Michael felt as if he'd swallowed ice. "She could be in danger."

"It's a possibility," Graham said. "We'll need to keep an eye on her."

"I offered to take her out on patrol with me," Michael said. "That way, she could collect her plants and I could make sure she didn't wander into anything dangerous."

"Not a bad idea," Graham said. "What did she think?"

"She was still pretty shaken up by the sniper thing." No sense admitting he'd blown it by coming on too strong. "She had some bad experiences in the war."

"You said she almost died?" Carmen asked.

"She did die." Michael didn't have to close his eyes to see her lying on that stretcher, pale as the sheets. "She coded in the helicopter on the way to the hospital. We brought her back, but she was pretty messed up."

"She was hit in the face?" Carmen stroked the side of her own face.

"She was hit all over, but the head wound was the worst."

"And you saved her life," Carmen said.

He looked away. "I did my job."

"Then you have a connection with her, whether she acknowledges that or not," Graham said. "Go talk to her. Tell her we want to offer her protection, in exchange for her help."

"What kind of help?" The idea surprised him.

"I have a sense she knows something she's not telling us," Graham said. He opened the file. "Now let's see if there's anything else in here we can go after."

"I'M DOING FINE, DAD. The research is going well." Abby held the phone tightly to her ear and paced the length of the travel trailer she'd rented for the summer. Four steps toward the bedroom at one end, turn and four steps back to the dinette at the other end, passing the galley kitchen in between. The research had been going well, until Michael Dance and his friends had thrown a wrench in her plans.

"Have you thought any more about coming home when you've wrapped things up there?" Her dad's voice, the velvety, well-modulated bass that was familiar to sports fans and channel-four viewers all over Milwaukee, seemed to fill up the trailer. "I've been talking to some people I know at the station. We've got a vacancy for a weekend anchor job. They'd love to give you a tryout."

Abby squeezed her eyes shut and suppressed a groan. "That wouldn't be a good idea, Dad." Any tryout they gave her would be because her dad—Brian Stewart, the voice of Milwaukee sports—had called in favors. Or worse, because they were playing the wounded-vet card. She wanted no part of it.

"Nonsense! You were always a natural in front of the camera. And if you're worried about your scar—it really isn't that bad. Stage makeup can cover a lot, you know, and you could have more plastic surgery."

How many times had he said the same thing? Did he

not hear her when she talked? "No more surgery," she said. "And no makeup. This is who I am."

"At least think about it. You know it would mean a lot to me."

And of course, this is all about you. She didn't say the words out loud. She wasn't that cruel. Practically since she could talk, her father had built the dream of her following in his footsteps. All the beauty pageants, the voice lessons and drama camps, had been part of his plan to turn her into an even bigger celebrity than he was.

"Are you sure you're okay, honey?" he asked. "You sound tired."

Maybe because she'd hardly slept last night, kept awake by memories of the day's events, mingled with flashbacks to the war. In the dark hours of the early morning, it had been hard to differentiate between the two. But she mentioned none of this to her father. He'd freak out and it would only prove what he had been saying for months now—that she was crazy to throw her life away on plants. Not when she had so much talent.

But did she really have talent? She had spent so many years getting by on her good looks. When you were blessed with beauty, people never looked any deeper or expected anything more. Their impression of you stayed on the surface. At least now when she made a discovery, she knew it was because she'd used her brain. "I'll be fine, Dad. It was good talking to you. I'd better go now. I have work to do."

"Goodbye, sweetheart. I love you. Your mom sends her love, too."

"I love you, too, Dad. Talk to you soon." She clicked off the phone and slid it into her pocket, then stared out the window at the distant mountains, the peaks still capped with snow. Maybe when she won the Nobel Prize for her work with medicinal plants, her father would give up his dream of making her a star, though she doubted it.

Knocking on the door of the little trailer startled her. She glanced at the gun, in its holster on the counter by the door, within easy reach if she needed it, then peeled back a corner of the blinds in the window beside the door.

Michael Dance stood on the ground below the steps, eyes shaded by dark sunglasses. He rocked back on his heels and glanced around the campsite, then leaned forward to knock again. She pulled open the door. "Good afternoon," she said.

"Good afternoon to you, too." His smile dazzled. It hit her like a spotlight, or maybe more like a laser beam, warmth blossoming in her chest.

"Come on in." She stepped back to let him pass her.

He stood in the middle of the trailer's one room and looked around—at the compact dinette with the padded bench seats all around that she used as a desk, at the half-size refrigerator and compact stove, microwave and sink, and back to the closed door of the bathroom and the queen-size bed. He nodded in approval. "This is nice. Cozy."

"It serves its purpose." She slid past him, the narrow space forcing them to brush together, the brief contact sending another wash of heat through her. She sat at the dinette, shoved her laptop to one side and motioned to the seat across from her. "Make yourself at home."

He eased his big frame onto the bench. "I didn't

mean to interrupt your work," he said, nodding to the laptop.

"I was just compiling the notes I've made so far. And cataloging my specimens, since I don't know when I'll be able to collect more."

"Listen, about yesterday—" he began.

"I'm sorry I went off on you like that," she said. "I was still upset about the sniper and finding that dead man and…and everything. I shouldn't have taken it out on you."

She was touched by how relieved he looked. "I understand," he said. "It was a lot to take in. Most people would be overwhelmed."

"I should have handled it better." After all, she'd had plenty of practice dealing with death and violence in her short time in the military.

"The offer to come with me on patrol is still open," he said.

Relief washed over her. She'd been prepared to beg if she had to, in order to continue her research. "Then, I accept."

"Great." He drummed his fingers on the table and looked around the trailer once more, avoiding her gaze.

"Is there something else?" she asked.

His eyes shifted back to her. "The G-Man— Graham—thinks there's something you're not telling us. About yesterday, when that man was shot."

So much for her acting ability. Or maybe it was just that she was having second thoughts about keeping her secret. What if Mariposa was somehow tied up with whatever was going on out there in the parkland? By not telling about her, was Abby endangering other peoples' lives?

"Before I tell you anything else, answer a few questions for me first," she said.

He sat back, hands flat on the table between them. "All right."

She couldn't look into that intense gaze anymore, so she studied his hands. He had long fingers and neatly trimmed nails, and he wore a silver-and-onyx ring on his right hand. They were masculine, capable hands—she remembered the feel of them at her back yesterday. Reassuring. Protective. "You work for Customs and Immigration, right?"

"US Customs and Border Protection."

"So when you encounter someone who's in this country illegally, your job is to deport them?"

"That's more Simon's territory. He's with ICE—Immigration and Customs Enforcement. They're part of Homeland Security, too. My job is more about protecting our borders, though we work with ICE sometimes. Why?"

She shifted in her seat. How to admit to this man that she'd been lying to him? "I did see someone else yesterday—before the man was shot. There was a woman. She was out collecting plants, too, but for food, not for scientific specimens. She spoke only Spanish and she had a baby with her. She told me her name was Mariposa. She was so young—and gorgeous. I wouldn't have stood a chance if I'd competed in a pageant with her. Here, I have a picture." She pulled her phone from her pocket and found the photo she'd snapped of Mariposa. She handed the phone to him.

"She looks young," he said. "A teenager."

"Maybe," Abby said.

He returned the phone to her. "She trusted you enough to let you take her picture."

"I didn't ask, I just snapped it in between shots of the plants I was gathering. She seemed surprised, but she didn't object."

"We'll run the photo by authorities, but I doubt we'll find anything," he said. "Still, you never know. Did she say where she lived? What she was doing out there?"

"No. Like I said, she didn't speak English and I don't know much Spanish. I gave her a couple of protein bars and she seemed grateful. She heard the people who shot that man shouting and she took off. I mean, she panicked and was running for her life."

"So she knew who they were?"

"That's what I think. Or at least what they were up to." She touched the back of his hand. "Do you think she's mixed up in all this somehow? Maybe she's being held prisoner by these people or something?"

"She's probably one of the workers. These drug operations bring illegals in to work their grow operations or make meth. They're as good as prisoners, isolated out here, kept under guard."

"Is that what happened to that man—he tried to escape?"

"We don't know for sure, but that's a likely scenario."

"No wonder she panicked and ran."

"Did she say anything else?"

"She said the baby was a girl named Angelique. And she showed me where to find some of the plants I was looking for. She seemed very familiar with the plants in the area. I got the impression she was hungry." She blinked back tears, thinking of the beautiful woman and the baby, alone and in danger.

"Maybe we can find her and help her. Even if we send her back to her home, that would be better than the way she's living now."

"I guess so." Better to return to home and family than to live with the threat of danger.

"You competed in beauty pageants?" Michael asked.

Of course he'd picked up on that. Why had she even mentioned it? "Don't sound so shocked. I was Miss Milwaukee my freshman year in college."

"How did a beauty queen end up in Afghanistan?"

"It's a long story."

"I've got time."

She sighed. She could try to blow him off, but he struck her as someone who wouldn't give up questioning her. It was probably a trait that made him good at his job. "I thought it would be a good way to get money for grad school," she said. "My parents thought I was wasting my time with more schooling, so they wouldn't pay. And I didn't expect them to. I was willing to do it on my own."

"So the beauty queen wanted to be a biologist all along," he said.

"I didn't know what I wanted to do," she said. "My undergrad degree is in communications. But I needed to get away from home. My father is a local celebrity. He does sports for the number one news station in the city, plus he does a lot of voice-over work—ads and public service announcements and things. Everybody knows him. He wanted me to follow in his footsteps, but I wanted the chance to prove myself doing something that was just mine. I never thought it would turn out the way it did."

"No one does," he said. "I mean, you couldn't, right?

No one would enlist if the first thing that came to mind was dying or being injured."

"My parents were horrified—first with my enlistment, then when I went overseas. When I was injured they freaked out. My mother burst into tears the first time she saw the scar. She still can hardly bear to look at me." She swallowed past the tightness in her throat. "My dad is always trying to fix me. He wants me to have more surgery, to try special makeup. He can't let go of the hope that I'll go into television after all. They think I'm wasting my time trying to be a scientist."

"Do you think it's a waste of time?"

"No. I'm happier doing this—something that's all mine—than I would have been competing with my dad. And I would have been competing, at least subconsciously. This is a chance to prove myself on my own terms. I guess it's what I was looking for in the military all along."

"Funny sometimes, how life has a way of working out."

"If you're talking about fate, I still don't believe in that. Things just happen for no reason."

"Hey, I didn't say anything." He grinned. "Is tomorrow soon enough for us to go out?"

"Go out?" She blushed, and hated that she did so.

"On patrol. You said you wanted to come with me, right?"

On patrol—of course. What was she, some sixteen-year-old expecting the class jock to ask her out on a date? "Oh, yeah. Sure. When can we go?"

"I'll pick you up about eight." He stood, and she rose, also, and followed him to the door. "Thanks for telling me about Mariposa," he said. "We'll try to find her and help her."

"I should have trusted you earlier, but…"

"Yeah, I know. It's hard to trust sometimes."

She followed him out the door, reluctant to say good-bye. Now that she'd confided in him, she felt closer somehow. As if she finally had a friend who really understood her. "What's that on your car?" he asked.

She followed his gaze to the box sitting on the hood of the Toyota Camry. "I don't know. I've never seen it before."

They walked to the car and she started to reach for the box, but he put out his arm to stop her. "Don't touch it yet. Let's take a closer look."

Following his example, she leaned over and read the writing on the outside of the small brown cardboard box. *Abby Stewart* was written in marker in block letters. "I don't see anything that says who it's from," she said.

"So you're not expecting a package from anyone?"

"No." She wrapped her arms across her stomach, fighting back a wave of nausea at the idea that a stranger had walked into her camp and left this.

Michael pulled out his radio. "Let's get Randall and Lotte over to take a look."

"The dog? Do you really think that's necessary?" She eyed the box. It looked both innocent and sinister.

"Better to be safe."

He made the call and Randall said he'd be right over. They retreated to the shade of the trailer's awning to wait. Abby fidgeted, but Michael leaned against the trailer, relaxed. "It's probably nothing," she said. "Maybe we should just open it."

"Let's wait," he said, and she didn't argue.

Randall pulled in beside Michael's Cruiser a few minutes later. He got out of the truck, then released Lotte. She trotted forward, eyes bright, tail waving. Randall showed her the box. "Lotte, *such*," he commanded.

The dog braced her front paws on the bumper of the car and stretched toward the box, ears flattened, tail low. She retreated quickly, whining, and circled the vehicle, clearly agitated. She paced, panting and whining, looking from the box to Randall and back again. "She doesn't look too happy about whatever is in there," Michael said.

"She's not alerting for bombs or explosives," Randall said. "But she doesn't like whatever she's smelling. Lotte, *komm*."

The dog came and lay at Randall's side. Michael took out a knife. "Let's see what we've got."

He picked up the box and balanced it in his hands. "It's heavy," he said. "Maybe three or four pounds." He opened out a blade on the knife and slit the tape along the sides of the box, then set it on the ground. "Better play it safe." He picked up a stick from beside the campsite's picnic table. "Stand back."

Abby retreated a few steps, chewing her lip nervously. They were probably going through all this drama for nothing, but the dog's behavior worried her. Whatever was in that box, it had upset Lotte, who still stared at it, her brow wrinkled.

Michael slid the tip of the stick under the edge of the box lid, and with a jerk, flipped it off. The box tilted to its side, the contents pouring out in a rippling, fluid motion. Lotte barked, and Abby screamed as she stared at the huge rattler, coiled and ready to strike.

Chapter Six

Michael pulled out his service weapon and squeezed off two shots. The rattler writhed and thrashed, then lay still. Lotte barked again and whined. Despite the heat, Abby felt chilled through. She stared at the dead snake, shaken more by the idea that someone had intended it for her than by the snake itself.

A gust of wind rattled the branches of the piñons that surrounded the campsite, and tugged at the awning of the trailer. "It's got to be five feet long." Randall picked up the stick Michael had used to open the box and lifted the snake.

"Careful," Abby said. "They still have venom in them, even when they're dead."

Randall nodded and glanced around. "Think we should bag it for evidence?"

"Photograph it, then bag it and tag it," Michael said. "The box, too. Maybe we can pick up some prints."

"I doubt it," Randall said. He let the snake drop again. It lay coiled in the dust, still menacing despite its lack of life. "Someone goes to all the trouble to box up a snake and leave it as a present, they're probably smart enough to wear gloves."

"Why would someone do this?" Abby asked.

"They're sending a message." Michael's expression was grim. "Warning you off."

"Warning me off what? I haven't done anything."

"You found that dead man and got us involved," Randall said. "We were close enough to something that sniper fired on us. Maybe they're trying to frighten you out of the backcountry altogether, in case you stumble onto anything else."

"I'm frightened, all right." She shuddered. "I could have been killed."

Michael rested a hand on her shoulder. "You might have been scared half to death. And you'd probably be pretty sick for a while," he said. "But the hospitals around here probably carry antivenin, so chances are good you'd have survived. But whoever did this probably doesn't care one way or another. You're a threat to them, so they're threatening back."

"I haven't done anything to anyone," she protested again.

"You witnessed an execution," he said.

She shuddered at the word. But that was what the murder of that man had been. They'd hunted him down and killed him, like predators hunting prey. "But I didn't see anything. I couldn't identify anyone."

"They can't be sure of that."

"But...how did they know my name?" She shook her head, the reality of what had happened refusing to sink in. "I hardly know anyone in the area—no one who would do anything like this."

"It would be easy enough to learn your name," Randall said. "They could look up your car registration, or get it off your camping permit at the park rangers' office. Using your name makes something like this more personal. More threatening."

She shuddered. She felt threatened, all right. And a little sick.

Michael squeezed her shoulder, then dropped his hand. "You can't stay here," he said.

"No, I can't." This time, whoever hated her had left a snake. What would they do next time? "But where can I go?"

"We'll find you a hotel in town," Randall said. "Register you under an assumed name. One of us can stay with you."

"One of you?"

"I'll stay with you," Michael said.

"You don't have to do that." She straightened her shoulders. "I have a weapon, and I know enough to be careful now. I can look after myself." She'd fought so hard to be independent. She couldn't let this faceless stranger or strangers take that from her.

Michael set his mouth in the stubborn line she was beginning to recognize. "Until we determine how big a threat these people are, I'm going to stay with you," he said.

"I don't need a babysitter." She especially didn't need him hovering. Just because he'd saved her life once didn't mean he was responsible for her the rest of her life. Now that the shock of what had happened was starting to fade, she could think more clearly. "Like you said, this was a warning. If someone had really wanted to hurt me, they wouldn't have bothered gift-wrapping the snake—they'd have turned it loose inside the car." She shuddered at the idea.

"I'm not going to give them a chance to get that close

again." His dark eyes met hers, their previous warmth replaced by cold determination.

"You might as well give up," Randall said. "He's stubborn."

"Fine," she said. "But I'm not sharing a room with you." Having him that close, that…intimate…would be too much.

"I can get a room next door to yours."

"All right." She'd have to learn to live with that.

Randall pulled out a camera and began taking pictures. "Let me see that box," he said. "Maybe Lotte can pick up a scent trail."

But the dog found nothing. Abby went into the trailer to pack while the two officers collected evidence and disposed of the snake. She came out with a suitcase in one hand, her laptop bag and purse in the other, her backpack on her back. "All right, I'm ready," she said. "But in the morning, can I still go out on patrol with you?"

"If you still want to." He took the suitcase from her.

"I want to. Working is better than sitting around brooding about the fact that someone I don't even know hates me enough to attack me with a snake. Besides, I have a lot of territory to cover and only a few weeks to do it. I can't let a threat from a stranger stop me."

MICHAEL TOLD HIMSELF he shouldn't have been surprised by Abby's toughness. She'd already proved she was a survivor. He glanced at her as they negotiated the winding road that led away from the park. The afternoon sun slanted across her face like a spotlight, glinting on the silver earrings she wore. She definitely looked like a beauty queen, or a movie star. "Can I ask you a personal question?"

She turned toward him, her dark blue eyes wary. "You can ask. I don't promise I'll answer."

He focused on the road again. "What happened after you came back to the States—after you were wounded?" he asked. "I mean, how long were you in the hospital? Did you have any kind of rehab, or did they just send you home?"

"I went to a hospital in Germany first. They did surgery there to remove shrapnel, and the surgeons saved my eye. They had to repair my broken cheek." She touched the scar. "I have a titanium plate holding everything together."

He winced. "Sounds brutal."

"I guess it was, but I was in a fog a lot of the time— partly from the drugs, partly from the trauma itself."

"I think that's a protective mechanism the mind has—blocking out trauma that way." In his PJ training, he'd been taught that the wounded seldom remembered what happened on the helicopters.

"I guess, but it bothers me sometimes that I can't remember," she said. "After I was transferred back to the States, to a hospital in Milwaukee, people came to see me and I have no memory of it. And yet the silliest things stay with me."

"Like what?"

"Like I remember I asked my mom to bring me some clothes to wear besides the hospital gown—sweats and things like that. She brought me this yellow blouse I'd always hated. I yelled at her for bringing it and she started to cry. My dad yelled at me for hurting her feelings and then *I* started to cry." She shook her head. "It was just so stupid—what did it matter what color the blouse was?"

"I don't know if it's so stupid," he said. "It makes sense to me. There were so many things happening to you that you couldn't control. The clothes you wore were one little thing you could control. And the medications, not to mention the brain injury, probably made it more difficult to manage your emotions. Your doctors should have told your parents that."

"They probably did. But my mom and dad's way of coping with this whole mess was to pretend nothing was wrong. We'd have these surreal conversations, where Mom would talk about boys I used to date who would be so glad to see me again, and Dad would tell me I should try out for a summer job with the community theater group. After a while, I couldn't stand it anymore and I'd say something horrible, like no one wanted a freak on stage. Then Mom would start to cry again. It was awful."

His hands tightened on the steering wheel. "You're not a freak, you know."

"I know. But I'm not who I was. I'm still coming to terms with that. I don't even want that old life anymore—I'm not sure I ever wanted it. But I'm still figuring out what my new life will look like." She shifted in the seat. "But right now, I'm more focused on figuring out where I'm going to be staying tonight."

"Carmen made reservations at a motel on the other side of town. We figured the farther from the park, the better."

The motel turned out to be one of those old-fashioned lodges with rooms lined up in two low-slung wings on either side of the A-frame lobby. "We have reservations for Ricky and Lucy," Michael told the desk clerk, a fleshy older man with skin the color of raw dough.

He handed over the keys and accepted Michael's credit card, then they drove down to a room on the end and parked. "Ricky and Lucy?" Abby asked. "Why those names?"

"Ricky and Lucy Ricardo? From *I Love Lucy*. I love those old shows. When I had to come up with a couple's names, that popped into my head."

His reply made her feel a little off balance—as if he really was a mind reader. "I love those old shows, too," she said. "When I was in the hospital, I watched a lot of them." Lucille Ball had been a beauty queen who wasn't afraid to make a fool of herself to get a laugh. Watching her had given Abby hope; maybe she could be more than a pretty face herself. But how could Michael know that?

He unlocked the door to the room next to the one on the end and did a quick tour of the space, then looked into the bathroom and checked out the closet. "What are you searching for?" she asked.

"Any sign that anyone's been here ahead of us."

"Why would they have been?"

"Someone might have heard about our plans to stay here. It's not likely, but it pays to be careful."

He unlocked the door to the adjoining room on the end of this wing. "Just to make it easier to reach each other in an emergency," he explained. "You can stay in this room. I'll take the one next door."

His room was a copy of hers, right down to the blue-and-green quilted spread and the bottle of water on the dresser. "What now?" she asked.

"Want to order pizza?"

She almost laughed. After everything that had

happened today, pizza seemed so ordinary. So safe. "That sounds like a good idea."

He pulled out his phone. "What do you like?"

"Anything but anchovies and onions."

He made a face. "Right."

She returned to her room and arranged her few things on the bed and table, then combed her hair and splashed water on her face. She hadn't bothered to do more than apply sunscreen this morning and it showed, her brows and lashes pale and unadorned. She thought about putting on makeup, but she didn't want Michael to get the wrong idea. Circumstances had thrown them together, but it wasn't as if they were dating or anything.

If she was ready to be in a relationship, he wouldn't be her first choice. She was glad he was with her now, and that men like him were hunting down whoever had killed the man in the desert, but he was too intense. Too protective. All his talk of fate and seeing meaning in random happenings unsettled her.

She booted up her laptop and tried to focus on the notes she'd made about desert parsley and its habitat. But that only made her think of Mariposa. She pulled out her phone and studied the picture of the beautiful young woman. Where was she right now? Were she and Angelique safe?

When Michael knocked on the door between their rooms and announced that the pizza had arrived, she gratefully shut down the computer and joined him in his room. The smell of spicy pepperoni and sausage, sauce and cheese made her a little dizzy, and she realized she was starving. "This was a great idea," she said, helping herself to a slice.

"Just what the doctor ordered." He filled his own

plate and sat across from her at the little table in front of the window. He'd drawn the drapes, shutting out the setting sun, and turned on the too-dim lamp behind him. The interior felt cool and cozy.

"Speaking of doctors," she said, "you seem to know a lot about medicine. Did you consider becoming a doctor?"

"Early on, I thought about it. That's why I signed up for the PJs. I thought I wanted a career in trauma medicine. I pictured excitement and the adrenaline rush and saving people's lives." He fell silent and picked a slice of pepperoni off his pizza.

"What is it?" she asked. "Is something wrong?"

"They don't tell you that you lose more than you save." He looked into her eyes. "You were my first save—that's another reason I remember you."

She wanted to look away from the intensity of his gaze, but she couldn't. This man had saved her life; she couldn't turn away from him. "I wish I remembered you," she said. If she did, would she feel that connection between them that he seemed to feel?

He shrugged his shoulders, as if shrugging off bad memories. "Anyway, by the time my tour was up, I'd decided I wasn't cut out for that line of work. I bummed around for a few months, not sure what I wanted to do. After the constant adrenaline rush of the war, civilian life was an adjustment. When my uncle suggested border patrol, I figured I'd give it a shot."

"Do you like it?"

"I like working outdoors, doing something different all the time. I'm not so crazy about the bureaucracy. And sometimes I question whether I'm really doing much good."

"You saved me from that snake." She smiled, letting him know she was teasing.

"If I hadn't gotten to it, Randall would have shot it." He took another bite of pizza and chewed, then swallowed. "Or you'd have killed it yourself. You're tough."

The words made her feel lighter—taller. She smiled. "You couldn't give me a better compliment."

"Is that all it takes?" He grinned, his teeth very white against his olive skin. "Maybe I'll try that line out on other women. I've been doing it all wrong, telling them they were pretty. Not that you aren't—pretty, that is."

Her smile faded. "I heard how pretty I was my whole life. And then I woke up and that was gone. At least something like toughness can't be taken away so easily."

"You talk as though you're horribly disfigured. It's one scar. With your hair down or in profile, it isn't even visible."

"I know it's there, and that affects the way I think about it. I can't help it. I'm not complaining, it's just my reality now."

"Well, just so you know, I think you're beautiful."

"You just admitted you say that to all the girls."

He was about to reply when his phone rang. He set down his slice of pizza and answered it. "Dance."

"Hey, you and Abby get settled in?" Randall's voice was hearty, audible from where she sat.

"We're fine. What's up?"

"I took that snake by the park rangers' office and let them have a look at it," he said. "One of the guys there is a wildlife biologist. He told me something interesting about it."

"Hang on a minute, I'm going to put you on speaker."

Michael glanced at Abby. "It's Randall. He found out something about your snake."

"It's not my snake." She made a face.

"Okay, go ahead," Michael told Randall.

"The snake you killed was a western diamondback," Randall said. "A common desert species, one responsible for most of the deaths from rattlesnake bites in the United States and Mexico."

Michael's eyes met hers across the table. She hugged her arms around herself, her appetite gone. "Why is that so interesting?" he asked.

"They don't have diamondbacks at this elevation," Randall said. "They don't have them at any elevation in Colorado. The only rattlesnakes around her are prairie rattlers—smaller and not as venomous as the diamondback. Whoever boxed up that fellow imported him from somewhere south or west of here."

Michael frowned. "Could you buy something like that at a pet store—you know, one that sells pythons and tarantulas and stuff?"

"It's against the law to sell venomous snakes. No, somebody caught this one in the wild and was keeping it around for special purposes."

"That's sick," Abby said.

"I heard about a drug dealer in Tucson who kept his stash in an aquarium with a venomous snake," Randall said. "It discouraged theft."

Michael sat back in his chair, legs stretched out in front of him. "So what do you make of this?"

"It tells us something about the people we're after," Randall said.

"Yeah, they're twisted."

"Twisted, and they won't stop at anything to protect what's theirs—or to make a point."

"Yeah, well, thanks for the information. I'll talk to you later."

"I'll let you know if anything new develops."

"Yeah. Do that." He hung up the phone and stuffed it back into the pouch on his utility belt.

"What point are they making with me?" Abby asked.

"You must have gotten way too close to something they want very much to hide," he said. "First the sniper, then the snake."

"What are we going to do about it?" She wasn't going to sit here, waiting to be a target.

"Tomorrow, I want to go back out to where we found the body and look around some more."

"I want to come with you."

He shook his head. "I know I said you could go on patrol with me, but this probably isn't safe."

"I've been in unsafe situations before. I want to go. I want to see if we can help Mariposa and her baby."

He paused, considering.

"You said I was tough," she said. "I won't hold you back or get in the way. And if these people are as dangerous as they seem, you shouldn't be out there alone. I can watch your back."

"All right. If I told you no, you'd probably follow me anyway."

"I probably would."

"At least this way I can keep you close, and maybe a little safer."

She started to protest that she didn't need him to protect her, but the words died in her throat. So far, she had needed him. The idea wasn't as disturbing now as it had been earlier. Maybe leaning on someone for help wasn't so bad—if it was the right someone.

Chapter Seven

Belted into the passenger seat of Michael's Cruiser, Abby couldn't shake the feeling that she was headed out on a mission, just like the missions in Afghanistan. The darkness here was like the darkness over there, deepest black, unsullied by the lights of houses or businesses. The nearest city, Montrose, was a dim glow on the horizon.

She leaned forward, straining against the seat belt, trying to see farther into the blackness. Her heart pounded and her nerves twitched with the same jumpy anticipation that had defined every trip she'd made off base during the war. They'd often left early in the morning, to take advantage of the cover of darkness. But their enemies had favored darkness, too, which had made every expedition fraught with danger.

The Cruiser's headlights cut narrow cones into the blackness, enough to illuminate the scraggly trees, jutting rocks and grasses of the park's backcountry. Once, a pair of silvery eyes looked back at them, and as they drew closer, a coyote stared at them, frozen against a backdrop of reddish rocks.

She shivered and pulled her jacket more tightly

around her. Even in summer, it was chilly at this altitude without the sun's warmth.

"You okay?" Michael asked.

"I'm fine." She slipped her hand into her pocket and rubbed her fingers across the little ceramic rabbit. Maybe it was silly for a grown woman to put faith in a good-luck charm, but the rabbit had gotten her through a lot of tough times since her injury. She wasn't ready to give up on it yet.

Michael leaned forward and switched the Cruiser's heat to high. "Tell me more about the research you're doing," he said. "What happens after you gather all these plants and leave here?"

"I'll take them to the lab and experiment with distilling certain compounds from them, and show the effect of those compounds on cells. For instance, if something inhibits cell mutation, it could help fight cancer, or if a substance encourages nerve cells to regenerate, or nerves to build new pathways, it could combat diseases like Parkinson's. I'll have to narrow my research to a single possibility for now, but the prospects for the future are endless."

"That's exciting, that you could be helping so many people. I'd like to do something like that."

She didn't miss the regret in his voice. "You're protecting people from danger," she said. "Making the park safer for visitors, trying to capture people who are hurting others."

"In theory I'm doing those things," he said. "But so far I haven't seen that anything I've done has directly made anyone's life better."

"Except mine," she said. "I wouldn't be here today if it wasn't for you."

He reached across the seat and took her hand and squeezed it. "Yeah. I'm glad about that."

She held his hand for a moment, letting the warmth and reassurance of his touch seep into her. But she couldn't let sentiment overwhelm common sense. Michael Dance was a good guy, but she scarcely knew him. He wasn't a knight in shining armor, and she definitely wasn't a princess who needed rescuing. She pulled away and focused her gaze out the windshield, on the faint band of gray on the horizon. "The sun will be up soon," she said.

If her sudden coolness caught him off guard, he didn't show it. "Check the GPS," he said. "We should be getting close."

She leaned over to glance at the dash-mounted GPS unit. "Looks like maybe another two miles."

"I'm going to cut the lights," he said. "Just in case anyone's watching." He switched off the headlights, plunging them into a disorienting void. She blinked, then he pressed a button and a dim glow illuminated the few inches of ground in front of the Cruiser's bumper. "Sneak lights," he said. "Mounted under the bumper."

She laughed nervously. "Good name."

The Cruiser crawled across the landscape. They'd left the road and followed what was little more than an animal trail—maybe even the same path Abby had followed when she was searching for specimens for her research.

Suddenly, Michael slammed on the brakes. She lurched forward against the shoulder harness. "What's wrong?" she whispered.

"I saw something out there. Movement." He waited a moment and she squinted, trying to make out anything. Though the eastern sky showed a faint blush of pink, it was impossible to make out details in the dim light. "Over there." He pointed up ahead and to the left. He eased his foot off the brake and angled the Cruiser in that direction, and turned on the headlights again. An animal ran in front of the vehicle, and then another.

"Coyotes," she said, and breathed a sigh of relief.

"They're feeding on something." His expression darkened. "We'd better check it out."

"Why? I mean, it's just a bunch of coyotes."

"They're scavengers. They eat whatever they find. For that many of them to be in one place, it must be something good-size."

Her stomach lurched and she swallowed past the sudden bitter taste in her mouth. "Like a body?"

He stopped the vehicle again and turned to her. "I have to check this out, but you can stay in the truck."

"Do you think it's another illegal, like the man we found day before yesterday?" she asked.

"It may not even be a person." The Cruiser rolled forward again.

"But you think it might be."

"It could be. But maybe not an illegal."

"Who, then?"

"A woman went missing in the park a few days ago. At least, she's missing and they found her car abandoned at one of the overlooks. She's a news anchor from a station in Denver—Lauren Starling."

The name sounded vaguely familiar, but Abby couldn't put a face with it. "What would she be doing way out here?" She looked toward the spot ahead where one lone coyote stood guard, his eyes glittering in the Cruiser's headlights.

"She might have stumbled into something she shouldn't have," he said.

The way Abby herself almost had. "I hope not," she said.

"She also might not be connected to this case at all," Michael said. "Some people see the park as a good place to take their own life."

"Suicide? But why in a park?"

"Maybe they think it will be easier on their families, not having to clean up the mess." He braked again, and the lone coyote trotted off. In the glow of the headlights she could make out a brown shape on the ground. There was definitely something there. Her stomach roiled again, and she gritted her teeth against a wave of nausea.

Michael shifted into Park and unfastened his seat belt. "Stay here," he said.

He didn't have to tell her twice. As soon as he opened the door she caught the scent of decay. Of death. She looked away, out the side window, but felt her gaze pulled back to him as he made his way to the formless shape on the ground. He stepped cautiously, his shoulders tensed, one hand on the weapon at his side.

Then he stopped and relaxed. He crouched down and studied the scene a moment longer, then stood and hurried back to the Cruiser. "It's a deer," he said. "There's not enough left to tell how it died. It could have been poachers, or maybe the coyotes managed to separate one from the herd."

She sagged against the seat, weak with relief. "A deer," she repeated. "I was so afraid…"

"I should have just checked it out and not said anything to upset you." He put the Cruiser into gear and turned back toward the track they'd been following.

"I'd have been more upset if you'd clammed up and refused to tell me anything," she said.

"I figured I could count on you to keep a cool head," he said. "I'm not sure how many other civilians would hold it together as well as you have, considering all that has happened."

Since coming to the park she'd stumbled over a dead body and been shot at by a sniper and threatened with a deadly rattlesnake. "I'm not exactly sleeping like a baby, but I'm okay," she said. "Maybe it's similar to being in battle—you do what you have to do at the time, then fall apart later."

He glanced at her. "I hope you don't fall apart."

"Maybe I'm stronger now." Despite a few flashbacks, she did feel stronger. Maybe the man beside her even had something to do with that.

"Give me the GPS coordinates on this spot." He took a small notebook from his shirt pocket.

She read off the coordinates. "Why do you need them?"

He shrugged. "You never know when someone might want to check this out. Maybe we suddenly have a rash of poaching and we need to document it."

"And to think I always pictured national parks as such peaceful, safe places."

"For most people, they are."

She stared out the windshield, at the expanding glow on the horizon. The gray light allowed her to make out more details in the landscape now—the silhouettes of trees and the distant mountains. "We're only a mile or so from the place where the sniper ambushed us," she said.

"I'm going to cut the lights again," he said. "It's getting light enough to see to drive, and if someone's watching, they'll have a harder time spotting us."

She watched the GPS as they crawled forward again. After a few more minutes, she held up her hand. "This is where I parked to hike into the area where we found the body, and where I saw Mariposa."

"And where the sniper fired at us." He put the Cruiser into four-wheel drive and turned off the faint track. "We'll drive a little farther into the backcountry, then get out and have a look around."

She pulled the zipper of her jacket up higher. "What exactly are we looking for?"

"Anything that looks out of place. They'll probably have used camouflage, but a building is tough to conceal. Look for a grouping of trees or rocks that stand out from the rest. Or they could set up a compound in a gully or canyon, where it's harder to detect." He tapped the console between them. "In here is a topo map. I highlighted some places they might try to conceal an operation. There's a Mini Maglite in there, too."

She found the map and light and when he stopped the vehicle she spread the heavy plastic-coated map between them. Yellow highlighter circled a box canyon, a dry wash and a small woodland. She studied the lines indicating elevation. "This wash is closest," she said, pointing to the area he'd circled. "And there's a seasonal creek nearby. This time of year, it will still have water from snowmelt. If I was going to set up a compound out here, that's what I'd choose."

"Let's give it a look, then."

She read out the GPS coordinates, and he turned the Cruiser toward them. "What do we do if we find something?" she asked.

"We call for backup. There's no sense going in alone when we don't even know how many people we're up against. This morning, we're just out sightseeing."

"I'm glad to hear it."

"But you were prepared to go in with just me?" He glanced at her, though she couldn't read his expression in the shadowed interior of the vehicle.

"I guess I trust your judgment," she said. "Is that a mistake?" After all, he didn't strike her as reckless. And he'd saved her life before—she couldn't imagine he'd be eager to throw it away now.

"You can trust me," he said. "Just like I trust you."

"Trust me how?"

"If we do get in a tight spot, I trust you to have my back."

"Of course." The words were casual, but the feeling in her chest was anything but lighthearted. Even the soldiers she'd worked with in Afghanistan weren't all so willing to rely on a woman for help. Michael's high opinion of her meant more than she was ready to say.

"What's that?" He hit the brake and leaned forward, gripping the steering wheel.

"What's what?" She saw nothing in the grayness ahead.

"I thought I saw a light." He switched off the sneak lights and the interior instrument lights. She stared out the windshield at a landscape of gray smudges, backlit by the first rays of the rising sun to their left. But she didn't see the light that had made him stop.

Michael opened the car door. "We better go in on foot," he said. "Stay close to me."

She slipped on her backpack and put one hand to the reassuring heft of the gun at her side. She was back on patrol again, minus the heavier pack and body armor. Even after so much time, the absence of that familiar weight made her feel vulnerable. Exposed.

She shut the door of the Cruiser without making a sound. But there was no way to move across the rugged ground without the occasional scrape of a shoe on rock, or the snapping of a twig that sounded as loud as a slamming door to her ears. Every sense felt heightened—sounds louder, sights clearer, the dawn breeze on her cheeks and the backs of her hands colder. She sniffed the air and grabbed Michael's arm. "Stop."

He halted. "What is it?"

"Do you smell that?"

He inhaled sharply through his nose. "Wood smoke."

"A campfire," she whispered. "I think we're getting very close."

"Which direction do you think it's coming from?"

She considered the question, then pointed ahead and to the right. "Over there."

They moved forward silently, slowly. The sky changed from gray to dusky pink to pale blue. The smell of wood smoke grew stronger, too, and with it came the scent of food—corn, maybe, or baking bread. Soon they were close enough to hear muffled voices, and the scrape of cutlery and clink of glassware.

Michael dropped to his belly and indicated she should do the same. They crawled on their stomachs, dragging themselves forward on elbows. She winced as a sharp rock dug into her forearm. At least here they didn't have to worry about land mines. Probably. She wished she hadn't thought of mines. Someone who'd employ a sniper, and maybe had access to a ghillie suit and military-grade weapons, might decide to use land mines, too.

She started to suggest as much to Michael when they moved around a clump of bushes and suddenly the whole camp was laid out in front of them, tucked into a wash, the depression deep enough so that the surrounding stunted piñons provided cover. Whoever had built the compound had piled brush between the trees to act as a privacy fence. They'd even pulled camouflage netting over the tops of the buildings, making the compound more difficult to detect from the air.

The camp itself wasn't impressive—four old camping trailers in a semicircle around a campfire ring and three warped wooden picnic tables. A brown tarp stretched between poles formed a crude shelter over the tables, where a dozen men and women sat, eating a breakfast of tortillas and beans.

A woman worked at the fire, baking more tortillas on a piece of tin balanced over the coals. When she turned to deliver a fresh batch of the flatbreads to another woman, Abby pinched Michael's arm. "That's Mariposa," she said. She wore the same plaid shawl she'd had on the other day, the baby wrapped securely in its folds.

Michael rose to squat on his heels and indicated they should leave. Reluctantly, she turned to go. She would have liked to talk to Mariposa again, to make sure she was all right. But staying here wasn't safe.

But as they prepared to emerge from the screen of bushes into more open ground, headlights suddenly cut through the darkness. Michael jerked her back into the underbrush and they crouched there, breathing hard and watching a truck make its way toward them.

The truck was bigger than a pickup, with a canvas-covered bed, similar to ones sometimes used by the military to transport troops. It lumbered into camp and stopped not far from the picnic tables. Abby and Michael crept to the edge of the brush once more and watched as two men, carrying semiautomatic rifles, climbed out and spoke to the men and women around the table in Spanish. But they were too far away to make out exactly what they were saying.

Suddenly, the camp sprang to life. The two men with rifles began directing the others to load the picnic tables into the back of the truck. A second truck arrived, and then a third. One man, who wore a white shirt and white straw cowboy hat, and who seemed to be in charge, picked up a bucket and thrust it at Mariposa. She spoke to him, clearly agitated, but he shoved the bucket into her hand and gave her a push. She turned and started walked toward the edge of the compound.

"He told her to get some water and put out the fire," Michael whispered. "They're ordering everyone to load the trucks and prepare to leave."

"I'm going around to the creek to see if I can talk to her and find out more."

Before he could stop her, she was on her feet, headed for the little creek that gurgled a few dozen yards from the camp. She moved cautiously, keeping the screen of brush between her and the activity in the camp. By the time she reached the water, Mariposa was already there, squatting on the bank and dipping the bucket in the shallows.

"Mariposa!" Abby called softly.

The woman looked up, startled. She dropped the bucket and it rolled away, under some bushes.

"Don't run. It's me." Abby moved closer, so the other woman could see her clearly.

Mariposa's expression changed to one of alarm. She spoke softly in rapid Spanish. The only word Abby could make out was *peligroso*—dangerous.

"I want to help you." Why couldn't Abby remember the word for help? She slipped off her pack and started looking for her phone. If she could get a signal out here, she could use a translator on the web to get her message across.

The shouting from camp grew louder. Mariposa glanced over her shoulder, then stood, the bucket abandoned in the creek.

Abby gave up the search for her phone. She dropped the pack and stood, also. "Come with me." She held out her hand. "I can help you."

Mariposa shook her head and started to back away. "No," she said—a word whose meaning was the same in Spanish and English.

"Por favor," Abby said. "Please."

Mariposa looked back toward camp. The shouting sounded closer now. She clutched the baby to her, and Abby was sure she was about to turn and run.

But instead, she untied the shawl and thrust it—and the baby—into Abby's arms. Then she whirled and fled, back toward camp.

Abby stared, stunned, the unfamiliar weight and warmth of the infant in her hands. The child stirred and whimpered, and Abby felt a primal response, a fierce desire to keep this tiny, helpless life safe. She cradled the child to her chest and turned to go back to Michael.

She collided with him just as she turned. For a second they were frozen, his arms steadying her, the baby cradled between them. She fought the instinct to lean into him, to draw strength and comfort from his solid presence. "What happened?" he asked.

"I saw Mariposa. I talked to her. But we couldn't understand each other. I don't know enough Spanish and she doesn't speak English. I think she told me it was dangerous for me to be here."

"She's right. We have to get out of here. They brought another truck in and they're breaking down the camp. We have to get back to the Cruiser and radio for help." He looked down at the bundle in her arms. "What is that?"

"This is Mariposa's baby." She folded back the shawl to reveal the infant's face. The child stared up at them with solemn brown eyes. "Angelique. Mariposa handed her to me, then she ran away. I think she wanted me to keep her safe."

"Come on, we've got to go." He put his arm around her and urged her forward.

They only traveled a few yards before they spotted the line of men and trucks in between them and the Cruiser. Michael swore under his breath. "We'd better risk a call for backup," he said. Huddled in the meager cover at the edge of the woods, he took out first his radio, then his cell. He swore under his breath. "The radio doesn't work this far out, and my phone can't get a signal," he said. "Try yours."

Abby felt sick to her stomach. "My phone is in my

pack, back there by the stream. I was so busy with the baby…"

"I'll get it." He started toward the creek once more, but just then a man stepped out in front of him and leveled a rifle at them. He wore a white shirt, a white hat and a menacing expression.

"You're in the wrong place, amigo," he said.

Chapter Eight

"Abby, run!" Michael shouted.

The last thing she wanted to do was abandon him to the man with the gun, but instinct compelled her to protect the child in her arms. Propelled by the urgency in Michael's voice, she turned and fled, running hunched over to shield the baby, darting and weaving, waiting for the gunshots she was sure would follow. She had no idea where she was headed, but every instinct told her she had to put as much distance as possible between herself and the camp. She could hide in the underbrush and wait until her pursuers were gone.

As for Michael, she prayed he'd find some way to escape. If she could think of any way to come back and help him without endangering the baby, she would.

She stumbled over rocks and brush, her lungs burning. The baby never made a sound. In her short life was she already so familiar with fear and flight? She ran until she was gasping for breath, fighting a painful stitch in her side. The infant was heavier than she looked. Abby stumbled and feared she might drop the child. She'd have to stop and rest for a moment. She needed to get her bearings and figure out her next move.

She huddled behind a pile of rocks, letting her breathing return to normal and her pounding heart slow its frantic racing. The rocks still held the chill of the evening, and she pressed her back against a boulder, letting the coolness seep into her and dry her sweat. She strained to hear any hint of approaching danger. She hadn't heard any gunshots from the camp, but would she have even noticed in her panic to escape?

She peered out from behind the rocks. No one appeared to be coming after her. She couldn't even make out the camp from this distance, but she could see the trucks on the edge of the wash and the bustle of activity around them. If only she had a pair of binoculars.

She needed to get to the truck. Michael probably had supplies and tools in there, maybe even a spare radio. If she could figure out how to start the vehicle, she could drive back to park headquarters and summon help.

She tried to orient herself. The rising sun had been on their left when they'd parked, and they'd walked straight ahead—south. She squinted in the direction she thought the Cruiser should be, but saw nothing. Michael had made a point of parking amid a grove of trees. She'd just have to set out walking in that direction and hope her instincts were right.

Cautiously, she moved out of her hiding place. Now that the sun was fully up, she felt exposed and more vulnerable than ever. But she'd seen no signs of pursuit. And no signs of Michael. Had the man in the white hat shot him and left his body beside the creek?

She pushed the thought away. She had to focus on Angelique now. She folded back the blanket and studied the child, who stared up at her with solemn brown eyes. She stroked the baby's soft cheek with her little finger and Angelique grasped it, holding on tightly. A wave of emotion rose up from deep inside Abby—a fierce protectiveness, longing and love. She would do whatever she had to in order to keep this child safe.

Keeping to the shelter of rocks and trees, she started moving north, on a trajectory she hoped would take her to the parked Cruiser but be well out of the way of the men at the camp. Every few yards she looked back toward the camp, but no one sounded an alarm that they had noticed her.

When she was confident she was well out of sight and sound of the camp, she increased her pace to a ragged trot over the rough ground. With the sun up it was getting warmer, and she wished she'd had some way to collect water back at the creek. If she didn't find the truck, she and Angelique were going to be in trouble.

She stopped to rest a moment and look around. Still no sign of the truck. She should have reached it by now. She couldn't see the camp, either, which made her uneasy. She wanted to be away from it, but she didn't want to accidentally stumble back onto it. She'd read that people who wandered off marked trails in the wilderness tended to walk in circles. Without a map or compass to guide her, she might be doing the same.

A movement somewhere to her right made her freeze. Slowly, she turned her head. Yes, there it was again, a subtle shifting of the brush. A shadow where a shadow shouldn't be. She wrapped her hand around the grip of the Sig Sauer and worked on controlling her breathing. A deep breath in…let it out slowly. She wouldn't shoot unless she had to, but if whoever was out there came too close… She clutched the baby tightly and slid the gun from the holster.

"Abby! Abby, it's me!"

She leaned forward and stared at the man loping toward her. Michael covered the distance quickly, with no sign of injury. She took a few steps toward him, only her grip on the pistol and the baby in her arms keeping her from greeting him with a hug. "How did you get away?" she asked when he stopped beside her.

He bent over, a rifle clutched in both hands, gasping for breath. A moment passed before he could speak, and in that moment she searched for any sign of injury, but he seemed whole and healthy.

He straightened. "When I shouted at you, it distracted the guy enough I was able to kick the gun out of his hands. We struggled for a bit, but I got away."

She nodded to the weapon he was holding. "With the gun."

He hefted the weapon. "He's probably not very happy about that, but I didn't give him any choice."

She glanced over his shoulder at the empty desert. "Are they coming after us?"

"I don't think so," he said. "Not right now anyway. They seemed pretty anxious to clear out." He nodded to the bundle in her arms. "How's the baby?"

"Good. She's very quiet. I'm not sure if that's a good thing or not." She adjusted the blanket to shield Angelique from the sun. "I was trying to get back to the Cruiser," she said.

"Good idea. But first, I want to get a closer look at their trucks before they leave." He turned back toward the camp.

"Wait." She grabbed his arm. "You can't go back there."

"I want to get pictures before they leave—of the

trucks and the people." He pulled his phone from his utility belt. "I can't get a signal, but the camera still works."

"It's too dangerous," she said.

"They won't expect me to come back. You can wait here with the baby."

"No, I'm coming with you." The two of them together, both armed, seemed a better idea than splitting up and forming separate targets. He might think no one was after them, but how could he be sure?

He didn't argue. "We'll follow the creek back to the camp," he said. "The trees will provide cover. We'll keep low and out of sight and just watch and take photographs."

"All right." She didn't like the plan, but she liked being left alone out there less.

They intersected with the creek farther up the wash and followed it down toward the camp. Soon, the slamming of vehicle doors and murmur of voices in Spanish filled the air. Michael stopped about a hundred yards from all the activity and crouched down. She huddled behind him, peering over his shoulder.

The men with guns stood guard as the other men and women filed into the trailers. Abby counted six people filing into one of the campers, which was smaller even than the one she'd rented for the summer. When all the people were inside, the guard reached up and locked the door, then pocketed the key.

"What are they doing?" she whispered, her lips against Michael's ear.

"I think the trucks are going to tow the trailers out of here."

Before he had even finished speaking, one of the

trucks had backed up to the trailer and begun the process of hooking on to the camper. Michael pulled out his camera and snapped picture after picture. Abby searched the camp for any sign of Mariposa, but couldn't find her. Was she already locked into one of the crowded trailers?

The man in the white shirt and hat who'd confronted them by the creek stood to one side. He'd found another rifle and held it across his chest, barking orders at the others. Within a quarter of an hour, the camp was clear. The man in the white shirt surveyed the area and seemed satisfied. He climbed into the vehicle at the front of the line and the trucks—four of them now, each with a trailer in tow—pulled away from the campsite. Two set out toward the main road, while the other two started cross-country.

When the vehicles were too far away for anyone to see them, Michael crawled out of their hiding place and stood to get a better look. "Where are they going?" Abby asked.

"There are a lot of old ranch roads and two-tracks cutting across this property. They're probably taking a roundabout way to the highway. My guess is the other two will turn off at some point, too. They won't want to risk being seen on the main park road by one of the park rangers or one of our team."

"What do we do now?" she asked.

"I'd like to get some people out here to comb this place for evidence."

"Are they going to find anything?" Except for an area bare of vegetation where the fire and picnic tables had been, there was little sign of the compound that had been here only an hour before. Even the rocks that had been used to make the fire ring had been cleaned and scattered, the footprints of those who had been here smoothed over with a branch of juniper.

"You never know." He stared at his phone. "Still no signal."

"Maybe mine will work," she said. "Now that they're gone, I can retrieve my pack."

"Good idea. Where is it?"

"Back this way." She led the way along the creek to the spot where she'd talked to Mariposa. She scanned the creek bank. "I don't see it," she said. "I could have sworn it was right in here."

"It was blue, right?"

She nodded. "Bright blue. It shouldn't be hard to spot." She walked along the bank, looking into the water and underbrush, even though she knew she had dropped it in the open. He searched, also.

"One of them must have seen it and taken it," he said. "What was in there besides your phone and the GPS?"

"Water, food, a first-aid kit. A space blanket, another pair of socks, a whistle, compass and fire starter." She ticked off the items in a standard backcountry emergency list—all things they could have used right now.

"They didn't leave anything behind," he said, looking around.

"Except this." She reached under a bush and started to pull out the metal bucket Mariposa had carried to the creek. "Though I don't see what good it's going to do us."

"Don't touch it." His hand on her arm stopped her and he moved up beside her. "We might get good prints off it that could help us identify some of the people involved."

"What should we do with it?" She stepped back.

"Leave it here. We'll want to get a team in here to go over the place—they can pick it up then." He tied his bandanna to a nearby tree branch to mark the spot.

"We just have to find our way back to headquarters," she said. "And find our way here again after that."

He straightened and looked around them, as if studying the terrain—the low hills and more distant mountains. "Which way is the canyon from here?" he asked. "Black Canyon." If they could find the canyon, they'd find the road that led to the headquarters.

"I don't know." She turned slowly in a circle, looking around them. "That's the thing about this place. The canyon isn't something you see from ground level. You have to be right up on it before you know it's there."

"What do we do now?" she asked.

"We can try to find the truck."

Her expression lightened. "I do know which direction the truck was in. All we have to do is walk right through there." She pointed to a cut in the fringe of trees along the edge of the wash, then set off at a brisk pace, Michael close behind her.

After twenty minutes of walking and backtracking, they didn't find the Cruiser. But they did find the tracks where it had been parked, and the tracks of the other vehicles that had passed. "What happened?" she asked.

"They stole it," he said. "Trucks don't just vanish, so one of them must be driving it."

"If they found the truck, they must know we're still out here," she said.

He nodded, his expression grim. "They'll probably send someone back to find us. We need to get out of here before that happens." He pulled out his phone and tried it, but it continued to show no signal. "We need higher ground." He looked around and spotted a low hill. "Up there."

She cradled Angelique in her arms as she climbed up the hill, praying that someone didn't have her in the sights of a rifle's scope as she climbed. She felt too exposed up here on the side of this hill. Anyone who looked in this direction would be able to spot them. She picked up her pace, anxious to find cover once more.

At the top of the rise, she ducked behind a low piñon and struggled to catch her breath. Michael stood a little ways from her, holding up his phone. "I think this is going to work," he said. "I'm getting a signal." He started walking backward, watching the screen, the phone in one hand, the radio in the other. "Almost there."

And then he was gone, dropping over the edge, a cascade of falling rocks and a single startled cry the only indication he had ever been there.

Chapter Nine

Michael scrabbled for a hold on the crumbling shale that continued to give way beneath his feet and slip from his hands. He dropped the phone and the radio—the radio somersaulting into the air and out of sight, the phone bouncing like a thrown rock as it, too, disappeared into the canyon. He kicked out his feet and found only air, and an image of his body, broken and bleeding, at the bottom of the gully flashed through his mind.

Frantic, he hurled himself toward a ragged piñon that jutted from the canyon wall. His fingers grasped the prickly needles, and he swung his other hand up to grip a branch. The tree bent and creaked, but held.

He hung there for a long moment, struggling to breathe and to slow the pounding of his heart. He found a toehold for one foot in the rock below and supported his weight partially on one leg, with the other resting uncomfortably against the slick, steep canyon wall.

He'd fallen about ten feet, though it had seemed farther. His instinct was to shout for help, but he checked it. All of the men from the camp might not have left in the trucks. He didn't know who was up there, looking for him.

And looking for Abby and the baby. He had to keep quiet for their sake.

Just then, Abby's face appeared above him. She was kneeling at the edge of the drainage into which he'd fallen, looking down at him, her forehead creased in a worried frown. "What happened?" she asked, her voice carrying to him in the clear air, though she didn't shout.

"I must have slipped. Stupid move." He should have known to be more careful on this unpredictable terrain, but it was too late to berate himself now.

"Can you climb up?"

He considered the almost vertical wall above him, lined with brittle shale and slick mud. Here and there tufts of grasses or wildflowers clung to the side—feeble handholds for a man who weighed one-eighty. "I don't suppose you have a rope," he said.

"Sorry. I'm fresh out."

"Yeah, I thought so." Already his arms were beginning to feel as if they'd pull out of their sockets. He couldn't hang here much longer. "What's happening up there?" he asked.

"Angelique is fussy—I think she's hungry. I've got her here beside me."

Of course her first concern was for the child. "No sign of the bad guys?"

"No sign of them. What can I do to help?"

"Maybe say a prayer." He focused on a clump of grass three feet overhead. "What do you know about native grasses?" he asked.

"Um, a lot, actually. What do you want to know?"

"Do they have very deep roots?"

"It depends. Some of them have very deep roots. That helps them find scarce water, and also prevents erosion."

And maybe they'd save his life. He took a deep breath, stretched up and took hold of the clump of grass. He lost his toehold and scrabbled for a new one, plastered against the side of the canyon, cool mud against his cheek, the scent of wet earth and sage filling his nostrils.

He clawed at the canyon wall and dug in with fingers, knees, toes—anything to keep from falling. Agonizing inch by agonizing inch, he crept toward the top, muscles screaming, mind fighting panic. Whenever he dared look up, he saw Abby's face, pale against the dark juniper and deep blue sky. Her eyes never left him, the tip of her thumb clenched between her teeth.

Having her there helped some. She gave him a goal to reach, a bigger reason to hang on. She and that baby depended on him to get them out of here safely. Giving up wasn't an option.

The climb to the top seemed to take an eternity, though in reality probably only fifteen minutes or so passed. When he dragged himself over the edge at last, he lay facedown on the ground, spent and aching.

Abby rested her hand on his back, a gentle weight grounding him to the earth and to her. "Are you all right?" she asked.

He pushed up onto his elbows. "Do we have any water?"

"No."

Of course they didn't. They also didn't have a phone or radio or GPS. They had two guns, the energy bar he'd stashed in his jacket, the hard candies he always carried and whatever Abby was carrying in her pockets. They also had a baby, who was going to get hungry sooner rather than later, and no idea where they were.

He sat up and pulled out his bandanna to wipe as much mud as he could from his face and hands. The baby began to whimper and Abby gathered it into her arms and rocked it. He studied her, head bent low over the fussy child, her blond hair falling forward to obscure half her face. She reminded him of a Madonna—a particularly beautiful one.

The memory of the way she'd touched him just now lingered, but he pushed it aside. He had to focus on how they were going to find their way back to headquarters. "Do you know where we are?" he asked.

She jerked her head up. "Don't you?"

He fought the instinct to play the macho man and lie to her, but lies like that only led to trouble. He shook his head. "We arrived in the dark, so I couldn't orient by landmarks. I made the mistake of relying on GPS." He looked around them, hoping to recognize some familiar rock outcropping or group of trees.

She moved up behind him to look over his shoulder. He became aware of her body pressed to his, her warmth seeping into him. "What do we do now?" Her breath tickled the hair at the back of his neck, sending heat sliding through him.

"I'm open to suggestions."

Abby cradled the child to her shoulder and rocked her gently. "We've got to get food for the baby," she said. "And water."

"The creek has water. I can't say how safe it is to drink, but it's a start." His own mouth felt as if he'd been chewing sawdust. He couldn't let dehydration cloud his judgment.

"So we'll walk back to the creek and get water," she said. "Then what?"

"Then I think we'd better sit down to wait."

"Wait for what?"

"For the Rangers to find us—or for whoever is in charge of the camp to return."

"Do you really think they'll come back?"

"They know we're still out here. Without a vehicle, we can't go too far. If they know we have the baby, they'll realize that will slow us down, even if we had a destination in mind. So yeah, I think they'll come back. We're a problem they won't let rest until they take care of it. The trick will be for us to take care of them first." He reached back and took her hand. "Come on."

ABBY'S FEET DRAGGED as she followed Michael back toward the creek and the deserted encampment. She hadn't slept well last night—the vision of the rattlesnake, alive and ready to strike, imprinted on the insides of her eyelids every time she closed them. Up at four this morning, then the tension and adrenaline rush of the events of the day, plus the ground they'd covered on their hikes around the area, had all taken their toll. She was exhausted, and the baby in her arms felt like a twenty-pound bowling ball.

But she could do nothing but keep moving. Going back to wait for the people who wanted them dead seemed foolhardy at best, suicidal even. But the move also made sense. Every survival manual she'd ever read stressed staying in one location if you were lost. Wandering aimlessly complicated the search for you and wasted precious energy. At least by the camp they'd have water, which they all needed, but Angelique, especially, had to have.

Michael looked back over his shoulder. "How are you doing?" he asked.

"I'm hanging in there."

"And the baby?"

"She seems to like the movement." She smiled down at the infant, who had fallen asleep. "She must have spent a lot of time moving around with her mother."

"It looked as if Mariposa was in charge of the cooking today. She probably spent a lot of time on her feet, gathering water, cleaning up and cooking the meals."

"What did the other people, the ones we saw eating, do?"

"They probably worked tending a crop of marijuana, or making meth, though I didn't see any signs of production around the trailer, and I didn't smell anything off. So probably marijuana."

"Are they here voluntarily?"

"Probably not. They may have crossed the border looking for work, but once they arrived here, they were prisoners."

"So they're slaves?"

"Pretty much, yeah."

"It…it's like something out of another century. Not something that should happen today in the United States."

"It happens more than people imagine—probably more than the statistics say, though the Justice Department estimates that more than seventeen thousand people a year are brought into the United States for trafficking purposes. They're forced to work in factories or on farms, and as household help. More than eighty percent of trafficking victims are sex slaves. Many of them are immigrants, though young Americans, runaways and homeless teens get caught up in trafficking, too."

"That's appalling."

"It is." He looked toward the now-deserted camp. "If these people are involved in that kind of thing, I want to stop them."

"I want to stop them, too," Abby said. "But we also need to get Angelique to a safe place. She's going to need to eat soon, and she'll need diapers." So many things they didn't have here in the middle of nowhere. Worry settled like a brick in her stomach. "How long do you think it will be before your team realizes we're missing?"

He glanced up at the sky, the color of purest turquoise. "They'll expect me to check in in a few hours, at the latest."

And it would probably be hours after that before anyone became really concerned, she thought. After all, their plan had been to spend the day in the backcountry, where it wasn't unusual to be without cell phone and radio signals. She shifted the baby to her other shoulder. They needed to find a place to settle and wait.

They had to cross a hundred yards of open prairie to reach the first cover that led along the edge of the wash to the creek. The wash itself began as a depression in the landscape, then gradually deepened and widened into the side drainage where Michael had fallen. That mini canyon was only about thirty feet deep—compared to the Black Canyon that gave the park its name, which plunged more than two thousand seven hundred feet at its deepest point.

Michael drew his gun. At least he hadn't lost it in the fall. "How do you feel about making a run for it?"

he asked. "Just in case someone is out there looking for us?"

"Do you really think they left someone behind to search for us?" she asked.

"I don't know. But we shouldn't take chances."

She nodded. "What do you want me to do?"

"Run as fast as you can to that clump of trees over there." He indicated a grouping of scrub oak. "I'll cover you. Then you can do the same for me."

She studied the expanse of ground, with its scant vegetation and rocky surface. "All right." Then she took off, cradling the infant to her, her feet raising little puffs of dust as she zigzagged her way across the ground. Within seconds, she'd reached the safety of the rocks; no one had fired.

He waited until she removed the Sig Sauer from the holster at her right hip and nodded in his direction. His darted out into the open, running hard, pumping his arms and legs, taking long strides, covering the ground as rapidly as possible. Then he threw himself on the ground beside her, too winded to speak.

"You looked good," she said. "Did you ever run track?"

He nodded. "In high school." He wiped his mouth. "A long time ago."

"I never liked running," she said. "Those drills were the worst part of basic training for me."

"I'm still trying to picture a beauty queen in boot camp."

She made a face. "I didn't tell anyone I was a beauty queen. If anything, I tried to make myself as plain as possible—no makeup, hair scraped back into a ponytail."

"I'll bet it didn't work," he said. "No one—no man,

for certain—would ever mistake you for homely." He stood and offered a hand to help her up. "You ready?"

"Ready." She stood, but didn't let go of his hand right away. When their eyes met, she offered a shy smile before turning away and moving toward the creek.

At the creek bank, Michael knelt to drink. Abby wandered along the bank, searching the ground.

He looked up, the cuffs of his sleeves and the front of his shirt damp from the creek water. "What are you looking for?"

"This." She held up a nearly new tin can she'd plucked from beneath a tree. She'd spotted the label earlier and it had vaguely registered as just another piece of garbage—a can that had once held corn and been discarded. "We can make a fire and boil water for Angelique," she explained. "You and I can deal with an upset stomach from anything that might be in that water, but a baby could die from the wrong bacteria."

"Good idea." He stood and pointed up the creek bank. "Let's move to that rock outcropping there. We'll be sheltered a little from the sun and wind, and we'll have a good view of anyone approaching the camp from this direction."

He led the way to a spot beneath a lone piñon that seemed to grow straight out of the surrounding rock. The stunted tree leaned crazily to one side, its branches spread like open arms, casting a pool of shade on the red granite. Michael began gathering pine needles and bark for tinder. "I had fire starters and matches in my pack," she said.

"See if you can find some broken glass around the camp. Otherwise, I can make a fire drill out of two sticks. It takes forever, but it does work."

She returned to the creek to wash out the can and fill it with water. She got a drink for herself and studied the plants that grew in or near the water. Ten minutes later, she returned to camp, feeling triumphant.

"What are you grinning about?" Michael asked.

"I found a good piece of glass." She held up what looked like the bottom of a jar. "And I found these." She opened the sling and began laying out the plants she'd gathered.

He took the glass and studied the plants. "What is all that?"

"Wild lettuce, cress and mustard. Wild onion. A few piñon nuts." She pointed to the various plants. "We can have a salad for lunch."

"If you say so."

"I'll see to the baby first, then I'll prepare some of this for us."

Using the piece of glass to focus sunlight on the tinder, Michael soon had a fire going. He fed the small blaze with more tinder, then twigs, and finally dead wood he'd salvaged from around the camp. Abby balanced the can of water on three rocks in the center of the blaze. When the liquid was boiling, she used the sleeve of her jacket like a potholder to remove it from the heat. "You still have Life Savers with you, don't you?" she asked.

"Sure." He fished the roll from his pocket.

"Let me have a couple."

He handed over the candies and she dropped them in the hot water. "They'll make a kind of sugar water for the baby."

"Clever," Michael said.

"The sugar will give her a little energy," Abby said.

"And the sweet taste might make her more willing to drink." While the water cooled, she set about stripping the stems from leaves and cleaning dirt from roots she collected.

Michael moved closer. "Is all that really edible?" he asked.

"Sure. All our native salad greens started out as wild plants. People think of this as a desert, but there are really a lot of edible plants here, if you know what to look for."

"What can I do to help?" he asked.

He'd already been a big help, keeping her calm and starting the fire. His steady, capable presence reassured her. "Just keep me company while I work. Were you a Boy Scout when you were little?"

"I was. And my family went camping a lot. Every other weekend in the summer, we'd pack the car with a tent and sleeping bags and a cooler and head to the national forest. We'd hike and fish and roast marshmallows around a campfire."

"And you liked that?"

"Are you kidding? For two days, my sister and I had our parents all to ourselves. We ran around outside, ate hot dogs and hamburgers, and no one cared how dirty we got. It was great." He smiled, remembering. "Those trips made me love being outdoors. They're probably why I was attracted to this job."

"You weren't worried you'd end up in an office, reviewing paperwork?"

"There's paperwork in every job, but from the first I applied for positions that allowed me to be out and on my own more. If it weren't for the crime and the bad guys, this would be the ideal job. What about you? Were you a Girl Scout?"

She shook her head. "Oh, no. My mother would not have spent the night outdoors unless forced to do so at gunpoint. I spent my weekends at dance recitals and beauty parlors and pageant practice."

"Boot camp must have been a big culture shock."

"It was and it wasn't." She tested the water in the can. Still a little too warm. "When I was in high school, I joined the school hiking club. It introduced me to a whole new group of kids—kids who liked to camp and hike and spend time outdoors."

"And they accepted you?"

"They were suspicious at first, but after I proved myself, they saw me as one of them. I discovered how much I liked spending time in the woods. A couple of my friends in the club went into the military right out of high school. Later, when I was searching for something to do with my life, I remembered them and thought, 'Why not?'"

She settled back against the trunk of the tree and unfastened the sling, using it as a blanket to swaddle the baby. Angelique fussed and began to cry. "I know, sweetheart. You're probably hungry." She dipped her finger in the can and brought it to the baby's lips. "Let's see if you'll take some of this for me."

The little mouth latched on to her finger and Abby felt a pull deep within her womb. She dribbled more water into the infant's mouth.

"I think she likes it." Michael had moved closer and watched the two of them with his usual intensity.

"At least it will keep her hydrated," she said. "But I hope someone comes for us soon."

"We might have to spend the night out here, but tomorrow, I know someone will come for us," he said.

The idea of a night without shelter, blankets or formula didn't thrill her, but whining about it wouldn't change anything. For now, Angelique seemed content, and that was all that mattered.

"Why do you think Mariposa gave her to you?"

She'd had plenty of time to ponder the answer to that question. "The only reason I can imagine a mother would give up her baby was because she thought Angelique would be safer with me." And Mariposa must have been desperate, to hand her child over to a stranger.

"Why didn't she give the baby to you the first day you two met?"

"Maybe she's learned some new information since then that made her fear for her safety—or the baby's safety."

"Maybe breaking up camp today didn't have anything to do with us finding that dead man," he said. "Maybe something else is up."

"Like what?"

"I don't know. But if she thought the baby was going to be in danger, she would have tried to protect her."

Anger at the thought of anyone trying to hurt this baby pushed away some of her weariness. "I want to find whoever's responsible and make sure they're punished," she said.

"I want to find them, too." He pulled out his phone and clicked over to the photos he'd taken earlier.

"Did you get anything useful?" she asked.

He squinted at the photos of the trucks lined up, ready to leave. "I can't make out the license plates," he said. "I think they've splattered them with mud."

"Who was the man you fought with?" she asked. "Do you have any idea?"

He shook his head. "Mariposa called him El Jefe—the chief. My guess is he's the boss, at least on this level."

"So there's probably someone else supervising operations above him?" she asked.

"Probably. Someone who doesn't get his hands dirty by dealing with people directly. He probably ordered them to move camp, now that we've gotten so close."

"Why didn't they leave yesterday, after the sniper fired at us?" she asked.

"I don't know. Maybe they had to get permission from someone higher up the chain of command. Or maybe they had to wait for the trucks to arrive from somewhere else."

"Yet they still had time to gift wrap a rattlesnake for me."

"If the two incidents are related. We don't know that for sure."

She leaned back against a tree trunk, the baby cradled to her shoulder. "I promise you, no one else hates me enough to send me a deadly snake."

"No jilted lovers or brokenhearted ex-boyfriends?" He kept his tone teasing, but she sensed a tension in the air as he waited for her answer.

"Not a one. I haven't been in any kind of relationship since before I joined the army. And none of them were serious. And please don't insult me with clichés like 'a pretty woman like you' or 'having so much to offer.' I get enough of that from my parents. I've been too busy—first with rehab, now with school—to worry about relationships."

"I wasn't going to say anything."

She shifted toward him. "What about you? Do you have a woman waiting for you back home—wherever home is?" Now it was her turn to hold her breath, waiting for his reply. She didn't like to admit how much his answer mattered to her.

"No. I didn't date a lot, though I always had women friends. The last long-term relationship I had, several years ago, she broke it off because she said I was too intense. I wasn't even sure what she meant."

Yes, he could be intense, a trait that both drew her to him and made her wary. "I think you're the kind of man who, when you do something, you don't give a half measure. You put everything you have into it, whether it's a job or a relationship. If someone else isn't ready for that level of commitment, that can feel too intense. It can be scary."

"Are you scared of me?"

She didn't look away from him, her gaze steady. He'd been honest with her; now it was her turn. "I'm not scared of you, Michael. But fear doesn't always— or even usually—come from other people. More often, we're scared of something inside ourselves. Of our own beliefs or emotions."

"I'm glad you're not afraid of me," he said. "I've got your back, remember?"

A hint of a smile curved her lips. "Yeah. I remember."

Chapter Ten

Michael kept his eyes locked to Abby's, willing her not to look away. What was she scared of inside herself, and how could he help her let go of that fear? But he got the impression if he tried to get that personal, she'd just pull back. As with the fall of hair that kept hiding her scar, Abby liked to keep layers between her and other people.

The baby started fussing, breaking the spell between them. Abby turned away and he sat back, stifling a sigh of frustration.

"I need your bandanna," she said. "The baby's diaper is soaked."

He handed it over, and she folded it into a makeshift diaper and handed him the soaked one. "Wash this out—downstream."

He made a face, but moved off to do as she asked. Washing dirty diapers wasn't on the list of things he had expected to do in this job, but there was something calming and grounding about the mundane, domestic chore. Yes, he was lost in the wilderness with the possibility that a killer was searching for them, but his duty was crystal clear—to protect this woman and this baby and somehow return them to safety.

The man in charge of this camp would be back.

Everything in the man's attitude and posture told Michael he wasn't one to overlook a threat. He'd been outsmarting the Rangers for weeks. The urgency of moving his people might have forced him to delay the hunt momentarily, but he wasn't going to let two people who had discovered his secret get away. When he'd stolen Michael's Cruiser he'd left the couple stranded, so he could be confident they were still close by. As long as Michael saw the man before he spotted them, they'd be safe. He'd make sure of it.

He had Abby to help, too. Thanks to her, they wouldn't starve. Roots and leaves weren't steak and potatoes, but his growling stomach would be thankful for anything he fed it. And being with Abby made him feel calmer and more certain that they'd come through this all right. She was worried, but not panicking. Anyone who mistook her for a dumb blonde was delusional.

He rejoined her and she sat up straighter, her hand making a fist in her lap.

"What do you have there?" He nodded to her fist.

She flushed. "It's nothing."

He spread the damp diaper on a tree branch to dry. "It's not nothing. What is it?"

She looked away. "I've been watching and I haven't seen any sign of anyone headed this way," she said.

Message received. She didn't want to talk about whatever she was holding. "We ought to be able to see the dust from a vehicle from a long way off," he said.

"How far do you think we are from the main road?" she asked.

"About five miles, I think. Maybe a little more."

"Where do you think they were taking those people?"

"To another camp in the park—or maybe all the way to Denver. I don't know."

"What a harsh life." She arranged the shawl to shade the sleeping infant. "Who's behind this?"

He sat beside her, wrists on his upraised knees. "We don't know that, either. There are rumors drug cartels have moved in from Mexico, but they need a local connection—a sponsor who can smooth the way for them."

"Who?"

"That's one of the things we've been trying to find out. It has to be someone with money. Someone powerful. Someone who thinks he's above the law."

"Do you have someone in mind?"

"We do. But we can't prove anything." Though law enforcement might rely on hunches to guide their investigation, they needed proof to stand up in court.

"Tell me. It's not as if I'll tell anyone else."

"Have you heard of a man named Richard Prentice?"

"No. But I'll admit, I've been so busy with school I haven't paid much attention to the news."

"He's a billionaire who owns the land at the entrance to the park."

"The place with the big stone pillars and iron gate?"

"That's the one. He's made a lot of money buying historic or critical wilderness properties and selling them to the government or conservation groups for inflated prices. But the Feds wouldn't bite when he tried to sell that place, and local governments passed restrictions that limited how he could develop it. So he made it his base of operations."

"I suppose it's a good location for overseeing a drug

operation within the park, but why would a guy like that bother with drugs? He's already rich."

"Some people never have enough money. But maybe it's not about the money for him. Maybe this is one more way to stick it to a government he seems to hate. Or maybe he gets a rush out of having control over so many people's lives."

"If he does have anything to do with this, I hope you can prove it and send him to jail for a long time."

"That's what we hope, too."

She shifted onto her knees. "Take the baby for a minute," she said. "I think our food is about ready." Not waiting for an answer, she shoved the infant into his arms.

The baby was heavier than he'd expected, warm and a little wiggly, too. As he tried to figure out the most comfortable way to hold her, she opened her eyes and stared up at him. She seemed so bright and alert, her gaze fixed on him, as if assessing him. "You're onto me, kid," he said softly. "I don't have the faintest idea what I'm doing."

She shifted, curling toward him with a little sigh that made his heart stop for a moment. He stared down at her, gripped by the most intense, protective instinct he'd ever felt. "I won't let them hurt you, little girl." He stroked her cheek with the tip of his finger, the skin softer than anything he'd ever felt.

"She likes you." Abby returned, holding a section of bark like a plate. "She settled right down."

"I don't have a lot of experience with babies."

"You're a natural." She set the "plate" on the ground between them. "I can take her again if you want."

"No. That's okay." The infant fit neatly in the crook

of his left arm, leaving the right arm free. "I don't want to disturb her." He leaned forward to study the items she'd arranged on the bark. "What's on the menu?"

"The salad greens I talked about earlier—no dressing, I'm afraid. The little white things are mariposa lily bulbs I roasted."

He popped one of the buds—about the size of a garlic clove—into his mouth and chewed. "Not bad. A little earthy, but a little sweet, too."

"They'd be better with salt or other seasonings, but they'll keep us going until help arrives."

"Not bad at all." He crunched down on another bulb.

They finished the meal in silence. Hunger sated, with the warmth of the sun off the rocks and the profound silence of the wilderness closing in, his eyelids began to feel heavy. He sat up straighter. He had to stay awake and watch for rescue—or the return of the camp boss.

"I think the early morning and all that hiking is catching up with me," Abby said.

"You can take a nap," he said. "I'll keep watch."

"I might have to." She looked around them. "Not that all this rock is going to make for a comfortable bed."

"Come lean against me." He patted the spot beside him.

She hesitated.

"Come on. I won't bite."

"You'd better not. I bite back." But she settled beside him.

He slipped his arm around her shoulder. "Just lean on me."

Again, she hesitated, but the gentle pressure from his hand coaxed her to lay her head in the hollow of his shoulder. She settled down with a sigh, her breast and side pressed against him, one hand resting on his thigh. He felt the same protective instinct toward her he'd felt toward the baby, but underneath the protectiveness was a more primal emotion, the awareness of her as a beautiful, desirable woman, and of himself as a man who wanted her.

The wanting was nothing new. He'd been physically attracted to her from the moment she walked into ranger headquarters. That in itself wasn't that unusual. He was attracted to women every day, a passing desire akin to seeing a luscious brownie and his mouth watering.

His desire for Abby went deeper. She wasn't a passing fascination. The more he knew her, as a complex, capable, sympathetic person, the more he felt drawn to know her more fully. Intimately.

She shifted against him and he looked down to find her head tipped up toward his. "You wanted to know what I was holding earlier," she said.

"You don't have to tell me if you don't want to," he said. "It's none of my business."

"No—I want to tell you." She held out her fisted hand and slowly opened her fingers to reveal the figure of a leaping rabbit, about three inches long. "It's just a kind of good-luck charm I keep. I know it's silly, but holding it makes me feel calmer."

"It's not silly." He was feeling anything but calm himself right now, but he didn't want to scare her by overreacting. "Do you remember where you got it?"

"I don't know." They both studied the little rabbit in her palm. It was white with brown spots, four legs outstretched as if running, ears erect. "When I came to in the hospital, I was holding it."

"I wasn't sure if you remembered." He could hardly

get the words out past the knot of emotion in his throat. He tried again. "Before they unloaded you off the chopper, I put it in your hand and you grasped it. It seemed like a good sign. Even unconscious, you were fighting. Hanging on."

She stared. He tried to read the emotion in her eyes and drew back a little. She looked upset. Maybe even angry. "Why did you do that?" she asked.

"My cousin gave it to me when I deployed," he said. "She said if one rabbit's foot was supposed to be lucky, she figured four feet, still attached to the rabbit, were even better. I figured you needed the luck more than I did right then."

She wrapped her fingers around the little figure again and returned it to her pocket, not looking at him. "Thank you," she said. "I always wondered where he came from."

"Did it help?"

She nodded. "It did. Whenever I was stressed or worried or needed distracting, I'd take him out and hold him. It reminded me that someone I didn't even know had been rooting for me to make it." She raised her head and looked at him, her eyes glinting with unshed tears. "Now I know that someone was you."

He couldn't speak, afraid of saying the wrong thing. Of breaking the connection between them. She sat up a little straighter, though she remained pressed against him. "I have a hard time warming up to people. Especially since I got home from Afghanistan."

"The things you went through over there—you can't really share them with others. They're like an invisible wall, separating you from everyone else who doesn't know what it's like. They can never see things from your point of view."

"But you can."

"Not entirely. But I have a better idea than some."

"Yes." She put her hand on his chest.

"Do you think that's all we have in common—the war?" He forced himself to look into her eyes, not sure he'd like the answer she gave. He hated the idea that she'd see him as just another damaged veteran with whom she could compare notes.

"I didn't mean it like that," she said. "Only that I felt comfortable enough with you to let my guard down a little. When you look at me, I feel like you see all of me—not just the beauty queen, and not just the scarred veteran, but the whole package."

He touched her cheek with his free hand. "It's a very nice package." He dragged his thumb across the corner of her mouth.

She let out her breath in a soft sigh and leaned closer. That was all the invitation he needed. He bent his head and covered her lips with his own. She returned the kiss, arching into him and sliding her hand around to clutch his shoulder. He wrapped his free arm around her and pulled her to his chest, her soft, feminine curves molding to him. He slanted his mouth more firmly against hers and she parted her lips, her tongue tracing the crease of his mouth, setting his heart racing.

She melded her body to his, urgent, needy. This wasn't a casual, flirtatious kiss, or one of tentative exploration. This kiss spoke of built-up longing, of a craving for a connection that went beyond words.

Angelique squirmed against him and began to whimper. Reluctantly, he broke the kiss and tried to comfort the baby. "I must have been crushing her," he said.

"I'll take her." Head down, hair falling forward to cover the side of her face and shield her expression from his view, she reached for the infant.

He slipped the baby into her arms, unsure of what he should say. Kissing was one thing—talking about it was another. Still, he couldn't let the moment pass as if nothing had happened. He reached out and brushed back her hair. "Are you okay?" he asked.

"I'm fine." She took a deep breath and raised her eyes to meet his. "We probably shouldn't have done that."

"Why not?"

"Because…" She bit her lower lip, then shook her head.

"Tell me." He cradled the side of her neck. "You seemed to be enjoying yourself at the time."

A warm flush crept up her cheeks—all the answer he really needed, but he held back a smile of triumph. "I don't want you to get the wrong idea," she said. "I'm not really ready…for more than kisses. For a relationship."

Her obvious distress touched him. "I'm in no hurry. No pressure, I promise." He sat back again. "If the baby's all right, you can take that nap now. I promise I won't bother you."

After a moment of hesitation, she settled against him once more, the baby wrapped in the sling and fastened around her. He stared out across the empty landscape and listened to the rhythm of her breathing slow and deepen as she fell asleep. At least with her this close, every nerve in his body aware of her, he wasn't too worried about falling asleep himself. He'd stay awake and keep watch, protecting her with his life if he had to.

MICHAEL WOKE WITH a start and stared out at the sun, which was sliding toward the horizon, the intense heat of midday fading toward the cool of dusk. He didn't think he'd dozed long; beside him, Abby and Angelique still slept. But every nerve vibrated with awareness. In the short time he'd lost his fight against sleep, something in the environment around them had changed.

All around them was silent—too silent. No birds sang. No lizards skittered on the rocks. No flies buzzed. The hair on the back of his neck rose, and he sat up straighter and started to turn around.

Hard metal pressed against the back of his head. "Don't move or I will blow your head off," a man said, in slightly accented English. "Give me the baby and I will think about letting you live."

Chapter Eleven

Abby gasped and clutched Angelique to her shoulder. The infant mewled and burrowed closer to her. An unfamiliar hand tightened on Abby's shoulder and she wrenched away and whirled to face an older Hispanic man. He held a gun to Michael's head. "Give the baby to me or I will kill your friend," he said. He held out his free hand for the baby.

"Who are you?" she demanded, clutching Angelique even more tightly to her. "What do you want with this baby?"

"You can call me El Jefe. Now give her to me or your friend will die."

"Don't give her to him." Michael spoke through gritted teeth. He still sat with his back to the man, his head wrenched to one side by the pressure of the gun barrel against his skull. But his eyes remained fixed on her, calm and determined.

Abby struggled to her feet and took a step back to put more distance between her and the man with the gun. She looked from him to Michael. Michael's face was pale, but nothing else about him betrayed agitation or fear. He'd gathered his legs under him, as if preparing to pounce. "Don't do it," he said again.

"Give her to me!" El Jefe insisted, and jabbed his weapon into Michael, who winced.

"What do you want with her?" Abby asked. She wrapped both arms around the baby. "She's an infant. She cries and wets her diaper. You don't look like a man who has time to change diapers."

"I will return her to her mother. She can take care of her."

Abby stared. Mariposa would certainly know how to take care of her own baby, but would this man really return the child to her? He was one of her jailers—the man who had ordered her to fetch water. Mariposa had wanted the child to be away from him.

"Her mother gave her to me to care for," Abby said. "I can't just hand her over to a stranger."

"You will give her to me!" He shoved the gun again, but this time Michael jerked his head to the side and swung his fist up and back, jamming it into the gunman's nose. El Jefe screamed, a wild, almost girlish sound, and blood poured from his broken nose. Michael shoved him back and grabbed for the weapon.

For an agonizingly long minute the two men struggled for the gun, rolling on the ground while Abby watched, heart in her throat, tensing herself for the explosion of the gun firing. She could have pulled her own weapon, but she didn't trust herself to get off a clear shot. El Jefe swore and struggled to grasp the weapon, but Michael was bigger and stronger, and he wasn't also fighting the pain and bleeding from a broken nose. At last, the older man gave up the fight, covering his face with his hands and shouting in Spanish.

Michael stood over him, breathing hard. "Who are you?" he demanded.

The man didn't look up, though he was no longer shouting, only muttering nonstop.

"Shut up and tell me who you are," Michael said.

The baby began to wail, and Abby rocked her in her arms, trying to comfort her. "Is she all right?" Michael asked.

"She's just hungry." And she was going to get a lot hungrier if they didn't get away from here soon.

Michael turned his attention back to the gunman, changing his line of questioning. "How did you get here?" he asked. "Where is your truck?"

Abby's spirits lifted. Of course. The man must have a vehicle somewhere nearby. A vehicle that could return them to safety—if they could find a road. But even the dirt tracks that crisscrossed the area must eventually lead somewhere. They could cover more ground searching in a vehicle than on foot.

"Why should I tell you anything?" the man asked.

"Answer my questions or I'll kill you." Michael's voice was hard; Abby shivered. She believed him.

"Kill me and you'll still be stuck out here with no way to leave," the man sneered. The bleeding had slowed. He patted gingerly at his nose, wincing.

A point for the bad guy. Abby looked around, hoping she'd spot the glint of sunlight off a truck hood or windshield, or maybe even see the vehicle, sitting in plain sight. Maybe it was too much to hope that the vehicle would come equipped with a GPS and a phone, but a woman could dream, couldn't she?

But instead of a lone truck sitting on the otherwise deserted plain, she saw something even better. "Michael, I think your friends finally found us," she said.

He kept the gun leveled on his prisoner, but glanced

over his shoulder at the line of Cruisers snaking across the desert. Then he pointed the weapon up and fired three shots. The baby wailed and Abby's own ears rang, but the signal had worked; the line of vehicles sped up, headed straight toward them.

"Now we'll deal— Stop!"

At Michael's shout, Abby turned. The gunman was running away, speeding over the rough ground like a jackrabbit, out of reach within seconds. Michael started across the rocks after him.

"Michael, no!" Abby said. "He's got too much of a head start. You can deal with him later."

"We may not have another chance." But he stopped and came to stand beside her. Together, they watched the Cruisers stop and park by the creek, then they walked down to meet them.

Graham greeted them as they picked their way across the creek. "What are you two doing out here?" he asked.

"Never mind that." Michael passed his boss, headed toward the trucks. "We need to try to catch up with the man who just ran away from here."

"What man?" Graham asked.

"He calls himself El Jefe. I'm pretty sure he's the guy who was in charge of this camp. If we can get him to talk, we may be able to break this case wide-open."

Graham and Michael left in Graham's Cruiser, leaving Abby with Carmen and Marco.

"Is that a baby?" Carmen stared at the bundle in Abby's arms.

"Her name is Angelique." Abby arranged the shawl to shade the infant's face. "And we really need to find some formula and feed her."

"Where did you get her?" Carmen smiled and stroked one of Angelique's tiny hands.

"Her mother was one of the workers camped here," Abby said. "How did you two ever find us?"

"We've been following the tracks of the trucks," Marco said. "We found Dance's Cruiser, wrecked and burning in a wash almost ten miles from here. We've been searching ever since."

"There was a camp of workers here," Abby said. "Four trailers—about two dozen people. Some men with trucks came and moved them this morning."

"Those must have been the trucks we were following." Marco joined them. "The tracks led right to here."

"Did the tracks lead from the destroyed Cruiser?" Abby asked.

"We found the tracks while we were trying to figure out how the Cruiser ended up in that wash," Marco said.

"But how did you two end up here without the Cruiser, and with a baby?" Carmen asked.

"It's a long story." Abby sighed. She was hot, tired, hungry and thirsty. "Right now, we need to get this child to a safe place."

She followed them to Marco's vehicle and climbed into the backseat. Angelique fussed and squirmed. "Somebody's not happy," Carmen said.

"She's hungry and her diaper needs changing," Abby said. "And she probably misses her mother." Mariposa probably missed her baby, too. Where was she now—and why had that man wanted her?

"Who's the guy Graham and Michael took off after?" Marco asked.

"He was in charge of the workers in the camp. He supervised the move. We hid and watched them hook up the trailers and drive off. I fell asleep and when I woke up, he was there, and had a gun on Michael. He demanded we give him the baby. When I refused, he threatened to kill Michael, but Michael broke his nose and took his gun. Your arrival distracted us enough he ran off."

When they reached the road and phone service, Carmen called headquarters. "Lance, I need you to run into town and buy a couple cans of baby formula, bottles and nipples, some baby wipes and a box of diapers." She looked over her shoulder at Angelique. "Size two." She grinned. "Yes, they're for a baby. Now, don't waste time arguing. We need these right away." She hung up the phone. "That's probably the oddest thing anyone's ever asked him to do. I wish I could see his face when he gets to the store and finds out how many different kinds of diapers there are. Let's hope he gets something that will work."

"You seem to know a lot about them," Marco said.

"I've got six younger brothers and sisters and half a dozen nieces and nephews," she said. "I've changed plenty of diapers in my day."

Abby cuddled the fussy baby closer. "We're going to make you more comfortable soon, little one," she said. She only hoped they'd be able to find Mariposa and reunite mother and child before it was too late.

MICHAEL STARED ACROSS the empty prairie. They hadn't found so much as a tire track that they could link to the man who had held him at gunpoint and tried to take the baby. "He couldn't have just vanished," he said.

"If he is the man in charge of the workers, he probably knows this country a lot better than we do," Graham said. He put his hand on Michael's shoulder. "Come on. Let's go back to headquarters."

"We need to go back to the campsite first. There's a bucket there that may have this guy's fingerprints on it. Maybe we'll come up with a match."

They returned to the camp and Michael retrieved the bucket from under the bush. "I'll get a team out to go over this place," Graham said.

"It's pretty clean, but maybe they'll find something," Michael said. He didn't like giving up the search for El Jefe so soon, but he doubted more time wandering around out here would bring them any closer to the man. He followed Graham back to the Cruiser.

"What happened to your face?" Graham asked.

Michael put a hand to the gash on his cheek. "I fell into a drainage. That's when I lost the phone and radio."

"Was that before or after you acquired the baby?"

"After."

"Where did the baby come from?"

"One of the workers gave it to Abby, when the bosses showed up to move them. Then we were spotted and had to make a run for it."

"But the guy in charge caught up with you?"

Michael shook his head. "That was later. Without the GPS or a phone or maps, we were lost. We needed water, so staying near the creek made sense. I knew you'd send someone to look for us when I didn't report in this evening. In the meantime, I figured the boss man might come back to look for us. I knew he'd stolen my truck, so he probably guessed we couldn't go far. I planned to get the jump on him when he returned, but it didn't work out that way." He fought down anger at himself for making such a hash of the whole day. Had his attraction to Abby distracted him so much he'd been less diligent?

"We'll find him," Graham said. "What did he want with the baby?"

"No idea. He said he would return her to her mother, but Abby got the impression the mom thought the baby would be safer with her."

"The two of you can fill us in on the details when we get back to headquarters."

At ranger headquarters, they found Carmen feeding the baby a bottle while Abby, dressed in a black task-force polo and hiking shorts she must have borrowed from Carmen, ate a deli sandwich from a tray in the middle of the conference table. She set aside the sandwich when he walked in. "Did you find him?" she asked.

Michael shook his head and sagged into the chair across from her. He glanced toward the baby. "How's Angelique?"

"She is living up to her name and being a little angel," Carmen said. She positioned the baby over her shoulder and patted her back.

"She's happier now that's she's eaten and had a fresh diaper," Abby said. "Though I don't think you're going to want your bandanna back."

"I have more where that came from." He helped himself to a sandwich. Abby's leaves and roots hadn't tasted as bad as he'd feared, but they hadn't been very filling.

Graham pulled out the chair at the head of the table. "Tell me about this man," he said.

"I'm pretty sure he's the one who was ordering everyone else around," Michael said. "I didn't have binoculars, but he was tall and thin, and was the only one wearing a white shirt."

"And he didn't say why he wanted the baby?"

"He said he would return her to her mother," Abby said.

"Maybe he's the father," Carmen said. When the others stared at her, she shrugged. "Even criminals can love their children. Or maybe he loves the mother and she changed her mind about giving up her child, and she sent him to retrieve the baby."

"Or maybe he sees the child as a tie to him and his operation and he wants to get rid of her," Marco said.

Abby shuddered at the idea. "What harm is an infant going to do?" she asked. "She can't testify against him."

"She might share his DNA, and that might tie him to a crime we don't even know about yet," Marco said.

Abby tried to push away the thought that the man might have wanted to harm Angelique. But a man who made slaves of other people might not balk at killing a baby.

"You said you were following tracks," Michael said. "Where did they lead?"

"Nowhere," Marco said. "Once they reached the highway, we lost them."

"But now that we know what we're looking for, it won't be so easy to hide that many people and trailers," Michael said.

"Unless they dismantled everything and took everyone straight to Denver or another big city," Carmen said. "Your guy could be long gone."

Michael shook his head. "I don't think so. He wanted Angelique badly enough to come back by himself to retrieve her."

"That part doesn't make sense to me," Marco said. "He had to have others helping him when he moved the camp."

"He had at least five other men with guns," Michael said.

"Then why didn't he bring them with him to retrieve the baby?" Marco asked. "Even one other man with him would have increased his chances of success."

"Maybe he didn't want anyone to know about the baby," Abby said.

"But they already knew about the baby," Michael said. "Mariposa didn't try to hide her from the others, that I could tell."

Abby stood and went to take the sleeping infant from Carmen. Angelique hardly stirred as Abby cradled her close. "Maybe Carmen is right and he came back for Angelique because she's his child," she said. "If that's true, he might not want the others to know, or to suspect he had a soft spot for the baby."

"We don't know that," Michael said. "He might have intended to kill her."

"Then maybe he didn't want the others to know that, either." The idea made her sick to her stomach, but they would gain nothing by refusing to consider all possibilities.

"Whatever the reason he wanted her, it doesn't really matter," Carmen said.

"Why not?" Michael asked.

"Because we know the baby represents a weakness or a secret he doesn't want anyone else finding out about," Graham said. "If you know a man's weakness or secret, you can find a way to exploit it."

"But if he's already on his way to Denver…" Abby sent a questioning look to Graham.

"I think Michael's hunch is right and he won't want to leave without the baby," Graham said. "We can use that against him."

Abby smiled down at the child, who had fallen back asleep. She'd never seen a more beautiful baby, with such long, dark lashes, and a perfect Cupid's bow of a mouth.

Aware that the room had fallen silent, she looked up to find everyone else looking at her—or rather, they were focused on the baby. "What is it?" she asked. "What's wrong?"

Graham cleared his throat. "If we spread the word around that you're keeping the baby for a while, and make you seem vulnerable, we could lure our guy out to take another chance. Only this time, we'd be waiting to capture him."

"You mean, use Angelique as bait to catch him?" She stared, sure she couldn't have heard them correctly.

Graham nodded. "You and Angelique, yes. Bait to catch what could be a very big fish."

Chapter Twelve

"No!" Abby and Michael spoke at the same time.

"It's too dangerous." Michael shoved back his chair and stood. "She could be hurt."

"He's right. You can't take that kind of risk with a baby," Abby said.

"I wasn't talking about Angelique." Michael moved around the table to stand beside her. "It's too dangerous for you *and* the baby." His eyes met hers and she knew he was speaking not as a law enforcement officer, but as a man who cared for her. The realization moved her, but she looked away. This wasn't a time to let sentiment cloud her judgment.

"We'd have someone from the team with you 24/7," Graham said. "And other team members stationed nearby. If our man makes a move, we'd be on him."

"It's our best chance to catch this guy," Marco said. "If we get to him, we're that much closer to finding the person in charge of the operation. We can stop him from enslaving other workers."

"Can you help Mariposa and the others?" she asked.

"There's a good chance we can," Graham said.

Abby looked down at the sleeping infant. As much as she cared for the child, she wasn't in a position to take her permanently. The baby needed to be with her mother, as long as her mother could take care of her.

Michael's hand rested heavy on her shoulder. "Abby, don't do it," he said. "Don't risk it. We'll find some other way."

"I can't risk anything happening to Angelique," she said. "We don't know what this man's intentions are toward her."

"She's right." Carmen spoke up. "We'll need to use a decoy for the baby and move Angelique into temporary foster care."

"Agreed," Graham said. "I don't want the child to come to harm. And I don't want you harmed, either, Abby. I promise we'll protect you. But the final decision is yours."

Michael's hand on her shoulder tightened, but he remained silent. That silence—his faith in her ability to make the right decision—moved her more than any words could have. "I'll do it," she said. "As long as Angelique is somewhere safe."

"Abby…" Michael spoke so softly she might have been the only one who heard.

She turned to face him. "I want to stop these people," she said. "I want Mariposa and Angelique to have a better life. If I can do something to help them, then I have to act."

"I want that, too," he said. "But I want you to stay safe."

"I'll be safe," she said. "I know you've got my back." She deliberately repeated the words he'd told her earlier.

"Carmen, you take care of transferring Angelique to foster care," Graham said. "We'll have to manage the switch without anyone who might be watching realizing what's going on."

"They make some pretty realistic-looking baby dolls," Carmen said. "I'll get one of those and a layette. Abby will pretend to care for it as she would Angelique."

"I might as well go back to my trailer in the park campground," Abby said. "That will make it easier for this guy to get to me, and put me closer to all of you."

"I'll go with you," Michael said.

Graham gave him a hard look. "It might be better to send someone else."

"No, sir. I can do this."

Graham's expression remained grim, but he nodded. "All right. Go on to the trailer. Carmen and Marco will meet you there later to pick up the baby and substitute the doll. Randall, you and Lance can take turns watching Abby's trailer. I doubt this guy will try anything so soon, but stay on your guard."

"Yes, sir."

Abby carried Angelique, while Michael gathered up the diapers, formula and other baby supplies, along with an overnight bag from his locker. "I'll be sure to bring a car seat when we come to get her," Carmen said, following them to her Cruiser, which Michael was borrowing until his could be replaced. "Right now, you don't have far to go to the campground."

Everything at her trailer looked just as she'd left it, though Michael insisted on searching all around the outside and checking out the inside while she waited with the baby. "I don't think anyone's been here since you left," he said at last, and held the door open for her to enter.

The baby started crying before they were through the door. "I think it's time for a diaper change," Abby said.

"I'll get the stuff out of the car."

When he returned, she was still standing in the middle of the room with the wailing baby. "What's wrong?" he asked.

"I don't know where to put her. I'm not exactly set up for a baby."

Michael looked around at the compact space, then set the box of supplies on the table and began emptying it out. "We can put her in here. It's about the size of a bassinet, and she won't fall out."

"You're brilliant." She grinned at him.

"I have my moments." He grabbed a towel from the counter and used it to line the box, then slid it toward her. "Instant cradle."

"Hand me a diaper first."

While she changed the baby, he put away the formula and other supplies. She wedged the box between the dinette and sofa and settled the baby inside. Michael sat beside her on the sofa. "Now what?" he asked.

"Why don't you take a shower, then I'll grab one," she said.

"Are you suggesting I need one?" He pretended to look offended.

"No comment." She stood. "I'm going to make some tea. The bathroom is kind of small, but I think you'll find everything you need."

While she filled the teakettle and took a mug from the cabinet, she listened to the water beating against the wall of the shower and tried not to think of Michael, naked, just on the other side of that barrier. But once the image was fixed in her mind, of his sculpted shoulders and arms and muscular abs, she could think of nothing else. Her imagination filled in the rest of the picture, until desire settled over her in a languid heat.

She forced her mind away from the fantasy and savored the memory of the kiss they'd shared earlier in the day. In that moment, kissing him had seemed the most natural thing in the world—the thing she had wanted most. She'd lusted after men before, but she couldn't remember ever feeling so close to one. She hadn't been in a serious relationship in years—before she went to war. A lifetime ago, when she was a different person.

Was it only because circumstance and danger had thrown them together that she felt this way? Did she feel so comfortable with him because they were both veterans? Or because he'd saved her life when she was injured in Afghanistan? Was he right, and fate had somehow brought them together? She slipped her hand into her pocket and caressed the little rabbit figure. All these years, she'd held on to the token, feeling it was somehow important. Had the caring the gift of the rabbit represented now grown into something more—even into love?

The bathroom door opened and he emerged wearing only a pair of low-slung jeans, toweling his hair. She stared at the drops of water glinting in the dusting of brown hair across his muscular chest and her mouth went dry. Michael Dance in uniform was an impressive sight, but Michael Dance half naked was enough to make her forget her own name.

He tossed the towel aside and grinned, and she blushed, sure he had caught her staring. "I feel almost human again," he said. He moved toward her at the same time she tried to leave the kitchen area, and they collided. The trailer suddenly felt too small to contain them. She mumbled an apology and tried to slip past, and he put out a hand to steady her, freezing her in place.

He smoothed his hand down her arm and a tremor rocked her. Her skin burned where he touched her, and she fought the urge to lean into him, to lose herself in the feel of his body against hers. She looked up and realized he'd shaved, the scent of his shaving cream filling her senses.

"Tight fit," he said.

Why did her traitorous mind turn those words into a come-on, with thoughts of how well the two of them would fit together? She looked away—at the floor, the wall—anything but those sensuous lips, beckoning. If she started to kiss him now, she'd forget all about the shower, and the baby, and everything but slaking the desire that rocked through her.

"I'll just, um, take my shower now," she said, pushing past him.

"Don't you need to wait for the water to warm up again?"

"That's okay." A little cold water might be just what she needed.

The water was warm enough, though. She took her time in the shower, washing her hair and shaving her legs. *As if I was prepping for a big date*, she thought.

But this was no casual date. Michael was spending the night here in her trailer. Considering the electricity they'd managed to generate with only a brief touch, she wasn't foolish enough to believe they wouldn't act on that attraction at some point. But when—and what might happen afterward—was anyone's guess.

She slipped into yoga pants and a T-shirt and blow-dried her hair, but didn't bother with makeup. She didn't want to seem obvious or desperate. Besides, the man had seen her at her absolute worst. A little mascara and lipstick weren't going to change his opinion of her.

She opened the bathroom door and was surprised to hear humming. She froze, listening, and made out a few words. "Hush, little baby, don't say a word. Papa's gonna buy you a mockingbird."

She peeked around the door and stared at Michael, standing by the sofa, holding the baby. The infant looked impossibly small in his arms, smiling up at him and cooing as he sang softly. More priceless still was the look on his face, the stern lines and angular features softened in a smile of such tenderness it brought a lump to her throat.

He turned and saw her standing there, and the tips of his ears turned pink. "She was fussy," he said by way of explanation.

"Obviously, you've made a conquest." She joined him in front of the sofa and he tried to hand the baby over, but she waved him off. "Oh, no, she looks very happy where she is."

She sat, and he sat beside her. Angelique gurgled happily. "I've never spent much time around babies," he said.

"Then, you're a natural," she said. "You'll make a good father one day."

He was silent for a moment, both of them watching the baby, who stared back with her solemn brown eyes. "Do you think about it much—having kids, raising a family?" he asked.

"Sometimes," she admitted. "More lately, now that

my life is beginning to settle down. Before, when I was in the army, and later, after I was injured, even the possibility of that kind of stability seemed so far away."

"Yeah, I haven't exactly had the kind of life that makes a wife and kids seem like a good idea."

"I have to finish graduate school and find a job—figure out what I'm going to do with the rest of my life." She leaned over and stroked the infant's satin-soft cheek. "But sometimes I wonder if those things are just excuses to keep me from focusing on all the emotional, personal things that are harder to deal with."

"I know what you mean," he said. "I can deal with the toughest situations in my job, but when it comes to relationships...sometimes that's a lot scarier."

Their eyes met, and her heart sped up, fluttering in her chest. "Do I scare you?" she asked, keeping her tone light, a little flirtatious.

"Oh, yeah." He cupped her cheek in his hand. "But I'm a big believer in the importance of facing your fears."

He lowered his head toward her, but the sound of tires on gravel made him straighten, instantly alert. "Someone's coming," he said, and handed her the baby.

He stood and walked to the window and peered out the blinds. Abby clutched the baby to her, aware that the vehicle had stopped outside her door.

"Hey, it's just us," a woman called. "We came by to see how you're settling in with the baby."

At the sound of Carmen's familiar voice, Michael's shoulders relaxed. He pulled on a T-shirt, then went to the door.

Carmen came in, followed by Lance. He carried a large cardboard box labeled Diapers.

"We brought you some more diapers and formula," he said, his voice loud in the evening silence.

He set the box on the table, made sure all the blinds were drawn, then took the top off the diaper box to reveal a realistic-looking baby doll, wrapped in a blanket identical to the one that swaddled Angelique. "It's a doll called My Real Baby," Carmen said. "Isn't it a kick?"

She lifted the doll out of the box, handling it as if it were a real baby, and passed it to Abby. "From a distance, I'm sure no one could tell the difference," she said.

Abby cradled the doll and turned to look at Angelique, who rested in the box on the sofa. "I'm going to miss the real baby, though," she said. "Where are you taking her?"

"The state put me in touch with a woman in Grand Junction who specializes in temporary foster care for infants," Carmen said. "She'll be safe there."

Safer than she would be here with her and Michael, Abby knew, but still, she hated to see her leave.

Carmen picked up Angelique and cooed at her, then transferred her to the diaper box. "I don't guess you've heard anything from our friend?" she said as she tucked blankets around the baby.

"Nothing," Michael said. "But we don't even know if he knows she's here yet."

"We talked it up in town," Lance said. "I stopped for gas and told everyone there about the baby we'd found."

"You'd think he lived for gossip." Carmen elbowed the younger agent in the side. "Everyone was all ears. Maybe some of the talk will get back to our guy."

"Maybe so."

"Call if you need anything." Lance fit the lid back on the diaper box and picked it up.

"Take good care of her." Abby curled her hands into fists to keep from reaching for the baby.

"We will," Carmen said. "See you tomorrow."

They left, and Michael shut and locked the door behind them. Abby sank onto the sofa and listened to the sound of their tires gradually fade to silence. She blinked hard, fighting tears, but they spilled over and rolled down her cheeks.

"Hey, what's wrong?" Michael hurried to her side.

"I didn't even get to say goodbye." She choked back a sob. He took her hand and patted it, but as she continued to sob harder, he pulled her to him. She buried her face against his chest. "I know it's stupid," she said. "I hardly know her, but I felt responsible for her."

"Shh. It's okay." He smoothed his hand down her hair and rocked her against him. "Of course you miss her. It's hard not knowing what's going to happen to her."

She raised her head to look at him. "You understand."

"I try." He kissed her cheek, but she turned and found his lips. She kissed him greedily, hungrily, wanting to blot out the sadness, to forget for a little while about the baby and Mariposa and a stranger who might want her dead.

He responded with the same fervor, wrapping his arms around her and pulling her tight against his chest. The tip of his tongue traced the seam of her lips and she opened to him, tasting the butterscotch candy he liked. They kissed until she was trembling and light-headed, her body humming with awareness of him, but still she wanted more.

She slid her hand beneath his T-shirt and pressed her

palm against his stomach, feeling the crisp line of hair that disappeared beneath the waistband of his jeans. He kissed his way to her ear and said, his voice low and husky with need, "If you keep that up, I'm not going to be able to stop."

"I don't want to stop," she said. "I want to make love to you." As if to prove her words, she pushed him back against the sofa, her body slanted over his. He dragged one hand up, over her rib cage, and cupped her breast through her thin T-shirt, the tip a hard bead pressed against his palm. He flicked his thumb back and forth across it, sending little shock waves of desire rocketing through her. Her breath came in gasps, and her eyes drifted shut as she surrendered to the onslaught of sensation.

Then his mouth was on her, the combination of heat and moisture and the gentle abrasion of the fabric driving her wild. She let out a soft moan and fumbled to remove the shirt. He sat up and helped her, then shed his own shirt, so they were both naked from the waist up.

"You're so beautiful." He slid his hands down her sides, as if cradling something precious. "So beautiful."

She believed he would have said the same thing if her body had been scarred like her face. The words wouldn't have been a lie; she believed when Michael looked at her, he saw more than what was on the surface. He always had; maybe that was why she'd fallen in love with him.

She stood and held out her hand. "Let's move to the bed, where we'll be more comfortable."

He grasped her hand and let her pull him up and lead him to the bed at the other end of the trailer. She pulled back the covers and he started to follow, then hesitated. "What is it?" she asked.

"Just a second." He turned and slipped into the bathroom.

She took off her jeans and underwear, so that by the time he returned, she was sitting up in bed, naked.

His gaze took her in, and the wanting in his eyes made her tremble all over again. "What took you so long?" she said.

He held up a condom in a foil packet. "I had to get this from my overnight bag."

She smiled. "You think of everything."

"I was a Boy Scout, remember? Their motto is Be Prepared."

"Something tells me they weren't thinking of situations like this." She moved over to make room for him.

He stopped to shed his own jeans and her heart beat faster as she stared—while trying to appear not to stare—at his body. He was as gorgeous as her fantasies.

They lay on their sides facing each other, the dimmed reading lights on either side of the bed providing soft illumination. He traced his hand down the curve of her side, then cupped her bottom and drew her close once more. "I feel as if I've been waiting for this moment for a long time," he said. "Does that seem crazy?"

"No." She felt the same way. As if her reluctance to go out with other men had been because she hadn't met *him* yet. Maybe those frantic moments on a helicopter over Afghanistan had forged a bond too deep for understanding. She only knew that with him, she lost the shyness and desire to close herself off and hide away. She wanted to open to him, to reveal everything, to be with him, in this moment, as she'd never allowed herself to be before.

"Make love to me," she whispered, and kissed him lightly on the lips.

He deepened the kiss, and soon they were entwined, arms and legs wrapped around each other, hands and lips stroking, exploring. He pulled away only long enough to roll on the condom, then he drew her close once more and entered her. She wrapped her legs around him, wanting to shout in joy or triumph, but then he began to move and she lost all power of speech or thought. There was only wave after wave of wonderful sensation building within her.

Her climax was the largest wave, washing over her, filling her with light and life, then releasing her, floating. Soaring. He tightened his hold on her and found his own release, crying out her name. "Abby!"

Afterward, they remained entwined, her head pillowed on his arms, her fingers stroking his chest. "I wasn't sure I'd ever feel that wonderful again," she said.

"I'm glad you don't feel you have to hide anything from me." He traced the scar on her face with the tip of one finger. With a start, she realized she lay with that side of her face to the light, her hair tucked back behind her ear. Even in sleep, she usually lay so the scar was hidden. But though this position felt a little awkward—exposed—it didn't feel wrong.

She snuggled closer to him. "You've seen me at my worst and didn't run away," she said. "I guess I really don't have anything to hide."

"I'll always be here for you," he said. "I won't let anyone hurt you again."

MICHAEL WOKE EARLY, long habit preventing him from sleeping much past sunrise. Gray light filled the trailer, and outside a bird was singing a morning chorus. Abby lay curled on her side beside him, her back to him, her face half buried in the covers. He rolled over, trying not to disturb her, and studied her sleeping form. Maybe he should pinch himself to make sure he wasn't dreaming. He'd had similar dreams often enough over the years. Sometimes he'd worried something was wrong with him; who let the memory of one woman with whom he'd never even spoken possess him so?

But it didn't matter why his attraction to Abby had stuck with him all these years, only that she was here with him now. Whether fate or chance had brought them together, he'd be her guardian and her lover. Neither of them would be alone again.

She stirred, as if feeling his gaze on her, and rolled onto her back and smiled up at him. "How long have you been watching me?" she asked.

"Only a few minutes." He moved closer; her skin was warm from sleep, so soft and smooth.

"Mmm. You're definitely awake." Smiling, she reached down to stroke him.

He resisted the urge to pull her onto him right away, and kissed her shoulder. "You're definitely nicer to wake up to than my alarm."

"Give me a second. I'll be right back." She patted his shoulder and slid out of bed. He rolled onto his back and stared up at the ceiling of the trailer, which was only a few feet above his head. He didn't want thoughts of the world outside to intrude on this moment, but of course they did. He wondered how Angelique was doing, and if El Jefe thought she was still with Abby.

She slipped back into bed, smelling of mint tooth-paste, her hair combed and the sleep washed from her eyes. "My turn," he said, and hurried to banish his own morning breath and retrieve another condom from his bag.

When he returned to the bed, she waited with open arms. He pulled her close, savoring the sensation of her breasts pillowed against his chest, the nipples already erect and hard. She draped her thigh over his, press-ing close, eager. "What time do you have to report in?" she asked.

"Not for another hour or so," he said. "We have plenty of time."

"Time for what?" she teased.

He snugged her more tightly against him. "Time for me to show you more of what you've been missing."

"Or maybe I'll be the one to show you a thing or two." She untangled herself from him and sat up, then pushed him back against the pillows and straddled him.

"Oh, you think so." He caressed her waist.

"I wasn't a biology major for nothing. Hand me that condom," she said. "Class is in session."

THEY FELL ASLEEP again and woke to the buzzing of Mi-chael's phone as it vibrated against the bedside table. He rolled over and snatched it up while Abby propped herself on her elbow and watched. She felt warm and relaxed and a little sore, but in a good way. She smiled, remembering how the soreness had come about. Clearly, all she needed was a little more practice with Michael to be in excellent shape.

"Nothing going on here," he said. "Did you get Angelique placed all right?...I'll tell Abby....She slept fine, as far as I know....Now, how would I know that?" The tips of his ears flushed red and Abby covered her mouth, smothering a giggle. She loved that he could still get flustered like that.

He hung up the phone and rolled onto his back. "That was Carmen. She said Angelique was settling in well when she left her last night. The woman is in her forties and has two teenagers. Angelique will be the only baby with her right now and seemed to really take to the woman."

"Thanks for letting me know. What did she say that made you blush?"

He turned even redder. "She wanted to know if I kept you up late last night—and if your bed was comfortable."

"So she knew you were attracted to me?"

"I think the whole team knew. I'm not so good at hiding my feelings."

"I guess I was the one who was slow on the uptake," she said. "At least for a while." She sat up. "And though I'd like to stay in bed with you all day, I guess we'd better get up. What's the plan for the day?"

"I guess you should be seen out and about with the baby. We want to give El Jefe every chance to find you and make his move."

"It won't be the same as having a real baby to hold, but I'll do my best."

Fifteen minutes later, they were both dressed and Abby had coffee brewing. "I'm going to go outside and look around," Michael said. He slid his gun into the holster on his utility belt. "I never heard anything last night, but you never know."

"We were both a little preoccupied last night," she said.

"True."

He opened the door and stepped out into the clear, thin light of early morning. The air still held a touch of the night's chill, and smelled of piñon and cedar. The campsites on either side of Abby's trailer were empty, and trees screened the view from any other site. Her car sat parked beside the picnic table and the empty fire ring, the borrowed Cruiser next to it. Nothing looked out of place.

He turned to survey the trailer and his heartbeat sped up. A folded sheet of paper fluttered against the door, held in place by a piece of blue tape.

He returned to the trailer and retrieved a knife from the drawer in the kitchen. "What is it?" Abby asked. She followed him to the door. "Is something wrong?"

"Someone left you a note." He slid the blade of the knife beneath the tape, detaching the note from the door. Holding it by the corner, he unfolded it and scanned the brief message.

"What does it say?" Abby stood on tiptoe, trying to see over his shoulder. "Let me see."

He held the note out to her. "Don't touch it. Just read it."

She frowned. "I can't. It's in Spanish."

He'd forgotten for a moment she didn't read the language. "It's from Mariposa. She wants you to meet her. She says she's safe and can take the baby now."

Chapter Thirteen

Abby stared at the note, wishing she could read the words for herself. "Does this mean she managed to get away from the people who were holding her prisoner?" she asked. "How did she know where to find me?"

"She didn't." Michael tapped the note with his index finger. "This is a fake. A trick to lure you away to a place where it will be easier to kidnap Angelique and get rid of you."

Her initial excitement over the note faded. Of course he was right. "Mariposa couldn't have known I was here," she said.

"Of course not. If she did, why not knock on the door and ask to see her baby right away?"

"I can understand why she wouldn't do that," Abby said. "If she's in the United States illegally, she wouldn't want to risk running into someone who works for border patrol. I mean, your car is parked out front."

"Point taken. But I don't believe she wrote this note," he said.

"Or she wrote it because someone forced her to," Abby said. Had El Jefe convinced Mariposa it was safe for her to have her child with her again? "I wish I knew why that man wants the baby."

"Does it matter?" Michael asked. "Even if it's because he's the father and loves her, what kind of life could she have with her mother as a prisoner?"

Abby hugged her arms across her chest, suddenly cold despite the growing warmth from the sun. "What do we do now?" she asked.

"I want to show this note to Graham and the rest of the team," he said. "Let's bundle up the baby and go over to headquarters."

Abby went through the motions of arranging the doll in the sling around her body. "This feels weird," she said.

"It may feel weird, but it looks real," he said. "That's all that counts. Just keep up the charade while we're outside, in case anyone is watching."

So she cradled the doll to her and pretended to coo and fuss over it as she walked to the Cruiser and climbed into the passenger seat. Michael started the engine. "Do you really think someone is watching us?" she asked.

"That note tells me they are." He checked the mirrors, then backed out of his parking spot.

"Then, they know you spent the night in my trailer."

He glanced at her. "Does that bother you? That other people know we were together?"

"No. But won't they be suspicious? The Cruiser makes it obvious you're with the task force, even if they didn't recognize you before."

"Just because I'm with the task force doesn't mean I was on duty last night. We're allowed to have personal lives. But just in case whoever is spying on us has doubts…" He shifted the Cruiser into Park and leaned across the seat and kissed her.

She let out a small gasp of surprise, then relaxed into him, reaching up one hand to twine her fingers in his hair as he deepened the kiss, his lips firm against her own, tantalizing and once again awakening desire she'd thought long dormant. When at last he broke contact, she stared up at him, a little breathless. "I'd say that was pretty convincing."

"I wasn't acting, if you were worried about that," he said.

"No." He hadn't been acting last night, either. The connection between them had been very real—and a little unnerving, if she was being completely honest with herself. She wasn't sure she was ready to jump into a relationship, especially with a man whose life was so complicated. She'd gotten through the years since her return from the war by keeping her life simple—no ties, no long-term commitments, no lasting obligations to anyone but herself. It was a shallow way to live, but a safe one. Michael was luring her into something much deeper—and scarier.

At ranger headquarters, they found Simon hunched over a computer in the front room. He frowned at the doll Abby unwrapped from the sling. "What are you two up to?" he asked.

"Someone left a suspicious note on Abby's door last night," Michael said. "Where's the G man?"

"I'm here." Graham emerged from his office. He looked tired, as if he hadn't slept well. Was he worried about her or Angelique? Abby wondered. Or did some new development in the case trouble him?

"This was taped to the door of Abby's trailer this morning." Michael handed Graham the note.

The captain took a pair of reading glasses from his

front pocket and slipped them on, then studied the torn scrap of paper. "Do you know who left it?" He looked at Abby. "Did you hear anyone? See anyone?"

"No, sir," Michael answered, brisk and military.

"No," Abby echoed, and looked away, focused on rearranging the blankets around the baby doll, as if doing so was an urgent task she could put off no longer. She marveled at Michael's ability to keep his expression neutral, revealing nothing. For much of the time last night, the two of them had been so focused on each other there could have been a drag race on the road outside her campsite and she wouldn't have noticed.

"Weren't Lance and Randall watching the place all night?" Michael asked.

"They were," Graham said. "If they'd seen anything suspicious, they would have called it in." He laid the note on the table. "We'll dust this for prints, though I doubt we'll come up with anything."

"We got a match off that bucket that was left behind at the camp," Simon said.

"Who is it?" Michael asked.

"The woman's prints didn't pull up anything, but the man's belong to Raul Meredes." Simon turned to Michael. "Ever hear of him?"

Michael shook his head. "No. Who is he?"

"He has ties to the Milenio cartel out of Guadalajara," Graham said. "He was the chief suspect in the murder of a sheriff's deputy on the Texas border, but they couldn't make the charges stick."

"He's been operating on both sides of the border for years," Simon said. "Smuggling drugs and people."

"I don't think he wrote this note." Carmen leaned

over Graham's shoulder and read the note. "The writing looks feminine to me."

"It does to me, too," Abby said. "But El Jefe—Meredes—could have forced her to write it. Or another woman might have written it."

"I don't suppose you saw any sign of a blonde American woman in the group at those trailers," Graham said.

"You mean Lauren Starling?" Michael asked. "So she's still missing."

"The Denver police are reluctant to call it a missing person. Apparently, she has a history of erratic behavior, and she pulled a disappearing act like this before. But the family is starting to make noise, so they've asked us to take a closer look—not that we have anything to go on. The car is clean—no note, map or anything indicating her intentions."

"I don't think she was at the camp," Abby said. "Everyone I saw had dark hair and looked Latino."

"Just thought I'd ask." Graham turned his attention back to the note. "What do we do about this?"

"It's a fake," Michael said. "Someone is trying to lure Abby and the baby into danger."

"The baby is safe," Carmen said. "Whatever we decide to do won't endanger her."

"We aren't going to do anything," Michael said. "It's too dangerous."

Abby froze in the act of tucking a blanket more securely around the doll. The voice was Michael's, but it could have been her father, telling her she couldn't join the army, or men in her unit protesting that she wasn't capable of leading a patrol, family members saying she couldn't go away to college, or she shouldn't study biology, or do research in remote areas. All her life, people had been telling her what she couldn't do or what she wasn't capable of. *Female* or *beautiful* or *wounded* had been labels they used against her that only made her want to dig in her heels and prove them wrong.

"We've had another new development, which may or may not be related," Graham said.

Abby stopped fussing with the blanket and turned to face the captain once more. He hadn't agreed with Michael. In fact, he'd changed the subject.

"What new development?" Michael arched one eyebrow and waited.

"Richard Prentice has blocked a park service road that crosses his land," Graham said. "It's a public road that predates the park. It's the shortest route—the only route, really—to some rare petroglyphs in the canyon. A group from the University of Denver has been studying them off and on for the past two years. This morning, they found barricades blocking the road. Prentice's lawyers filed an injunction yesterday and a judge ordered the road closed, pending a hearing."

"Why is he closing the road now, after all this time?" Michael asked.

"Because he can," Simon said.

"Or because he's doing something he doesn't want anyone getting close enough to see," Lance said.

"Something like what?" Abby asked.

Graham frowned. Maybe he was weighing the wisdom of discussing a task force case with a civilian. Abby wished she'd kept her mouth shut. Now he might send her from the room. "Abby is part of this now," Carmen said. "And she knows how to keep what we say confidential."

"Of course," she agreed, and sent Carmen a grateful look.

Graham nodded. "Sensors we planted on the public road to measure traffic into the park indicate an increase in the number of vehicles turning onto Prentice's ranch," he said. "More than we can credit to a few college students on their way to the petroglyphs, or Prentice and his various workers and visitors."

"Who do you think is going in and out of there?" Michael asked.

"We've been doing frequent drive-bys, but we haven't seen much," Randall said.

"Prentice complains loudly and long—to the press, to government officials and to anyone else who will listen—that we're harassing him," Simon said.

"We've tried taking a look from the air, but we haven't spotted anything suspicious—yet," Graham said.

"Do you think whatever is going on there has anything to do with Mariposa and Raul Meredes and the illegal workers we saw in the trailers?" Abby asked.

"We just don't know," Graham said.

"But those trailers and people had to go somewhere when they left that wash," Simon said. "Prentice's ranch makes a convenient place for them to disappear quickly. We can't find anyone who saw them after they left you two that morning, and once they hit the park road, the tracks disappeared."

"If I go to this meeting with Mariposa or Meredes or whoever, you can find out more," Abby said. "You might learn something really useful that would help crack the case."

"No!" Michael's protest drowned out whatever

Graham had been about to say. Even a stern look from his boss didn't make him back down. "We shouldn't endanger a civilian," he added.

"This is what we wanted all along, isn't it?" Abby asked. "To lure him into the open so that you can capture him."

"It's too risky," Michael said. "Our original plan was to lure him here, where we have more control over everything. If you move into his territory, the control shifts to him."

Was he so worried about control over the outcome of this plan—or control over her? She tried to tell herself Michael wasn't like that, but her past experiences with the men in her life told her otherwise. After all, how well did she really know this man? He'd first made a claim on her because he'd saved her life. In the golden afterglow of lovemaking, had she misinterpreted an unhealthy obsession for love?

She forced herself to look directly at him, to try to read the true emotion in his dark eyes. But she found only stubbornness. "I'm not helpless," she said. "I've been in dangerous situations before. Much more dangerous. I'm trained to look after myself."

"You don't have an army behind you this time," he said. "Don't confuse foolishness with bravery."

The words stung like a slap. "You don't have a right to tell me what to do!" she protested.

"Abby's right." Graham stepped between them. "This could be the break we've been looking for. If we can get to Meredes, he could lead us to the person behind this whole operation."

"We might find a link between him and Prentice," Simon said.

"This might help save Mariposa and a lot of other innocent people," Abby said. "How could I not do it?"

"We'll set up the meeting for a neutral place," Graham said. "And we'll have plenty of our people watching, on guard if Meredes tries to pull anything."

"If you try to take him there, he's liable to use Abby as a hostage," Michael said.

"If we can't get to him without endangering her, we'll follow him after he leaves," Graham said.

"I want to do this," Abby said. "I want to help these people."

"I still don't think—"

But she didn't get to hear what he did or didn't think. Graham's phone rang, the old-fashioned clanging silencing them all. "Captain Ellison," he answered. He stood up straighter, shoulders tensed, expression alert. "Where?...How many?...We'll be right there."

He ended the call. "That was Randall. He and Marco think they've found the trailers from the camp, or at least some of them."

"Where?" Simon was the first to speak.

"Are there any people in them?" Carmen asked.

Graham turned to the map on the wall behind him. He studied it for a moment, then pointed to a spot on the edge of the parkland. "There's a wash through here. The trailers are there."

Michael joined Graham in front of the map. "That's on the very edge of Richard Prentice's ranch," he said, pointing to the white area marked Private Property on the map.

"And they almost certainly crossed Prentice's land on that road he closed in order to get there," Simon said.

"How did Randall and Marco get there?" Carmen asked.

"They hitched a ride on a BLM chopper," Graham said. "Someone who owed Randall a favor."

"The bigger question is, how are we going to get there?" Michael asked. "Prentice still has the road closed."

"Then we'll have to persuade him to open it." Graham fished car keys from his pocket. "Let's go. Michael, you'd better stay here with Abby."

"I'll come with you," Abby said.

"I can't let you do that," Graham said.

"You need Michael with you, and you can't leave me here unguarded as long as Meredes is looking for me and the baby. Instead of sacrificing one man to babysit me, let me come along. I promise to stay in the vehicle, out of your way." She hesitated, then added, "Please. I need to know if Mariposa is there—if she's safe."

Graham glanced at Michael, then back to Abby. "You can come, but you're to stay well away from the action. Ride with Simon."

"Thank you," she said.

"She can ride with me," Michael said.

"No. I need you focused on the job, not her," Graham said. "Carmen will ride with you. Now let's get going."

Abby tried to arrange the baby doll more comfortably in the sling as the others gathered their gear and prepared to head out. Michael approached her. "I just want to talk to you for a minute," he said in response to her wary look. He pulled her to a corner of the room, away from the others.

"I know what I'm getting into," she said. "I don't need you to protect me."

"I'm not saying you're not smart and capable," he said. "I know you are. But I just found you." He stared into her eyes, pleading. "I don't want to lose you."

"This isn't about you. Or me. It's about doing what's right." She eased from his grasp. "If the captain thinks I can help by agreeing to meet with Meredes, then I have to do it."

Instead of telling her that he didn't like it but he understood—words she wanted, even needed, to hear from him—he turned away. He retreated to the other side of the room, arms folded over his chest, expression sullen.

She struggled to compose herself, to face the others as a strong, determined woman, not letting them see her heartbreak. One night and a few kisses didn't mean Michael had a claim on her, though the pain in her chest as she thought this warned her he might have already staked out a territory she didn't want to relinquish.

Chapter Fourteen

"You hold on to that steering wheel any tighter it's going to come off in your hands. Might make driving awkward."

Carmen spoke lightly, making the words a joke, but when Michael glanced over at his coworker in the Cruiser's passenger seat, she was studying him intently. "You need to relax," she said. "An overbearing attitude isn't going to go over well with a woman like Abby."

He glanced in the mirror at the car behind him, which contained Abby and Simon, but the glare of the sun on the tinted windshield made it impossible to see into the vehicle.

"Leave her alone for a while," Carmen said. "Give her some space and she'll come around."

"What do you know about it?" he asked, annoyed. "Were you eavesdropping?"

"I didn't have to hear a word to know she was upset. Her body language when you ordered her to stand down told the whole story. She wanted you to back her up on this and instead, you tried to shut her down." She shook her head. "Wrong move."

"Shut up." He didn't need anyone telling him where he'd gone wrong with Abby. He'd known he was making a mistake as soon as the words were out of his mouth, but he couldn't stop himself from saying them. She needed someone to look out for her. She'd been pushing through on her own for so long she didn't know how to stop fighting. He'd tried to tell her he was there for her, but instead of reassuring her, he'd come across like some big bully. And he didn't know how to correct that impression now.

Instead, he was stuck watching while she remained determined to put her life on the line to deal with a man it was his job to take care of. His only hope was that something would happen between now and then to make a meeting between Abby and Meredes unnecessary.

Graham, leading the trio of vehicles, slowed for the turn onto Prentice's ranch. The big iron gate was open, allowing them to pass beneath the massive stone archway. "Smile, you're on camera," Michael said, nodding to the lens mounted on the side of the arch.

"And here's the welcoming committee," Carmen said as a Jeep blocked the road ahead. Three beefy men in desert camo, semiautomatic rifles slung across their chests, piled out.

"Armed guards?" Michael shifted the Cruiser into Park and pulled in alongside Graham's vehicle. "Who does this guy think he is?"

"Maybe one of the richest men in the country feels like he has a lot to protect," Carmen said.

"Or a lot to hide." He unsnapped his seat belt and climbed out of the Cruiser and joined the others—except Abby, who'd remained in the car, as ordered, as they gathered around Graham.

"I need you all to get back into your vehicles," the

tallest of the trio, his white-blond hair buzzed into a flattop, said.

No one moved. Michael glared at the other two guards, who took up positions at the front and passenger side of the vehicle. They kept their assault rifles pointed toward the ground, but their manner was still threatening.

"Sir, I'll have to ask you to turn around," the tallest guard said. "This is private property."

"Captain Graham Ellison, Colorado Public Lands Task Force." Graham flashed his badge and credentials. "I'm here to see Mr. Prentice on official business."

"Mr. Prentice doesn't see anyone without an appointment." The guard's expression remained impassive, his gaze fixed on Graham. The credentials might have been bubblegum cards for all he cared.

"I think he'll want to see us," Graham said. "We've discovered what appears to be illegal activity taking place on his property and we need to bring this to his attention."

A single crease formed in the middle of the guard's brow at the words *illegal activity*.

"If you call Mr. Prentice's office, they'll put you in touch with his legal team," he said.

Apparently, one lawyer wasn't enough for this guy— he needed a whole team.

"We don't need to speak to a legal team." Graham's tone grew flinty. "We need to speak with Mr. Prentice. Call him and tell him he needs to talk to us now, or the next time he sees us, we'll have a warrant for his arrest."

The threat was a bluff. While they might find a judge to issue a warrant, they were just as likely to come up against one who was friendly with Prentice. But

Graham did a good job of making the words sound like a promise. The guard hesitated. "Call him," Graham said.

The guard turned away, though the other two remained in position by the Jeep. Michael tapped his foot. If it was up to him, he'd hit the siren and drive forward, forcing the guards to jump out of the way. But maybe that was why Graham was the commander and he wasn't.

The guard finished his phone call and turned back to the car. "Mr. Prentice will spare a few minutes for you. You can follow me to the house." He pointed to Graham. "Just you. The others can stay here."

"Dance, come with me," Graham said. "The rest of you stay here."

Michael moved toward Graham's Cruiser. The guard started to argue, but Graham cut him off. "I'm not going in alone. You wouldn't."

The guard frowned, but nodded and returned to his Jeep. A quarter mile down the drive, a second Jeep fell in behind them. "These people are really beginning to annoy me," Michael said.

"That's probably the point," Graham says. "He wants to rattle us."

"I didn't say I was rattled—just annoyed." He scowled at the building that loomed in front of them. Richard Prentice's "ranch house" was a castle, complete with gray stone walls and a round tower. The three-bay garage to one side was larger than most homes.

Graham parked the Cruiser behind a black Escalade that sat in front of the door, and they climbed out and followed the guards into a dark foyer. After the bright light outside, Michael couldn't make out much about the interior of the house. A long hall seemed to lead farther into the dwelling, but the guard ushered them into a small room just off the foyer. Lined with bookshelves, this room seemed to be a library, though Michael wondered if their host had ever opened most of the matched leather-bound volumes that filled the shelves in neat, coordinated rows.

They waited a full ten minutes, Michael pacing while Graham sat quietly. Neither man said a thing. Michael was sure Prentice had the room bugged—all those books could conceal a lot of recording equipment. "He's not going to see us," Michael said finally. "I think we should go ahead and call the judge, get the warrant."

Thirty seconds later, the door to the room opened and a short man in an expensive suit strolled in. "Richard Prentice." He offered his hand. "Sorry to have kept you waiting."

Based on his reputation for outsize behavior, Michael was startled to find that the man himself was so unimpressive. The ring on his finger was probably worth more than Michael made all year, but Prentice was barely five-eight, and his hair was thinning.

"The phone call I received led me to believe you're accusing me of some illegal activity," Prentice said.

"Not at all," Graham said. "But we wanted to alert you to some illegal activity going on on your property— I know you'll want to cooperate in getting the criminals off your land and in jail where they belong."

"Won't you sit down?" Prentice indicated a pair of wing-back chairs arranged on either side of a small table. He and Graham sat, while Michael remained standing.

Prentice perched on the edge of his chair, gripping

his knees. "You'll need to explain things a little more clearly before I decide if I'm going to 'cooperate.'" He didn't exactly make quote marks in the air around the word, but Michael heard the qualifiers in his tone of voice. Prentice hadn't gotten where he was by cooperating with anyone.

"We've been investigating a possible human trafficking case on federal lands adjacent to your ranch," Graham said. "A man named Raul Meredes, with ties to a Mexican drug cartel, may be behind the ring."

Michael studied Prentice, watching for a reaction to Meredes's name. Did he imagine the way Prentice's lips compressed and the muscles of his jaw tightened? "I've never heard of him," Prentice said. "What does any of this have to do with me?"

"Our aerial reconnaissance has revealed a possible camp where we believe Meredes is holding a number of illegal aliens captive, located just outside the borders of your property."

Prentice's frown deepened at the words *aerial reconnaissance*, but he let it pass. "Let me make sure I understand you, Captain," he said. "This isn't happening on my property."

"No, but—"

"Then, it really isn't my concern." He stepped aside. "You may leave now."

Graham held up his hand. "We have reason to believe Meredes has been using the area—including portions of your estate—for the manufacture and production of narcotics, and as a way station for a human trafficking pipeline from Mexico and South America into Denver."

"Drugs and human trafficking. Those are pretty serious charges. I think I would have noticed if anything like that was taking place around here, and I can promise you, I haven't."

"Your property encompasses over five hundred acres," Graham said. "I think it would be impossible to monitor everything that takes place on an estate that size, especially when so much of it is roadless and rugged. We believe an operation that began on public lands has spilled over onto your property."

"But you don't have proof of that." He looked as calm as if he was discussing the weather.

"If the trailers we spotted from the air are part of the illegal camp, the only way they could have reached their current location is by crossing your land," Graham said.

"I don't put much stock in speculation." He stood back, a clear signal of dismissal. "Thank you for letting me know about this, gentlemen. I'll have my men investigate the matter and I'll let you know what I find."

"This isn't a matter for civilians," Graham said. "We'll need to conduct the investigation. That means we need access across your land to the site."

Prentice looked as if he'd bitten into something rotten. "I see where this is going. This was all a ruse to gain access to my property."

"The lives of innocent people are at stake here, Mr. Prentice."

"If, as you say, they're in this country illegally, and involved in the manufacture and distribution of drugs, then they are far from innocent."

Michael wondered if Prentice practiced that sneer in the mirror, or if it came naturally.

"All we're asking is permission to bring our crews and equipment across your land," Graham said. "On a road that until your court action was a public thoroughfare."

"The court has sided with me in agreeing that the road is private. And my property is private. I won't have you using it to harass me further."

"Mr. Prentice, this may be hard for you to believe, but the world does not revolve around you," Michael said. "This is about other innocent lives that are in danger. Any momentary discomfort for you is incidental."

Prentice glared at him. "I'll ask you to leave now." He turned to Graham. "If you do try anything, my private security force will prevent you from proceeding further. You'll also be hearing from my attorneys."

Graham took a step toward Prentice. He towered over the businessman by at least six inches, and outweighed him by fifty pounds. He didn't raise his voice, because he didn't have to. Years of command, first in the marines, then in law enforcement, had imbued him with a sense of authority. "You can either cooperate and give us access to the approach to that canyon, or I *will* obtain a warrant to search this property. We'll bring in dog teams and helicopters and CSI and everyone else we can think of. We'll search every inch of this place. And I'll make sure the press knows why."

Sweat beaded on Prentice's upper lip, though his expression didn't change. "That's an invasion of privacy."

"Yes, it is. But one that would be necessary."

Michael could practically hear the man's teeth grinding, but Graham had him backed into a corner, and he knew it. He might successfully stall for a while, but if Graham carried out his threat—especially if he got the media involved—Prentice would have no peace for weeks, even months. "You don't really give me any choice, do you?" he said.

"Not really," Graham answered.

Prentice stepped back. "Fine. Use the road. But my men will be watching, and if you travel too far afield, you will need that warrant."

Graham nodded. "Thank you. We appreciate your cooperation." He moved past the businessman; Michael followed.

They'd reached the front door when Prentice's voice rang out behind them. "What will you do with Meredes?" he asked.

Graham looked back. "We'll arrest him and question him. We don't believe he's acting alone. We believe he has someone in Colorado—someone with money and power—who is funding his operations. Possibly a large landowner with a history of antagonism toward the government."

Prentice's face reddened. "What are you saying?"

"I'm not saying anything, Mr. Prentice. Merely answering your question." He nodded. "Goodbye."

Michael waited until they were back in the vehicle before he spoke. "I don't trust him," he said. "He's hiding something."

"He's probably hiding a lot of things," Graham said. "Whether it's anything we're interested in or not, I don't know."

Right. What did they care about Prentice? "What next?"

"Now we see what Randall and Marco uncovered."

They returned to the others, who stood in a cluster around the two Cruisers, Abby with them. Their eyes met, hers full of questions. He resisted the urge to go to her; now wasn't the time. "We have Mr. Prentice's permission to use the road," Graham said.

"We'll escort you," the guard said.

Graham shrugged. "Do you know where we're going?"

"We'll follow you." The guard looked toward the others.

"Don't even think about suggesting they stay behind," Graham said.

They returned to their vehicles and formed a caravan, this time with the guards' two Jeeps bringing up the rear. "What happened in there?" Carmen asked as Michael guided his Cruiser behind Graham's.

"About what we expected—he pretended all of this has nothing to do with him, that his private property rights trump any other concerns. I don't trust him."

"We've never trusted him," Carmen said. "That doesn't mean he's guilty of anything. Maybe he really did close the road after noticing an uptick in traffic. He might not have anything to do with Meredes."

"Then why not cooperate with our efforts to stop him?"

"He's made his reputation out of not cooperating with the Feds on anything. What does he have to gain by doing so now? And he did cooperate in the end. How did Graham manage that?"

"He promised to come back with a warrant and a search team to tear the whole place apart. That worried Prentice enough to give in. But I'm sure we'll be hearing from his lawyers."

"And probably a few journalists. I've noticed he likes to make his case in the press, and they eat it up."

He didn't care about the press. "I wish now Abby had stayed at headquarters."

"Then you would have had to stay, too. Meredes might have decided that was the perfect time to swoop in and take her and the baby."

"You could have stayed with her." Not that staying with Abby was a hardship, but he had a job to do. Staying out of the fray when people needed help struck him as wrong.

"Uh-uh. You signed on for bodyguard duty, not me. Why would I want to sit out the action?"

"I know Spanish. A lot of these immigrants don't speak any English."

"I know Spanish, too, amigo."

They stopped at the edge of the wash. Graham climbed out of his Cruiser and the others joined him. "Randall and Marco said they think the trailers are down here," he said.

"In the bottom of the wash?" Simon looked skeptical.

Graham walked to the edge the ravine and took out a pair of binoculars. "I see something." He passed the glasses to Michael. Sunlight glinted off metal at the bottom of the wash.

One of the guards had out his own binoculars. "Looks to me as if the rancher who owned this before used it as a dump site," he said. "People did that back then—when a ravine was full of junk cars and metal, they'd haul in a load of dirt to cover it up."

"There's no rust on that metal," Michael said. "It hasn't been sitting there for decades."

Graham reached into the Cruiser for his pack. "We'd better go down there."

"We'd better hurry," Carmen said. She'd taken out her own pair of binoculars. "I see movement." She focused the glasses closer. "It's a woman, and she's waving something. I think she's signaling for help."

Chapter Fifteen

Abby stood on tiptoe, trying to see what was happening in the ravine, but here by the Cruiser, she was too far away from the action. Apparently, they'd found some people alive down there, but she had no idea who. She wanted to be helping, instead of stuck up here with this hot, heavy baby doll strapped to her torso. She was tempted to stick the doll in the back of the Cruiser and join the others at the ravine. Who would even notice? Prentice's guards ignored her, their attention focused on the action below.

Michael emerged from the trail that led into the canyon and she started toward him, eager for news. Despite the tension between them earlier, she was sure he wouldn't shut her out.

"Send every ambulance you can spare. And hurry." He spoke not to her, but into his phone, as he hurried toward her.

"What's going on?" she asked, meeting him in front of the vehicle.

"Hey. Are you okay?" He squeezed her arm and looked into her eyes.

"I'm fine. But what's happening down there?" She nodded toward the canyon. "Who's hurt?"

He released her and moved to the back of the Cruiser and began pulling out emergency gear—a first-aid kit, blankets and water. "It's pretty bad down there," he said. "Maybe a dozen wounded. Some dead." He crammed supplies into a pack as he spoke.

"But how?" Abby tried to take in this news.

"Looks as though somebody—Meredes and his men, probably—pulled the trailers up to the edge of the ravine and pushed them over—with all the people locked inside."

She stared at him, unsure she'd heard him correctly. "Is Mariposa there?" she asked, afraid to say the words.

"I haven't seen her yet, so maybe she wasn't there or she got away."

She hugged the baby closer, as if she could take some comfort from the doll. "Why do something so horrible?"

"I guess they weren't useful to the operation anymore. They were a liability, so he got rid of them."

Nausea rose in her throat. The man responsible for this was the same one who wanted Angelique. Thank God the baby was safe. "What are you going to do?"

He shouldered the pack. "We're going to go after him," he said. "We're going to make him pay for this."

"I have to meet with him," she said. "If that's the best way to draw him out, I have to do it."

He grasped her hand and gave it a gentle squeeze. "I know," he said. "I don't like it, but I understand. I'm sorry I came on so strong before. It's just… I don't want anything to happen to you."

"I'll be okay." She managed a brief smile. "I have a lot to live for."

He glanced over his shoulder at the ravine. "I'd better get back down there."

"What can I do to help?" she asked.

"Nothing right now. Stay up here. Out of the way."

When he was gone, she felt even more useless and worried. The sun beat down with searing intensity. Still cradling her fake charge, she moved into the shade, the shouts of those below drifting up to her as they worked to save the injured and dying. She felt numb, the way she'd felt in Afghanistan after encountering tragedy, the horror of the events too much to take.

She leaned against the tree and closed her eyes, willing herself not to fall apart. This wasn't about her. The others didn't need anyone else to look after right now. She had to keep it together.

Something tugged at her arm and she jerked upright, eyes wide, mouth open to scream, but a hand clamped over her lips silenced her. "Don't make any noise, senorita. While the others are busy, you will come with me." She stared into Raul Meredes's eyes, fighting panic, as he covered her face with a cloth and the world went black.

ABBY CAME TO in the backseat of a vehicle, wedged between the door and the body of a man who sat with a rifle resting across his knees. The vehicle hit a bump and her head knocked against the door. She grunted, the only sound she could make against the gag that all but choked her, and the man turned to look at her, then said something in Spanish to whoever was driving.

Her arms and shoulders ached from where one of her captors had tied her hands behind her back, and the bandanna in her mouth tasted of cotton and dust. Her captors hadn't bothered covering her eyes, though all she could see from here was the back of the seat in front of her, and the profile of the man beside her. He wore fatigues and dusty boots, and the hands that cradled the rifle were dirty, the nails bitten.

This man wasn't Meredes. She wondered if he was driving. Was there another guard in the front passenger seat? She and Michael had seen at least three other men with guns when they came to move the trailers, but for all she knew, Meredes had a dozen at his command.

She couldn't see the baby. They would have figured out quickly that it was a fake. They must have been watching, and seen that the others were preoccupied with the goings-on in the canyon. Or maybe Prentice had called Meredes to warn him of the task force's discovery. He couldn't resist the opportunity to snatch the child. Was he furious at being frustrated in his efforts to obtain the baby? Would he take that frustration out on her? A man who would callously push imprisoned people to their death in a canyon wasn't likely to have qualms about hurting a woman who had crossed him.

She wondered how long it would be before Michael and the others realized she was missing. They ought to be able to follow the trail of this vehicle over the rough terrain, but then what? If Meredes planned to use her as a hostage and bargain for the baby, she might have a chance to escape. But what if he wanted to send a different kind of message—by killing her and disposing of the body?

She shuddered and pushed the thought away. That kind of thinking would get her nowhere. In the army, she'd been trained to focus on escape and survival. If she could do the first, she knew how to do the second. She could find food and shelter in the wilderness. All she needed was an opportunity to slip away from Meredes and the man beside her.

The vehicle jerked to a stop, the brakes squealing. The guard got out, then came around to her side of the vehicle, opened the door and took hold of her bound arms and dragged her out of the car. A hot breeze buffeted her as she steadied herself, and she squinted at the surrounding landscape. They'd stopped at the edge of the canyon—Black Canyon, the one that gave the park its name. This must have been part of the gorge that wasn't in the national park, away from tourists and traffic.

She'd correctly guessed that Meredes was driving. He walked around the vehicle and stood in front of her. Though not a big man, he was tall, and wiry. He wore his sideburns long, but was clean shaven, his white shirt stiff with starch, his jeans precisely creased. It seemed odd to find a dandy here in the middle of the wilderness.

He said something in Spanish and the guard pulled a large knife from his belt. Her terror must have shown on her face. He laughed and waved the knife in front of her nose, then bent and cut the restraints from her ankles.

The passenger door of the vehicle opened and Abby received another shock to her system as Mariposa stepped out. The other woman frowned at her. What was she thinking? Was she upset that Abby hadn't brought the baby? Had she known about the plan to kill her co-workers by pushing the trailers into the ravine, or was she an unwilling pawn? What was her relationship to Meredes? Was he her lover? Her captor? Both?

The guard shoved Abby toward the edge of the canyon. Her heart hammered in her chest and she dug in her heels. Did they intend to throw her into the chasm and leave her to die, as they'd done with the workers in the trailers?

Her guard said something in Spanish and Meredes addressed her. "Follow me," he said, and indicated a narrow trail that led along the side of the canyon.

The barrel of the rifle pressed to her back told her she had no choice in the matter. She fell into step behind Mariposa, the guard behind her. Meredes led them along the canyon rim and then down into the canyon itself, the trail cut into the canyon wall. They descended about twenty feet, to a narrow ledge where someone had built a cabin. The stone-and-wood structure hugged the side of the gorge, blending perfectly with its surroundings. It would be invisible from anyone who didn't already know it was there.

Inside, the cabin was furnished simply but comfortably, with a double bed, a sofa and a table with four chairs arranged around an iron woodstove. The guard knelt before the stove and began building a fire. Despite the heat on the canyon rim, the air here in the shadowed chasm held a chill. Meredes shoved Abby into a chair. Mariposa filled a kettle from a water barrel by the door and set it on the stove to heat.

Meredes faced Abby and removed the gag. "What have you done with Angelique?" he asked.

"She's safe," Abby said. She watched Mariposa as she spoke; the woman's shoulders sagged with relief.

"You were stupid to think you could fool me," Meredes said. "Do not make that mistake again."

She said nothing, only glared at him. "Where is the child?" he asked.

"She's somewhere safe," Abby repeated. "She's in a

good home." She hoped Mariposa knew enough English to understand the words.

"She belongs here."

"Why? So you can make a slave of her the way you have these other people?"

He slapped her, a hard, stinging blow that snapped her head back and made her ears ring.

"That is not your concern." He shoved her into a chair, then settled onto the sofa. Mariposa brought him a mug; Abby caught the aroma of coffee. He sipped the drink and settled back against the cushions, a man comfortable in his home.

"Why did you murder those people?" she asked.

His expression didn't change. "What people are you accusing me of murdering?"

"The people who worked for you. The ones in the camp. You locked them in their trailers and pushed the trailers into the ravine."

Crockery rattled, and they both turned to look at Mariposa, who quickly turned away. Had she not known about the fate of her fellow immigrants? "I don't know what you're talking about," Meredes said, though his eyes told a different story. The hatred she saw there made her shiver.

"Some of them survived," she said. "The Rangers rescued them. They'll be able to identify you as the one who held them prisoner, then tried to murder them."

"They cannot identify someone who was not there," he said.

"I don't believe you," she said.

"It doesn't matter to me what you believe," he said. "Once I have the baby, you will be no use to me anymore."

"Do you think you're going to trade me for the baby?" she asked.

"Trade?" He sipped his coffee. "That is what I will let the Rangers think, but I promise you, senorita, you will never leave here alive."

MICHAEL HELPED LOAD the last stretcher into the waiting ambulance. The man strapped there had borne the rough ride up from the canyon floor in stoic silence, only occasional grunts betraying the pain from his broken leg and ribs. "You're going to be okay," Michael said in Spanish, and patted the man's shoulder. The man stared back at him, one unspoken question in his eyes—*why*?

Michael had asked himself the same question a dozen times in the past two hours. Why would someone do this to innocent people who worked for him? "If Meredes had no use for them anymore, why didn't he just turn them loose in the nearest town to make their own way back to the border or to find work elsewhere?" he asked Carmen as they headed back to his Cruiser. "Why go to so much trouble to harm them?"

"Maybe he wanted to make a point," Simon said. "To let word get around about what happened to anyone who crossed him. Fear is power to a man like that."

"Maybe he's just a psycho who gets off on hurting people," Randall said.

And this was the guy they were willingly going to let Abby face? Michael shuddered, and looked around for Abby. Just seeing her would make him feel better.

"Where's Abby?" he asked.

The others looked around. "Is she in the car?" Carmen asked.

"She's not here," Simon said from beside his Cruiser.

Heart racing, Michael ran to the clump of trees where he'd seen Abby last. He stared at the scuff marks in the dirt, not wanting to believe what he was seeing. "Randall, get Lotte over here," he said.

The young ranger looked up from adding a bottle of water to the dog's dish. "What is it?" he asked.

"Just bring her over here. Now."

"Lotte. Come."

The dog obediently trotted along beside Randall, to where Michael crouched next to the scuff marks. "Abby's gone," he said. "I think this is where they took her. She struggled. I need Lotte to help us find her." He struggled to keep his voice calm and dispassionate, though inside he wanted to scream.

"We don't need a dog to follow this trail." Simon pointed out across the desert. "The tire tracks are easy enough to see in this terrain."

Michael stood and clamped Randall on the shoulder. "Come on," he said. "Maybe we have time to catch up with them."

"Wait just a minute." Graham's command stopped them. He joined them in studying the tire tracks headed into the desert. "You can't go tearing off without a plan."

"Meredes probably isn't alone," Carmen said. "If you corner him, you put Abby in danger."

"She's already in danger," Michael said. "The man's a murderer."

"He took her alive." Graham pointed to the ground. "There's no blood. He probably plans to use her to trade for the baby."

"Which we can't give him," Carmen said.

Michael took a deep breath, struggling to control his emotions. "So we follow him, but we don't make any rash moves. We find out where he's taking Abby and scope out the situation. Then we formulate a plan to rescue her."

"All right." Graham nodded. "Carmen, you go with them. Keep me posted about whatever you find."

Michael pulled out his keys. "Come on," he said.

They piled into the Cruiser, Carmen in the front with Michael, Randall and Lotte in the back. Carmen rolled down her window and leaned out. "It should be pretty easy to follow the tracks through here," she said.

"He must have some kind of hideout," Randall said. "Either that, or he knows a shortcut back to the main road."

"Get the map from the console and tell me if you see any likely hiding places," Michael said. He hunched over the steering wheel, following the faint depressions made by the vehicle's tires across the prairie. He wanted to tear out across the empty expanse, but the rocky ground forced him to reduce his speed to scarcely above a crawl.

The stiff paper of the map crackled as Randall spread it out. "There's half a dozen side canyons branching off from the main gorge in this direction," he said. "Careful you don't drive us into one."

"Do you see any place that would make a good hideout?" Michael asked.

"Dozens of places," Randall said. "There's the canyons, old buildings left from the days when this was a ranch. And he could pull a trailer in anywhere. No roads, though, so he's probably not headed to town."

"Just keep following the tracks," Carmen said. She leaned forward, squinting out the windshield. "And keep your speed down, so you don't kick up dust. We don't want him to know we're tailing him."

"He's far enough ahead he can't see our dust," Michael said, but he forced himself to ease off the accelerator.

He guided the Cruiser along a dry creek bed, around an outcropping of rock. The remains of an old corral appeared on their left, ancient fence posts sticking up from the eroded land like broken teeth. "The map indicates some old ranch buildings around here," Randall said. "Keep an eye out for vehicles."

"I see something." Carmen grabbed his wrist and he braked to a halt. She pointed to the ruins of an old log cabin. "There's a car parked there."

He peered closer and could make out the front bumper and headlights of a vehicle. "Looks like an older Jeep," Randall said.

"Let's get out and take a look." He backed up and parked the Cruiser in the shadow of the outcropping they'd just passed, out of sight of the old Jeep. Michael looked through the gap between the boulders out on what must have been an old bunkhouse or line shack, the roof caved in, glassless windows showing grass and piñons growing up from the dirt floor. The vehicle, an older Jeep Cherokee, had been parked against the remains of a log wall, partially hidden from view.

He settled into position behind the right-hand boulder and took a pair of binoculars from the pack.

"See anything?" Randall asked.

"Just the Jeep. It wasn't one of the vehicles Abby and I saw at the camp. Maybe it's been parked there awhile. It doesn't look as though anything but coyotes have been out here for years."

"The maps designate the ruins as a historical structure," Randall said. "Part of the ranch that operated here before the park."

"Doesn't the park date back to the thirties?" Carmen asked.

"Something like that," Randall said. "Amazing how long things last in this dry air." He snapped the leash on Lotte. "She'll tell us if anyone's been here recently, and where they've gone."

Moving quickly and quietly, they shouldered day packs, and Michael picked up the assault rifle he'd removed from the gun safe at headquarters that morning. The memory of that first day Abby had walked into headquarters, when they'd been pinned down by that sniper, still burned fresh. He could still recall the feel of her body beneath his, and the fierce protectiveness he'd felt for her even then. Multiply that anxiety by twenty now.

They approached the Jeep from an angle, spreading out and putting Lotte in front. The dog remained relaxed, tail up, ears erect, nose alert. "She'd tell us if anyone was around," Randall said. "Whoever parked there is long gone."

"Not too long." Michael pressed his palm against the hood of the vehicle and felt the heat of the engine.

Carmen dropped to one knee at the front of the Jeep. "The pattern on the tires looks the same as the ones we've been following," she said.

He scrutinized the landscape around them, alert for any sign that someone was near. But he didn't have the sense that anyone was watching. A hot wind buffeted them, bringing the scents of sage and piñon. The only sounds were the scrape of their boots on rock and the occasional creak of a pack strap or the clink of the rifle stock against the pack. Whoever had driven this Jeep seemed to have disappeared.

He pulled a pair of thin latex gloves from his pocket and slipped them on, then carefully opened the driver's door. The brown cloth seats were worn, a rip in the back repaired with duct tape. The cup holder was empty, as was the center console and the glove box. No dust collected on the dash. "It looks like they wiped it clean," he said. "But we'll get someone to check for prints anyway."

He moved to the backseat. More of the same. He might have been looking at a used car for sale on a dealer's lot. He started to close the door when the glint of something on the floorboard caught his attention. He bent to get a closer look and his heart stopped beating for a moment. Carefully, he reached down and picked up the little ceramic figure of a brown-and-white rabbit.

"What have you got there?" Carmen came to stand beside him.

"It's Abby's," he said. "She was here." He folded his hand around the good-luck charm and looked at the seemingly empty prairie around them. A few hundred yards away, the ground fell away, into yet another canyon. Abby had been here, maybe only moments before. But where was she now?

Chapter Sixteen

"Please, make yourself comfortable." Raul Meredes motioned to the chair across from the sofa in the little cabin.

"I can't be comfortable with my hands tied like this," Abby said. She'd never be comfortable as long as she was held prisoner here, but she saw no sense in pointing that out to a man whose whole livelihood revolved around imprisoning people against their will.

In answer, he reached into the pocket of his neatly pressed jeans and pulled out a large knife. He pressed a button and a blade sprang out, sharp and gleaming. Abby shrank from it and he laughed, then grabbed her shoulder and turned her around.

Having her hands free again felt wonderful, then it felt awful, as blood flow returned and with it sharp pains like needles, up and down her arms. She massaged her forearms and wrists and looked at Mariposa, who had watched the exchange without a word. The other woman turned away, her attention on the kettle on the stove.

"Sit," Meredes ordered, and Abby did so, perched on the edge of the chair as if poised to run at the first opportunity. But she had nowhere to run, with the deep canyon on one side of the cabin and guards all around it. She wanted to ask what he intended to do with her—but she wasn't sure she really wanted to know the answer to that question, or that Meredes would tell her the truth.

She focused again on Mariposa. The stove made the cabin uncomfortably warm, even with the windows open. Standing next to it, Mariposa must be burning up, but she showed no signs of discomfort. She spooned instant coffee into two cups and added boiling water, then took one cup to Meredes. He smiled and caressed her hip, then pinched her bottom. Her expression never changed, though when she turned away, Abby thought she read disgust in the woman's eyes.

Mariposa brought the second cup to Abby. *"Gracias,"* Abby said. She sipped the brew to be polite, though she wasn't a fan of instant coffee; this concoction tasted particularly nasty.

"What happened to your face?"

The question startled her, both because she hadn't expected El Jefe to talk to her, and because most people—most adults anyway—were too polite to ask about her scar.

"I was injured in the war," she said.

"You should have plastic surgery to fix it," he said. "Without the scar, you would be beautiful."

Her hand tightened on the cup. She wanted to hurl the hot liquid into his face, but she wanted more to keep living, unharmed, so she simply said, "Some things can't be fixed."

"This is what happens when women try to fight," he said. "They are too sentimental to make good warriors. And they make the men around them soft."

She'd heard similar opinions from some of the men

she'd served with in the army. But the majority of her fellow soldiers had respected her and trusted her skills and training.

"Do you have other injuries from the war?" he asked.

Everyone she knew who'd fought had injuries, even though many of them weren't visible. "I don't see how it matters to you," she said.

"I was making conversation. Passing the time." He looked offended.

She sat back in the chair, determined to appear relaxed, even if she wasn't. "How long do you intend to stay here?" she asked.

"As long as necessary," he said, which was no answer at all. She was sure he was purposely trying to frustrate her, so she said nothing.

"I will offer to trade you to the Rangers for Angelique," he said after a moment.

"If Mariposa wants her baby back, she can petition the court to return her to her." Though Abby wasn't sure how the court would view an illegal immigrant who had willfully handed over her infant to a stranger.

"Why would I waste my time with courts and judges? My way is much faster, and more effective."

He sounded so sure, but she doubted the Rangers—even Michael—would hand over the child in exchange for her. "Why do you want the baby?" she asked.

He scowled. Clearly, he didn't like being on the receiving end of nosy questions. She braced herself for an angry retort. Instead, he sipped more coffee, then said, "Mariposa is sad without her. I don't like to see her sad."

Mariposa, bent over something in the sink, hunched her shoulders.

Abby looked back at Meredes. "Are you the baby's father?"

His scowl made deep lines, like gullies, on his sun-damaged face. "Does that surprise you?" he asked. "Do you think a man like me would not value a daughter? One of the things that makes something valuable is rarity. With my wife in Tamaulipas, I have four sons. But I have only one daughter. She will be a great beauty."

Of course. Beautiful women were the ones who counted. Hadn't she been hearing that all her life?

She stood. "I'll help Mariposa in the kitchen." Surely he would think that was an appropriate place for a woman.

He made no objection, so she moved to the sink and began drying the cups the other woman washed. *"Gracias,"* Mariposa whispered, her voice barely audible.

Abby had so many questions she wanted to ask: *Why are you with this man? Has he hurt you? Why did you give your baby to me?*

But Meredes's looming presence, not to mention the language barrier, prevented them from communicating with anything beyond looks.

As she stacked the dried dishes on the shelf above the counter, she looked for a knife or other weapon. But even if she found one, what good would it do? One knife was no match against Meredes and his guards. She could see one of the men out the kitchen window, pacing back and forth, weapon slung across his chest, a cigarette pinched between his lips.

Michael and the others would be looking for her. The

Jeep tracks wouldn't have been too difficult to follow across the prairie, provided they'd discovered them and linked the tracks to her disappearance. Meredes hadn't tried to cover the tracks—maybe because he'd known that once they reached the remote canyon, locating the cabin would be more difficult. A visitor had to be practically on top of the building before it was visible, and the guards would see any intruder long before he'd be aware of them.

If he planned to trade her for the baby, he'd likely arrange some kind of meeting. That would be her best opportunity to escape. Until then, she'd remain alert and bide her time.

The dishes done, Mariposa indicated that Abby should sit once more. Abby reluctantly turned to the chair across from El Jefe. Mariposa started to sit at the table, but El Jefe held out his hand to her. *"Sentarse conmigo,"* he said, and pulled her into his lap.

Abby looked away as he stroked his hand up and down Mariposa's thigh. The other woman looked miserable, but she didn't try to fight him. Maybe she'd learned doing so was futile. And maybe he was only fondling Mariposa because he sensed it made Abby uncomfortable. She assumed a disinterested expression and tried to think of some way to distract him.

"Did Richard Prentice supply this cabin?" she asked.

His hand stilled and something flickered in his eyes—was it anger, or fear? But he quickly recovered. "I do not know this Richard Prentice," he said.

"You don't know the largest landholder in the county?"

"Maybe I have heard of him, but I do not know him."

"You're practically on his land. Maybe you *are* on

his land." She tried to remember the layout of the map Michael had shown her. The park boundary must be near here.

"I am on public land. There is a great deal of public land in Colorado, free for anyone to use. So much of it is empty. No one ever visits. This suits our purposes well."

"What is your purpose here?" she asked.

His expression transformed to a sneer, but he remained silent.

"What happened to those people we saw at the campground?" she asked. "Who were they? What were they doing?"

"There were no people," he said. "No campground."

"But I saw them. There were four travel trailers and all of these people. You moved them away with trucks." *And pushed them to the bottom of a ravine.* She swallowed hard, wondering if she dared confront him again with what she knew he'd done.

His eyes met hers, and the look in them made her feel cold in spite of the summer heat. "Senorita, if you know what is good for you, you will accept that you never saw such people," he said.

"Lotte tracked Abby right to the edge of the canyon, here." Michael pointed to the place on the map on the wall of ranger headquarters. "She was there, I'm sure of it." The frustration of being so close and not being able to reach Abby gnawed at him.

"Meredes must have some kind of hideout nearby, but it's well guarded," Randall said. He rubbed his shoulder where a fragment of rock had nicked him after the guards started firing. One minute, the three of them and Lotte had been standing on the rim of the canyon, peering down. The next they'd been forced to retreat to the Cruiser. Even Michael had reluctantly agreed they needed reinforcements.

"That's almost at Prentice's boundary." Graham traced the blue line on the map that marked the edge of park lands.

"*Almost* only counts in horseshoes and hand grenades," Randall said.

"Don't tell me a man with ties to a Mexican drug cartel is hiding out that close and Prentice knows nothing about it," Michael said.

"It's what he'll say," Simon said. "And we can't prove any different."

"Then, find me some proof that links him to Meredes," Graham said.

"What do the workers we pulled from the rubble in that wash say?" Graham asked.

"Simon and I interviewed a couple of the victims at the hospital," Marco said. "But they're terrified to say much. The man they know as El Jefe promised them work—jobs paying more than they'd been told they could earn working for the farmers or ranchers in the area. When they agreed to do the work, he brought them here and made them prisoners. During the day, they worked growing marijuana. They traveled to and from the grow sites under armed guard. At night they were locked into the trailers and more guards kept watch."

"They can't tell us where the grow operation is," Simon said.

"Do you believe them?" Graham asked.

"I do," Marco said. "It's easy to get turned around out there in the wilderness, and the guards didn't take them over any recognizable roads. They moved around a lot, to avoid detection."

"What about the woman—Mariposa?" Carmen asked. "Where does she fit in all this?"

"She didn't work in the fields with the others," Marco said. "She did most of the cooking and cleaning. El Jefe singled her out. She wasn't exactly his girlfriend, but she had special privileges."

"So he might be the baby's father," Carmen said.

"We didn't ask about that," Simon said. "We were more interested in determining how the organization is structured."

"They all said they had never seen a man who looked like Richard Prentice in their camp," Marco said. "But they didn't get many visitors of any kind—just El Jefe and the guards."

"Prentice wouldn't dirty his hands mingling with the workers," Michael said.

He paced the conference room, unable to sit. Abby had been in or near that canyon, with Meredes, he was sure. She'd definitely been in that Jeep, and left the rabbit behind. Had she accidentally dropped it, or had she left it on purpose for him to find? "We need to go back there, find Meredes and rescue Abby," he said. "Go in there with everything we've got."

"We're not going to do that." If Graham shared Michael's rage toward the Mexican, he didn't show it. "We've got a potential hostage situation. We're going to approach this cautiously and minimize the risk to everyone."

"But those people are killers." Saying the word out loud made him shake.

"That's why we won't rush in."

Graham's calm only increased Michael's agitation. *Get a grip*, he told himself, and walked away, fighting to keep his composure. Everything the captain said made sense. But his emotions where Abby was concerned didn't always respond to logic.

"You got it bad, don't you?" Randall joined him in the corner of the room and spoke softly.

"I care about her."

"Just don't let it mess with your judgment."

"My judgment is fine." But even as he said the words, he wondered. By focusing on Abby, was he losing sight of the bigger picture, the reason he was doing this job in the first place? He wasn't here to protect just one woman, but to make life safer for many people—visitors to the park, the illegal immigrants who fell victim to the drug dealers' scams and the people whose lives could be ruined by the drugs they imported. So much more was at stake than his relationship to one woman.

When had she become so important to him? He couldn't identify a single moment when she'd changed from someone who'd made a strong impression on him in the past to the woman he loved. When she'd walked back into his life that afternoon at ranger headquarters he'd been impressed by her strength and bravery, touched by her compassion, and yes, physically attracted to her. All that had come together for him sometime over the past few days. They'd clicked, and last night at her trailer, he'd been sure she felt the same.

Then he'd blown it by coming on too strong.

A ringing phone shook the tense silence of the room. Carmen answered. "Public Lands Task Force."

Her expression of calm dissolved into one of agitation. "Just a minute." She held the phone out to Graham. "It's for you. Raul Meredes."

Graham took the receiver and punched the button to put the call on speakerphone. "I have something you want." Meredes's voice, heavily accented but clear and precise, filled the room. "Since you also have something I want, I think we should make a trade."

Graham said nothing, but nodded to Simon, who went to the computer and began trying to trace the call.

"Are you listening, Captain?"

"I'm listening."

"You will bring the baby to the old water tank by the old ranch corral at eight o'clock tonight. The women and I will be there, waiting."

"We can't meet that soon," Graham said. "The baby isn't close and we have to get her. We can meet you in the morning."

Michael took a step toward the captain. Was he serious about leaving Abby with a killer overnight? Randall took his arm. Michael tried to shake him off, but the younger man held tight.

"You will bring her this evening." Meredes's words were clipped—an order, not a request.

"We can't," Graham lied. "She's in Denver. Even if we chartered a private plane and left now, we couldn't get her back here by eight." The captain's gaze found and held Michael's, sending the message to keep quiet and trust him.

Michael remained tense, but he nodded to Randall, letting him know he didn't have to restrain him anymore.

"In the morning, then. 6:00 a.m."

"How do we know Abby is safe?" Graham asked. "We don't have a deal if you've harmed her."

The thought that Abby might be injured—or worse—made Michael's stomach roil. He balled his hands into fists and waited for Meredes's answer.

"If you want to see her safely, you will bring the baby to me in the morning," Meredes said.

Before Graham could reply, a woman's breathy gasp replaced the Mexican's gruff voice. "Captain, is that you?" Abby's words were high-pitched and strained.

"Yes, it's me. Abby, are you all right?"

"Do as he says, Captain," she pleaded, on the verge of tears. "Please."

With a click, the call ended, the hum of dead air filling the room.

Randall patted Michael's back. "We'll take care of him, don't worry," he said softly.

"Oh, we'll take care of him, all right," Michael said. He blinked, trying to clear his vision of the angry red haze. He straightened and nodded to Randall to show he was all right. Rage wasn't going to get Abby back.

He turned to Graham. "What's the plan?"

Chapter Seventeen

Meredes lifted the blade of the knife from Mariposa's throat and Abby let out a gasp of relief. One moment he'd been talking on the phone with Graham and the next he had jerked Mariposa to him and pressed the knife to her throat. "Tell them to do as I say or I will cut her," he'd growled.

Mariposa, eyes wide with terror, had whimpered as a trickle of blood had formed along the edge of the knife. Meredes had thrust the phone into Abby's shaking hand. "Tell them," he'd commanded.

She'd forced the words past the fear in her throat, terrified that Meredes would kill Mariposa right in front of her.

He'd brought the women with him out of the cabin and up onto the canyon's rim. He'd refused to say where they were going, but when he'd stopped only a short distance away and pulled out his phone, she'd realized he'd only been moving to where he could get a good cell signal.

He replaced the knife in the sheath on his belt and took the phone from her. "He says the baby is in Denver. Is this true?" he asked.

The last she'd heard, Angelique was with a woman

in Grand Junction. But maybe she'd been moved to put her farther from danger. Or maybe Graham was putting off Meredes to buy time. Maybe he had a plan to rescue her. "I don't know where they took her," she said. "But the offices for the state child welfare services are in Denver, so it makes sense they'd take her there."

The answer didn't seem to please him, but he said nothing more on the subject. "Come." He motioned for her to move ahead of him, then took hold of Mariposa's arm and dragged her after them. She held one hand over the cut on her neck and stared at the ground. Abby thought of dogs who cringed at their master's abuse, yet continued to follow after them. Did Mariposa seriously care about Meredes, or did she simply think she had no other choice but to try to stay in his good graces?

Inside the cabin once more, she followed Mariposa to the sink. "Let me," she said, and took a cloth and wet it under the faucet, then pressed it to the cut. Mariposa winced, then tried a wavering smile. *"Gracias,"* she whispered.

"Leave her," Meredes ordered.

Abby ignored him. He still needed to be able to show her to the Rangers when they arrived if he had any hope of retrieving the baby. As long as he thought that, he wasn't going to do her any serious harm.

"Do you want me to cut her again?" he asked. "I said, leave her."

Mariposa understood his harsh tone of voice, if not his words. She pushed Abby away from her. Reluctantly, Abby returned to the chair across from Meredes. "As a former soldier, you should understand the importance of obeying orders," he said.

"I pledged to obey my commanders in the army," she said. "I never made that kind of promise to you."

"I am more powerful than you," he said. "That is all the authority I need."

She couldn't argue with his assertion that he had power over her for the moment, but she held on to the hope that that would change. Michael and the others would come to rescue her. But she had a long night ahead of her first.

Night came early to the little cabin. The canyon walls blocked the sun and cast the dwelling in twilight in early afternoon. The shadows continued to lengthen until full darkness shrouded the hiding place. Mariposa moved to the kitchen and began taking cans and packages from the cabinet. "Can I help?" Abby asked.

Mariposa glanced at her, then at Meredes, who sat by the woodstove, cleaning his nails with the blade of the knife. He looked up when Abby stood and moved into the kitchen, but made no objection. Mariposa handed her a can of beans and an opener, and pantomimed that she should dump the contents of the can into the large pot she'd set on the stove.

While Abby opened cans, she stared out the window over the sink. She could no longer see much of the landscape, but she already knew that the window looked out into the canyon itself. If she tried to climb out it, she'd only fall to her death, hundreds of feet below. The two guards watched the front of the little house; occasionally she heard them talking in Spanish, or smelled the smoke from their cigarettes. The back of the house rested against rock. El Jefe had chosen his hideout well for its protected position.

She glanced up at the low ceiling, then quickly away.

The gunshots she'd heard earlier must have been the guards firing at the Rangers. They'd retreated for the moment, but she didn't believe they'd give up so easily. They'd wait until dark, and come in with reinforcements.

With canned vegetables and some spices, Mariposa made a soup that was more delicious than Abby would have thought possible. Though nerves stole her appetite, she forced herself to eat a little. She needed to remain strong for whatever ordeal lay ahead.

After the women washed the dishes and put them away, Mariposa went to the bed in the corner and lay down, her back to them.

"Is she all right?" Abby asked. The other woman's sudden retreat alarmed her.

"Leave her," Meredes said. "She misses the little one."

"She must have thought the baby would be safer with me than staying here with you," Abby said.

"It wasn't me she was worried about, it was Denver. She's afraid of cities."

"Denver?"

"I told her I was taking her and the baby to Denver. She should have been happy to leave this desolate place."

"What was she going to do in Denver?"

He shrugged. "Nothing difficult. I would set her up in a house there. Occasionally, she'd entertain some friends I would send to her. Nothing difficult."

Abby watched Mariposa as he spoke. Her back stiffened, then she smothered a sob. Understanding washed over her in a sickening wave as she remembered what

Michael had told her. She forced herself to look at Meredes again. "You wanted her to be a prostitute."

"It's easier work than any she'd have found if she'd stayed in Tampico. And she could have kept the baby with her."

Except Mariposa wanted more for her daughter than a life of slavery. So she'd given her away. Abby swallowed the emotions that threatened to overtake her.

"She wants the baby back now, so I told her I'd get her for her," he said.

"How thoughtful of you."

He must not have missed the sarcasm in her voice. "She'll work better if she's happy," he said.

But how could anyone kept a prisoner be happy? She had to do something to help her new friend, and to help herself in the process. But what? She returned to her seat on the sofa and tried to think, but her thoughts spun in circles. After a while, lulled by the silence and weary from the stressful day, she dozed.

"THE WATER TANK where Meredes wants to meet is here." Graham indicated the dot on the map labeled Historic Structure.

"And the Jeep was parked about here." Randall pointed to a second dot, several hundred yards from the first.

"And we were fired on from here." Marco indicated a spot on the edge of the canyon. "So the hideout is probably very near there. The shorter distance he has to travel to make the exchange, the less chance of our intercepting him or Abby making a run for it."

"Would she do that?" Carmen asked. "Make a run for it, I mean?"

Michael realized she'd addressed the question to him. "How should I know?" he said. He'd make a run for it, but Abby was a woman, and he was clearly no expert on the female sex.

"You know," Carmen said. "You've spent more time with her than anyone. Is she the type to be paralyzed by fear, or would she save herself?"

He thought back to how Abby had handled herself that first day, when they'd been trapped by the sniper. Even fighting flashbacks to the war, she'd held herself together. She'd faced her fears. And when they'd been lost in the backcountry, she hadn't panicked or blamed him, or any of the things other people might have done under similar circumstances. She'd looked after the baby, found food for them to eat and settled in to wait. "She wouldn't panic," he said. "She's the type who assesses a problem and tries to find solutions. And she'd fall back on her military training. In the army, they train you to focus on escape if you're captured, so she'll be looking for opportunities to get away from Meredes. And she'll fight back with everything she's got if she's in danger."

"That's good," Graham said. "We can count on her to help us when we get to them."

"How are we going to get to her?" Randall asked. "From what Lotte told us, they're down in the canyon."

"That's why we're going in at night," Graham said. "I'm counting on catching them unawares. And I want to take Meredes alive. We need him to tell us what he knows about the operation."

The others nodded, but Michael kept silent. He understood the importance of Meredes to the investigation, but when it came to protecting Abby, all bets were off. He hadn't saved her life once to lose her now.

ABBY WOKE WITH a start, unsure at first what had roused her, then the noise reached her ears again: a low thump, like something—or someone—landing on the roof. She stood, heart pounding. Meredes looked up from the book he'd been reading. "What is it?" he asked.

Was it possible he hadn't heard? She clutched her stomach. "I have to use the bathroom," she said. "Something in the soup didn't agree with me." Earlier in the afternoon, she'd made a trip to the outhouse perched on the edge of the canyon. A guard had waited outside the door, then escorted her back to El Jefe, who had waited for her in front of the cabin.

He frowned at her now. She bent double and moaned, loud enough to cover what she was sure was the sound of footsteps on the roof.

He went to the door and opened it, and called something in Spanish. Gunfire from in front of the cabin cut off his words as plaster rained down from the ceiling overhead. Abby looked up in time to see the blade of an ax pierce the ceiling. The ax struck again and again, then Michael dropped down through the resulting hole, landing a few feet from her.

"Are you all right?" he asked.

"I'm fine. I knew you'd come."

Meredes whirled to face him, one hand on the gun at his side. "Give it up, Meredes." Michael leveled his pistol at the Mexican. "You're surrounded. We already took care of your guards outside."

"You won't take me." Before she or Michael could react, Meredes lunged for Abby. He wrenched her to him and pressed the barrel of the pistol against her temple. "One move and I'll blow her head off," he growled.

He was as rigid as a statue, the hand clamped around her arm digging in like an iron restraint. He smelled of sweat and fear—of desperation. He pressed the gun to her head as if trying to bore a hole. She gritted her teeth against the pain and, trying to rein in her own panic, looked to Michael. His gaze burned into hers, equal parts anger, determination and caring. "Let her go, Meredes," he said. "You'll never get away from here alive if you don't."

"She'll be the one who dies if you come any closer." He moved toward the door, dragging her with him. "Call your bosses. Tell them I want a helicopter here in half an hour."

"There's no way—"

"Tell them!"

Gaze still locked to her, Michael pulled the radio from his belt. "He's got Abby," he said. "He wants a helicopter and safe passage out of here or he'll kill her."

And when he got those things, he'd kill her anyway, Abby thought. Would he push her body out of the helicopter in the United States, or wait until he was safely over the border? She had to do whatever she could to avoid getting onto that helicopter with him.

"Tell them to stand back and give me room," Meredes said.

Michael repeated the instructions. "He's coming out," he added.

Would they have had time to position a sniper in the rocks along the canyon? Abby wondered. Did they have night-vision goggles to make the shot possible?

Maybe Meredes wondered the same thing. He hugged Abby to him, his arm pressed tightly beneath her breasts, his head positioned behind hers. Even an expert would have trouble getting off a safe shot now.

Outside, the moon was a silver sliver of light amid a glittering array of stars. Dark shapes stood at a distance—other agents of the task force. "I've radioed for the helicopter." Graham's voice spoke from the darkness. "They'll be here in forty-five minutes."

Three-quarters of an hour to stand in this man's cruel embrace. Would either of them be able to endure it?

"Don't come any closer." Meredes backed away from the agents. Where was the drop-off into the canyon? She tried to remember how much room they might have, but the darkness made it difficult to orient herself. With no electric lights in the cabin and no light pollution from a nearby town, not to mention the canyon walls closing in on either side, the darkness was like a physical shroud, thick and unyielding.

"Let her go," Michael said from somewhere to their left. "Take me instead."

Meredes's laughter abraded her raw nerves like fingernails on a chalkboard. "How chivalrous of you. But you are worthless to me."

He took another step back and Abby cried out in protest. "Careful," she said. "We must be close to the canyon."

He stiffened and stretched one foot carefully behind him. Abby wondered if she could trip him, then throw herself forward, to the ground. But his grip on her was too strong. If he fell over the edge, he'd be sure to drag her with him.

"Over to the cabin," he said. "We'll wait on those rocks."

He dragged her toward the boulders piled against one corner of the cabin, then leaned against the rocks, keeping her tight against him, cradled between his legs. Her head and heart pounded in unison, a drumbeat of fear and adrenaline.

Light blinded them, a white glare that hit them full-on. "Cut it out!" Meredes shouted, enraged.

"Shut it off!" Graham ordered, and they were plunged into darkness again, blinded now, spots dancing before her eyes.

"We'll have to turn on lights to guide the helicopter in," Graham said.

"Then, wait until it arrives," Meredes said. "I still have the gun to her head, even if you can't see it." As if to emphasize his point, he dug the barrel in harder. She felt a trickle of blood run down the side of her face and flinched. He moved his free hand to cup her breast, his fingers digging in. "Just holding on tight," he murmured.

She forced herself not to react, to remain rigid in his arms. She wouldn't give him the satisfaction of knowing how afraid she was. She wouldn't let him see any weakness. He was used to people being afraid of him, of using weaker women like Mariposa. She wouldn't be another victim for him to gloat over.

Mariposa. For the first time in minutes, she thought of the other woman. Was she still asleep on the bed in the cabin? Surely she hadn't slept through this chaos. Maybe she'd followed them out and was safe with one of the Rangers, invisible in the dark. Abby hoped so. She hoped Mariposa could be reunited with her baby, and safely returned to her home, wherever that was.

Something scraped on the rock behind them, along the side of the cabin. El Jefe jerked upright. "If anyone tries anything—" he shouted. But the words died in his throat. Mariposa landed on top of them. Meredes fell to his knees and Abby kicked out against him, scrabbling away from him even as a gun exploded, deafening her. She screamed and rolled away, then Michael was pulling her up, into his arms. Light blared around them, blinding her.

"Are you okay?" Michael smoothed the hair back from her face.

"I'm fine." Her head still throbbed, and she'd have a few bruises tomorrow, but she was alive and safe. "What happened?"

"Mariposa crept up from behind and tried to stab Meredes with a kitchen knife."

She twisted around. "Is he—?"

"He's dead." Michael pulled her closer and together they watched Carmen help Mariposa from the ground and gently pry the knife from her hand. The Mexican woman was sobbing and staring at the man on the ground in front of her, blood pooling around him.

"She didn't kill him," Michael said.

Abby stared at the body of the man on the ground. "I don't understand."

"A sniper shot him." Randall joined them. "As soon as you moved out of the way, they fired. They must have been watching, waiting for a chance."

"I wondered if you'd position a sniper," she said.

"It wasn't one of ours," Randall said.

She frowned. "Then, who?"

"Someone else wanted him dead," Michael said. "Before we could question him."

Mariposa's sobbing broke the silence. The pitiful sound tore at Abby's heart. "What will happen to her?" she asked.

"We'll question her, but I doubt there will be any charges filed," Michael said. "We'll want to know whatever she can tell us about Meredes's operation. Then we'll try to find her relatives in Mexico and arrange for her and the baby to return there."

"I hope she can find a place where she can be happy and safe," she said. Wasn't that what they all wanted? She studied the man on the ground again; he looked so small and harmless in death. Yet he'd destroyed so many lives. He'd almost destroyed hers.

"I'm not sorry he's dead," Michael said. "But I'm just sorry we didn't get the chance to question him."

"You want to know who's backing him?" she asked.

"He's only one small part of the operations in the area," Michael said. "Our guess is, he was in charge of the labor force. Other people must be overseeing production and distribution."

"What about the people you found in the canyon earlier today—the workers from the camp?" she asked.

He smoothed his hand along her shoulder. "Three of them died, and some of them are seriously injured, but will probably live. We'll question them, but it's unlikely they know much. They probably never saw anyone other than Meredes and the guards. They'll be processed through ICE offices in Grand Junction and sent back home."

She looked at El Jefe's still body once more. "He got off too easy," she said.

"Forget about him." Michael gently turned her away from the dead man. "I have something that belongs to you," he said. He opened his hand to reveal the little ceramic rabbit.

Seeing the familiar token was like being reunited with an old friend; she felt a surge of relief. "I wondered what happened to it." She took it from him. "Thanks for saving it for me. I'm not sure I really believe in luck, but I like having it around."

"I thought maybe you'd left it for me to find."

"I didn't think of that." She glanced up at him. He radiated caring and concern, two emotions she'd spent a lot of time warding off, as if letting people worry about her made her somehow weaker. Michael had helped her to see things differently. Other people's compassion could make her stronger. "Besides, I knew you'd come for me."

"You did?"

"You haven't let me down yet."

He put his arm around her. "Come on. I want a paramedic to take a look at that cut on your head."

"It's nothing." She touched the tender spot and felt the blood matting in her hair.

"Humor me."

"All right. I'll let someone clean me up and slap on a bandage. Then what?"

"Then maybe we'll stop by your trailer and you can pick up a few things."

"Why do I need to do that?"

He turned her to face him and cradled the side of her face in his hand. "Because I want you to come stay with me."

"Do you think I'm still in some kind of danger?" she asked.

"No. I want us to be together."

There her heart went, racing again. So much for play-

ing it cool and not letting him see how much this mattered to her. "For how long?"

"For as long as you like. Though forever would be
fine with me."

She put her hand over his and took a step back, wanting to see him more clearly—to see all of him, not just
his eyes regarding her so intently. "What are you saying?"

He swallowed. "You're going to make me spell it
out, aren't you?"

"Yes."

"All right. I love you. I want to be with you. Always.
I want to marry you, but if you think it's too soon for
that, I'm willing to wait."

"It seems to me you've already been waiting awhile
now," she said. "Five years."

"But part of that time, I didn't really know what I
was waiting for."

"Neither did I." She moved into his arms once more
and tilted her head up to kiss him. Here in his embrace
felt like the safest place she'd ever be. As long as he held
on to her, she'd be capable of anything. "I don't want to
wait any longer," she said. "I don't want to waste any
more time."

"Are you saying you'll marry me?"

"Now who wants everything spelled out?" She
smiled. "Yes. Yes, I'll marry you. I love you and I want
to be with you." Here was a man she could trust to love
her, not for what she looked like, but for who she was.
When a woman found that kind of gift, she'd be smart
to hang on and never let go.

* * * * *

MILLS & BOON®

The Thirty List

At thirty, Rachel has slid down every ladder she has ever climbed. Jobless, broke and ditched by her husband, she has to move in with grumpy Patrick and his four-year-old son.

Patrick is also getting divorced, so to cheer themselves up the two decide to draw up bucket lists. Soon they are learning to tango, abseiling, trying stand-up comedy and more. But, as she gets closer to Patrick, Rachel wonders if their relationship is too good to be true...

Order yours today at
www.millsandboon.co.uk/Thethirtylist

MILLS & BOON®

The Chatsfield Collection!

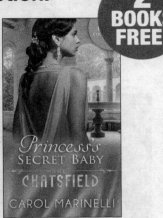

Style, spectacle, scandal…!

With the eight Chatsfield siblings happily married and settling down, it's time for a new generation of Chatsfields to shine, in this brand-new 8-book collection! The prospect of a merger with the Harrington family's boutique hotels will shape the future forever. But who will come out on top?

Find out at
www.millsandboon.co.uk/TheChatsfield2

0615/46